The Man from Dahomey

Two brothers are returning from a slave auction in Virginia. In the back of their wagon sits a tall silent Negro. They have unknowingly bought a great chief of Dahomey, a magnificent man of position and power, governor of a province, husband of six wives, one of them the daughter of a king. This is the story of his life—from boyhood and youthful romance, through the terrors of war, passionate grief in bereavement, great love, to honour as a hero and leader of men, and beyond . . .

Delving deep into the West African past, *Frank Yerby* re-creates a great nation of the early nineteenth century—Dahomey, home of a rich culture where knowledge and religious conviction mingled strangely with barbaric ceremony. Based on intensive research, given an unusually exotic setting and written with Yerby's unique vitality, THE MAN FROM DAHOMEY is an impressive successor to Mayflower's all-time bestselling THE SARACEN BLADE, GOAT SONG, PRIDE'S CASTLE, THE GOLDEN HAWK, THE DEVIL'S LAUGHTER and JUDAS, MY BROTHER.

The Man from Dahomey

An Historical Novel

Frank Yerby

Mayflower

Granada Publishing Limited
Published in 1973 by Mayflower Books Ltd.
Frogmore, St Albans, Herts AL2 2NF

First published in Great Britain by
William Heinemann Ltd 1971
Copyright © Frank Yerby 1971
Made and printed in Great Britain by
Richard Clay (The Chaucer Press) Ltd
Bungay, Suffolk
Set in Monotype Times

A NOTE TO THE READER

This novel is based, in so far as its historical sociological aspects are concerned, upon that very fine anthropological study, *Dahomey: An Ancient West African Kingdom*, by the late Melville J. Herskovits (Northwestern University Press, 1967). Of course, many other works on Dahomey, both in English and French, have been consulted. But Herskovits' magnum opus has the great virtue of correcting, with cool, scientific detachment, the usually prejudiced viewpoint of the earlier observers, such as Bosman, Lambe, Snelgrove, Smith, Norris, Dalzel, Duncan, Wilmot, Burton (who deserves to be set apart as the best, fairest, and most accurate of the lot), Skertchly, Foa, and La Herisse.

The writer mentions this only to assure the reader that every detail in this book that he laboriously piled up, is as accurate as it is humanly possible to make it; and the more strange, bizarre, and outlandish the detail may seem to the reader, the more he can be certain that the writer *didn't* invent it.

The purpose of *The Man From Dahomey*, apart from the only legitimate purpose of any novel, entertaining the reader, is admittedly to correct, as far as possible, the Anglo-Saxon reader's historical perspective. For among the countless tragedies caused by North American slavery—indisputably the most abysmally cruel system of bondage in the whole of human history—was the destruction of the high, and in many ways admirable, culture of the African, reducing in the process the proud, industrious, warlike people described in this work to the state of tortured, neurotic, self-hating caricatures of humanity from which the Afro-American* minority is hopefully, and

---

* This writer prefers the term Afro-American as being linguistically accurate. The current use of the word black to describe a racially mixed, multihued minority seems to him an abuse of language: to call the young Georgia legislator, Julian Bond, Cong. Adam Clayton Powell, and Sen. Edward Brook, 'blacks' is quite simply to reduce a descriptive adjective to meaninglessness. While the angry controversy over the use of black in English as against black in Spanish (Negro) leaves him shaking his weary and greying head in bemused admiration for the human capacity to exercise itself over semantic irrelevancies.

5

at long last, beginning to emerge.

The thoughtful reader will observe that the writer has *not* attempted to make the Dahomeans either more or less than what they were. He is aware that truth is an uncomfortable quality; that neither the racist, the liberal, nor the advocates of Black Power and-or Pride will find much support for their dearly held and perhaps, to them, emotionally and psychologically necessary myths herein.

So be it. Myths solve nothing, arrange nothing. But then, as the protagonist of this novel is driven in the end to put it, perhaps there are no viable solutions or arrangements in life for any of the desperate problems facing humanity in an all too hostile world.

Madrid, Spain   April 27, 1970.

PROLOGUE

'Swear to God, Matt,' Monroe Parks said to his brother Matthew, 'I don't know why you bought this here nigger. I plumb downright plain don't know.'

Matthew Parks looked back over his shoulder from the front seat of the farm wagon he was driving at the huge Negro, all of six feet five inches tall and a shade more by actual measurement, who sat in the back of the wagon, his dark eyes lid-hooded, brooding.

'Straight out o' Africa!' Monroe went on querulously. 'That there thieving bastid of an auctioneer is a mealy-mouthed liar! This big buck ain't never been nowhere's nigh Jamaica! Look at him, will you? Got the tribal scars on his temples and his chest. And you won't even put the cuffs on him, nigger what ate hisself a missionary and his daughter for breakfast every morning, likely!'

'Now that ain't a half bad idea,' Matthew said, 'the daughter, anyhow. Seen some hymn-singing fillies what rightly did look good enough to eat. Now be quiet, Mun, won't you? I got some thinking to do. And stop squirming around like a nervous Nellie. This here nigger's gentle, Big as he is, he don't have that wild, trouble-making look.'

'But an *African* nigger!' Monroe said. 'A cannibal! Why . . .'

'Feed him your old woman, then,' Matthew said, 'in quarter sections. Though skinny as she be, she won't last him long. Be one way to shut her up, though . . .'

The wagon rolled on, skirting the bay. The brothers didn't say anything more for nearly half an hour. Then Monroe said, 'Y'know, Matt, you could be right. He don't look fierce. Just big. But he plain gives me the creeps being so quiet. You done gone and found out effen he can talk, ain't you? He ain't deaf 'n' dumb, maybe?'

'He can talk. Sensible, too. When I asked him what he knowed how to do he said, "Work iron." And we could do with a blacksmith on th' place for a fact. Give him a try at it as soon as we git home. But that ain't the main reason I bought him, Mun . . .'

'Then what in tarnation *be* your reason, Matt?'

'Put him out to stud. Look at the size of that there nigger,

7

Mun! You know damn well the money's in breeding niggers these days up here in Virginia. Land's plumb played out. But down south in Alabama 'n' Mississippi they're purely weepin' an' acryin' for prime hands. Put this big buck atop all the lone wenches first thing! Betcha he'll make 'em mighty happy, too!'

Monroe Parks stared back uneasily at the huge black.

'All right,' he said, 'whatcha gonna call him, Matt?'

'Dunno. Maybe he's already got hisself a name.' Matthew turned then in the wagon seat.

'Hey, nigger,' he said. 'You got a name? What folks call you?'

The black man's voice, speaking, was like a drum. Soft, but endlessly deep. It awoke echoes.

'Hwesu,' he said, 'I be Hwesu, Cap'n.'

'Hell, that's too damn heathenish!' Monroe Parks said. 'You gotta change it, Matt.'

'Hwesu. Hmmmmmm. Wes! That's it. Look, nigger, folks ask you, you named Wes. Wesley Parks. Understand?'

'Yessir, Cap'n,' the Negro said.

The wagon rolled on under the oaks.

'Give me the creeps, being so quiet. Don't grin or talk or do nothing niggerish,' Monroe complained. 'Matt—you ever wonder what he was like—back there? In Africa, I mean?'

'No, and I don't aim to start now. Now will you shut up? You chatter more'n your old woman does. . . .'

And the wagon creaked on under the oaks towards the few miserable scrawny acres the Parks brothers called their plantation.

For Nyasandu Dosu Agausu Hwesu Gbokau Kesu, son of Gbenu, a great chief, and himself lately governor of the province of Alladah in Dahomey, husband of six wives, one of them the daughter of the king, a notable, a 'personage with a name' in his own lilting Ffon or Fau language, life was over.

But for Wesley Parks, a beast of burden, an owned thing, a slave, it had just begun.

The rest—this chronicle of his African days—is memory.

8

ONE

From where he lay in the bush on the edge of his 'evening field', Nyasanu could see the road. It wound through a grove of the sacred loko trees and out past the *augaudo*, the special palm tree that had his own umbilical cord buried under it, and hence was the guardian of his *fa*, his fate. He lay there on his belly watching the hard-packed serpentine, grey-white ribbon, draped with sun-glare and leaf-shade, very carefully, for trouble was going to come to him over that road. His father's diviner, the *bokono*, who read the *du*, the magic lots, had been sure of that. And the *bokono* was almost never wrong.

Nyasanu lay there gripping the handle of his hoe, so hard that the knuckles of his black hands turned grey from the strain. The feel of it was good. He had made the hoe himself, for he was of the *xenu* of the Ayatovi Gaminu, and the *vudu* of that clan was Gu, the God of Iron. Therefore Nyasanu had been sent to the chief of the blacksmith's guild when he was only twelve years old as an apprentice. He had learned the ironworker's craft, and its rites, spells, charms, and tabus, very well indeed. In a way, because of the love and skill which had gone into its shaping, something of Gu, himself, had entered into that hoe, making of it a sort of *gbo*, strong magic against most of the dangers in this world.

But today, Nyasanu didn't have much faith in its powers. For the *bokono* had said, 'These dangers will come from without—over the king's road. They are alien dangers, foreign to this land. I do not see clearly what they are.'

'So,' Nyasanu thought, 'how do I know it will work against them? It, or any other *gbo*? Aido Hwedo, protect me, Gu, aid me. Mawu-Lisa, gods of the sky. Xevioso, God of Thunder. Sagbata, God of Earth. Fa, who is fate, Legba, the Divine Trickster, give me cunning. Danh, the serpent . . .'

He stopped there. It didn't make any sense to appeal to the *vudun*. He'd have to make sacrifices to them, or they wouldn't listen. So he'd have to wait, anyhow. Simple common sense told him that the best thing to do was to have the *bokono* cast the lots again to find which god was sending the trouble. After that they could make sacrifices to appease him. But first, they had to let the trouble get there so they could see what kind of trouble it was.

That was bad. But what else could they do? He, Nyasanu, had been born two years after His Royal Majesty Gezo, the tenth king of Dahomey, had been enstooled at the Capital, Ahomey, which meant he was only seventeen years old.* He had been given his partial *fa* at thirteen, as custom dictated for every Dahomean boy; but he couldn't have his complete *fa* established until after he had been circumcised, which should be done this very year. He shuddered, thinking about that. He had seen it done to last year's group of seventeen- and nineteen-year-olds, and it had been awful. Some of the boys had screamed. Several had fainted. It had taken a month for the wounds of the lucky ones—those who hadn't got infected—to heal. The others had taken three months. Two had taken forever. For the gangrene had crawled up their swollen penises into their bellies, and they had died.

But, because he hadn't had his complete fate established, couldn't in fact go through the ceremonies and sacrifices by which a man's destiny was revealed to him until he had been circumcised, declared an adult, married, it was very hard for the diviners to determine his immediate future with any accuracy. They, the *bokonoe*, admitted that. And that was why he, Nyasanu, second son of Gbenu, *toxausu*, or chief of the City of Alladah, couldn't know what the trouble that was coming to him was.

That upset him. That and the *bokono*'s certainty that it was going to be foreign trouble. Because both conditions took it out of the categories he was accustomed to dealing with. He was very good at dealing with trouble as his common, or everyday, name indicated. For Nyasanu meant 'man among men'.

And he was. He knew that without complacency, but without any false modesty either. At seventeen, he stood five fingers taller than the chief, his father, and Gbenu was an imposing man more than six feet tall. Everyone said that when he, Nyasanu, filled out, he was going to be bigger than his father, too. Right now he was as slender as a loko sapling; but he was well muscled, for all that. He was also aware of the fact that he was the handsomest young man in Alladah. He

* Gezo, according to most authorities, became king in 1818.

10

couldn't escape knowing that. The way the *nyaukpovi*, the village maidens, dropped their gaze silently or burst into fits of hysterical giggling when he passed demonstrated that to him every day without any need of the added confirmation of having his *novichi nyqnu*, female children of his same mother, repeat their remarks to him, as they always did with sisterly pride.

Yet, as far as girls were concerned, he realised sadly that he was as innocent as it was possible for a well-to-do Dahomean youth to be. Which meant he had played kissing and touching games with only one girl, Agbale; and she, herself, no later than last night, had again easily prevented him from going any further than the usual few and brief caresses. Since they were already engaged to be married, and had been from infancy, Agbale had said very simply and quietly, but with immense dignity:

'No, Dosu, I want to be able to show our sleeping mat to your father and to mine the morning after our wedding night.'

And that had been that. He'd been angry and sullen at her rebuke; but he'd stopped at once, awed by her purity and her pride.

He looked at the road. It was still empty. Maybe the *bokono* was wrong. Maybe the trouble wouldn't come. He hoped so, but he doubted it. Zezu, his father's *bokono*, was the best of all the diviners. Nobody could bring up a provable instance when the great diviner had been wrong about the future.

So, Nyasanu lay there, keeping his vigil. Today was Lamisi, Thursday, the day sacred to Gu, the *vudu* of the ironworkers, so he didn't have to go to his forge. And the field he lay beside was his very own. It was the *badagle*, or 'evening field', given to every Dahomean boy by his father, so that he didn't have to share the produce from it with anyone and therefore he could work it, or not work it, as he saw fit. Usually, Nyasanu worked it, and used his produce to buy gifts for his future father-in-law and mother-in-law, and even occasionally for Agbale herself. Although the number and the nature of the gifts he was allowed to buy his betrothed was sharply limited by the stern Dahomean concepts of propriety and morality. But today, it was more important to watch that road. . . .

Only, once he'd started thinking, or rather dreaming, about Agbale, he was lost. From that moment on, a legion of ghosts, evil spirits, an army of Auyo, Hausa, Fulani, or Ashanti war-

11

riors, or even a rogue elephant, could have stormed up that road, and he wouldn't have noticed it.

Agbale was so beautiful! She was absolutely the blackest girl in the whole village. She was so black that his pet name for her was Nyaunu wi, 'black woman'. He wondered whether he dared give her that name as her married name once they'd been wed. He could if he wanted to. It was the Dahomean custom for a husband to rename his bride. But, since blackness was one of the conditions of beauty, the first condition, in fact, followed closely by the pattern of a woman's decorative scars, it might sound too much like boasting. And, as a chief's son, he had been taught that it was beneath his social position to indulge in that commonest of all Dahomean vices.

'Beautiful,' he thought. 'Like a night when the sky has eaten the moon and there aren't any stars. And chaste. Pure—as—as spring water in the rain forest. Oh what a fool I was last night! I almost lost her! I almost drove her away from me!'

Because, although he'd stopped his clumsy efforts to seduce Agbale at once, he had been angered by her refusal. So he had replied to her quietly stated wish to be able to show with honour their nuptial sleeping mat to their respective fathers, with an ugly and cruel joke:

'With or without soldier ants?' he had said.

The moment the words were out, he was sorry. It was a bad joke. Everybody knew that girls who had been unchaste put zaxwa, night warrior ants, up inside themselves the night before their wedding, allowing the biting, stinging insects to so irritate their vaginal tracts that the lightest sexual contact thereafter produced bleeding. That way, many a girl who'd lain with practically everyone in the village except her own bridegroom was able to convince the poor fool that he had wed the purest maid in Africa.

But Agbale had stood there looking at him, and the horror in her eyes would have melted the thunderstones of Naete, wife of the thundergod's son. Then her eyes went out, walled out by her tears, so that he couldn't see them any more.

'Agbale . . .' he said.

She went on looking at him and letting the tears chase one another down her cheeks. They looked like the tracery a falling star makes across the night. Her wide, wonderful, heavy-lipped mouth trembled. He couldn't bear watching that, but he couldn't take his eyes off it either.

12

'Agbale——' he groaned.

'Give me your knife, Dosu,' she said. 'For this night I must go to the ancestors. If you think *that* of me, what need have I to live?'

'Agbale!' he said. 'Nyaunu wi! You can't! I won't let you! I . . .'

'How can you stop me, Dosu?' she said. 'If not with your knife, then with my father's. Or I will go to the *azaundato* and buy a poison. Because you have sent me beyond the river. If you think me one of the *ko-si*, they who sell their favours, or one of the free women who are like the dogs always in heat—it is *your* hand that strikes me down; *your* wish that eats my breath. . . .'

Then, he did the only thing possible. He knelt before her, pressing his forehead to the ground, clawed up a handful of damp earth, and poured it on his head. So, in the land of Da's Belly—Dahomey—does one honour a queen.

A moment later he felt her small hands tugging at him and came to his knees, and she was kneeling before him, kissing him in every place she could reach and crying like someone whose brains Legba had eaten, and he was crying too, quite shamelessly, and all the night blazed with splendour and they clung to each other like lost and demented children until they were quiet.

And then it was all right. Perfectly all right.

'Nyaunu wi,' he said tenderly. 'Little black one. My love.'

'Dosu,' she said. 'You—you don't trust me. You—you love me, I think; but you don't trust me. So how can you marry me? How can you make me your number one wife?'

He smiled at her then. He was a Dahomean and no Dahomean ever lacks guile.

'I don't trust you?' he said. 'Tell me, Nyaunu wi, what name did you call me by just now?'

'Dosu,' she said at once. Then: 'Oh! Your—secret name! The name that . . .'

'Only three people know: my mother, my first friend eldest, and *you*, little black one. Not even the *vuduno* or my father. The name you could take to the *azaundato*, the sorcerer, and enslave me forever. Blow out the light behind my eyes. Eat my brains. Send me across the dark river to the ancestors. Dosu, which my mother called me because I was so big that she thought I was going to be twins. So now, listen: here are the rest of my secret names: I am also called Agausu, because I was born feet first; Hwesu, because the first light I saw was the noonday sun; I had my umbilical cord wrapped about my neck so that it was a miracle of *fa* that I did not choke to death, and for that my mother named me Gbokau. Moreover, I had a caul over my face which my grandmother had to rip from me with a knife to keep me from smothering, so I am also called Kesu. And now that I have given all three of my souls into your keeping, how can you say I don't trust you, Agbale?'

She kissed him. Then she raised her small, black, beautiful face towards the sky.

'Mawa, hear me!' she said. 'Lisa! Fa! Legba. All the *vudun* —of sky, of earth, of sea, of thunder! If ever I betray—this my husband—this my warrior and my prince, even in my thoughts, I pray you in that same moment to eat my breath. Stop my heartbeat. Send me to the ancestors. And—and leave my body unburied so that my souls must wander lost forever between the worlds.'

'Agbale!' he said, his voice shaking with pure terror, 'you must not say these things! You must not!'

'I didn't say them,' she said, 'I swore them. So now, will you, my Dosu, swear me a thing?'

He stared at her.

'What thing, my Nyaunu wi?' he said.

'That you—that you will take no other wife. I know! I know! Your father has forty wives. My father has ten. And a man needs many sons and daughters to establish his worship among the ancestors once he has crossed the river, gone to Them. Only—Dosu, Dosu, when I think of another girl kissing you—touching you—sharing thy sleeping mat—something on my insides dies. And—and not quietly. It screams and screams and screams until it dies. I am strange. I know that, too. But I mean to give thee twenty sons all by myself! All *novichi sunu* —male children of one mother—*me*! Not *to-vichi*—of various women scheming against one another, hating each other, as your father's firstborn, the *medaxochi* of your house, that weak and ugly Gbochi, hates thee! Will you swear me this, my husband, father of *all* my children, the *only* man who will ever know my body, lie with me?'

He hung there staring at her, stunned by the enormity of the thing she asked of him. In Dahomey, for a man to have only one wife meant that he was practically a beggar. Was—and

14

remained. For children—especially girl children—were wealth. The gifts a prospective son-in-law had to make to the father of the bride was one of the sources of a man's fortune. Another was the house building, repairs to his walls, work in his fields that the young man and his *dokpwe*, as the communal organisation of young males was called, did free of charge for the future father-in-law. But sons were valued too. Sons married, and though weddings of sons were costly to father and son alike, this expense was more than compensated for by the fact that the sons brought their wives into the father's compound, or enlarged it into an extended compound, and they, plus their *dokpwe*, plus their ever increasing children were an important source of labour.

But the most important thing many sons did for a man was to insure him an imposing funeral—the Dahomean's dearest wish, and greatest pride—and guarantee his deification after death and the establishment of his cult as an ancestor-*vudu* or god.

So a man needed children by the tens, twenties, hundreds. And such numbers no one woman could supply. For what tender, wild, headstrong, loving Agbale was forgetting were the tabus surrounding childbirth in Dahomey, chief among them being that a woman must absent herself from her husband's sleeping mat as long as she suckled her child. That meant, since Dahomean children were not weaned until they were two or three years old, that no woman could possibly give her husband a large number of children. The tabu was both deliberate and wise. Too frequent childbearing, the elders held, was bad for the health of both the woman and the subsequent offspring. So what Agbale proposed to do was, by the very customs of her people, impossible. Along with the menstrual tabus, the religious tabus, the ancestral cult tabus, the funeral and mourning tabus, and all the other tabus that sharply reduced the frequency of sexual intercourse between a man and any one of his wives, the possibility of her bearing him even ten children before reaching her menopause was slight. No; more than slight. It was practically non-existent.

Therefore, religiously, economically, and socially, what Agbale was asking of him was a terrible thing, destructive to his honour, position, and peace of mind. Yet, on the other hand, approaching the matter as nearly as he could from her point of view, he conceded at once that jealousy was natural enough

15

among women, forcing a man to be impartial with his favours, and to rule his compound with an iron hand. Out of a simple desire for peace he was willing to compromise with Agbale on the practical grounds that it was better not to have too many wives. Nyasanu had always considered four or five enough. That many a man could manage. That many he could keep reasonably contented sexually and in all other ways. But when a man had forty-three wives, as his father had, or hundreds, as the King had, was it any wonder that some of his children resembled him not at all?

Of course, if he became *toxausu* or chief of the village when his father died—an event not at all unlikely, considering how many times Gbochi, the *medaxochi* or firstborn of his father, had incurred Gbenu's displeasure now by his weakling's bearing and whining ways—he would have to marry a great number of women to insure that the people respected his manhood, his wealth, and his social position. In that case, what became of a promise made in youth to a foolish and lovelorn girl?

Another thing. What could he say that would negate the institution of *chiosi*? *Chiosi* was a sacred thing. When a man died, his wives were divided among his sons, either by his own testimony as given to his best friend, or by the *xenuga*, the chief of the dead man's *xenu* or clan. And there was no way a man could refuse an inherited wife. What's more, he *had* to lie with her in turn until age had stopped the fountain of her blood, no matter if she was twenty years older than he and physically repulsive to him. If he did not, he was offering injury to his father's cult, and the ancestors would promptly eat his breath.

As swift as thought is, thinking all that took him considerable time. Agbale tossed her close cropped, woolly little head.

'I see,' she said. 'I ask too much, don't I, Dosu? Very well. This night or tomorrow, my father will return your gifts, pay ...'

'Agbale!' he got out.

'... you and your *dokpwega* for the work you've done in our fields, compensate the *bokono* and the *vuduno* for the sacrifices already made, for I ...'

'Agbale!' he was frankly crying now.

'... will not be even Number One among the many wives. I will not share thee, Dosu! Not with anyone. So since you will not be satisfied with me as I am and must remain with thee—

goodbye.'

'Wait!' he said. 'I *am* satisfied with you, Agbale. I want no other wife. And I'll swear thy oath, if you'll let me change it a little. . . .'

She stared at him suspiciously.

'Change it how?' she said.

'By all the *vudun* of earth, sky, sea, and thunder; by Danh the Serpent, Dangbe his son; by Aido Hwedo, the rainbow snake who eats his own tail, and holds up the world so that it doesn't fall into the sea; by Fa who is Fate; and by cunning Legba, Linguist of the Gods. I do most solemnly swear I will take no other woman than Agbale to wife *of my own free will.*'

She stood there staring at him.

'Oh!' she said.

'Do you accept my oath, little Nyaunu wi?' he said.

'No!' she said furiously. 'You are trickier than Legba, Dosu! Now you can say "How can I injure the clan of X or Y or Z by refusing their offer of a girlchild of that *xenu*?' It's a deadly insult! Or . . .'

'How can I refuse the widows of my father, since that would be to desecrate his sacred cult? How can I refuse my wife for one night, the *tasino* so old that her moonblood no longer flows, who must lie with me for that one night at the risk of her life to appease the *vudu* of the knife that cuts my fore-skin? You are not a fool, Agbale. You know a chief's son acquires wives more by obligation than by love or lust. What I do swear is to love no other woman but thee on my heart. And if this oath be not true, may Legba eat my breath!'

She stood there, trembling, and again her eyes were wet. Then with a doe thing's skip and scamper, she was in his arms.

'I will die,' she wailed, 'my heart will stop from too much pain when thou'rt with the other wives, Dosu. But I cannot give you up. I cannot. That would be to have an evil spirit eat my brains before crossing the river, and go screaming to the ancestors. But, oh, my Dosu—I will suffer so!'

'No you won't,' he said, 'having all my love, you . . .'

She drew back then, stared at him, her eyes night black in her ebony face.

'Time changes a man,' she said, 'and women grow old. One day when my hair is white, our sons grown or even before,

17

there will come one who moves like a palm tree in a little wind; whose voice is as sweet as the Otutu bird's is when she cries for rain; and whose body will have been made by the *vudun* of the brass workers and wood carvers out of the stuff of the night. And you will love her, despite your oath. And you know what I shall do then, Dosu Agausu Hwesu Gbokau Kesu Nyasanu, lord of my life?'

'No,' he said, 'what?'

'Die,' Agbale Nyaunu wi said.

He was thinking all that, dreaming it, remembering it, when a shadow fell across his face, shutting out the sun. He looked up into the stern faces of three men.

One half of their heads had been shaved so that half of their craniums gleamed like polished ebony in the light; but the other half had not known scissors or razor in many years, so that an immense thatch of kinky wool covered it.

By that token he knew them at once. The Half Heads, the royal messengers. His trouble had come. And from the highest, the most merciless of sources.

The king.

TWO

'Get up,' the eldest of the three Half Heads said.

Nyasanu got up. The royal messenger represented the king. To disobey them was to die—unpleasantly. He stood there looking into their faces, at the bamboo fronds they bore as the emblems of office; at the necklace made of the teeth of the enemy warrior each of them had personally slain in battles that they won. Looking at the necklaces sent a thrill stabbing through him. His *vudu*, Gu, was also the god of fighters as well as of iron. One day he would have such a necklace. But with more teeth in it. Many more!

'Lead us to your village chief,' the eldest Half Head said.

Nyasanu bowed.

'I hear and obey, respected older persons,' he said.

He led the three visitors into the compound of his father, winding his way through the many, many houses in it, for due to the fact that Dahomean custom demanded that each wife be

18

given an individual house for herself and her younger children, and also because a personage of importance, as Gbenu was, gradually accumulated a host of hangers-on, young brothers, older sons, destitute widows of deceased relatives, and the like, the compound of a wealthy man soon became a small village in itself. So the boy and the royal visitors moved towards Gbenu's house through a great shrilling and gabbling of women and the shouts and laughter of the children. A crowd formed behind them, growing every time they passed a house. Gbenu's dwelling was the second biggest house in the compound. The reason it was only the second biggest was that the biggest was the cult house of the ancestors, where the bones of the *tauhwiyo*, the founder of the clan, were buried. No men would show disrespect for the forefathers by building a more imposing house than theirs. The very idea was unthinkable, even for a chief.

When they reached Gbenu's bungalow finally, the *toxausu* was lying in his hammock outside it. He was attended by four of the youngest and prettiest of his wives. One of them held the highly ornamented chief's umbrella over him to protect him from the sun, two of the others were fanning him with huge palmetto fans to keep him cool, while the fourth crouched beside his hammock and held his brass spittoon, so polished that it shone like gold, for him to spit into.

The minute Gbenu saw who his visitors were, he dismissed his wives with a wave of his hand. Nyasanu watched three of them scurrying away in the direction of their houses; but the fourth went into his father's house, for it was her turn, or she had been chosen, to cohabit with the *toxausu*. And it came to the boy that keeping his vow to Agbale to love no other woman but her in his heart was going to be difficult indeed. There were so many beautiful girls in the world!

His father stood up and bowed to the Half Heads. They bowed to him in their turn, but much more deeply than he had. Nyasanu felt his heart swelling with pride. His father was an important personage in Dahomey. The respect the Half Heads showed him was evidence enough for that. . . .

'What is His Majesty's pleasure, my lords?' Gbenu said.

'First, send all these people away,' the eldest Half Head said.

Gbenu raised his huge, powerful hands and clapped them three times. At the third clap the space before his house was empty. But Nyasanu didn't go. After all, he was his father's second son and almost surely his favourite.

'And the boy,' the Half Head said.

'He is my son,' Gbenu said.

Something in the way his father pronounced those words brought a sting to Nyasanu's eyes, a tightening to his throat. He would be the next *toxausu*! He would be! Of course Gbochi was his elder by three days, and normally should be named chief when their father died. But not only was Gbochi ugly, he was also so weak and cowardly that nearly everybody was already sure that Gbenu was going to pass over him and name Nyasanu as his heir. Another thing that Nyasanu knew about his half-brother was that Gbochi was guilty of *gaglo*, that is, indulging in homosexual practices with the only two other boys in Alladah who were so inclined. But he didn't tell his father that. Tale-bearing would have sharply decreased Gbenu's gruff fondness for him. Besides, being a Dahomean—of that race before whose ingrained deviousness Machiavelli himself would have been forced to bow—he knew how effective it would be for him to say on the day his father finally asked him about that unsavoury matter: 'But I did not want to distress thee, oh my father!'

The Half Heads had turned towards him now, and were studying him with some care.

'A young lion, oh Toxausu!' their spokesman said.

'Thank you, my lords,' Gbenu said, and waited.

'Has he seen the *adagbwoto*?' the Half Head said.

Nyasanu stiffened, for the word *adagbwoto* means 'he who cuts the foreskin'. The memory of last year's witnessed horror came flooding back. He could feel a trembling crawling up his legs and held hard against it.

'No,' Gbenu said. 'We are waiting for the rains.'

'That is wise,' the Half Head said. 'It is too dangerous when the heat is on the land. But see to it—for him and for all thy sons, and the sons of thy clan who are of age. The king so orders it.'

Gbenu inclined his massive head, regal under the embroidered green skullcap he wore, in a slight bow.

'Are there further orders, my lords?' he said.

'Yes, you are to bring the pebbles of the men to the court within twelve days.'

'Is there to be war, then?' he said.

'The king, himself, will inform you of that,' the Half Head said.

Again Gbenu nodded.

'I pray you, my lords,' he said, 'to stay here tonight. I will assign you a house in which to rest—and make a feast in your honour. It goes without saying that if any unmarried women of the village please you, I shall put them at your disposition.'

The Half Heads looked at each other. Nyasanu saw temptation wage a short, brisk skirmish with duty in their eyes. Duty won. However rich the feast that the *toxausu* Gbenu offered them, and the charms of the ebony maidens of Alladah, such brief pleasures would not compensate them for being strangled before the royal court for failing to obey orders.

'We thank thee, noble Toxausu,' their spokesman said, 'but we cannot. We must reach three more villages before night falls. Only in the last of them can we rest. Perhaps the next time. . . .'

'We shall be honoured, whenever you come,' the chief said, 'but surely your haste is not such that you can't take a cup of palm wine with me?'

'That, yes,' the oldest Half Head said.

After they had gone, Nyasanu lingered at the house of his father.

'Da,' he said, 'tell me . . .'

His father stretched out his huge hand and let it rest on his son's shoulder.

'Does the knife hurt?' Gbenu teased. 'Yes, my son. But do not fear, I will send four warriors to hold you down, and stuff your mouth with five woman's headcloths so that you will not disgrace me with your screaming.'

'I shall not scream,' Nyasanu said simply. And he wouldn't. He'd die first. Both of them knew that.

'Good,' Gbenu said. 'There is something you want of me, my son?'

'Yes, Tau,' Nyasanu said.

Gbenu frowned. In Ffon, the language of Dahomey, *tau* is formal and means 'father'. On the other hand, *da* is affectionate, and has no precise meaning. Nyasanu called both his grandfathers—for Gbenu hadn't inherited the chieftainship, but had been awarded it for his valour in battle by the king, hence Nyasanu was able to enjoy the company of his father's father, the *xenuga*, the 'elder' or chief of the clan, as well as that of his mother's father, since both spry and vigorous and somewhat mischievous old men still lived—his granduncles, and his uncles all 'Da', when addressing any one of them directly. Years later, when Legba the Trickster, or whoever the *vudu* was who so terribly mishandled his Fa, his fate, had forced Nyasanu to learn English, he told white people that *da* meant 'Daddy'. But he only told them that out of his Dahomean conviction that all white men are idiot children, thus making it unnecessary to go to the trouble of explaining what *da* really did mean, which was practically impossible to do in the language of the Furtoo, anyhow. The closest he could get to it was 'old man I am too fond of to have to be polite to', or words to that effect.

The trouble was that Nyasanu's choice of the one form of address instead of the other was deliberate, and his father knew it. Ffon, or Fau, is a subtle language, as befitting the subtle people who speak it. So Gbenu frowned when his beloved second son addressed him as 'Tau'. It was warning enough that Nyasanu was going to ask him something he couldn't, or wouldn't want to, answer.

'May I go with you to Abomey when you take the pebbles to the king?' Nyasanu said.

Gbenu's frown deepened.

'No,' he said.

Nyasanu bowed his head.

'But, Da . . .' he whispered.

Again Gbenu put his huge hand on his son's shoulder.

'Next year I will take you,' he said, 'after you have been married.'

'Thank you, my father,' Nyasanu said. 'You are wise. So I know your reason for the delay is also wise. But could you not share it with me? I am no longer a child, you know.'

Gbenu hesitated.

'Listen, Vi . . .' His use of the small and tender Dahomean word for 'son' was also a signal, designed to let Nyasanu know that his father approved of him, was proud of him, even loved him, which took most of the sting out of his refusal. 'What happens to even the cub of the lion, if he attempts to hunt among the leopards?'

Nyasanu considered that. It was a Dahomean characteristic to use metaphoric language, especially when speaking of forbidden things. He didn't need to ask what his father meant.

The royal house was of the clan Gbekpovi Aladaxonu, which can be interpreted, 'Children of the Leopard, who, of old, came from Alladah.'

'But you have the king's favour,' he said. 'He made you *toxausu*!'

'My predecessor also enjoyed it,' Gbenu said. 'But one day he fell into a pit after having been carried before the people in a little basket and wearing a red cap. And in that pit, someone cut off his head.'

'Oh,' Nyasanu said. What his father had described to him was the manner of royal executions; what Gbenu meant was that the favour of the king was not to be depended upon.

'You mean that if you take me to Abomey, I might do or say something that . . .' he persisted.

'No. In the presence of the Leopard, dogs do not bark,' his father said. 'I mean you are young—and good to look upon. There are the Leopard's wives, the *kposi*, who are often bored because there are too many of them for him to husband properly. Many of them are young and very beautiful. And there are also the *kpovi nyqnu*, daughters of the Leopard, with whom it is unwise to have any dealings either . . .'

'Why?' Nyasanu said. 'They are allowed to marry commoners, Da. In fact, they usually do. . . .'

'Nearly always,' Gbenu conceded drily. 'Whereupon their children take their names, are initiated into the Leopard Clan, and owe neither obedience nor respect to their fathers. Whereupon, if upon his wedding night the husband finds he is ploughing a field worked many times before, not only can he *not* return his beautiful Leopardess to her father, but even a whispered complaint would ensure his joining his ancestors. Whereupon, if he returns unexpectedly from his fields and finds his princess wife entertaining a male visitor upon his sleeping mat, he must avert his eyes, bow politely, leave the house, and return only when he is sure the visitor has gone. Whereupon, not only does he not divorce his faithless wife, but neither does he beat her with a peeled rod or even with his hand. Instead, he makes no mention of what his eyes have seen and even "dashes" her with silver beads and silken clothes. Whereupon . . .'

'That's enough, Da!' Nyasanu laughed. 'Should I meet a princess, I shall run!'

'Even so,' the *toxausu* said quietly, 'next year will be a better time to present you at court. After you have been married. For, judging by what I have seen of that little black witch . . .'

'Father!' Nyasanu said.

'I chose her for you, remember,' Gbenu chuckled, 'thus making it all too easy for you to be a dutiful son. What I have seen of Agbale convinces me that after you've spent some moons with her you can mingle with the beauties of the court and keep your head. I mean that in both senses. Now, is there anything else you wish to know?'

'Yes, Da,' Nyasanu said. 'Only it is hard to say what it is because I am not sure of how to put it. Does a man beat cold iron on his forge? Does the otutu go on singing once the rain has begun? Why is the Leopard always hungry, though . . .'

'Everything,' Gbenu sighed, 'including us. So much so that we are called "things of the Leopard" instead of men. I enjoy Da Da Gezu's favour—so far. But in any relation to the Leopard Clan—how much of love is there involved, and how much of fear?'

'There!' Nyasanu said. 'You have said it for me, O my Father.'

'Only because we are alone,' Gbenu said, 'and thou'rt my son, and worthy of my trust. Tell me, you have worked for the chief of the ironworkers at the Sogbwenu forge, have you not?'

'Yes, Da,' the boy said.

'And what is made there, oh my son?'

'Hoes,' Nyasanu said. 'And—*ase*.' *Ase* were the small iron alters that are placed in the *dexoxo*, the cult house of the ancestors.

'Nothing else?' Gbenu said.

'Nothing else,' Nyasanu said.

'You are wrong,' his father said, 'as I will presently demonstrate to you. But just tell me, beyond the head blacksmith, his assistants—like you, Nyasanu—and the boy who works the bellows, who is always present at a forge?'

'Why, the *felikpautau*, of course.'

'He who watches at the forge. And what does he, *felikpautau*, do?'

'Just that. What you said. He watches.'

'Why?' Gbenu said.

'For the king.' Nyasanu whispered.

'Aye, Nyasanu,' the *toxausu* said. 'For the king. And on each hoe he stamps a mark, said mark having been assigned to

24

that particular forge by the king. Then the hoes are sent to market, are they not? Or each one buys a hoe directly at the forge?'

'No, my father,' Nyasanu said.

'So at the market, the *axino*, the chief of the market, has twelve boxes, each bearing the mark of one of the twelve forges in Dahomey. Each time a hoe is sold, he notes the mark and puts a pebble in the proper box. When full, the box is sent to the king, and a new one started. At the end of the year, your chief, like all the blacksmiths, had to go to the palace, didn't he?'

'Yes, Da,' Nyasanu said.

'Whereupon the king asked him how many hoes he had made, because our ruler hath need of knowing—he says—how many blades there are available to wound the earth. Now, tell me, could your chief possibly lie to the king?'

'No, Da, because the *felikpautau* was there to contradict him if he spoke falsely,' Nyasanu said.

'And the *naye*, the "mother" of all the *felikpautaui*—an old and put aside wife of the king who hath been given the office of storing such matters in her head, is there to memorise the answer. Then, after the number of hoes made have been compared with the number sold, by the simple method of counting the pebbles from the boxes bearing the forge's mark, the king "gives" a bar of iron to the chief of the forge, and orders him to make cartridges for the army—the product that *you*, my boy, forgot!—in proportion to the number of hoes remaining to be sold, for which cartridges he is *not* paid. What doth this suggest to you, my son?'

'A—tax?' Nyasanu said.

'A tax. As upon all else in Da's Belly!' Gbenu said. 'Can one bear an el of cloth on one's head from Alladah to Abomey without passing a dozen toll houses where one is forced to pay a fraction of its value? Is there not an *agucha* at court to whom every miserable, scrawny antelope a hunter shoots must be reported? A *tauvi* to whom every finger-long fish must be told? Doth not the *galano* scare all the peasants with the fear of his river god's rising and causing the animals to sicken if they do not take a cowry shell representing each beast to the king? To which, of course, the king himself adds a large, showy personal contribution to conceal from those sweaty oafs that they are being taxed. Whereupon they praise him for

25

saving the animals that were never in danger while he takes the yams out of their children's mouths.'

'Father . . .' Nyasanu said.

'A *zamaiza* counts the hives of the beekeepers. The *guno* counts the knives of the hunters. A *taukpau* counts the fruits of the soil. An *akwedenudje* controls the makers of salt, a *deno* sits athwart every road to tax the goods that pass that way. A *dokpwe gbunugu* taxes the gravediggers! A *binazo* collects the rattles the priest uses to honour even the dead! From birth to death we are taxed, taxed, taxed, my son—so that the princesses and princes may live in licentious idleness—that is, if even our lives are not required of us for some small fault, or because the king needs a certain kind of worker—a blacksmith, say, to be sent to the ancestors to make *ase* or hoes for the royal dead!'

'Is there no escape from this, oh my father?' Nyasanu whispered.

'One—to leave Dahomey. But there is only one way to leave the land of Da's Belly. . . .'

'And that is?' the boy said.

'To be sold as slave to the Furtoo—those hideous creatures who come in huge canoes from across the sea—and who have no skins. . . .'

'They have no skins?' Nyasanu said. 'But if they have been flayed, they would die!'

'They have skins, I suppose,' Gbenu said, 'but the colour of those skins is that of the carcass of a flayed beast; pink and red and pale purple. They call themselves white men, but they really aren't white, but rather the colours that I said. When they have been in the sun a while, their faces, hands, and arms begin to darken, becoming almost human looking, finally. But once I saw some of their women at Whydah—and as the females do everything they can to shield themselves from the sun, they *were* white; the colour of a fish's belly, or a corpse dug up for the second burial. Some of them had hair the hue the grass turns after a long dry season. And none of them had any discernible hips or breasts under their clothes. I have never seen more hideous creatures!'

'Do they,' Nyasanu asked, 'reproduce after the manner of people?'

'How should I know? I think not. Their smell was very rare and very unpleasant. And they held themselves very stiffly apart from the men and showed no signs of fondness towards even those of the Furtoo who were supposed to be their husbands. I think they have a method of spawning without bodily contact. But enough of talk! Tomorrow I must make preparations for my journey. . . .'

'Father,' Nyasanu said, 'why does the king need the pebbles of the men?'

'To know how many men there are, Nyasanu—so that he may call them up, as soldiers, to attack some defenceless Maxi village in a war that hath no other purpose than to supply him with slaves to sell the flayed ones. . . .'

'And the pebbles of the women and girls?'

'We are told it is to compensate the widows and female children of men who fall in battle. . . .'

'But it isn't for that, is it, Da?' Nyasanu said.

'No. It is to keep a steady supply of good-looking young girls for his harem, and ugly, tall, and strong ones for the *ahosi*—the female soldiers,' Gbenu sighed. 'Now leave me, my son—for I must rest. . . .'

Going away from his father's house, Nyasanu walked with his head down, a prey to the depression his father's sombre interpretation of Dahomean life nearly always awoke in him. So he sought his usual remedy for that: he directed his steps towards the house of his mother.

When he entered her house, Gudjo, his mother, looked up at him and smiled. She and her eldest daughter—whom, when he spoke of her, Nyasanu was forced to call 'novichi nyqnu', that is, 'mother's child female', since there is no word in Fau for sister, nor for brother for that matter—were weaving straw mats. Axisi, for so the girl was called, because she had been born in the market-place where Gudjo had gone to peddle the mats and baskets and clay pots that she made, grinned at him and made an impish face.

Today thy little black monkey cannot sit upon her bottom,' she said. 'And 'tis thy fault, Novichi sunu.'

'Axisi!' Gudjo said.

'*Kafla, No.*' Axisi said. This was formula. It meant 'Do not listen, Mother!' And once a girl, especially a spoiled favourite daughter such as Axisi, had pronounced the ritual words, she was permitted to say whatever absolutely outrageous things that came to her head.

'How is it my fault, Axisi?' Nyasanu said.

'Because you detained her last night, Novichi sunu,' Axisi mocked. The fact that she went on calling him the clumsy Dahomean circumlocution for brother, 'mother's child male', indicated that she was sure she held something over his head. Ordinarily, brothers and sisters call each other by name.

'Detained her?' Nyasanu said.

'Yes. Or perhaps you were playing *gbigbe*. But are you not too old for hide and seek, oh male child of my mother? What is certain is that thou were seen not only kissing thy little black monkey on the mouth, but also investigating to see whether the *tokono* had done her work well. . . .'

'Axisi!' Gudjo said, outraged now, truly outraged.

'*Kafla, No*,' Axisi said again.

'A lie,' Nyasanu said calmly. But he was shaking on the inside. It was truly wicked of Axisi to even mention such forbidden things. For the *tokono* was the young married woman into whose charge the prepubescent girls were placed. And her chief function was to perform some mysterious and frequently repeated operation upon them that was supposed to greatly increase their capacity to give pleasure to their husbands once they were wed. He didn't know exactly what the operation was. All he'd been able to get out of Agbale was that it was intensely painful. But he'd guessed that it was also designed to augment the woman's enjoyment of love as well. To which Agbale had responded: 'How would I know, Nyasanu? Perhaps it does; perhaps it doesn't. Let's not talk about it any more. It's not a thing for talking. . . .' She was right, of course. In Dahomey, life was hedged about with so many tabus.

'So,' Axisi went on merrily, 'after examining her to see how much damage thou hadst done to that which thou hast not the right to injure until thou'rt wed, her father's mother stripped thy Agbale naked and beat her with many rods. So, great swordsman, thou'rt guilty of . . .'

'Mother,' Nyasanu said, 'put her out of here.'

'Go, Axisi,' Gudjo said.

'Ah, Mother . . .' Axisi began.

'Go!' Nyasanu said. 'Or I will propose that our father hasten your wedding to Asogbakitikli, Axisi! And he will heed me, doubt it not, little woman!'

Asogbakitikli was Axisi's husband to be, chosen for her, as was usual among well-off Dahomeans, by her father. The result of the choice was that—also as usual, or almost—Axisi hated her fiancé with all her rebellious heart.

She stood up then and faced her brother. Like all the children of Gbenu and Gudjo, she was tall.

'Hear me, Nyasanu,' she said very quickly. 'I shall *never* marry that fat and clumsy idiot. Never. And if our father forces me to, I shall cut my throat before the door of the cult house of the ancestors on the day that Asogbukitikli's kinswomen come for me. I don't mean to marry at all, for all men are hateful, even you, male child of my mother! But if I should change my mind, be assured that my marriage shall be *xadudo*, for that is the only honourable way for a free woman to wed!'

And with that awful word drumming in their ears, Axisi turned on her heel and marched out of there. Mother and son stood there, looking at one another, their heavy-lipped mouths slack with worry. There were thirteen different ways of getting married in Dahomey. And of these thirteen, each of the first twelve had its respective rites, ceremonies, tabus, guarantees, and laws. But the thirteenth had no rites, no ceremonies, no tabus, no laws. Under it a young couple simply ran away and lived together. That thirteenth was *xadudo*. It was considered all right for slaves, tenant farmers, and other people of no importance. But for a chief's daughter, it would be a disgrace, and for her family a social disaster. In the past, both Gudjo and Nyasanu knew, *xadudo* elopements of high-born maids had been the cause of more than one ferocious tribal war.

'We,' Nyasanu said, 'must do something about Axisi, Mother.'

'True,' Gudjo groaned. 'But *what*, oh my tall and handsome son?'

'Leave it to me,' Nyasanu said. 'I will find out whom it is she loves and talk to Father. He has had of Asogbakitikli few gifts and even less work, so it will be no problem to return them . . .'

'None,' Gudjo said drily, 'except the stubbornness of thy father, oh my son.'

'Father will listen to me,' Nyasanu said, 'for I have his love.'

Gudjo smiled.

'You do, don't you, son?' she said. 'And no wonder. You've always been dutiful—even in your marriage you've bowed to your father's choice. . . .'

'Because he chose well,' Nyasanu said. 'Agbale is the most

beautiful girl in Alladah.'

'Humph!' his mother said. 'I'm not so sure of that!'

Nyasanu bent over and kissed her cheek.

'Don't be a jealous female, Mother!' he said.

Gudjo laughed aloud.

'You know, you're right,' she said. 'We mothers are always jealous of the wives of our sons. Especially the first one. I don't know why, but we . . .'

'Mother,' Nyasanu said, 'why does so great a chief as my father look upon life in so dark a fashion?'

'That is a matter of his *fa*, my son,' Gudjo said. 'He cannot help his destiny or the way he's made. . . .'

'But,' Nyasanu whispered, 'much do I fear that he is right, Nochi. Sometimes this world seems a cruel place. . . .'

Gudjo took his arm.

'Sit down, Nyasanu,' she said, 'and listen to me. You are tall and strong, but you are a child for all that. I fear that all men are children and remain so until they die. . . .'

'Nochi,' Nyasanu said, 'little mother, I . . .'

'Listen!' Gudjo said. 'Hath not the year rainy seasons and dry? So hath our lives both joy and sadness. Life is good, my son! The otutu calls for rains, singing with a sweetness that pierces one's heart—and is not the sound of her singing good, my son? When you go out with your *dokpwe* and wound the earth with your hoes, working in unison, striking, turning the earth with your heels, until the sweat runs down, and chanting to the strokes, is that not good, my son? When the rain whispers down and the maize and millet and cassava and yams spring up from the earth's bosom to feed the children of men, is that not good? When the small boy pumps the bellows so that the coals glow in the forge and thy hammer rings against the red-hot iron, shaping it to thy will, is not that a pride in thee?'

'Yes, Nochi,' Nyasanu said, 'but . . .'

'Is not love good, Dosu?' Gudjo said. 'When thy lust in the night with thy love . . .'

'Mother!' Nyasanu said in an agony of shame. 'I . . .'

'Not even Agbale?' Gudjo said.

'Especially not Agbale,' Nyasanu whispered. 'She . . . she won't! She says she wants to show our sleeping mat—afterwards to her father.'

'Bless her,' Gudjo laughed. 'And bless you, my son. My tall, fine son—who is also clean. I like that. Go to your bride like

30

that, for that is also good.'

'Mother ...' Nyasanu said, 'what of the *tasino* I must be with after my circumcision is healed to appease the spirit of the knife? Agbale is troubled about that....'

'Tell her not to be. For such a one is old and ugly and comes to thee in the dark and goes before it is light. You will never even know who she is, and hence will take no pleasure of it. Therefore it is no sin. But speaking of thy circumcision. When ...'

'Now,' Nyasanu said gloomily. 'That is, when the rains come.... The king hath so ordered it....'

Gudjo looked at him.

'Have no fear, oh my son,' she whispered, 'for thou'rt a young lion. And thou knowest I shall pray for thee....'

And with that comfort, which, come to think of it, was not small, Nyasanu had to be content.

THREE

When Nyasanu came out of his mother's house, he found his best friend, Kpadunu, waiting for him. This did not surprise him, because among Dahomeans, a man's best friend is not only a beloved comrade, as he is among all peoples, but also the holder of a very definite ritual, religious, and legal position, involving certain obligations towards the one who has so chosen him. And among the obligations Kpadunu had towards Nyasanu was the pleasant one of visiting him at least once every day.

The two boys embraced solemnly. Then, although it was now night, so that Nyasanu couldn't see Kpadunu's black face clearly, something in the boy's attitude—an unaccustomed stiffness, perhaps—told Nyasanu that his friend was badly troubled.

'Speak, oh my brother!' he said.

'It's Gbochi,' Kpadunu said. 'He's been to my uncle, the sorcerer. And I saw him sniffing around the *fedi* in thy father's grove, so ...'

'Xevioso, blast him!' Nyasanu said. 'Come on!'

The two of them went racing down the road in the moon-

31

light towards Gbenu's grove of sacred palm trees. Each of those fedi palms was the *augaudi*, the guardian of the fate of some member of Gbenu's family. That is, the *vuduno* of Fa, the Priest of Fate, had buried the umbilical cord of each of Gbenu's children under a fedi palm on the day that that particular child had been born. Thereafter that palm became the child's *augaude*, 'fate watcher'.

So if Gbochi could find Nyasanu's guardian tree—even thinking about the horrible possibility made the boy stumble. Kpadunu reached out and caught his arm.

'It is nothing,' Nyasanu said. 'Come on!'

The fedi grove was in sight now, so they stopped running. They fell into the half-crouching, stalking attitude of hunters. Neither of them had a weapon. But then, who needed a blade against such a thing as Gbochi?

Nyasanu drew ahead then, for he knew where his fate watcher tree was. So did Kpadunu, for that matter. In fact, Kpadunu knew absolutely everything about Nyasanu, including his 'strong' names, the secret ones his mother had given him at birth. When Nyasanu had made Kpandunu his *xauntau daxo*, his 'first friend eldest', he had revealed all his secrets to the boy, thus proving his trust. For a man, knowing the things that Kpadunu knew about Nyasanu, could go to the *azaundato*, the sorcerer, and gain control over all three of his souls, which was why Nyasanu telling his 'strong' names to Agbale had been so foolish.

Nyasanu stopped suddenly and put out one hand, palm turned backwards, to halt Kpadunu as well. But Kpadunu had already seen the little fire flickering among the palm trees. They crept forward again, ghost silent, intent, until they were very close to the place where Nyasanu's *augaude* was. Then they hung there, frozen, despite the warmth of the night. Gbochi had found the right tree all right. And he was busily engaged in killing it, in murdering the guardian of Nyasanu's *fa*, thus making sure that there wouldn't be any future for his hated younger half-brother. For when you killed the guardian of a man's *fa*, his fate, you exposed that man to unimaginable evils: that his luck, at the very least, would be uniformly bad from then on, or that Legba the Trickster would eat his brains, leaving him mad, or worse still, his breath, forcing him to cross the river, join the ancestors because of some sickness that no *vuduno* could define, not to mention cure.

Gbochi was working with great care. He had already ringed his brother's tree with deep cuts. And now he was searing those cuts with irons he had heated in the fire that would stop the sap from flowing upwards in Nyasanu's sacred palm tree and it would die. Then his *fa*, his destiny, would have no home and would desert him. To the Dahomean mind, what Gbochi was doing was murder. A great deal more subtle than thrusting a blade through your enemy's guts, but murder just the same.

With a howl Nyasanu fell upon his elder half-brother. Gbochi tore free of him, already running. But before he'd taken two steps, Kpadunu blocked his path.

'Stay and fight, O he who does with men what should only be done with women,' Kpadunu said contemptuously, 'and from the nether position at that.'

'Worse,' Nyasanu said. 'He confuses the penis with the teat. But no more. Tonight he will join his ancestors, the pigs. . . .'

'Spare me!' Gbochi wept. 'It was a joke! I didn't mean to . . .'

Then Nyasanu hit him very fast and very hard. On his big, blubbery nose, which was a mistake.

For Gbochi's nose began to bleed, frightfully. They could see by the light of the fire he had lit to kill Nyasanu's tree, a flood of thick ropy red pour out.

Gbochi put up his hand and touched his nose. His fingers came away covered with his blood.

'I am killed!' he whispered. 'You have murdered me.' Then he fell down on the ground and didn't move.

Kpadunu looked at Nyasanu worriedly.

'Isn't he of the . . .'

'Ayanavi M'mulanu?' Nyasanu said. 'I don't know. His mother, Yu, is. But a man is of his father's *xenu*, isn't he?'

'Sometimes,' Kpadunu said, 'sometimes not. Depends on *how* they got married. And . . .' He stopped then, confusion in his eyes.

'If the man he calls father really is,' Nyasanu said. 'That's what you were going to say, wasn't it?'

'Yes,' Kpadunu said. 'Exactly that, my brother! Look at him. Who but the Xenu Ayanavi M'mulanu, the Stubborn Pig People, Yu's clan, have noses like that?'

'Nobody,' Nyasanu whispered, 'and none that bleed like this, anyhow. So now, first friend—I'm in trouble, bad trouble. It is forbidden to hit a pig person in the nose. They get very sick

33

when you hit them there. Very often they . . . die. . . .'

'See how he bleeds!' Kpadunu said.

'Come, help me pick him up,' Nyasanu said.

Kpadunu bent and took Gbochi by the legs. Nyasanu already had his hand beneath his half-brother's armpits.

'And now?' Kpadunu said.

'We take him to his mother's home. Being of that clan, maybe she's got a special *gbo* to stop the bleeding. In the name of all the *vudun*, Kpad—come on!'

They bore Gbochi to his mother's house. Yu looked up from the bloody, swollen face of her only son, for all the rest of her children were girls, and stared at them. But she didn't say anything. It wasn't until they were halfway across the compound that she began to scream.

'Da . . .' Nyasanu whispered.

'Silence, oh son of Gudjo!' Gbenu said.

Nyasanu was troubled, hearing those terrible words. For by calling him neither Vi nor by his name, Gbenu was publicly disowning him.

'This,' Gbenu said, 'constitutes a court. I, your chief, have enstooled myself before it. This boy, Nyasanu by name, stands accused of a grave crime, that last night he did strike a member of the Stubborn Pig People Clan in the nose. I need not explain that the members, Ayanavi M'mulanu, because of their clan history, cannot be struck there, for due to a structural weakness of their facial bones, inherited from their *tauhwiyo*, their clan ancestor the Boar Ya, such a blow can prove fatal. . . .'

Gbenu paused, looked around the counsel of elders.

'In my judgment,' he went on solemnly, 'I shall not be swayed by the facts that this boy is my second son, and his victim my first son eldest. Until all the testimony is in, both are but members of the Dahomean nation, citizens of the village of Alladah.'

Again he paused. In the silence, there was only the whisper of the great fans, moved by two male slaves, for no woman could take part in, or even witness, a trial that did not concern her directly.

'First, before I call for testimony,' the chief continued, 'has any of the respected elders a question to ask, or a statement to make?'

'A question, Great Toxausu!' an old man said.

34

Nyasanu looked at the man who had spoken. His name was Hwegbe, he was a woodcarver, and he was actually Nyasanu's *taugbochinovi,* or granduncle on his father's side. Of those three facts, only his profession counted now. Woodcarvers, every Dahomean knew, were notoriously unstable people. Hwegbe, for all that he was Gbenu's uncle, had only recently come to Alladah. In his youth, he'd wandered far and wide, as woodcarvers will, returning to live upon his nephew's bounty in his old age, because he'd never remained in any one place long enough to found his own compound. As for wives, Hwegbe's had all been *xadudo*—or common law; and he had deserted each of them as soon as he'd tired of her, many of them the morning after his wedding night.

Which was why he didn't know the answer to the question he asked, that question he shouldn't have asked at all.

'How is it, Great Chief,' he cackled, 'that thy just son eldest is not of *thy* clan? Thou'rt of the ironworkers and ...'

'My marriage to his mother was *avaunusi,*' Gbenu said. 'The lady Yu was given to me by the king's daughter. Hence, my eldest son—and all my children by this marriage—are of their mother's clan. You know the law, venerable elder!'

The answer, Nyasanu realised, was a good one, princesses often gave a favoured lady-in-waiting in marriage, retaining for their dainty, regal selves the same privileges ordinarily held by the father of the bride. And *avaunusi* 'woman with cloth', marriages, so called because the husband was spared all other gifts except a fine headcloth for his bride, were matriarchal, the children taking their mother's name and clan. But his father's answer didn't really lay to rest the malicious implication of his granduncle's query. 'Isn't this boy actually a bastard and a fruit of an ignored or pardoned infidelity?' Because even in an *avaunusi* marriage, a child ought to have at least some of his father's characteristics and Gbochi hadn't—not any at all!

'Any further questions?' Gbenu said. He was visibly annoyed. 'Could it not be,' Nyasanu thought, 'that you, too, have often suspected the Pig woman's virtue, oh my father? And looking upon that ugly and perverted monster—surely since thou'rt no fool, father mine—you have doubted more than twice that you sired him? That being so—why in the name of Legba the Trickster did you not put Yu by?'

Then the answer came to him. Yu had been given to his father by the Princess Fedime, King Gezo's eldest daughter, probably at the Pig woman's own instigation. But by that long ago event the road to greatness had been opened to Gbenu. The king had marked him and made him chief, given him a general's rank in the army. Any attempt to divorce Yu would have reversed the process, brought down Gezo's royal wrath upon Gbenu's head. 'So even if my father actually knows,' Nyasanu reasoned painfully, 'he dares not . . .'

But his thought was interrupted by the words of his own maternal grandfather.

'Just one question more before you proceed, Great Chief. How fares the injured boy?'

Gbenu frowned. Then he said quietly:

'Ill. The scorcerer says he will live, but that his health will be permanently impaired. . . .'

'I see.' Nyasanu's *nochitau*, or maternal grandfather said, 'Let us proceed, then. . . .'

'First,' Gbenu said. 'Do you, Nyasanu, son of Gudjo, admit to having struck thy *medaxochi*, thy elder brother to whom obedience and respect is owed by you, upon the nose?'

'Yes, Da,' Nyasanu said.

'Do not call me Da, not even Tau!' Gbenu thundered. 'Today I am not thy father but thy judge!'

'Yes, Great Chief,' Nyasanu said. 'I struck him, all right, but . . .'

'Silence!' Gbenu said. 'It's not your place to testify on your own behalf! Is there anyone present who knows of an extenuating circumstance? Of any reason why I should not condemn this boy to be beaten with many rods?'

At once Kpandunu pushed his way forward and stood before the chief.

'I, Great Chief,' he said.

Gbenu looked at the boy.

'And who are you?' he demanded.

'Kpadunu, son of Tedo, of the *xenu* Azimavi Xaukaunu Xaukau,' the boy said.

At the boy's words, an audible gasp went up from the assembled elders. Naturally, considering the swarms of youngsters there were in every African village, some of the old men didn't know Kpadunu, but there were those who did. Nyasanu could hear the contrapuntal whispers.

'Son of Tedo, the greatest of the sorcerers! And a member of the Peanut Leaf Clan, those workers of dark and evil

36

magic! It cannot be! How came he to be among us?'

And the response, snorted, angry:

'The boy lies! He's M'butu's son! His mother is Kolo. He was born in Alladah, and Dangbe witness that there are none of the Azimavi Xaukaunu Xaukau among us!'

Gbenu looked at the boy before him. That his father knew Kpadunu perfectly well, that the chief could not have avoided knowing his son's first friend, a boy who was in and out of his compound at all hours was, Nyasanu realised, evident. And yet Gbenu stared at Kpadunu calmly, gravely, as though the boy were a stranger. 'Careful, Kpadunu! Softly, first friend!' Nyasanu wailed inside his heart. 'My father hath more guile than Danh, Dangbe, and all the serpents put together! Think well what you will say . . .'

'Stretch forth your hand, my son,' Gbenu said.

Kpadunu put out his hand. The chief ran his fingertips over it lightly.

'Thy skin is rough,' Gbenu said slowly, 'which is the sign of the Peanut Leaf Clan. But the Azimavi Xaukaunu Xaukau live far to the north among the Maxi, so how . . .'

'My mother,' Kpadunu whispered, 'is of the Golonuvi Tofaunu . . .'

At that, all the elders nodded their heads as though it were explanation enough. It was, in a way, Nyasanu decided. All the world knew that the clan called Children of Golo from the 'River Tofa' had very strange customs. One of those customs was that a bride *always* went on a journey before her marriage, and lay with a casual stranger while far away. The reason for this was that a man who had sexual intercourse with a virgin of the Golo-Tofa Clan inevitably died soon thereafter. So, in order to preserve the lives of their husbands, Golo maidens always contrived to lose their virginity beforehand with a man they didn't care about. But how could Kpadunu be sure his father was Tedo, the greatest *azaundato* or sorcerer in the world?

And although the question had no apparent bearing on the case on trial, Gbenu, out of simple, understandable human curiosity, asked Kpadunu that.

'My mother is very kind,' Kpadunu said slowly. 'She was reluctant to cause the death of even a man she did not know, even one of our enemies, the Maxi, so it occurred to her, there in the far-off land, to consult a sorcerer. That *azaundato* was

Tedo. He consented to take my mother's virginity, since he, himself, possessed powerful *gbos* against sudden death, and besides, my mother was pleasant to look upon then, for she is so still.

Gbenu said gently 'Very well. We accept your identification. Now, one thing more: what relationship do you bear to Nyasanu, the accused?'

'Don't tell him!' Nyasanu prayed silently. 'Don't tell him you are my first friend! Don't you see it will ruin everything? Why should the judge believe the words of one who bears the accused so special a love?'

But there was no way he could warn Kpadunu, not even with a frown or shake of his head. He stood before the elders with fifty watchful pairs of eyes upon him; and of them all, the keenest, most observant were those in his father's head.

Kpadunu didn't even hesitate.

'I am his *xautau daxo*,' he said proudly.

'I see,' Gbenu said. 'Thy name is Kpadunu, he who forms the hedge, a fitting name for a first friend. But, now, son Kpadunu, tell me this: why, in view of the special loyalty that first friends bear one another, should this court believe your words? Would you not lie to save thy almost brother from his punishment?'

'Yes,' Kpadunu said. 'I would lie, Great Chief, if it were necessary. But it is not, because I can prove my words. Last night, O Toxausu and assembled elders, Nyasanu struck his elder brother. That is true. I was there, and saw the blow. But I also saw the provocation. . . .'

'Which was?' Gbenu said.

'That Gbochi deliberately tried to kill Nyasanu's fate-watcher tree. How he found out which fedi palm was Nya-sanu's *augaude*, I do not know. Through some sorcerer, prob-ably, though which one, only Minona, their goddess, knows. . . .'

Gbenu was staring at the boy before him. When he spoke, his bass voice actually trembled.

'You say that Gbochi . . .'

'Ringed Nyasanu's sacred fedi palm about with cuts. And after that, he scored those cuts with fire. I say that. And also that this morning when I passed thy fedi grove, Great Chief, the fronds of Nyasanu's *augaude* were already turning brown. . . .'

Gbenu turned his gaze upon his son's face now. And what

swam in his eyes' depths were deep and moving things: pity, love, loss, anguished pain.

But the elders stared at Nyasanu in horror. To them he had become a living ghost. A man already dead.

'Come,' Gbenu said, his big voice vibrant with pain. 'Let us go to my fedi grove, O elders! I, your chief, command it. Come!'

They stood there a long time, staring at the fate-watcher palm. It was very clearly dying. In the heat of that January day it would not last until nightfall.

'I pronounce the trial over,' Gbenu whispered, 'and this my second son free of guilt, for surely this offence equals and cancels the other, even though Gbochi die of it . . .'

'It is not!' Akili, Nyasanu's maternal grandfather cried out, his voice almost woman-shrill with rage. 'For all my grandson's blow could cost that perverted little swine would be his life; while to kill a man's *fa* is to destroy all three of his souls!'

'Still,' Gbenu said, 'we must hold the two offences equal for the time being. Tomorrow I must go to Abomey to bear the pebbles of the men before the king. There I will consult the king's diviner, the head *bokono* of the realm. Perhaps he can suggest . . .'

Gbenu's voice choked, hung in his throat, unable to force itself over the mountain of his grief. The great tears stood and glittered in his eyes.

At once Nyasanu ran to his father, fell to his knees before him, bent, and kissed his sandalled feet.

'Do not weep for me, O my father!' he whispered. 'I am not worth thy tears!'

Gbenu bent and raised him up.

'Thou art—my future, O young lion who roars within my heart,' he said, 'and very dear to me.' Then he faced the elders, sternly.

'Court is dismissed!' he said, and walked away from there, his great arm about the shoulders of his son.

About the shoulders of a ghost, a man already dead.

FOUR

The sound of wailing throbbed against the night: high, ululate, shrill. Far above the loko trees, the moon heard it and veiled her face with a wisp of cloud. Out on the savanna, a jackal lifted his head and howled. And now, for a moment, the wailing ceased before the house of Gudjo, as the women listened to the pulsations of the beast-dog's voice. Then their multi-throated cry rose again, louder, shriller, and more hopeless. A night bird screamed in the baobab tree, making a rusty blade of a shriek that cut through the women's wailing; but now they didn't stop their crying, but went on with it, shredding the thick, hot darkness with their grief.

Nyasanu stared at the wailing women. How strange it was to hear the *avidochio*, the ritual wailing with which Dahomean women honoured their dead, while yet he lived. All three of his *novichi nyqnu*, female children of his same mother, were there. And it was a tribute to his great beauty and manly charm that no less than ten of his *tauvichi nyqnu*, that is to say, daughters of Gbenu by other wives than Gudjo, were also present, howling as loud as his full sisters; no, louder since there were more of them. Strangest of all was the fact that Alogba, daughter of Gbenu by Yu, and therefore Gbochi's full sister, led the group, tears streaming down her big-nosed, rather porcine face.

Poor Gbochi, Nyasanu thought, not even his own *novichi nyqnu* love him ...

He turned towards his mother and his aunts, both *nochino-vinyqnu*, as his mother's two sisters were called, and his *tauchinovinyqnu*, or sole paternal aunt. The grief of these middle-aged women was hard to bear, especially that of Chadasi, his father's sister, whom Fa had not blessed with children. Her heartbreak equalled Gudjo's, if it didn't actually exceed it ...

'Mother,' Nyasanu groaned, 'Aunt Chadasi, don't weep! I am not worth——'

Nearby, startlingly close at hand, a hideous, whooping sound of laughter drowned his voice. Far out on the rolling, grassy savanna another answered it. Then another and another until all the night rocked with obscene laughter.

40

Nyasanu bowed his head. There was no hope. His death was at hand. When the hyenas laughed in the night, someone always crossed the river, went to the ancestors. And with his fate watcher dead, who else stood doomed but he?

That awful noise stopped the women's weeping. They hung there, their mouths half opened, the tears glittering on their black faces in the moonlight. And in the heavy, suddenly oppressive silence, a new sound rode in upon them: the soft, slow sobbing of someone not wailing aloud, not making the terrible *avidochio*, 'the tears to give the dead' howling shriek, but simply crying her heart out in pure, sincere, absolutely inconsolable grief.

They turned then, all of them, and saw her: there, in the shadow between Gudjo's house and the next, a figure was crawling on her belly like a wounded dog.

'Agbale!' Nyasanu got out, 'O, Agbale, O, Nyaunu, little black one——'

He bent and raised her up. Then he hung there while the baobab trees, the lokos, and the fedi palms swung dizzily above his head, the moon made a circle of white fire around the night. There was a sudden trilling of birds, xetagbles, otutus, and others he didn't know. He realised dimly that the brush birds were imaginary, for these don't sing in the dark. He caught his souls to him, so that he would not faint, for to show such weakness would be unmanly.

Then the dizziness passed.

'Oh, Agbale!' he wept.

She had on dark purple cloth, such as widows wear; the black sash of a bereaved wife was wound about her tiny waist; she had shaved her head, as widows do, and plastered it with mud and ashes as a sign of grief; but what it was that stopped his heart, his breath, was the awful fact that she was crying blood.

He raised his trembling fingers to her cheeks, and took them away, staring at the thick, hot, bloody tears that covered them. He caught her by the shoulders and turned her to face the moon. By its light he saw the two deep cuts she had made in her cheeks just below her eyes, from which the blood poured down and mingled with her tears.

He couldn't get her name out. He tried; but he simply couldn't form the sounds of it at all.

'For thee,' she whispered, 'the tears of my eyes were not

41

enough. I offer thee, my warrior and my prince, those of my heart as well——'

He put out his arms to her before them all. But she backed away from him.

'No,' she said, 'for I have not yet honoured thee enough. . . .'

Then she was gone from him, down upon the hard-packed earth. She lay there, her two arms wrapped around his ankles, kissing his feet and crying.

For some obscure reason, embedded deep in the female psyche, this extravagant display of grief angered Nyasanu's mother.

'Get up from there, girl!' she snapped. 'You're not his wife. And now, you'll never be. Which is just as well, I think. For such a bold and shameless one as you——'

'Mother!' Nyasanu said. 'How dare you! She——'

But Agbale came up slowly before their eyes. Stood there facing Gudjo.

'You're right, my Lady Gudjo, mother of my love,' she said. 'I am not your son's wife. And here in the land of the living, I can never be. But across the river, in the other world—who can say what the Sky Gods will or won't allow?'

Gudjo looked at the girl.

'You're young,' she said wearily, 'you'll take another as your husband. You'll go swinging through the fields before the first rains come. So stop this, will you? You offend the *vudun* of earth, the gods of fertility, by pretending to be what you're not—a wife. And you blaspheme against the *vudun* of the sky by putting on these widow's robes you have no right to. But most of all, you sin against any grief, which Dangbe knows is real. . . .'

'And mine is not?' Agbale whispered. 'Mine is not?'

Something in her tone hit Nyasanu in his belly's pot. It felt like those straps of bronze Dahomean boxers put over their knuckles when they mean to maim or kill. 'Agbale,' he said, and started towards her; but she danced away from him with effortless grace.

She stood there looking at him, not only with all the love and longing in the world in her eyes; with something else as well, something very great and very terrible. Her fingertips strayed over the nipples of her breasts for, like all the women present, she was naked from the waist up, as was the sensible Dahomean custom for summer wear. She went on looking at

42

Nyasanu, half opened her mouth to say—

What? He didn't know. Perhaps he would never know; for it was at that precise moment that Kpadunu and his Uncle Mauchau, the sorcerer, came. Just behind them, towering over them, Gbenu, chief of Alladah followed, his eyes filled with—hope.

Kpadunu was dancing as he approached the now silent women. Which revealed to Nyasanu how great his friend's emotion was, for to Dahomeans dancing is the supreme art. Their absolute mastery of the craft of casting bronze, their sculpture in this metal, in silver, in iron, and in wood, which awes all other peoples who have seen it, the appliqué figured cloth which is their substitute for painting, the beauty of their weaving, their splendid pottery, their finely made jewellery, these things the Dahomeans dismiss with a shrug, not knowing and caring even less what the alien pale-skinned races see in them. But to dance! To mould the pliant air with supple bodies; to stamp out intricate rhythms upon the hard-packed earth to the myriad, polyphony—sound woven into sound, music interspaced with brooding silences—of the drums until the world reels and the *vudun* enters a man's heart, his mind, this—this!—is to be god-drunken, worshipper, artist!

So Kpadunu had no need to speak. His ebony litheness sculptured joy out of the moon-drenched night for them all to see. He leaped—no, soared!—effortlessly to a height taller than Gbenu stood—drifted to earth like a leaf, and his bare feet beat out a marvellous interweaving of syncopated rhythms. He strutted, chest out, his teeth flashing in the glistening blackness of his face, his arms made sinuous, serpentine weavings about Nyasanu's slim form. He swooped to earth, rose slowly, his body a treetrunk shooting up, his arms not only palm fronds, branches, but also the twittering of the birds within them. And the tears that burst from his eyes were tears of joy.

'Great are the *vudun*!' Gbenu said. 'You mean my son's *fa*——'

'Hath found another tree!' Mauchau the sorcerer said.

Gbenu clapped his great hands. At once his menservants and his slaves came flying towards that sound.

'Bring torches,' Gbenu said, 'come!'

Kpadunu and his uncle, the *azaundato*, led the way to the fedi grove. Before Nyasanu's fate-watcher palm, they stopped.

43

Nothing had changed; the palm fronds were brown and dry; the tree was totally dead. But Kpadunu, with a dancing step, strutted and pranced to a spot five yards away. Swiftly he bent and pointed.

'Torch bearers!' Gbenu said. The slaves leaped forward, their torches pushing the night back, bloodying the sky. And now instead of 'the tears give death' funeral wail, the women split the night apart with a great cry of joy.

But Agbale did not cry out with the rest. She stood a little apart and looked at Nyasanu. And there was no joy in her eyes, no joy at all.

By then all the people were dancing. Gbenu led the dance, his mighty body become a fluid mass of twitching muscle, totally without bones. The women whirled, their naked breasts bobbing to the rhythms, for from the nearer compounds, the musicians were already streaming out, shaking their gourd rattles, beating their tall drums.

But neither Nyasanu nor Agbale danced. They both stood there, bemused, lost, staring at that tiny palm shoot some three inches high, sprung overnight from the dark bosom of the earth, their mother. And then, suddenly Agbale started to tremble. She shook all over like a loko sapling in a high wind. The bones melted inside her legs. She dropped to earth, lay there, crying.

At once Nyasanu was kneeling at her side.

'Why do you weep, Nyaunu wi?' he whispered. 'Why dost thou weep, Agbale my love? This is a thing of joy! My *fa* has found a new home and——'

But she could not tell him. She lay there on the earth, remembering the smallest details of the appalling thing she had done, the great and terrible act that instead of uniting them for ever as she had planned it, had now left her finally and completely and eternally alone.

Unlike Nyasanu she was a cult member—a *vudunsi*, or spiritual bride of the Sky God's cult, so she had been given her *fa* at age thirteen, all of two years ago now. Not her complete destiny, of course, because a woman partakes of her husband's fate, her *fa* only is completed when she weds. So when they'd told her of the murder Gbochi had gone to Nyasanu's fate-watcher tree, she had known instantly and at once what to do.

First thing in the morning she had stolen out of her grandmother's house, and gone to the sacred place where the image of her *fa*, her fate, was kept. With her she bore a sack of *ataki* peppers, a jar of *afiti* mustard, and a live rooster. Slowly, deliberately, and with great care, she had rubbed the *ataki* peppers across the ugly image's eyes, thus blinding her own destiny. Then she'd smeared *afiti* mustard across its mouth, leaving it speechless and without the powers of prophecy. Last of all, she'd killed the cock, and dripped its blood into the face of her *fa*. And since in the Dahomean Ffon phase, *fa* eats neither *afiti*, nor *ataki*, nor does he drink cock's blood, by which the *vuduno* meant these things are tabu to him, Agbale had—murdered her own *fa*, ended her own destiny, and death, before many moons were gone, as sure to beckon her to cross the river, join the ancestral dead.

This she had done, believing him doomed, whom she loved more than herself or life. Out of her youth, her hot blood, her impatience, her folly—she'd ended her own future, become a ghost—'While you, my Dosu,' she wailed inside her heart, 'live on to take other wives!'

But she didn't say it aloud. Something inside her heart, rather than in her mind, instructed her, swifter far than even thought. 'If I even have a year with him, a month, a week, a day—an hour—it will be enough. He must not know that I am doomed and damned for love of him. No! Not by my love for thee, my Dosu, but by my own folly and my haste....'

'Agbale,' Nyasanu groaned, 'Little black one! Why do you cry? It's going to be all right! I tell you! It's——'

'I—weep for joy, Dosu,' she whispered. 'Oh yes, I weep for joy!'

FIVE

Nyasanu and Kpadunu lay on their bellies beside Nyasanu's evening field. Since it was late January, Midsummer, the big day season, all planting had come to a stop. With the earth baked into stony hardness by a pitiless sun, there was nothing they could do until March came, and the first whisper of the early rains started the slow rhythms of the earth anew.

Of course Nyasanu had work enough at the forge. Ever

since Gbenu had left Alladah to carry the pebbles of the men to King Gezo at Abomey, all the blacksmiths had been busy hammering out spear points—the razor-edged *assegai* that the Dahomeans had copied from their sometime allies the Ashanti —and brass cartridge cases, moulding bullets, making brush knives—in fact, getting ready for war.

'Think your father will come back today?' Kpadunu said.

'Don't know,' Nyasanu said; then, his voice going tight and dry in his throat, 'He has to! He's been gone fifteen days, Kpadunu! Tomorrow the moon will change. If the king is going to order us to march against the Maxi, he has to give the command soon, or else it will be too late to even start. Their villages are far away. And, if it comes to a siege, why the rains will catch us before——'

'I,' Kpadunu said judiciously, 'don't believe Dada Gezo means to go to war this year. . . .'

'Why not?' Nyasanu said.

Kpadunu grinned at him.

'Because in spite of all the talk of great victories we heard last year, we were badly beaten. The Auyos came in to help the Maxi, not because they love those grubbing mountain swine, but because they hate us, so badly that they'd ally themselves with the evil gods who live beneath the earth if they thought that would be to their good, and to us, harm. . . .'

Nyasanu looked at his first friend.

'You mean to say you think King Gezo's *afraid*?' he whispered.

'I mean to say I think King Gezo is wise,' Kpadunu said. 'Though the two words often amount to the same thing. It's awfully hard to tell a hero from a fool, at times. In fact it usually is.'

'Nyasanu!' Kpadunu said.

'I know. I make strong talk, don't I? But look, first friend mine, tell me this: why do we fight the Maxi?'

'Well,' Nyasanu floundered, 'they're our enemies and——'

'And the Auyo are not? The Hausu? The Fanti? Even the Ashanti three quarters of the time. The Yoruba? Tell me, first friend eldest, who does not hate us? Of what people have we the love?'

'It's envy!' Nyasanu said. 'We're the strongest nation, the best fighters, the——'

'Dung,' Kpadunu said. 'Goat dung at that. Have you ever

46

been to Kumassi, the capital of the Ashanti? Why think you that Gezo made that treaty by which the king of the Ashanti lends him two army corps every time we go to war? Because the Ashanti are the world's best warriors, not us! In fact our women soldiers win all our wars. . . .'

Nyasanu grinned at his friend suddenly.

'Naturally,' he mocked, 'when you keep a herd of females locked up all the time, and guarded by eunuchs so that no man can do to them what they dearly long to have done, they get to be more ferocious than starving leopardesses. So how can mere men stand again them?'

'I'd suggest,' Kpadunu said solemnly, 'that if our enemies were to unsheath their natural weapons and wave them at the *kposo*, *we'd never* win a war!'

The two boys stared at each other. Then they both threw back their heads and roared with laughter.

'But seriously, Nyasanu,' Kpadunu said. 'Why among all our enemies do we nearly always choose the Maxi to attack?'

'Don't know,' Nyasanu said, half angrily. 'Why do we?'

'Because they are the weakest. Because we *know* we can beat them if the Auyo or the Hausa don't come in to help them. So year in year out we fall upon a peaceful, mountain people who are no danger to us at all——'

'Kpadunu!' Nyasunu said. 'You talk treason!'

'I talk sense. But that's the same thing, isn't it? In Dahomey sense is always treasonable. We attack the Maxi, *xauntau daxo* mine, so that Dada Gezo can procure a supply of slaves to sell for gold, iron, and gun powder to the Furtoo, those hideous skinless people from beyond the sea. Thus he adds to the great wealth he has already gained by taxing us nearly to death and enables himself to support his many wives and those puffed-up idlers and eternally rutting she-jackals he *thinks* are his sons and daughters in lascivious idleness. . . .'

Nyasanu opened his mouth to protest, but then closed it again. Had not his father said the same thing in almost exactly the same words? Kpadunu was no fool; and most certainly Gbenu wasn't either. The tyranny of the Dahomean kings was a soul-crushing thing. How many lives did the king take each year in his monstrous 'customs'? More than thirty or forty, surely. And if rumours had it right, as rumour often did, the king sent a man and a woman of his household *every* morning to the ancestors to thank them for allowing him to see a new day. Which meant, since the year had three-hundred-sixty-odd days, that Gezo sacrificed over seven hundred human beings a year simply to bid the ancestors good morning!

He didn't like to think about those things. They made him sad. More, they made his stomach sick. They awoke a longing in him to leave Da's Belly, travel to some fairer, less oppressive clime, where—but then he remembered his father's words: 'How can one leave Dahomey? Only by being sold to the flayed ones, the Furtoo?'

'I wish Father would come home!' he said aloud.

'Look!' Kpadunu said. 'I see someone now! Maybe it's your father——'

Nyasanu shook his head.

'My father always travels on horseback, like the great chief he is,' he said proudly. 'You should know that, Kpadunu. And whoever that is down there is——'

'Walking,' Kpadunu said, cupping his hands about his eyes to shade them against the sun's glare. 'What's more, it's a woman. No, a girl. Why, it's Agbale. Another thing I should have known. My sister told me that she comes here every day to——'

'Water my fate guardian tree,' Nyasanu whispered, 'lest it die before the rains come——'

Then he didn't say anything else. He lay lost, watching Agbale as she came towards the sacred fedi grove with a tall waterjar balanced on her woolly little head. She did not so much as put up her hand to steady the jar, but walked easily, gracefully, so that the jar, her beautiful conical breasts, the figured skirt draped over her wide hips all swayed to the same rhythm.

'How she loves thee!' Kpadunu said.

'Yes,' Nyasanu said, 'but——'

'But what?' his first friend said.

'There is sadness in her,' Nyasanu said. 'A bad sadness. Often, when she doesn't know I'm watching her, she cries. And she does not go to her cult houses any more. The priestess of Mawu—for Agbale is of the Sky Goddess cult, you know— has complained to her father that she neglects the sacrifices and the rites——'

'That's bad,' Kpadunu said. 'Why does she?'

'She says it doesn't matter any more. That nothing

48

does——'

'Except thy new fate watcher. She comes and waters it every day without fail. If nothing matters any more, why does she do that?'

'Well, Nyasanu said. 'Look, Kpad—I don't know! When she says nothing matters, I think she means nothing in her own life!'

'*You're* in her life,' Kpadunu said.

'Yes. But since she has already had her *fa* established, at least to the extent that women can, I cannot influence what happens to her. I think—a *bokono* or a dream—has told her something bad about her future. In fact, I'm sure of it. But she won't tell me what it is——'

'Let me talk to her,' Kpadunu said, 'I'll get it out of her. I'm good at finding out secrets. . . .'

'Kpad,' Nyasanu said, 'have you decided to become a—sorcerer?'

'Yes,' Kpadunu said; then, 'it's an honourable profession, Nya!'

'I didn't say it wasn't,' Nyasanu whispered, 'still——'

'It frightens people. Even—you,' Kpadunu said soberly. 'Though it need not. All the magic I'll ever work as far as you're concerned will be good magic. In fact, it already has been——'

'It has been?' Nyasanu said. 'How?'

'Don't ask me that. I can't tell you. I'm not permitted to. Well—do you want me to talk to her? It wouldn't be very smart of you to take as your number one wife a woman who—who's accursed, say. Or condemned for some secret sin. Or even who's been chosen as a wife by one of the ghosts of the ancestors. . . .'

'Well—all right,' Nyasanu said. 'But whatever you find out, Kpad, I'm warning you now, I *won't* give her up. I can't.'

'She is—beautiful,' Kpadunu said, 'but there are other beautiful girls, my brother. And, besides——'

But it was then that they heard the hoofbeats of Gbenu's horse; still far off and faint in the distance, but sounding clearly, growing louder, coming on.

Agbale saw them as they went racing down the road towards the sound of the hoofbeats. And she saw them once again as they came back, clinging to the ornamented stirrups of

49

Gbenu's horse. As they reached the second of the roads just abreast of where she knelt before the tiny, newly sprouted fedi palm, they loosed their grip on the stirrups and began to dance their joy.

Agbale's eyes narrowed, watching that, then widened again, became luminous.

'So,' she whispered to herself, 'he is safe for another year! There will be no war....'

Had anyone asked her how she knew this without having been told, she would have stared at him, astonished at the degree of stupidity foreigners were capable of. For, of course, no Dahomean would have asked so idiotic a thing. A Dahomean would *know*, just as she knew. She had needed to see only the first of their movements, perhaps five or six of the swoops, soaring leaps, earth-pounding stomps, and struttings to know they were writing the word 'peace!' with their black bodies on the naked air.

Of course Kpadunu was the finest dancer in Alladah and Nyasanu only a little less skilled; but it wasn't that. The dance itself was a language, speaking to her mind and her heart in ways she didn't really understand herself and lacked the words to explain. Pressed to do so, she would have had to proceed by indirection; by pointing out what was not, rather than what was.

'It's not a war dance,' she would have said. 'They don't make the motions of brandishing weapons. They don't throw the spear, shoot the gun, stab with the sword. Nor do they pretend to be cutting off heads....'

But the rest of it, she couldn't have said. It was too abstract, too stylised. The import of it—what it suggested, rather than stated, to her mind—was that life would go on. March would come and with it the patter of the early rains. Then the *dokpwe* of the young men would move out into the fields, clearing them of the dried bush, then stooping over the rows with their short-handled hoes, swinging the broad blades in perfect rhythm, wounding the earth. April would drift across the land in mists and whisperings, and she, along with all the other women and girls, would move down the rows, sowing the first crop, maize, beans, peanuts, cassava, for—except for yams, which were planted in hillocks in the iron-hard earth late in February by the men—seeding the earth was a thing of women. And a good thing it was, too: cradling the sack in one

50

elbow, though its cords slanted upward diagonally across one's upper trunk and were looped around one's neck and left shoulder, while the right hand dipped up the seed, swinging out in an arc, broadcasting the kernels in an iridescent arc, and the feet making a heel-toe movement, covering them, the whole of it a kind of sober, ritual dance that worshipped the dark earth gods, fertility, the sky that sent the rain, the benevolent ancestors who protected life, all in this one good rite or sowing....

In May, the millet, sorgho, and cotton would be planted. Early in June, white beans. Later, while June still lingered golden and misty over the plains, she and the other women would crop the ears of maize designed for human consumption; left too long, the corn became hard, and fit only for animal fodder.

In July, the rains would lessen, and she'd have to help with weeding at the end of the month when the rains ceased; and the small day season begun, she'd work at harvesting first the maize and yams, then as August blazed the earth with a kind of spring, all other crops.

Nor during this time would Nyasanu, Kpadunu, and the other boys and men be idle. Apart from their specialities—such as ironworking for Nyasanu and the preparation of *gbos*; for Kpadunu, charms and spells under his uncle's direction—they, like every male Dahomean, would join their socialist collectivities called *dokpwe*, for communal work. They'd tend animals, sheep, goats, pigs, horses, a very few cows—beef animals don't prosper in Dahomey; build houses; thatch roofs; burn brush and clear the fields for next year's planting—for Dahomeans are a hardworking people, among the most industrious races in all the world....

Betimes there'd be the great rites and ceremonies dedicated to the earth gods, the sky gods, the gods of thunder and the sea. And the lesser ones: the deification of the ancestors, the rites of birth, the twelve different kinds of ceremonies for the twelve kinds of marriage, the solemn and imposing mourning and funeral rites....

Life, Agbale thought, is a complicated business! There're so many things to do and learn! She remembered suddenly her girlhood school where the *tokono* had taught her the domestic arts—and also done the intensely painful things to her female genitalia which were designed to give her husband-to-be so

51

great pleasure in love that he'd never leave her. Only one thing remained—a thing she should have done two years ago, when she'd first entered into puberty, but hadn't—out of fear of pain. To be beautiful, her body should be covered all over with decorative scars. She'd have to submit to being cut with a sharp knife in more than one hundred separate places and then to having soot and other irritants rubbed into her wounds. When they healed, she'd have beautiful scars made in patterns in order that even naked, she'd seem to be clothed in a twining network of leaves, vines, ridges, crosshatches, cords, standing up high above the glossy ebony of her skin—so that Nyasanu could touch them, so that his fingertips could move over them, would linger. . . .

Thinking all that brought a wave of heat beating about her small head.

'I'm wicked!' she thought. 'Depraved. But I want him. Mawu Lisa witness that I want him so——'

Then abruptly, she remembered that she had killed her own *fa* and had no future at all. She bent her lovely little round head and wept stormily. A long time, a very long time. After that, she raised her oval, soft, nightshade face towards the sky.

'Mawu!' she prayed, 'I am pledged to him. Save me! I was a fool. I could not let him die alone. But now that he's saved, save me, too! Do not make me cross the river all by myself——'

She stood there listening for one sign, some answer. But there was none. She hung there, her slim body sculpturing defeat.

'If,' she whispered, 'you will not spare my life—at least do not eat my breath—before—before I have known—his love——'

Then, head down and blindly, she whirled and ran up the curving path towards the compound of her father. . . .

Nyasanu stared at Gbenu.

'Da,' he whispered, 'could not the king's *bokono* be wrong?'

'Yes,' Gbenu said, 'he could be. Any diviner can be mistaken, my son. Still what he read in the *du*, the sacred lots, hath a certain force. Your *auguade* was killed—and sprang up again some distance away. And the royal *bokono's du* say that you will leave Dahomey—that your life will be renewed in a far-off

52

land——'

'Da,' Nyasanu said.

'Yes, my son?'

'Couldn't we have Zezu read my *du* again? Just to make sure, I mean?'

Gbenu considered that.

'Yes,' he said slowly, 'we could. But it seems to me that in light of all that has happened, we'd better establish your *fa* once and for all. . . .'

'Da,' Nyasanu said, 'we can't. Not yet. I haven't yet seen the *adagbwolo*! And until I do—until I have been circumcised, declared officially a man—how can my fate be established? 'Tis against all custom, and all law. . . .'

'There you're right, my son,' the *toxausau* said. 'But it is only a short month until the rains begin. I suggest we wait, then call in the cutter of foreskins, have the circumcision performed, and thereafter once you're healed, establish your *fa*. . . .'

Nyasanu looked at his father.

'Da,' he whispered, 'would it be too much to ask—I mean—could you see your way clear to—to advance me the money to——'

'Marry Agbale!' Gbenu said.

'Yes, Father,' Nyasanu said.

'Think you it would be wise to take a wife with so uncertain a fate hanging over you?' Gbenu said.

'I don't know,' Nyasanu said. 'All I know is that I cannot live without her. So if I am not permitted to take her unto me soon—my fate will end in any case! Oh, Da, can't you understand?'

Gbenu smiled at his favourite son. He was not so old that he could not remember how he'd felt at the first sight of Gudjo—the lovely woman who had given him this young lion of a son. Of course, he'd already had a wife by then, Yu—who despite her ugliness he'd been forced to take because she'd been offered him by the Princess Fédime, Dada Gezo's eldest daughter. A man didn't refuse a bride offered him by a member of the royal family, not if he were wise. Besides, there had been in his first marriage several flattering circumstances and not a few advantages. To begin with, though nobody's beauty, Yu, in her youth, had been very exciting in the carnal, sensual sense. He had never loved her, but he had desired her—for Pig Clan

53

member or not, Yu had been desirable. That was one thing. Another was that Yu, herself, had instigated the whole thing, as she candidly confessed after they were wed. She'd seen Gbenu on one of the visits all prominent Dahomeans had occasionally to make to the court, and as she put it: 'One glance and I was afire! So I sought out my Lady Fedime and——'

'And brought me to the attention of the royal house,' Gbenu thought now. 'Which had—and has—its advantages. I have become *toxausau* of Alladah. I am a general in the army. My wealth is great. I have many wives and many sons and daughters. So what does it matter that Yu early began to use her privileges as an *avaunusi* wife to remedy my neglect of her? Having the princess's support, as she does, she knew I could not beat her with many rods. Gbochi now—my eldest—is he truly mine? Ugly as he is—weak—effeminate——'

'Da,' Nyasanu said.

'I am thinking, son,' Gbenu said. But he wasn't really. What he was doing was remembering. Gudjo had been very like his son's bride-to-be, Agbale. Perhaps it was that fact that had caused him to choose Agbale for Nyasanu. So he could understand his son's feeling towards that tiny, exquisite, nightblack girl. It wasn't lust. Not, at least, entirely. Lust was a far more simple thing. Lust a woman like Yu could satisfy. But when you wanted a woman at your side—on your sleeping mat, of course, but also walking beside you under the trees, hand in hand; when her laughter was your music; her voice talking commonplaces was sweeter than all the birdsong under heaven —that was something else, a finer, purer thing. When you could tell her your dreams, consult her about your problems— when the babies she brought forth from her swollen belly (being even in that state, the loveliest of women!) were as beautiful as the sky gods themselves, children shaped from the very stuff of night, tall as *vudun*, eyed with stars! That was a rare thing— and very fine. Never he remembered, lying with Gudjo, had he raged and roared and pounded her with doubled fists, as he had Yu—and other wives of his. Never had she bit his throat, clawed his back, screamed the '*aga gbe*', adultery language, words at him as many women did to demonstrate their passion. No. Still, Gudjo was the most passionate of all his wives. Only her love was deep and fine and true and tender. Lying together they kissed each other and smiled and moved together like dancers and worshipped each other with their bodies and

54

there was no ugliness in it. What he did with Yu and his other wives was what a beast does with his mate on heat. What he did with Gudjo was what a man does with his wife; what maybe even the male and female *vudun* did together. And the result of it, the proof of its quality, was here before him: this boy as beautiful as the night itself, godlike, tall, with a commanding magic about him. How slowly how lovingly had he and Gudjo shaped this young lion—taking all of a night about it, until the morning sun was in her eyes before she cried out with the voice of the otutu saying:

'Now, my husband, now!' And the thing was done.

'Da,' Nyasanu all but wept, 'please!'

Gbenu smiled at his son then.

'Send her your calabash, son,' he said, 'for I will do it!'

When Agbale got the beautiful calabash bowl, carved with myriad figures declaring Nyasanu's love, and more, his desire that the wedding take place this very year, she went in search of her mother.

'Nochi,' she said, 'call the knife man, for I must have my scars——'

Adje, her mother, looked at her.

'Will he pay for it, this chief's son who hath proved that Legba hath devoured his brains by choosing you, idiot girl of mine?' she said.

'Yes, Mother,' Agbale said.

'Hummmphf,' her mother snorted; then, 'I will speak to your father, foolish child!'

That same afternoon, Nwesa, Agbale's father received a visitor. The young man, clad in a modest Dahomean toga of white cotton and wearing neither ornaments nor jewellery nor any sign of rank, came accompanied by his mother, the Lady Gudjo, his aunt, the Lady Chadusi, his paternal grandfather, the *xenuga*, or head of his clan, the venerable elder Adjaemi, and the equally venerable elder Akili, his maternal grandfather. With this group of distinguished Dahomeans, came another, much larger, group of slaves, some of whom bore burdens on their heads.

The princely young Dahomean fell to his knees and kissed the ground before Nwesa's feet.

'Rise, O Nyasanu, son of Gbenu!' Nwesa said.

Nyasanu got up.

55

'My lord,' he said, 'I beg of you the privilege of calling you father.'

Nwesa frowned.

'Your meaning is not clear, chief's son,' he said.

'Long ago, when your daughter was but a "things-peddle-person", and I but newly a "killer of lizards",' Nyasanu said, using the metaphoric Dahomean terms which indicate middle childhood in a girl, and preadolescence in a boy, 'my father and you, my lord, had a talk. Modesty forbids me to publicly state the subject of it. I ask only, do you, my lord, remember what was discussed at that time?'

'I do,' Nwesa said.

'Also at that time,' Nyasanu went on, 'my father's *bokono*, Zezu, and my lord's, Agasau, both found the cast *du* of Fa favourable to the matter under discussion. So now I ask you my lord, hath anything happened since to cause my lord to change his mind?'

'No, nothing,' Nwesa said gruffly.

'Then, before these members of my family, before these two venerable elders, ancestors of mine whom Fa has permitted to live on, I ask thee, my lord Nwesa, for thy daughter, Agbale, as my number one wife, to be honoured by me lifelong, above all others!'

Nwesa didn't answer that. He did not, because at the moment, by age-old Dahomean custom, he was not supposed to.

Nyasanu turned and clapped his hands. At once a slave came forward and fell to his knees before the chief's son, holding out to him a package. Nyasanu took it and turned to Nwesa.

'Tobacco,' he said solemnly, 'for my lord's pipe. May it make a pleasant smell in my lord's nostrils.'

Nwesa took the tobacco. It was quite heavy, being about one kilogram, in fact. He nodded, turned to one of his own slaves.

'Call the *xenuga*!' he said.

The *xenuga*, or head elder of his clan, the Guduvi Adjalenu, by interpretation, 'the Children of Gudu, the People of Adja', one of the very few sacred clans in Dahomey, for it was devoted wholly to the worship of Mawu-Lisa and the Sky *Vudun*, was Nwesa's own granduncle Azauvidi. He, a tall and stately man with a thick white beard, came at once.

'This young man would have of us our daughter,' Nwesa said, 'and comes bearing gifts for thee, O *xenuga*, tobacco.'

'I thank you, son Nwesa,' Azauvidi said. 'I will divide it among the clan members.'

'Then you look favourably upon his suit?' Nwesa said.

'Well,' Azauvidi said, 'to smoke tobacco, one needs fire. . . .'

At once Nyasanu clapped his hands again and another slave knelt before him holding out a beautifully carved calabash filled with *dekwe*, bamboo tinder, and a box containing the flint and iron necessary for striking sparks.

Azauvidi, the clan elder, accepted this gift, too, from the hands of his nephew, Agbale's father.

'Do you now look upon this young man's plea with favour?' Nwesa said.

Slowly and solemnly the *xenuga* shook his head.

'The ancestors have thirst,' he said.

Again Nyasanu clapped his hands and a group of slaves scampered forward, bearing in their hands many clay bottles of *lixa*, a kind of whisky made from millet grain.

'Let us all retire to the cult house of the ancestors,' Azauvidi said.

Then all those present—Nyasanu and his family, Nwesa and his wife Adje, Agbale's mother, the *xenuga* Azauvidi, and those members of the clan who had begun to gather for the occasion by then—went towards the *doxoxo*, that large and imposing thatched bungalow which housed the *ase*, those slim and delicately beautiful wrought-iron altars of the mighty dead, many of the newest of them made for Nwesa's clan by Nyasanu himself. There, with great solemnity, Azauvidi passed over the bottles of strong drink to the *tauvoduno*, or priest of the ancestor cult.

'I bid thee drink, O *tauvudun*!' the priest cried out in a loud voice. 'A young man comes bringing liquor for you, ancestor gods!'

Then he poured out all the *lixa* before the altars.

The *tauvoduno* knelt before the great *ase* of the founder of the clan and prayed silently. Then from beneath the wrought-iron altar, he took a silver *fa* cup. It was bowl-shaped and borne on the back of a most realistic Xwensuvo bird between its outstretched wings. The legs of the Xwensuvo and its claws gripping a branch embedded in a small mound of silver formed the stem and base of the cup. It was, Nyasanu decided, the single most beautiful *fa* cup he'd ever seen. He'd ask Amosu to

57

make him one like it, when it came time to establish his own *fa*.

In the cup were sixteen silver beads, representing the palm kernels or *du* of Fa. The priest laid it down, and beside it a board covered with white clay. Then, pouring the beads into his hand, he began his divination, which consisted of opening his hand so that only one or two beads fell into his other hand. Immediately they were retransferred into the hand holding the beads, and the priest made two marks on the white board with his fingertip if one seed had fallen, a single mark if two had fallen. This he did eight times, while all the spectators held their breath.

'What says the *fa* of the *tauhwiyo*?' Azauvidi said at last. 'What answer does the guardian destiny of the great ancestor, the founder of our clan give to this match?'

'That he favours it, let it proceed,' the *tauvoduno*, the priest of the ancestor cult, said. And all the people cried aloud their joy.

Outside in the compound once more, Nyasanu called his father's slaves and gave a huge sack of millet to his future mother-in-law, Adje. This, too, was part of the ceremony, but it was also prudence. For while all the things he had already done for Nwesa, such as to come with his *dokpwe*, his communal work group, to clear his future father-in-law's fields and hoe them for the planting, repair the roofs of his houses, and build him new houses, new walls, dig deeper wells, and forge *ase* for his ancestors were obligatory, the tasks he'd done for Adje, such as cutting whole forests of firewood for her cook fires, sending his father's slaves to bear her goods to market, showering her with women's clothes, beads, bracelets, and jewellery, weren't. But being a sober, prudent youth, Nyasanu had done them just the same, for mothers-in-law are as much mothers-in-law in Africa as they are in the rest of the world, and a wise son-in-law to be did well to court their favour. After that, Nyasanu made the final gift, a money payment of five thousand dowry shells, the Dahomean currency.

Of this sum only eight hundred and fifty were required as the ceremonial bridal price, thus symbolically lifting the approaching marriage into the highest *akwenusi*, 'money with woman' category: but Nyasanu had demanded and got this tremendous sum from Gbenu to demonstrate how great his love for Agbale was and also to show how rich and powerful a chief his father was, thus giving vent to that number one Dahomean vice, excessive pride.

And now, once Nwesa had accepted his gift, Nyasanu bowed before him once again.

'When can your diviner meet with my father's *bokono* to determine a favourable day for the wedding?' he said.

He saw a look of embarrassment come into Nwesa's eyes. The reason for Nwesa's shame he did not, could not, know; but actually, it was simple: Agbale, always headstrong, had flatly refused to have any of her beauty cicastrisations made before this very day. Usually a high-born Dahomean girl received the hundreds of cuts that transformed her into a beauty, roped all over with interesting scars, little by little over a period of years, beginning a week or two after her first menstrual period. But not Agbale!

'I won't have anybody cutting me!' she had howled; and that had been that—at least up until now. So, the fact that all of a sudden, as women will, she had abruptly changed her mind, was going to delay matters seriously. For, if she could not endure all the hundreds of cuts at one time, the wedding might be held back years, until she had all the scars. 'And,' Nwesa reflected grimly, 'if she does have them all at once, it is likely never to take place, for surely so slim and delicate a girl as she will die!'

'My daughter, O son of mine to be,' Nwesa said sadly, 'asks a delay. It seems that now, at last, she'd have her scars!'

Nyasanu bowed his head in assent. There was no way he could refuse Agbale what was a woman's age-old right. But he was sick at heart when he considered the long delay—doubled or tripled by the fact that he himself had to be healed of his own obligatory circumcision as well before he could wed—and terrified by the terrible risk of a complete scarification at one time. That Agbale would run that risk, he knew. Agbale would have done anything, run any risk for his sake.

But man among men that he might be, telling his father of his fears that same night, Nyasanu broke down and cried.

That next afternoon Nwesa was honoured by a visit from no less a personage than the chief of Alladah himself. The two men sat on low stools, while attendants held umbrellas over them. This, too, was a great honour for Nwesa, since only chiefs were entitled to the gaudily decorated parasols. In fact, Gbenu had the second great sunshade brought along as evidence of his respect for the father of his son's bride-to-be. With him was Zezu, his personal *bokono*, or diviner. Solemnly Zezu cast the sixteen *du* that were the lots of Fa, and declared that tomorrow itself would be a propitious day to begin the cicatrisations. . . .

Nwesa frowned. To him, logically enough, it seemed that it was still too hot to have his daughter cut all over in hundreds of places. The risk of fatal infection was grave. This was one of the things that made intelligent Dahomeans suspicious of diviners: they so often read the *du* in a way that was calculated to please the rich and the great.

Of course, the marriage of his daughter to the chief's son was a source of joy to Nwesa, too. But he loved his pretty, stubborn, headstrong daughter truly. He wanted this wedding to take place. He wanted Agbale wed to Nyasanu. But by all the dark and ugly *vudun* of the earth, he didn't want her dead! And when a girl died of mortification of her beauty cuts, her final agony was terrible.

'Great Chief,' he said slowly, ' 'tis very hot. . . .'

'I know,' Gbenu said.

'Had we not better consult still another diviner?'

At that Zezu leaped to his feet, his face twisted with rage.

'Don't trust me, eh?' he shrieked; 'Tell him, oh Toxausau! When have I been known to fail?'

'Never,' Gbenu said mildly, 'but there's always a first time, Zezu. Besides, I want a wife for my son. I don't want him mourning a corpse? Agreed, O Nwesa. Call your own diviner!'

At once retainers were sent to find Nwesa's diviner, Akausu by name. But there was one element in the matter that no one had taken into consideration: Akausu was so terrified at being brought into the presence of the chief, and even more into that of the number one *bokono* of Alladah, Zezu, that having been informed en route what Zezu's reading of the *du* had been he immediately read his own magic kernels the same way, confirming Zezu's interpretation to the letter. Which meant that poor Agbale had to receive her ceremonial cuts at the end of the dry season, before the rains came, while the heat was still on the land.

They made, of course, a great feast of it, Nyasanu brought the knife man a brand new *kisi*, or ceremonial knife. He came with all his *dokpwe*, his work group, and his *gbe*, his fraternal

60

society.... All Agbale's girlfriends were there, too; and all the world was merry—except Agbale herself. Despite the palm wine she had been given, she was both sober and afraid.

Then she saw Nyasanu smiling at her. His teeth were very even and white, because Gudjo had refused to allow the boy to have them filed into points or one or two of them knocked out by the *adukato*, the tooth breaker, in conformity with the Dahomean idea of male beauty. Agbale was glad he hadn't had it done. It seemed to her he was handsomer with all his teeth. And, at the sight of his smile, courage came to her. She'd bear it. She would! She'd endure the whole series of cuts without crying out.

Then the knife man bent above her and she flinched. But Nyasanu took her hand.

'I am here, little black woman,' he said.

The knife flashed in making a zigzag line of cuts above her nose. She knew then that she was going to be able to bear it. It hurt, but not so terribly as she'd feared. The knife was new, and very sharp, so the pain was less. A dull, old knife, badly sharpened, would have hurt more. The *nukpante,* the 'there one sees', cuts were done in a flash. Then the knife man made the *djixuse* cuts close to her hair; those, 'the rain wet straw', cuts were made to emphasise the beauty of her close-curling, woolly coiffure. She was trembling now, and the blood came down in little rivulets over her face. Nyasanu bent and put a fine silken cloth in her lap.

She smiled at him, knowing the gift was to give her courage. Kpadunu poured a handful of cowry shells onto the cloth. As Nyasanu's best friend, it was his duty as well to encourage his friend's bride-to-be in her ordeal.

And now the knife man made the sacred *tadu*, 'head word', cuts. When a woman talks to the man she loves, the scars of these cuts on her temple stand out and pulsate with her blood, thus giving her lover visible proof of her love. Agbale bore these well, and also the *gbugbome* circle, the 'kiss me' scar cut in her left cheek.

Then, assisted by her girlfriends, Agbale stood up. She was quite naked except for a loincloth, for the operation of cicatrisation necessarily could not make any concession to modesty.

And now the knife man began slicing at her back, making the first of the *meitau le kpau* cuts, 'he who goes will turn to look!' which were placed on the small of her back. There were twenty-four of these cuts, but Nyasanu cried out 'Stop it!' at the fifteenth, because he was already gut sick at the sight of her pain.

'Here, old one, take a sip!' Kpadunu said. 'Do not be less brave than she is!'

Nyasanu drank deeply, then gave Agbale a silver bracelet. Then turning to his *dokpire* and his *gbe*, he cried out:

'Push me!'

Then all his fellow society members showered Agbale with gifts. And since he was a chief's son, the gifts were expensive and fine. Agbale knew she'd have to stand all the cuts now. She couldn't give up and wait for another occasion. So she drew in her breath and whispered, 'Give me to drink, Nya——'

He held out his bottle of palm wine to her, she drank a little sip, no more.

'Now—kiss me!' she said.

He bent and kissed the bloody circle on her cheek. All the spectators roared. By now there were a great number of them, for all her relatives had come, and a goodly number of Nyasanu's as well, including her father, the chief, which was a great honour indeed.

So now the skilful butchery went on. The *kodjau*, 'the neck good to touch', was cut into Agbale's throat. The *gblime*, 'the hands pass over', cuts—meaning that Nyasanu would caress her there once they were wed—were carved into her bare buttocks. Then the knife man began the eighty-one cuts on the inside of her thighs that are called *zido*, or 'push me', the connotation being purely sexual—and all the men and boys crowded forward to see, gleefully crying out obscenities, describing what Nyasanu was going to do when these nine rows of ridged scars clasped about his body in the embrace of love.

This made Nyasanu furious but he couldn't show it. Instead, he asked the knife man to scar his cheeks so that he might 'share the heat of the knife' as a demonstration of his love.

'No!' Agbale shrilled, 'Oh no, my love! Your face is beautiful! Do not ruin it!'

'Cut me!' Nyasanu cried.

'On the chest then,' the *kisi* man said. He'd had much experience of overwrought lovers before this time.

'All right,' Nyasanu said, and the knife man cut him five times above his heart, thus giving Agbale the excuse she needed to sob aloud.

It went on for hours. Agbale submitted without a whimper to having the *sifanu*, the water glass, sign cut into the back of her left hand. This was done because there a man is permitted to kiss his women in the presence of others without giving offence. Then a *lizard* design was carved into her belly just above the loincloth. This was called the *adaumehwe*, or 'stomach over', cuts. Then the *abotahwe* cuts were made around and between her breasts. . . .

By this time, poor Agbale was more than half unconscious from pain and loss of blood. Nyasanu and all his friends and fellow society members were drunk as lords, so were Gbenu and Nwesa, the fathers of the young couple soon to be wed. And their wives Gudjo and Adje were sobbing in each others' arms, overcome by the bravery Agbale had displayed. . . .

It did not end there, though all the cuts were made. The women rubbed crushed azoma leaf mixed with palm oil and soot into the wounds. This they did on the third day, while Agbale lay on her sleeping mat in a darkened room, and they continued rubbing this irritating compounds into the cuts until the huge ridged scars began to form, standing up high above her ebony skin.

Nyasanu visited her daily during this time, as custom permitted him to. For even the grandmothers held that a girl was unlikely to sin with her body striped all over with aching, itching cuts. The grandmothers were right. Even a kiss was too painful.

But Agbale, gazing with adoration at her lover, held in her heart her deepest fear: that the wounds would mortify in the terrible heat, drip pus, and she would die. For had not she murdered her own *fa*?

Only miraculously, they did not. When the first rains sighed down, she was able to rise and go about her normal tasks, proud of her new, exquisite beauty, the lines of ridged scar tissue that made her seem clad in a network of grey pink rope even when completely nude.

But now it was Nyasanu's turn to suffer pain for her sweet sake, as she'd endured it for his.

SIX

And now all the sacrifices had been made, the lots cast. So they, the group of twelve boys to be that day made into men, marched together to the compound of the *adagbwoto*, he-who-cuts the foreskin. It was a cool day, mist-laden; for no one would dare perform so dangerous an operation as circumcision in the dry season, while the heat was still on the land.

Nyasanu, as son of the chief, led the procession. In sober fact, as *medaxochi*, or eldest son of Gbenu, Gbochi should have headed the group; but he hung back, his porcine face greyish with fear. And as the boys marched along behind Nyasanu and Kpadunu, Gbochi fell farther and farther behind, until by the time they'd passed the shrines to the *fa* and the *legba* of the surgeon, and had gone under the protective *gbo* placed over the gate, Gbochi was nowhere to be seen.

There was a crowd of spectators of both sexes waiting for them within the compound of Alihonu, the knife man, for Dahomeans did not hold it shameful for women to witness this operation. Agbale was there, standing between her own mother Adje and Gudjo, Nyasanu's. Under the great, ornamented umbrella, Gbenu stood, with Nwesa, Agbale's father, a little behind him, as a mark of favour to the head of the family so soon to be united with his own. Then, as was to be expected of him, Hwegbe, the woodcarver, Nyasanu's paternal granduncle, came edging forward, mischief in his sly old eyes.

'Where is thy eldest son, Gbenu?' he cackled, 'Is he not to be cut this day?'

Gbenu frowned. His gaze roamed over the group.

'Nyasanu!' he boomed. 'Where is thy elder brother?'

Nyasanu bowed his head. For him to tell the truth, that Gbochi had run away from the ordeal, was both bad form and worse policy. So he compromised and told another truth:

'I—I do not know, Father——'

'Kpadunu!' Gbenu said. 'Do *you* know where Gbochi is?'

'No, Great Chief,' Kpadunu said. '*Where* he is I do not know. Why he is not here, I do.'

'And why isn't he, O rough-skinned son of the sorcerer?' Hwegbe, the ancient mischief-maker, said.

'Silence, Hwegbe!' Gbenu said. 'You are my *tauhinovi*,

64

brother of my father, and a venerable elder. For these things I owe you respect. But I am chief here, and I must ask you to respect my office, if not my years. I will ask the questions. All right, first friend of my son, where is Gbochi?'

'He has run away, Great Chief,' Kpadunu said, mockingly.

'You imply my eldest son is afraid?' Gbenu said.

'I imply nothing, Great Chief,' Kpadunu said. 'I say only what I know: Gbochi has run away. Or perhaps he has gone to kiss Hugbadji and Kokame goodbye. On the mouth, as one kisses women.'

A roar of laughter went up from the crowd. Hugbadji and Kokame were *gaglo*, homosexuals; and though they did their best to conceal practices that Dahomeans hold in utter contempt, one had but to look at them to know it.

Gbenu clapped his big hands together, making a sound like thunder. The laughter stopped, abruptly, as though it had never been. The chief turned to his retainers. Two of them big men, who wore the human-teeth necklaces of successful warriors.

'Find him,' Gbenu said grimly. 'Bring him here. He is my son, and the eldest. I will not allow him to disgrace me.'

So now, there was nothing to do but to wait until the warriors came back with Gbochi. Which, best said, didn't take them long. Kpadunu's mocking words had given them enough of a lead. So they went straight to the compound of Hugbadji's father—and found all three fugitives from virility and responsibility there.

Leaving Hugbadji and Kokame crying like the hysterical women they essentially were, Gbenu's two guards dragged Gbochi back to Alihonu's compound. Long before they got there all the spectators could hear him screaming.

'No! I won't be cut! I won't be! It hurts! It hurts, I tell you! I'll bleed to death! I'll die!'

But the warriors paid no attention to his words, except to mock him.

'Why do you weep, Gbochi?' one of them said. 'Alihonu's knife is sharp. Whisper but two words in his ear, and he'll cut it all off and carve you a cunning little cleft beside, thus making of you the woman you want to be....'

'He still wouldn't have any breasts,' the other warrior said.

'Oh, he'd grow them fast enough,' the first warrior said, 'once he's lost these feeble evidences of manhood that Legba tricked his *fa* into giving him. . . .'

'You aren't being just to him,' the second said. 'I find him heavily enough hung. Strange, isn't it? For a man to be born with a woman's soul, I mean?'

'A punishment for his mother's sins, surely,' the first warrior said. 'Which, *Dangbe* witness it, are many. Well, here we are. . . .'

Gbenu stood there beneath the umbrella looking at his eldest son. And what was in his eyes, or his heart, then, no man present could discern. His voice when he spoke was quiet.

'As my eldest son,' he said, 'let Gbochi be first!'

They led the twelve boys—for Gbochi was no longer resisting now—to twelve small holes dug in the ground. And there they sat them down. Their legs wide spread, each above one of the holes, so that the blood and the severed prepuce could fall into it. Two men stood beside each boy, ready to hold him, should he give way to fear.

And now Alihonu, the *adagbwoto*, came towards where Gbochi sat. He put out his right hand, caught the boy by the foreskin and pulled it, hard. At once Gbochi let out a scream loud enough to wake the ancestors from their eternal sleep beyond the river. The two men caught him by the arms; but as strong as they were, they were no match for the strength lent Gbochi by his terror.

Nyasanu sat there watching the struggles of his ugly, pig-faced elder half-brother. Pity tore his heart. Turning his head towards where the *toxausau* stood, he said:

'Let him go, my father! What need has he to lose his fore-skin, who will never husband a woman?'

But his words only served to anger Gbenu the more. In one great stride, the chief left his umbrella bearer and stood beside his eldest son. Gbochi went on struggling like a wild thing.

Then Gbenu raised his mighty fist and brought it down like a hammer on Gbochi's head. The boy went limp, inert. His mother, Yu, screamed out:

'Do not hurt my son! I'll go to the Princess Fedime! I'll——'

Gbenu didn't grant her the courtesy—or the importance—of a glance.

'Cut him!' he said. And the thing was done.

And now it was Nyasanu's turn. The knife wielder knelt before him and laid that wicked, still bloody blade on the boy's

bare thigh. At once the two attendant warriors caught Nyasanu by the arms. He looked at them, his head thrown back,
his eyes flaming like a leopard's in the night.

'Release me!' he spat. 'I am not Gbochi. I am a true son of
my father—and a man. You have no need to hold me!'

Gbenu smiled then, his white teeth, filed to glittering points,
flashing in the light.

'Release him!' he said.

The *adagbwoto* picked up his knife, and reached out his left
hand to take Nyasanu by the foreskin.

'Wait!' Nyasanu said, and his voice was harsh. 'I bid you
wipe your blade, O Alihonu! I would not mingle my blood
with that of such a one as this!'

'Wipe it, knife man,' Gbenu growled.

The cutter of foreskins wiped his blade, knelt there looking
into Nyasanu's eyes.

'It does hurt, you know,' he said. 'The knife hath fire in it. It
is not a disgrace to be held. If you jerk away, I might injure
you badly.'

'Agbale!' Nyasanu cried out then. 'Bring me a bowl of
water!'

Agbale scampered away, came back with the bowl, knelt, and
held it out to Nyasanu. Her small hands shook.

'It is not full enough,' Nyasanu said, aping perfectly the
tone of a long-married man towards a wife who has failed to
please him. 'Fill it to the brim, little black woman!'

Wonderingly, Agbale did so. Nyasanu took it from her
trembling hand and placed it with great care atop his own
head.

'Now,' he said quietly. 'Cut me, O knife wielder! And if I
spill a single drop from this bowl, you have leave to call me
coward.'

Gbenu turned then, stretched out his great hand, and
brought it down on Nwesa's shoulder so hard that Agbale's
father quivered under the impact.

'Look you, Nwesa!' he roared. 'Look what a husband I give
thy daughter!'

The knife man pulled on the foreskin hard, but smoothly.
The knife flashed out; the blood spurted. But Nyasanu sat
there like a statue of polished ebony, his head erect, so still the
water in the bowl atop his head did not even ripple.

All the spectators clapped their hands and cheered at that—

except one, Agbale; by then she was sobbing aloud.

'He bleeds!' she wept. 'Oh, how he bleeds! Stop it! Oh, Lisa! Oh, Mawu, I——'

She bowed her head, her black face greying out of life, of thought, bent forward, and would have fallen if Adje and Gudjo between them had not caught her. She, who had lost far more blood than this for his sake, and from a hundred wounds.

The *adagbwoto* put down his knife, opened his medicine pouch and took out a handful of spiderweb. He'd gathered it this morning, in case one or more of the boys should haemorrhage like this. Quickly he brought the bleeding under control, picked up a cloth to wipe his blade.

'Do *not* wipe it,' Kpadunu, who was next in line, said. 'I am his first friend and his brother! To mingle his blood with mine would honour me.' Then, as the warrior took hold of his arms: 'Turn me loose. I would not be less than he . . .'

But all the rest of the boys consented to be held. Most of them screamed. Two of them fainted. No one held such weakness against them. From that hour on they were all brothers of the same knife, and would defend each other to the death. Yet everyone knew who their leader was: Nyasanu, man among men, and future chief of Alladah. For when the people saw Gbenu call his own first friend eldest, one Zumadunu, or as he was better known by his common name, Kausu, aside, they knew at once with what command the chief had charged him:

'Nyasanu is to succeed me. After I have gone to the ancestors, see to it, O Xauntau Daxo!'

But Agbale stared at Nyasanu in a strange and troubling way. He did not like that look. It had far more sorrow in it than joy.

They, all twelve of them, had one month of purest torment, during which they sat most of the time, with their male organs buried in heaps of heated sand, which was the only way to make the excruciating itch of their healing bearable.

Gbochi, of course, and one other boy, had not the will power to keep their hands off themselves. They scratched their itching wounds and infected them. The result was that Gbochi was abed three months with his penis swollen to the size of a huge sausage and dripping pus. The other boy was less lucky still.

68

He started screaming in his terrible pain and went on screaming until he died.

But in the end the eleven brothers of the same knife were examined by the cutter of foreskins and pronounced cured. Then, in the village, there commenced a great deal of secret visiting among the women. Agbale, who knew the purpose of these visits, grew thinner every day, because she had quite simply ceased to eat at all.

'Foolish girl!' Adje, her mother screamed at her. 'To harm yourself out of jealousy of a *tasino*! Don't you know it must be done? If Gudjo cannot persuade some old woman, a widow, or divorced, to lie with him to cool the heat of the knife, paying her for the task with many rich gifts for so risking her life—then, oh idiot daughter who now resembles a sack of bones, so ugly that he must turn from thee, the risk must fall upon thy head! Would you die for the privilege of appeasing him?'

'Yes,' Agbale said.

'Fool! Fool! Fool!' her mother shrieked, and slapped her, hard. Whereupon, head down and sobbing, Agbale fled her mother's house.

What she did next was a proof of devotion and of cunning, though hardly of intelligence. She began to follow Gudjo secretly, everywhere her fiancé's mother went. And very soon she knew who the *tasino* was who had agreed to take from Nyasanu his clean young male virginity.

The minute she was sure, she went to see the woman.

'Don't do it!' she wept. 'I will double the gifts you've had from his mother! Only leave him alone! He's mine, you hear me! Oh, Mawu-Lisa, above, I couldn't stand——'

The old woman sat there, looking at wild, tender, headstrong Agbale with great compassion. She stretched out her arms to her, in a gesture so maternal that Agbale understood at once that she was no enemy and came to her.

The *tasino* sat there holding the weeping girl and talking to her gently.

'You'd take my place?' she said. 'Listen, daughter, gladly would I let you—if it were not for certain things——'

'What things, No?' Agbale said, deliberately calling the *tasino* 'No', the Fau word for mother, as evidence of respect.

'First of all, it is dangerous. Very often, the woman who

69

cools the heat of the knife dies. . . .'

'I don't care,' Agbale said. 'For him, I'd——'

'Die. I'm sure you would, child. And leave him to weep his eyes out over you, whom he loves. Is it not better to follow the ancient customs: to select a woman, a *tasino* like me, whose moonblood has ceased, whose life is over? Who, having neither husband nor sons, can be easily spared, leaving no one to weep for her?'

'I—I will weep for thee, Nochi!' Agbale said.

'Thank you, daughter. I know you will—if I die. But death is not the chief danger, though it does come of this more often than I dare think of, now. The chief danger is that she who cools the heat of the knife is *always* left barren. Always. That's why a woman of my age is chosen. Having passed our years of childbearing, this risk is nothing to us. But you, child: would you surrender the joy and glory of giving him children? Tall sons and lissome daughters to bless his old age?'

'No!' Agbale said. 'Never! I mean to bear him twenty sons!'

'You'll have your work cut out for you then, little Agbale,' the *tasino* said. 'Now look me in the face and hear my words: I will take no joy of this. A youth so tall and powerful is likely to hurt me badly. And I have lived beyond the hungers of the flesh, the sweet torments of love. I do my duty, only. And while it's being done'—she stopped, loosed a soft, knowing chuckle—'a matter of incredible brevity with the young and hot of blood! I shall think only of thee, daughter, and pray to Mawu, the Sky Goddess of whose cult thou art, that she grant thee long life and many sons!'

Agbale lay there looking at the *tasino*. She had been pretty once, perhaps even beautiful. In a way, she still was.

'Nochi,' she whispered, 'my mother—I—I'd like to kiss you. And ask you—your blessing.'

'You have it, child,' the *tasino* said.

Afterwards, had she not been bound by terrible oaths, the *tasino* would have gladly told Agbale what happened on that night. The first part, anyhow, for that would have eased the girl's jealous and rebellious heart. For Nyasanu refused her, flatly, saying:

'I want no other woman except the one I love!'

She had to use much the same argument she'd employed before to calm Agbale, herself, to convince him. And of them

70

all, the fear of rendering his bride barren was the telling one.

But thereafter, to her own astonishment, all the *tasino* knowing predictions failed her: Nyasanu was very gentle with her, almost tender. And, since he felt no lust at all for this clean perfumed, rather plump and pleasant presence in the dark, featureless and unknown, being, actually, only a kindly maternal voice, dissociated somehow from the rather good body he became tangibly aware of now, he was not driven into haste.

So what passed between them then could not be told to Agbale and left the *tasino* obsessed with a sense of sin. For she reached not once, but several times that night, the peak of carnal joy, was forced to cry out at the last, like a lovesick girl, a bride.

No, she could never tell Agbale that. Nor could Nyasanu.

The others of the group, the other brothers of the same knife, behaved, as men will, as their individual temperaments dictated. One, Kpadunu, gave his *tasino* even more pleasure than Nyasanu had forced his to reach, having cunningly procured a foaming drink and several *gbo* from his uncle, the sorcerer, to that purpose. Some of the others were driven by fleshly desire into unseemly haste; one or two, rendered temporarily impotent by nervousness, had to be stroked and petted into an acceptable degree of virility.

Only one failed completely: Gbochi. When, in a desperate last attempt to awake some semblance of manhood in him, his *tasino* kissed him on the mouth, he turned his head and vomited.

Thereupon, reflecting upon the obvious fact that he would never husband a woman in any case, the *tasino* stole out into the night and left him there.

So was it done. They were men now and could be wed. Which, very promptly, two of them did: Kpadunu, the apprentice sorcerer, and Nyasanu, son of Gbenu, *toxausu*, or chief of Alladah. And both weddings were long remembered in the land of Da's Belly, not because the persons involved were notables, which they were, of course, but long after marriages among people of even higher rank, greater distinction, were quite forgotten, people were still talking about those two.

For both were so surrounded, permeated, shot through with dark and bright magic, that they could have occurred only in that vast and brooding continent where the natural and the supernatural meet and melt together, and no arbitrary line can be drawn between them.

Men say that Ku, Death, danced at Nyasanu's wedding to Agbale.

And as for Dangbevi, Kpadunu's bride, there was some doubt that she was even of the race of man.

SEVEN

And now that the day of his wedding to Agbale was almost at hand, Nyasanu found that, chief's son or not, man among men, Gbenu's lion cub that he might be, he was no more immune than any other prospective bridegroom to a sudden, unexpected, but none the less shattering, attack of prenuptial nerves.

First of all, he had a dispute with his father that bordered perilously on the edge of an open quarrel.

'Son,' Gbenu said to him, 'it's only a week until your wedding day. So go call the *bokono*. Everything has been provided. Here are your *dokpo* sack, your hoe, your bottles of strong drink. Your mother has sixteen chickens for the lesser sacrifice already caged; and, for the greater, I've told my goat keeper to give you the six best goats in the whole herd. My diviner, Zezu, will be waiting for you in his *fazume*, any night you say the word. . . .'

'In his *fazume*,' Nyasanu thought, 'his *fa* Forest. Ready to establish my complete *fa*. The full destiny I don't want to know. Because if the king's diviner had it right I——'

'Well?' Gbenu said.

'Father,' Nyasanu said, 'I—I don't want my *fa* established. Not—not yet. After I'm married will be time enough to——'

'*After* you're married will be too late!' Gbenu said. 'I know what you're going to say: a good many men don't establish their *fas* until after they're wed. But those men, Vi, have had peaceful, uneventful lives up until their wedding days. Can you say the same? Here of late, too many things have happened: that ugly business of Gbochi's killing your fate-watcher tree, the fact that you bled far too much at your circumcision,

72

some dreams I've had about you, and the king's *bokono* said——'

'That my life would end here in the land of Da's Belly, only to begin anew in a far off place. Tell me, Father, when he said that, did he mention whether or not Agbale would go with me?'

Gbenu frowned.

'No,' he said. 'The king's diviner didn't mention your little black sorceress. But then, why should he have? A woman partakes of her father's *fa* until she's wed, and afterwards of her husband's. So——'

'Father,' Nyasanu whispered, 'what if—my *fa* is bad?'

'Then you have no right to inflict it upon Agbale!' Gbenu said sternly. 'Nwesa is my friend. I could never look him in the face again if I let his daughter come to evil days because I didn't—or my son wouldn't—bother to find out his destiny!'

'So,' Nyasanu said, 'if *Bokono* Zezu says my fate is to be a bad one you—you won't *let* me marry Agbale?'

'Well,' Gbenu hesitated, 'I wouldn't go so far as that. What I should do, Nya, would be to acquaint Nwesa with the facts——'

'And allow him to forbid it in your stead,' Nyasanu said. 'Thus keeping my love, Da. Don't worry. That you have no matter what you do. But Tauchi, father mine, hear me, listen to my words: if I can't have Agbale, do you think it'll matter *who* it is that forbids the marriage? To me it won't, not even if it's Dada Gezo, himself for by then I shall be dancing outside the compound, my head on the ground, my feet in the air!'

Then seeing—not without a perverse satisfaction—his father's broad black face so grey with shock, Nyasanu whirled and ran out of the house.

Gbenu sat there, gathering all three of his souls together, until his breath came back. For, in Dahomey, it is held that a man's ghost dances thus, at his own funeral. Even suicides. Even the invisible phantoms of the self-slaughtered dead.

The chief got up, and went to the door of his bungalow.

'Nya!' he called out, hearing to his own disgust, the rather piteous quaver that invaded his voice, 'Nyasanu, wait!'

But no answer came back to him, except the sound of Nyasanu's feet drumming against the hard-packed earth, as the boy ran blindly down the road, under the loko trees.

From his father's compounds Nyasanu went to that of Mauchau where Kpadunu and his mother lived under the protection of the sorcerer, since M'butu, the boy's at least adoptive father, and Mauchau's brother, had crossed the river, gone to the ancestors a long time ago. But Kpadunu wasn't there.

'He went into the forest with the Azaundato to—to gather things,' Kolo, Kpadunu's mother, said.

'Things to make *gbo*,' Nyasanu thought. 'Charms for me, likely. To protect Agbale and me against——'

Against what? The divided future hanging over me? Against whatever it is that is making my little black one sick with fear?

But he didn't say that aloud, he said, 'I thank you, mother of my first friend eldest,' made Kolo a reverent bow, and left her there.

Outside the *azaundato*'s compound, Nyasanu stood a long time. Inside his belly a host of night warrior ants were on the march. A plague of locusts whined up and down his throat. The air he breathed tasted green—like swamp slime. His head pounded.

'I'll go to Amosu's, he thought, and after that to Taugbad-ji's. . . .'

Amosu was his second friend. In Dahomey, where everything is ritualised, a man must choose from all his friends three of paramount importance. The first was the *xauntau daxo*, first friend eldest, guardian companion, dearly beloved, almost brother, repository of all secrets, and keeper—in his head, carefully memorised since Ffon or Fau is not a written language—of a man's last will and testament.

The second was *xauli-si-me*, he who stands against the wall, which means that a certain distance separated him from the one who had chosen him; and, as a matter of policy, only half a man's secrets are told to his second friend. For this position, not without honour, Nyasanu had chosen Amosu, son of Wusa, the brassworker.

The third friend was called *xauntau gbe ka ta*, the friend who stands on the threshold, the implication being that the intimacy is less still, so that the third friend must stand in the doorway and hear what he can, nothing being directly told him. Nyasanu's third friend was Taugbadji, son of Gbusu, head of the Clothworkers' Guild.

Nyasanu started out at once, but after taking no more than

two strides, he stopped, his handsome young face frowning.

'They'll think it's because I want to see what wedding gifts they're making,' he thought. 'And I don't—not really. I just need somebody to talk to. And Xevioso alone knows where Kpad is——'

He hung there. Then he decided, 'Let them! What harm is there in that? If I stay by myself, worrying about the future, Legba will eat my brains! Every time I think that if my *fa* is bad, and I link my Nyaunu wi to it, I'll drag her down to whatever awful thing's going to happen to me, I get sick.'

'Zezu said trouble was coming to me over the king's road. Then Gbochi killed my tree. Then the king's *bokono* said that I was going far away—and Agbale cries all the time. And——'

He started running then towards Wusa's compound, towards Amosu's house.

Amosu wasn't at home, either. But he was at his father's forge, hard at work. On the far side of the enclosure, protected from the heat of the furnaces by woven screens, lay a number of figures moulded out of beeswax and covered with wet cloth to make sure that not even the sun's heat would melt them. At the moment Amosu was deftly putting lumps of wet, sticky clay all over a large wax figure of a man, until the clay hid the figure completely, transforming it into something that looked like a child's mud house.

He looked at Nyasanu and grinned.

'Couldn't wait, could you, Nya?' he said. 'Well, you're out of luck. They aren't finished yet. But, since you're here, you can help me work. Even a clumsy oaf of an ironworker knows how to pour!'

Nyasanu smiled at his second friend's gibes. It was a rather feeble smile, but, at the moment, the best he could manage. Everyone made fun of a young man who was marrying his first wife. He had to expect that and accept it. So if Amosu today showed less than the required respect due to this high-born youth, he couldn't resent it. In fact, he didn't. It just didn't matter. Besides, the brassworkers and the ironworkers always taunted each other out of a professional rivalry which, if keen, remained friendly, since all metalworkers were members of related clans.

'All right,' he said, 'but aren't you afraid I'll break something?'

'No,' Amosu said cheerfully, 'you aren't that clumsy, Nya.

75

In fact, given ten years, I might even make a decent brass-worker out of you!'

Turning, Amosu lifted several lumps of shapeless clay off the edge of the furnace. They had been placed there so that the wax that had formed the figures would melt and run out of the hole in the top of them when Amosu turned them upside down with his long firetongs. Once the wax had run out, the fire-hardened clay remained hollow, forming a mould which conformed to every curve and plane and angle of the now lost wax figure's form.

'Now!' Amosu said, and Nyasanu dipped a long-handled spoon ladle into the molten brass. Carefully he poured the molten brass into the hole in the top of each lump of clay until it ran over a little.

'Come with me, Nya,' Amosu said. 'I want to show you something. . . .'

Nyasanu followed his second friend out into the yard. There under the shade of a baobab tree, Amosu had placed several clay moulds to cool. The young brassworker bent and touched them with his finger. Straightened up, grinning.

'They're cool enough,' he said. 'That one, Nya. Bring it back into my workshop.'

The workshop was a little apart from the forge, since in the forge room itself, the heat was all but unbearable. In the workshop, the brassworkers finished their figures. There they filed away the rough spots, buffed and polished them until they gleamed like gold, and last of all, hammered the designs into them with a hammer and pointed iron dies.

And once again, as he stood inside Amosu's little workshop, a feeling of envy stole over Nyasanu. The figures the brass-workers made were so beautiful! They were amazingly lifelike, except that a certain artistic convention caused the brass-workers to shape them proportionally taller and more slender than the people and animals represented actually were. But they seemed to be alive, so realistic and graceful were the forms. Here a group of dancers worshipped Mawu-Lisa to the music of drummers who held their drumsticks in various positions so progressive that the illusion of motion was nearly complete. Here a rather skinny elephant lifted an unfortunate hunter in his trunk, ready to dash him to death while others pointed over-sized guns and spears at the beast. Here a lion tore an antelope, a leopard crouched to spring upon a monkey;

here a woman with a baby in a sling on her back pounded corn in a mortar. The figures were endless, and endlessly lovely.

Nyasanu wondered suddenly why the figures that woodcarvers made were so squat and thick—though, in their way, they had a certain compelling power, that made of their ugliness a sort of beauty—while the brass figures were so lithe and beautiful. So he asked Amosu that.

'Apart from the fact that woodcarvers have all their brains eaten by Legba and are crazier than a jackal bitten by a viper,' Amosu said, 'it's the stuff we work with that makes the difference. You can do anything with wax, Nya! Anything at all! Look at this leopard's tail. If your old duty-minded granduncle Hwegbe tried to carve a piece of wood this thin, what would happen? It would break, as sure as Xevioso sends the thunder. But in wax we can make it this delicate, because the wax is only temporary. After we pour in the brass——'

'Or the silver,' Nyasanu said.

'Or the silver, it's plenty strong. Which reminds me. Put that mould you're carrying down on the bench. There, that's it. Now break it with that hammer. A light tap will do. It isn't iron, you know, you Gu worshipper, you!'

Nyasanu put the shapeless lump of clay down, took up the hammer, and tapped at it tentatively.

'Harder than that, anyhow,' Amosu laughed. 'Even clay has a certain strength. . . .'

Nyasanu gave the clay a smart tap. It broke all at once, and a woman's figure stood revealed. It had been cast in silver and was naked except for a loincloth. And it was the single most beautiful thing Nyasanu had ever seen, except——

'Except the girl it was a portrait of.

'Why,' Nyasanu whispered, 'why—it's Agbale!'

'Yes,' Amosu said gruffly. 'I'm making you a wedding group, Nya. The big figure I was covering with clay when you came in is you, old friend. Now, get out of here, and let me work!'

Nyasanu stood there, a sharp pain digging into his middle, watching Amosu picking up the die that would make the marks to represent Agbale's lovely woolly hair. Others would represent her beauty scars, others her beads and jewellery. But what held Nyasanu there, motionless, was a disquieting thing—The recognition that a masterpiece such as this could only be born of love.

And was. Looking at Amosu's usually cheerful face, frowning now, intent, he knew all at once and completely that his second friend was in love with his chosen bride. Hopelessly, helplessly in love.

Could this be part of my divided fate, he thought, part of the evil that is to come to me?

No! The *bokono* told me it was a foreign evil, alien to this land. O Mawu, who is *her* god, help me! I——

'Get out of here Nya!' Amosu said. 'You make me nervous. I might spoil it with *you* here——'

And without a parting word, Nyasanu went.

He found Taugbadji busily stitching away at an appliqué cloth pillowcase that was part of a set that his third friend was making for Nyasanu's wedding mat. Among Dahomeans needlework is purely a masculine art; women do not sew at all.

Nyasanu looked at the design, made by cutting figures, people, animals, birds, trees, flowers, instruments of labour, weapons, and the like out of variously coloured cloths, with scissors, free handed, and sewing these upon the larger cloth that formed the background. But he could make nothing of it. Like all designs in appliqué, which Dahomeans consider one of their fine arts, equivalent to painting among other people, it was allegorical. And it wasn't finished enough for him to search for its meaning. Afterwards, he'd be able to read it, just as he could read the fables other artists carved upon the calabash bowls that served young Dahomeans as love letters. Though 'read' wasn't the right word. Interpret would be better. It was another language, unrelated to spoken Fau—a language of signs, symbols, allusions that were hauntingly beautiful. . . .

Taugbadji made no attempt to explain his design to Nyasanu. What to talk about was another, more troublesome thing.

'You really should do something about your *taugbochinovi* Hwegbe, Nya,' he said. 'Of course, all woodcarvers are crazy, but he exceeds all limits——'

'Why *are* they like that?' Nyasanu said.

'Don't know,' his third friend said. 'They claim it's artistic temperament. But *you're* an artist in iron, you make the most beautiful *ase* in all Dahomey——'

'Hardly that,' Nyasanu said.

'Yes that! Nobody makes finer or more beautiful iron altars

for the ancestors than you, my friend. And Amosu has a gift from the *vudun* on his fingertips. Even I, in my humble way——'

'Make glorious things,' Nyasanu said, 'for which my wife to be will bless your name before Mawu once they're finished——'

'I thank you,' Taugbadji said solemnly. 'But what I was getting at is that all three of us are artists in different ways, but we don't ask the world to put up with absolutely outrageous behaviour the way the woodcarvers do! Do we disappear into the forest for weeks at a time to search out one particular kind of wood, leaving our wives and children to starve while we're gone? Do we make a figure—fine, I'll grant you—and then fall so in love with it that we refuse to deliver it to the man who ordered it, even though our children whine with hunger about our knees? Are we held to be so disreputable that if a man wants to carve a little figure out of wood, for fun say, or as a toy for his child, he has to hide to do it, lest people think he's turning into the kind of shiftless scoundrels all woodcarvers are? No one respects them, Nya! No one at all!'

'No,' Nyasanu said, 'but everyone loves them. Strange isn't it?'

'No,' Taugbadji said severely. 'Most scoundrels are charming. The two things go together. Which is what makes them so dangerous. Take your granduncle Hwegbe, now. People flock to him to hear his outrageous lies.'

'And even more outrageous truths,' Nyasanu said.

'Granted. But because a thing is true *must* it be told?' Taugbadji said. 'Hasn't a person a right to some privacy, Nya?'

'Yes,' Nyasanu said, 'why yes, of course. Go on, Badji....'

'People flock to your granduncle to laugh at the outrageous things he says about other people. When he says things about *them,* they get mad. I suppose the reason nobody's given him a good beating, or cut his evil throat for him and thrown his carcass in the brush, is that he's your father's uncle....'

'So?' Nyasanu said.

'So he goes too far! The things he's spreading all over the village now about your father and this wedding of yours, you wouldn't believe, Nya. Which is one of the reasons I'm not going to descend to his level by repeating them. Besides, I don't have to. Pay him a visit, Nya—using as pretext that you want to see the protective *agbadome* he's carving for your new home —and inside of two minutes, he'll repeat his dirty-minded lies himself. Then, if I were you, I'd take action. Have your father run him out of Alladah, say. . . .'

'Father wouldn't,' Nyasanu said. 'He respects age too much. But I'll think of something. And thanks, Badji. Now, I go. . . .'

Nyasanu sat there watching the little wooden figure taking shape under the blows of his granduncle Hwegbe's chisel. The figure was to be a *bauchie*, one of the pair called *agbadome*, one male, one female, which are to Dahomeans *lares et penates,* guardian of a man's house.

'*Agbadome,*' Hwegbe cackled, 'to protect the *hwe*, the home of a warrior and a man! But will you protect the *goxau*, the play-house of a partridge-chaser-person, who merely wants to push his tiny little waterspout up a things-peddle-person?'

Nyasanu smiled. Hwegbe was running true to form. His jibe had to do with Nyasanu's and Agbale's youth. A boy became an *asau nyan tau,* 'he who chases partridges' at age eight or thereabouts. And a girl was given her supplies of soap, chewing sticks, lump sugar, salt, cakes to peddle in the market at the same age, since buying and selling was a thing of women, thus making her a *nu djalu tau,* 'a peddler of things'.

'Don't you exaggerate, Taugbochinovi?' he said. 'Let's say a *kpo ijdo alautoe* wants to share his sleeping mat with an *adjanle vu. . . .*'

Hwegbe laughed at that.

'You're cleverer than your old rutting billygoat of a father, nephew!' he said. 'Instead of getting mad and puffing up like a bullfrog, you merely diminish my jest. But I won't have it! *Not* "a lizard killer" who is really quite a big boy, big enough in fact to get his weapon up, and a "little woman" who's had her sheath stretched enough to receive it; but a partridge chaser and a little whining peddler, a snot-nose and a ninny! Will my *bauchie* protect such a house?'

'Don't know,' Nyasanu said, 'but since I'm not going to become a woodcarver, my house won't need so much protection!'

'Meaning we neglect ours?' Hwegbe said. 'We *have* to, nephew! What we do is sacred. Nothing you metalworkers do—except your *ase* altars and the brassworkers' *xevioso* axes —compares with it! Who, I ask you, makes the *fa* cups in which the sacred divining seeds are kept? Who, the figures of Fa, of Legba, of Danh, of Dangbe, of all the male and female

80

vudun? The wooden bowls to catch the blood of the sacrificial victims? The intricate stools of the kings and the chiefs?'

That was true, Nyasanu reflected. The products of the wood-carvers' art were greatly prized. And the men who make them would be, too, he added wryly, if only they behaved a little better!

By then, Hwegbe had finished blocking out the male figurine with his chisel, using the blunt end of his adze as a hammer. So he lay the chisel down and began to work with the adze itself, using that little hoe-shaped implement with delicate surety to shape eyes, nose, mouth, the rough masses of the hair, and the male genitalia. As usual, he made the organs of mas-culinity disproportionately huge, and the bent legs far too short.

Again it occurred to Nyasanu how strange the contrast was between the slim, delicate, but largely lifelike figures that brass-workers such as his second friend Amosu made, and the brutal, powerful grossness of the carved wooden figures. Cert-ainly people didn't look, nor were they built, the way wood-carvers represented them. The male *agbadome* his granduncle was chipping out of the block of wood could couple with neither a cow elephant nor with a woman. He couldn't mount a she-elephant because his legs were too short, nor a woman, because his parts were too big.

But Nyasanu kept that completely outrageous thought to himself. Aloud, he said:

'Taugbochinovi Hwegbe, why do you carve him like that? I mean so short and—and thick? People aren't——'

'Hummph!' Hwegbe snorted. 'It's *su dudu* to carve slender figures.'

'It is *su dudu* to leave one wife the morning after your wed-ding night, Granduncle!' Nyasanu shot back at him. 'So why do you observe this tabu, and not that one?'

Hwegbe grinned at him.

'Good!' he cackled. 'Thou art smart, Grandnephew! When a fool asks a person in authority *why* one does this or that, the great chief, or king, or *vuduno* always answers it's forbidden, *su dudu,* by the gods. But since you are *not* a fool, and there probably aren't any gods anyhow——'

'Taugbochinovi!' Nyasanu said.

'Grandnephew!' Hwegbe mocked Nyasanu's tone of out-raged shock. 'Perhaps thou'rt a fool after all. Tell me this: when five or six perfectly healthy sheep are found dead in a herd, and all the people rush off to pay their cowries to the River God's priest in order to save the rest of their animals, is it really the River God who murders the poor beasts, or the servants of the priest, himself?'

'The servants, likely,' Nyasanu said. 'Father says that all the indirect ways used by Dada Gezo to scare us into paying our taxes are fakes and——'

'So are the gods,' Hwegbe said imperturbably, 'who were invented by kings, priests, and nobles to keep the people in subjugation. So now I'll tell you the truth: we make our figures thick like this because the wood itself compels us to. Carve them too thin, and they break before you're halfway done. The reasons, Nya, why one does *everything* one does are somewhat less than noble.... Take your wedding, for instance——'

'Granduncle Hwegbe!' Nyasanu said.

'Oh, I wasn't going to discourse upon the fact that that woolly little treasure between your sweetheart's thighs, with its lips carefully thickened for your pleasure by the *tokono*, is what you actually mean when you say you've won Agbale's heart——'

'Taugbochinovi,' Nyasanu whispered, 'don't make me forget the respect I have for you....'

'The respect you don't have for me!' Hwegbe cackled. 'Come off it, Nyasanu! What I meant was that you run a great risk with this *tochesi* wedding of yours....'

'*Tochesi!*' Nyasanu said. 'My wedding's going to be *akwenusi!*'

'The money with woman ceremony,' Hwegbe said with a sly grin. 'The highest, most solemn type of the twelve. Or of the thirteen, if you count *xadudo*, common-law matings. But nephew mine, *tochesi* weddings *are akwenusi*, the only difference being the source of the money. So naturally you, a beginning blacksmith, not yet eighteen years old, are so rolling in cowries that you can purchase a bride?'

'No,' Nyasanu said slowly, 'I haven't any money, as you know well, Granduncle. Father's letting me have——'

'Ah!' Hwegbe said. 'And *what*, son Nya, does the word *tochesi* mean?'

'Wife from my Father,' Nya whispered, 'but——'

'But what?' the woodcarver persisted. 'Has my large and exceedingly lusty nephew Gbenu stated his conditions for advancing you the money?'

Nyasanu stared at his granduncle. Not once had his father said that the money was an outright gift. So the wedding *could* be *tochesi. Tochesi* marriages were entirely legal and respectable, the only trouble with them being that the bride had to live among the father's wives until the son paid off his debt to his father, and the bridegroom could only visit her by stealth. Which was maddeningly awkward and inconvenient.

But, he realised with sudden horror, *that* wasn't the difficulty his granduncle meant!

'Don't worry about it, Grandnephew!' that evil-minded old scoundrel cackled. 'Since you look more like your father than most sons do, nobody will call your firstborn's paternity into question.'

Nyasanu sat there, looking at the ground between his feet. He felt sick. Not only were the implications of Hwegbe's remark outrageously immoral; they were cruel. Of course, there were stories of men who'd made carnal use of a son's wife left in their charge, just as there were stories of men believed to be impotent who never the less 'fathered' a large number of children by closing their eyes to their wives' comings and goings. Gossip was not the least of Dahomean failings. But generally, no one put much stock in such scandal-mongering. *Näiveté* was not a characteristic of the Fau-speaking peoples. So any Dahomean's reaction to the teller, the bearer, the spreader of such ugly tales, was to instantly wonder what the teller's own motives were.

Only, in this case, Hwegbe hadn't any motives. He never had in all the mischief that he worked. Simply, he had a love for evil for evil's own pristine sake. So poor Nyasanu was left to contemplate bleakly his father's proven record of lustiness, forty-three wives and literally hundreds of children, and set that knowledge against his own aching, tormented awareness of Agbale's great beauty.

'Not Nyaunu wi!' he mourned inside his heart. 'Not my little black woman, more beautiful than the night!'

Then a comforting thought came to him. He raised his head to face his granduncle and said:

'If my father had ever wanted Agbale, he had but to say the word and Nwesa would have given her to him as wife. What say you to that, Taugbochinovi?'

'That men generally don't desire girl-babies still pulling at their mother's teats,' Hwegbe said, 'and that was what Agbale was when her father promised her to you. But in the last year or two Tovichivivu mine? Since she hath grown breasts that sway this way, while her hips are swaying that. And with all those lovely cicastrisations to call one's eyes to her salient points, why——'

'Why you're a dirty old man, Granduncle!' Nyasanu said, and got up from there. 'And may the Earth *Vudun* punish you for your sins!'

'There aren't any *vudun*, son,' Hwegbe began, but Nyasanu had no intention of listening to that. He had troubles enough hanging over him now without increasing them, which was precisely what bringing down the wrath of all the myriad gods upon his head by listening to what was clearly a blasphemy would surely do. So he clapped his hands over his ears and got out of there.

Once again he went to Mauchau's compound, but this time he didn't enter it. Instead he squatted on his slim haunches and waited as silent as a statue of polished ebony, and as motionless, before the shrines of Legba and Fa, under the protective *gbo* over the gate, until Kpadunu came home again.

Kpadunu listened quietly to his first friend's recital of his renewed onslaught of troubles.

'What should I do, Kpad?' Nyasanu wailed. 'I—I can't go to Father with this! He'd be insulted——'

'And he'd have some right to be!' Kpadunu said.

'Yes—but——' Nyasanu said.

'But Agbale is—lovely, and your father *is* a lusty man,' Kpadunu reasoned slowly. 'So you're afraid that Old Dung Spreader is right. That left in the chief's care too long, Agbale's beauty might make resisting temptation a little too hard for him to bear, considering how little practice he'd had in enduring that particular variety. I see. And I ask only that you leave the matter in my hands, First Friend! Go home and sleep. I promise you I'll arrange it. . . .'

But Nyasanu could not sleep. He lay night-long upon his mat, tormented by desire, by fear. Actually of course, he gave Kpandunu too little credit. The young appretice sorcerer arranged things very well indeed—and on two levels; one diplomatic and the other magical.

Early that next morning, Gbenu received a visit not from

Kpadunu's Uncle Mauchau, the *azaundato*, or sorcerer, to whom Nyasanu's best friend eldest had taken the matter, but, with characteristic Dahomean indirection, from Zezu, the *bokono*, or diviner, to whom Mauchau had taken it in his turn. And the upshot of much rambling, metaphorical talk was this: the Chief called a council of the elders and after taking up two hours in discussion of matters of astonishing unimportance— who'd stolen a chicken from whom; the boundaries of certain inherited fields that were in dispute between two neighbours; the announcement of the rites, sacrifices, and ceremonies to free one of his wives from her burdensome obligation as wife of the ghost of the *tauhwiyo*, the clan founder, which was what Zezu had declared her to be; and to confirm her newborn child—'probably', Gbenu reflected sadly, 'because it looks too little like me'—in the high position of having been conceived by the ghost of the mighty departed, the chief let fall with elaborate casualness:

'Let me see—let me see—there was something else.... Oh yes. Touching the wedding of my second son, Nyasanu, it is to be *akwenusi*. As a token of my esteem for the boy, I am making him a free gift of the money. So whatever sons, or grandsons more likely, of yours may belong to his *dokpwe* or his *gbe* have my permission to begin to build him his bridal house....'

Thus, in his subtle Dahomean way, Gbenu, without even mentioning his uncle's name, made absolutely sure that Hwegbe's malicious stories would no longer be believed. But Kpadunu was not content with that. He knew only too well that seeing one lie frustrated the woodcarver would only invent a better one. So that same afternoon he called together his mutual aid society. Since this particular *gbe* was confined to the sons of sorcerers and diviners, Nyasanu could not be a member of it. But such was Mauchau's prestige among the *azaundatoe* and *bokonoe,* that as his nephew, Kpadunu had been elected *gbega*, or president of the *gbe*, or society.

When they had all assembled in the rather scraggly clump of loko, baobab, and cottonsilk trees that served Mauchau as his *fazume*, his fate forest, where he went to work good or evil magic and to tell the future, Kpadunu addressed his fellow members:

'Blood brothers,' he said, 'I call upon you all to push me in aiding a friend....'

The members of the society listened impassively. They were

not surprised by their president's opening remarks. That was
what a *gbe* was for: to 'push' a fellow member in times of
need. Few Dahomeans were rich enough to bear unaided the
crushing expenses that fell upon their heads at such times as
weddings, funerals, the establishment of the ancestors as *tauvudun*, or family gods, the scarring of a promised bridge, and
many more occasions when a man stood disgraced if he didn't
make a brave show. So all Dahomeans were members of *gbe*,
which were social clubs and insurance companies at one and
the same time. Everyone contributed sums of money monthly
to his *gbe*, and when a need arose, the *gbe* had funds enough to
bear what no man could bear alone: the cost of rich gifts and
showy sacrifices that determined a man's proud place in this
world.

But when Kpadunu went on, they *were* surprised. For what
he was asking them to do was to form a subsociety within the
gbe, and this society was to be a secret one, having for its
purpose police action, that is, the apprehension and punishment of good-for-nothings, vagabonds, and criminals.

Now, of them all, only Kpadunu and one other boy, Kapo,
son of the *bokono* Akausu, who served as diviner to Agbale's
father, Nwesa, and all his clan, had been to the seacoast region
of Dahomey, Kpadunu having visited Whydah several times
with his uncle, and Kapo having journeyed to Porto Nova with
Akausu, his father.

Therefore, Kpadunu and Kapo alone knew of the existence
of the coastal secret societies, which had no counterpart in the
interior of the country. So now they sat bolt upright and listened with an interest that slowly became enthusiasm as Kpadunu described the Zangbwetan, 'the Hunters of the Night' of
Whydah, who under shapeless costumes of net and reed, and
wearing hideous masks, dance in the night before their victim's
house, convincing him by certain tricks that they were ghosts
of the departed ancestors, and by this means alone often
frightening him so much that he mended his evil ways.

'But I think we'd better give old Hwegbe a good beating,
besides,' Kpandunu said, 'he's both tough and smart. Only to do
that, we'll have to catch him outside his house, and Aido
Hwedo knows *that* won't be easy. . . .'

'I know how!' another boy, M'bula, said: 'I've got a big
piece of Anya wood in my house. I'll show it to the old rascal
and tell him where the fallen tree trunk can be found. . . .'

'Good!' Kapo laughed. 'A woodcarver would follow you down to the abode of the Earth *Vudun* in order to get his hands on a good block of ironwood!'

'Now let us plan it carefully, O my brothers!' Kpadunu said.

As the boy himself had predicted, that next night Hwegbe, the woodcarver, eagerly and greedily followed M'bula into the forest, chuckling at the chance of getting his hands on a whole trunk of Anya ironwood. The reason for the old man's eagerness and his greed was very simple: Anya is sacred to Gu, the God of Iron, and hence cannot be cut down; which meant that woodcarvers had to content themselves with finding an Anya tree that had been uprooted by a storm or had fallen for other, natural causes. And, in Africa, as in all the world, scarcity increases value.

But, once deep into the woods, Hwegbe had no time to express his growing impatience, for suddenly, he and his guide found themselves surrounded by towering, ghostly figures. Whereupon M'bula gave a terrible shriek and fled into the deeper brush.

Sceptic that he was, Hwegbe did his best to follow the boy; but his years were a weight upon him, so his phantom pursuers easily cut him off.

Then, in the thick, hot silence, they began to dance all around him. In the midst of the dance, two of the figures swayed together. Then one of them sank slowly to earth, leaving only a bundle of reeds not two fingers high under which no human being, not even the smallest child, could have hidden himself.

Hwegbe's bloodshot old eyes bugged out at that. There weren't any men behind those masks or under those bundles of reeds! These were ghosts! And by Xevioso, they were real!

If it had been less dark, or if he'd watched the second figure closely, Nyasanu's granduncle would have seen that it danced away on four legs now, which explained why the first reed and net costume had become totally devoid of human flesh. But the others kept him so distracted that he didn't notice that, nor the fact that M'bula had crawled out of the brush a moment later and was worming his way under the collapsed costume.

So when they all fell back two paces and Hwegbe saw the 'empty' bundle of reeds slowly come upright again and begin to dance, his shriek tore the night apart.

'Silence, O miserable woodcarver!' the tallest figure said.

This one, poor Hwegbe saw, had a head of gleaming bronze.
It was utterly lifelike and utterly beautiful, Kpadunu had borrowed it from Nyasanu's second friend, Amosu, the brassworker. And now, before the woodworker's terrified eyes, the
ghost took off his gleaming bronze head and sat it upon the
stump of a tree.

From whence to Hwegbe's utter horror, it began to address
the others. If Hwegbe had not been frightened out of his
usually keen wits by then, he would have heard how the head
was almost choking to death in its effort to suppress its
laughter. In fact, Kapo, who lay on his belly behind the stump
in the dark, and supplied the severed head with a voice, was
literally strangling upon his own mirth. So much so that
Kpadunu, who was the now headless body, had to arrange
matters.

'Why do you laugh, O my head?' he growled.

'At the sight of a fool,' his head shot back at him.

'And what has the fool done?' the body demanded.

'Spread filthy lies about the honour of a great chief, and of
his son, soon to be wed!'

'And what, O my cut-off-head, that aches me so in the place
where my neck bleeds no blood, should be done with the fool?'
the body said.

'Beat him with many rods!' the head thundered.

So now poor old Hwegbe found himself seized by hands that
were hard and hot and young and anything but ghostly. They
ripped the toga-like garment from his skinny old body. Then
they bent him over with his hands tied to a stick run through
the crook of his knees. They tied his ankles to the outer end of
the same stick, and thus forced him to arch his body like a
bow, drawing his poor old hide so tight that every blow of their
peeled rods brought blood.

Inside of five minutes, he was unconscious.

'Stop it!' Kpadunu cried out. 'It wouldn't do to kill him!'

'That is, if we haven't already!' Kapo said worriedly.

One of the others bent and felt Hwegbe's chest.

'No, his heart is beating strongly enough, only what'll we do
with him now?'

'Carry him to his house,' Kpadunu said, '*before* he comes to
himself. He'll wake up thinking he's had a bad dream till he

feels those stripes. Then maybe he'll think twice before letting his evil old tongue wag so about other people's affairs!'

So it was done. But in Hwegbe's house they found many bottles of strong drink, which they immediately stole. They retired to the woods again and proceeded to get as drunk as lords. Within an hour, they were all dead to the world and snoring lustily—except Kpadunu, who had drunk considerably less than the others.

Less than they, but quite enough to swim the moon, the stars, the thicker night of the tree tops in concentric circles above his head. He got up from there and wandered deeper into the brush, singing, as he went, the song of Legba, the Messenger or Linguist of the Gods and the trickiest of all the *vudun.*

> *If the food is good, and the house is in order,*
> *If the field is fertile, and its yield tenfold,*
> *I shall be content.*
> *Legba will not feel the pangs*
> *Of an empty belly*
> *And Kaunikauni will come to lie with*
> *him and ease the ache*
> *of where he aches forever*
> *without surcease....*

He was singing that magical song when he saw the three snakes. They were pythons, sacred to Dangbe and Danh. So reverently he bent down and kissed the earth before them.

Then he saw that two of the bigger snakes were grappling fiercely while the third one lay in a languid coil and watched the battle. And one of the pythons was getting much the worst of it. So while Kpadunu squatted there, bemused with liquor, the python who was losing the battle cried out to him:

'Help me, nephew of Mauchau! I am her husband! And this scoundrel would take her away from me!'

It didn't surprise Kpadunu at all to hear a python speak Fau. Pythons are sacred animals, and who could define the limits of their powers?

'How do I know you're not lying?' he said with drunken gravity.

'Ask her!' the losing python gasped.

'Is he your husband?' Kpadunu asked the female serpent.

'Yes,' the she-snake said.

'Tell me, Lady Pythoness,' Kpadunu said, 'which of the two of them do you prefer?'

'My lover, of course,' the she-snake said. 'He's younger and stronger and makes much better love.'

Whereupon Kpadunu got up and gave her a kick in the ribs.

'You're a whore,' he said solemnly, and taking out his brush knife, cut off the younger python's head.

'I thank you, O Kpadunu!' the serpent husband got out between gasps, 'and I shall reward you this very night!'

'Reward me, how?' Kpadunu yawned. This business of standing there holding a long conversation with snakes was beginning to bore him.

'I shall give you my daughter as your bride,' the serpent said and slithered off into the underbrush. A moment later, his faithless wife followed him.

Kpadunu considered that.

'But how does one lie with a snake?' he thought, and plunged into the brush after them to ask them that. Only by then the two pythons were nowhere to be seen. So Kpadunu walked away from there. He stepped carefully over the body of the dead serpent and started homeward. But he did not reach his uncle's compound, for a few minutes later a terrible weight of darkness fell out of heaven and hit him on the head.

When he opened his eyes it was still dark, but the darkness was beginning to grey a little, and things were growing edges, form was being reborn out of night and chaos. His head ached as though Xevioso had struck him with a thunderstone.

Then he remembered the pythons.

'What a silly dream!' he said disgustedly, and got unsteadily to his feet. The minute he did so he came face to face with the girl.

She wasn't a Dahomean. He saw that at once in the rapidly strengthening light. Her nose and lips were as thin as those of the Furtoo he'd seen in Whydah. But her skin was as black as his own. Her hair was neither kinky nor woolly, but neither was it as thin and stringy as that of the skinless people who came from across the sea to buy slaves. So he decided that she must be a Fanti, who lived far to the north and had mixed her blood so thoroughly with the Arabs that, though they had black skins, they were in all other ways like Furtoos. Only he couldn't speak Fanti so he hung there, watching her.

She was beautiful. Her eyes were huge, like melted pearls on the half-shells in which some *vudun* had plunged two rounded, jewelled pieces of the night. She had no beauty scars at all, and she didn't need them. Strangest of all, she was naked, wearing neither a skirt or a loincloth. And her body was a miracle made by all the *vudun* of the night sky.

'Who are you?' he groaned.

'I—I don't know,' she whispered, speaking to him not in Fau, but in Ewe, which was the language of the Yoruban people to the east of Dahomey. And since Ewe actually is only a dialect of Fau, he understood her perfectly.

'Where did you come from?' he said, then.

'I don't know that either,' she said.

'Who are your parents?' he demanded, beginning to get angry, now.

'I—I don't remember!' she wailed, and there were tears in those glorious eyes. 'I don't remember anything before now, my lord! I seem to have awakened from a long sleep and——'

Kpadunu stared at her, drums in his blood. She was! She was! She had to be!

'Walk over to that tree,' he said and pointed. The girl did so. Her walk was poetry, music. She didn't walk, she flowed, lithe-slender, sinuous. This—this daughter of the *vudu* Dangbe! This child of Aido Hwedo, the great snake who holds up the world!

'I know who you are,' Kpadunu said.

'Then who am I, my lord?' the girl said.

'Thou'rt Dangbevi, Serpent's Child, and my bride!' Kpadunu said in a voice so great it shook the trees.

Thereupon he led her to his uncle's compound and slipped her into his own house before anyone was awake. Then he made love to her. He must have hurt her terribly, because when the light of morning was high and strong, he saw that his sleeping mat was soaked through with blood.

But she hadn't cried out and had loved him with great tenderness. So he got up from there and took the sleeping mat up off the floor. She knelt there staring at him, and there was blood on her thighs, and her eyes were like twin moons at the full.

'Where dost thou go, O my husband?' she said to him then.

'To show the mat to my uncle, and then to your father, my Dangbevi,' Kpadunu said, his voice bubbling with exultant laughter and tenderness and joy. 'And after that to take the goats and the cloths and the salt and the money into the forest to give them to the python, thy father, so that the wedding be legal, for I would not make a *xadudo* of thee, whom I love more than life!'

'Wait,' Dangbevi said gently, 'first I will cook food for thee, for is that not the duty of a wife?'

So was it, in this fashion, in Dahomey where men do not separate the real from the dreamed, the spirit from the flesh as other peoples do, that Kpadunu, Nyasanu's first friend eldest, acquired his number one wife.

EIGHT

Nyasanu's *taugbochinovi*, or granduncle, the woodcarver Hwegbe, woke that same morning to the consciousness of pain. More pain than he had ever felt before in his seventy-odd years of existence. He put out his long, powerful fingers and felt himself in various places. So far as he could tell, none of his bones was broken. But reaching gingerly around his ancient, skinny form, he ran his hands, as far as they could reach over his upper back and his buttocks. As light as he touched himself, he almost screamed. His shoulders, back, and seat were a mass of stripes, crusted over with dried blood, and from neck to kneecrook, he stiffened, ached, and itched all at the same time.

With a groan, Hwegbe eased himself back down upon his sleeping mat. He lay, of course, on his belly, pillowing his white-bearded chin on his crossed arms. And, lying there like that, he reasoned out what had happened to him.

'A trick, of course. An elaborate trick, carefully planned.

'And I got scared—like any other superstitious fool. Just as if I hadn't lived in Whydah and spent years at Kumassi among the Ashanti. Just as if I didn't know that the body is a dung sack that stinks to high heaven living, and even worse than that, dead. The soul's breath. All three of them. Ha! Couldn't we worms in the tripes of Da be content with *one* as other peoples are?'

He stared towards the door of his mud and wattles hut.

'Their hands—hard. Hot. And young. A ghost's would be cold. Clammy cold. That's logic. The logic of believing that the ghosts I don't believe in would have hands I could feel! So—who? Ah, that's the question! My grandnephew, of course! Because I wouldn't grant divinity to his goddess. Offended by my suggestion that what his black pearl passes when she squats to relieve herself isn't perfume from the front, and honey from the rear! So he called his *gbe* together. Aided by that friend of his who claims to be the son of one sorcerer and the nephew of another——

'Well, they've asked for it! Oh, evil spirits from beneath the earth—if I could only move! I need to consult an *azaundato*. Which one doesn't matter—any one of the gibbering old fakers will do. Nyakadju, now; he of the rough skin! A Peanut Leaf Clan marker: they're the best. And wholly my man, since his own *du*, cast by his own hands, told him his life is inseparately linked to mine. Nonsense, thou hast thy uses! But he lives at Umpegume, a half day's journey from here. If only there were someone I could trust enough to send him a message bidding him to come to me!

'Only, there isn't. I am Hwegbe, a windy old fool of a wood-carver, who has offended all the world because his sense of the ridiculous is too keen. Yes, a fool. Why can't I let people keep their pomposities, idiocies, superstitions, all the cotton-silk batten of nonsense with which they enwrap their lives—to protect themselves from reality, whose clasp is too rough, whose blows are too hard?

'So nobody. Nobody to aid this windy old goat in his favourite sport of cutting fools down to size. O Legba of the ever-erect penis, aid me in performing a rude fornication upon the tenderest parts of their pomposity! For I'd have my vengeance upon randy Gbenu and his too handsome son. But for that I need——

'Someone who hates them as much as I do. No more, because come to think of it, I don't hate them at all. I'd only revenge this affront to my dignity, cleanse them of pomposity and pride. But who can I find that——'

He lay there, his eyes suddenly afire. Lifted his chin off his arms and loosed his shrill and evil-sounding old man's cackle.

'Gbochi! That son of a pig! No—of an ever-rutting sow. The *medaxochi* of Gbenu's house—though Yu under pain of ordeal couldn't swear with any certainty who his father is!

The elder son clearly displaced by his younger brother. Whining effeminate that he is, for this at least he'll do!'

So Hwegbe waited on his bed of pain for some small child to pass his opened door. It was hours before one did; but Hwegbe wasted no time in bemoaning that fact. He simply called out, when a naked, pot-bellied little urchin finally did appear:

'Come here, my son!'

Ten minutes later, the child, with chewing sticks, cakes, and sweetmeats clasped lovingly in his grimy fists, was on his way to Gbochi's house.

And now all the preliminary rites had been accomplished.

The *du* or lots cast once again by both Zezu and Akausu declared that there was no reason that he, Nyasanu, could not take Agbale to wife, a thing that afterwards caused him to remember another of the almost blasphemous mockeries his *taugbochinovi* Hwegbe was always giving vent to:

'The *du*, ha! The sacred seeds cast from the thrice sacred *fa* cup to determine a man's fate! Tell me, Nephew, whenever do they predict ill fortune for the rich, the powerful, and the great? Even when a man's ant-cleansed skull is going to decorate a stake over an Auyo or a Maxi village gate, do not his *du*, as read by his own *bokono*, the day before he marches off on one of those slaving raids Dada Gepo calls wars, *always* predict for him—if, mark you, Nephew, he be a noble, or a *gletanu*, or a chief—that he'll come back covered with glory and bearing many heads?'

But on that bright morning, as he set out to bear the sacred *xaungbo* payments to Azauvidi, the *xenuga* or head of Agbale's father's clan, Nyasanu carefully pushed all such disquieting thoughts from his mind, dismissing not only Hwegbe's mockery, but his own keen-witted observation that the *bokono* more often interpreted the lots in a manner to please an important client than not; and that when they did place a rich man's son in jeopardy—as both his father's diviner Zezu, and the head *bokono* of the realm had placed him—it was usually to receive a large sum of money from said rich man by performing a spectacular rescue of the jeopardized one with their *gbo* and other charms.

At the moment, however, clad in princely finery and followed by a host of his father's servants and slaves, the first four of whom bore the sacred gifts, Nyasanu took great comfort from the two diviners' predictions of long life and happiness for him and his bride. And truly on that bright morning, the young Dahomean was a sight to see. He was dressed in his finest clothes: a toga of green, watered silk draped over one lithe muscular shoulder, a green chief's cap—worn with his father's permission—on his proud young head, bracelets of bronze and silver encircling his powerful arms, iron and shell beads about his neck, sandals of antelope hide, dyed green to match his toga, stitched with red threads and white and decorated with cowry shells on his slim feet. And what was more, he walked under his father's gorgeously decorated umbrella, also lent him for the occasion by Gbenu, as a mark of favour, which was held over his head by a slave, a Maxi captive like all the rest of his retinue, the lot of them taken by the chief in one or another of his many displays of valour during King Gezo's wars.

The visit Nyasanu was now making was not to Nwesa, Agbale's father, but to her granduncle Azauvidi, the *xenuga* or head of the clan Nwesa belonged to. Custom demanded—because, from the religious point of view, the clan head's authority over any girl was held to be greater than that of her own parents—that the young bridegroom solemnise the approaching marriage by making 'strong' gifts to the clan head, as he had already done, on the occasion of formally asking Agbale's hand, to the father of the bride.

Behind him as he marched, head up and striding proudly and occasionally fanning away those true lords of Africa, the flies, with a Gnu-tail fly whisk, came his father's retainers, bearing his gifts to the *xenuga* of Agbale's clan. One of them carried a leather purse containing seven hundred and twenty cowry shells. Another bore carefully folded on his head one large man's cloth, white in colour and woven from the fibres of the local cottonsilk tree, and a woman's cloth of the same material. A third bore a huge sack of salt, so heavy he had to wear a cushion between it and his head to absorb some of its weight, thus demonstrating Gbenu's immense wealth, for salt, in the interior of Dahomey was costly indeed. And, as custom also demanded, the fourth slave led a gelded goat, exactly twelve years old and of that dwarf breed that stands no more than two feet high.

And now the whole procession came trooping into Nwesa's compound. Nwesa was there, of course, but he held back, and let the clan head receive them.

Nyasanu bowed low before Agbale's *taugbochinovi* Azau-vidi.

'I bring you strong gifts, O great Xenuga!' he said. And at the first snap of his fingers, the slave led forward the little goat.

'I accept this gift on behalf of the ghost of the founder of our clan!' Azauvidi said. Then: 'Bind him!' The clan members sprang forward and bound the little goat so tightly with cords it could not move. Then they bore the poor little creature, bleating piteously all the while, to the cult house of the ancestors. There Azauvidi deftly cut its throat while one of his followers caught the hot blood in a bowl. This the *xenuga* carried inside before the *ase*, or iron altar sacred to Ghosikpan, the *tauhwiyo,* or founder of the clan.

'I give you to dinner, father of us all, great Ghosikpan!' the *xenuga* said, 'and inform you that one of thy daughters is to wed!' Then he poured the blood on the ground before the altar.

They came out of the dim and shadowy interior of the cult house—a fitting abode for ghosts, Nyasanu thought—into the full light of the morning sun.

'Bring the salt, O captive taken in battle by my father!' Nyasanu called out, then. At once the slave shuffled forward and knelt before his young master, going down on his knees carefully so that the huge sack would not fall from his head. At the sight of its size and weight an audible gasp went up from the spectators. Several of them snapped their fingers loudly in the most African gesture of admiration and approval. 'Verily this is an *akwenusi* wedding, and of number one class!' several of them whispered 'for though cowry shells represent money, who can argue with the fact that salt is true wealth!'

'I offer thee, O great Xenuga, this small and humble gift,' Nyasanu said quietly, trying to keep the pride he was almost bursting with out of his voice.

'I accept your salt, new son of our family,' the clan head said, 'on behalf of this household.'

Nyasanu bowed, and taking from the hands of the fourth slave the large white cloth, he gave it to Azauvidi.

At once the clan head turned to Nwesa and said:

'Take this cloth, son Nwesa, to replace the one upon which you lay with thy wife on the night you got her with the daughter who tomorrow becomes a bride!'

Nwesa took the cloth and bowed silently.

Then Nyasanu took the woman's cloth and gave it to Azauvidi. Again the *xenuga* turned and held the cloth out to Adje, saying:

'Take this cloth, woman, to replace the one you used as a sling to bear upon thy back the girl-child who tomorrow becomes a bride!'

Then everyone bowed, snapped their fingers loudly, and the ceremony of the *xaungbo* gifts was over.

Nyasanu went back home again. There before his house he found not one, as custom demanded, but literally dozens of *axa* baskets such as women use to carry cloth in, placed there for him by his mother and sisters. All the baskets were filled with the very finest of women's cloths, bought for him by all his female relatives. And not only had his sisters, both full and half, his mother, and his aunts spent every cowry they'd managed to save from their own not inconsiderable earnings from the things they grew or made and then sold in the marketplace, but all the really lavish sums Gbenu had put at their disposition out of his determination to see that his favourite son had the biggest wedding, not only in the history of Alladah but, if possible, in that of all Dahomey as well.

Nyasanu examined all the cloths carefully and added some headcloths and silk handkerchiefs brought that very morning from Whydah by a relay of runners. They were of European manufacture, Italian silks, and Portuguese brocades, and Gbenu had ordered them for him from the great seacoast town, which was the only place in Dahomey such exquisite luxuries could be had. After that the young bridegroom lay atop the cloths a string of beads of the kind called *lisadje*, since Agbale was of the Sky *Cudun* cult, and those snowy beads were sacred to Lisa, the husband-brother of Mawu, goddess of the sky. With it, he put a flask of *adiminhwe*, a perfume made from almond blossoms, the scent customarily worn by brides in Dahomey.

Having done this—which was in all probability his last act as a single man—Nyasanu went in search of his grandfather, Adjaemi. Now Adjaemi was not only the boy's *taugbochi,* or paternal grandfather, he was also the *xenuga* of the Ironworkers' Clan. It was in this high capacity that Nyasanu now sought him.

'Taugbochi,' he whispered, when he had found that still spry

97

and decidedly mischievous old man, 'the bridal gifts are ready——'

Adjaemi took the long pipe he was smoking out of his mouth. Good, Vivu, son of my son,' he said calmly: 'I will send the messenger tomorrow night.' Then he put the pipe back into his mouth and went on smoking.

'Grandfather,' Nyasanu said, 'couldn't you send them—to-night?'

'No,' Adjaemi said. 'Such haste is unseemly, grandson.' He took the pipe out of his mouth once more and pointed with the stem of it towards the general area of Nyasanu's pelvis.

'If *that* aches you,' he cackled, 'pour cold water on it, for you have two more exceedingly long nights to wait, Vivu!'

Nyasanu stood there, trying to control his anger. Why did they—especially all these dirty-minded old men—assume that a young bridegroom-to-be was fairly burning up with desire? He, at least, didn't feel that way towards Agbale. What he really felt was faint with tenderness, his bones water within him, and so nervous, weak from emotion, afraid, that he was almost sure that his wedding night was going to be a disaster.

'Strange,' he said.

'What's strange, son's son?' his grandfather said.

'How often I forget that you and Taugbochinovi Hwegbe are, after all—brothers, Taugbochi,' Nyasanu said, and turning on his heel marched away from there.

That next night, the *xenuga* of the Ironworkers' Clan sent two sons of his, half-brothers of Gbenu, and two daughters, both married within the clan, to the collectivity of many compounds of which Nwesa's was the original unit. Now, ordinarily, they would have borne Nyasanu's gift among themselves; but the *toxausu* had so outdone himself on behalf of his beloved son that once again a long procession of bearers had to accompany the messengers of the clan head in order to carry all the *axa* baskets filled with fragrantly perfumed cloths.

When they arrived, the matter was conducted with the weighty ceremony dear to the Dahomean heart. Nyawi, Adjaemi's *medaxochi* or eldest son, but only *tovichi*, half brother, to Gbenu, stepped forward. Already in the autumn of his years, for he was far older than Gbenu, Nyawi was a man of imposing girth and presence. Solemnly he bowed to Nwesa and said in a deep and stately voice:

'The *xenuga* of our clan sends us with these gifts to tell you that he is hungry. At his home he has millet and maize and cassava and yams, but there is no one to prepare them for him. He asks, therefore, that you send him a woman.'

Then Nwesa bowed in his turn and said:

'The will of the venerable head of the Ironworkers' Clan is our command.' He called out: 'Let my daughter Agbale be brought!'

All the people assembled cried out:

'Agbale, Agbale! Come, child! Thy husband's people await thee!'

But there was no answer. In her mother's house, Agbale hid behind Adje's skirts and trembled. No one was surprised at this behaviour; thus always, in the land of Da's Belly, does a bride-to-be display her modesty.

Nwesa clapped his hands and a group of female slaves came out of the cook house bearing many platters. A table was brought, and stools, and the platters of steaming antelope flesh, pork, brushhen, and wild birds were placed upon the table along with bottles of palm wine. The slaves went back and forth bringing still more platters: yams and cassava and corn and fruit of many varieties.

'Sit and eat, august visitors,' Nwesa said.

The four messengers sat down and began to eat. No one said anything until they had finished; then a woman came rushing out of Adje's house and said with great, and obviously theatrical, emotion:

'Thy daughter, O Nwesa, hath fled to the forest! Searchers must be sent after her!'

'Hmmm,' Nwesa said. 'That will call for money. Searchers ask a lot!'

'Allow me the honour of paying them,' Nyawi said, and all the spectators snapped their fingers in astonishment and joy, just as if the same charade had not been a part of every *akwenusi* wedding in Dahomey since the institution of marriage began.

Nyawi then poured out several hundred cowry shells into the hands of the woman who had brought the bad news. She went back into Adje's house, and almost instantly came out again, her black face beaming:

'Thy daughter hath been found, O Nwesa!' she cried.

And almost at the sound of her words they heard the sound of drumbeats.

A moment later, a huge crowd of drumming, dancing, singing young men appeared. These were the members of Nyasanu's *gbe*. They were dressed in their finest clothes and bore banners of appliqué cloths showing the society's motto and giving some indication of its functions. Behind them came the members of his *dokpwe*, his communal work group, also dressed in gaudy togas, and bearing their own appliqué cloth banners and dancing, drumming, and singing as loudly as the *gbe* members, which—since the tune they drummed, danced to, and sang, was completely different from the tune of the mutual aid society, deafening even the jackals out on the savanna—lent a certain colourful confusion to the scene.

Next came Nyasanu's first, second, and third friends. In his enthusiasm and new-found joy, Kpadunu seemed determined to negate or repeal the laws of gravitation. His soaring leaps were miracles of the dancer's art. He rose into the air, tree-top high it seemed to the watchers, he floated, a wind-borne leaf, thistledown upon an evening breeze, a warm thundercloud drifting, drifting over the fields of spring. . . .

Amosu and Taugbadji could not hope to equal Kpadunu's performance, but they provided a fitting accompaniment to it with their sweeps and struts and stompings before that matchless great hammock of rainbow-hued appliqué cloth attached to a carved ironwood pole borne fore and aft upon the shoulders of massive slaves in which lay, not Gbenu, but wonder of wonders, a thing unheard of in Dahomean history—his son.

The finger-snapping of the spectators was as the crackling of a brush fire at that sight. Surely no wedding in memory had been so great as this! Surely no father so indulgent with a second son; for always, always the bridegroom walked to the compound of his wife's father; it was unheard of for him to be hammock-borne like a chief.

After Nyasanu's hammock came another one, even more imposing, in which Gbenu lay. Last of all came a huge group, literally hundreds of men and women. Heading this group were both Nyasanu's grandfathers followed by their wives. Then his granduncles, among whom be it said, was the woodcarver Hwegbe, hobbling along with surprising agility, aided by a stout walking stick. Then Gudjo, the mother of the groom, surrounded by a regal court of women attendants, most of them volunteers, and including, surprisingly enough, Yu,

100

Gbochi's mother, to whom this open display of favouritism upon Gbenu's part for his second son must have been a bitter pill to swallow indeed.

But among the swarms of lithe and lovely young women— many of them either full or half sisters (*novichi or tovichi nyqnu*) of the princely young man being married on this day— was one who walked totally and terribly alone. And this one— whose sinuous, flowing stride marked her, whose body's perfection was incredible even among a race whose young women have the most beautiful bodies in all the world—was Dangbevi, Serpent's Child. She moved thus, head up, erect, hiding her great hurt, for already throughout all Alladah had spread the whispers: 'She's not a human being! She's an evil spirit, born of a snake!'

And now Nyasanu and his father, the chief, got down from their hammocks. There was a great scurrying about of servants and slaves busily engaged in making piles, to the right of the spot where Nyasanu stood, of all the gifts he had made his bride. The cloths alone made a mound taller than he was, and Nyasanu was fully six feet five inches tall. As each gift was placed on the ground the wedding guests snapped their fingers, especially when Amosu's gift, the little group of figures cast in silver and soldered to a common silver base, was displayed. In Dahomey silver objects were seldom seen except in the homes of nobles or the king.

Then Nwesa's wives and his female servants came forward and began to pile up Agbale's belongings to Nyasanu's left. First they made a huge pile of her cloths, with those she had bought with the money she had herself earned on top, thus subtly hinting to the groom what a treasure of a girl he was getting. Then all her jewellery, rings, bracelets, beads, her perfumes, her calabash dishes, and her brass cooking pots, polished until they shone like gold. In front of Nyasanu another group of Nwesa's people piled up the wedding gifts that her father had himself given the bride, and those included more cloths, more calabashes, more jewellery, and a showy pile of money.

And now Agbale came out of her mother's house and took her place beside her bridegroom. She was dressed in a red silk skirt covered with white appliqué flowers. She had many strings of beads around her neck and around her waist; her wrists were heavy with bracelets, as were her ankles. She wore no earrings, because it was a tabu of her clan to pierce their ears; and not only had her mother personally bathed her at least three times that morning for fear that she might smell of sweat like a peasant, but she was literally drenched with almond blossom perfume.

As she came towards her fiancé, she was so lovely that Nyasanu could feel his bones melting inside his legs. He was sure he was going to faint from nervousness, love, longing, and desire. She was, of course, naked from the waist up, but she didn't appear to be, because the greyish pink ridges of her decorative scars coiled all over her upper body like a network of vines. And now that she was close to him, he could see how she was trembling, perceive the sacred *tadu*, or 'head word', scars on her temples pulsating like wild, tender, living things from the anguished beat of her blood. Even the *gbugbomi*, 'kiss me', circle on her cheek was alive and afire and trembling.

What saved them both from the terrible tension of that moment was the fact that Aauvi, the priestess of the ancestor cult, who is second only in importance to the *tauvodunu* or high priest of the father gods himself, came forward to pronounce the nuptial blessing.

'I bless you, my daughter,' she said, 'and you, chief's son, who bears her away from us. I pray you to love and cherish and honour her all her days. Do you so promise?'

Nyasanu forced sound over the mountain of agonising tenderness in his throat, and whispered:

'I do so promise, venerable Aauvi. . . .'

The old woman turned to Agbale then, and said slowly, impressively, the wedding words:

'My daughter, you are going to be married. You will bear sons who in time to come will watch over the family of your husband, and the clan of his father. You will bear daughters who will leave you to marry into other clans, and they will spread among those to whom they go the name of the Clan Guduvi Adjadenu to which you belong. We hope to see born of you a girl-child who, one day, will increase the clan you are now leaving. May your husband love you always, and may evil and bad luck and sickness be forever absent from your wedding house. May you be well cared for and live to carry the children of your grandchildren in your arms. In the name of the *tauhwiho*. the clan founder, and all the great ancestors, I bless you!'

102

Then from the hands of another, younger priestess, the *Aauvi* took a large urn of water and poured it in a circle all around the young couple.

'Go, child,' she said now, 'with thy husband to his mother's house!'

And now, once again, Agbale was to prove what an individualist she was, how wanting in prudence, how great of heart, for as she started towards Gbenu's compound on her new husband's arm, she noticed on the edges of the crowd of young women who were crowding in to form her escort, a strange girl who stood apart, looking sad and lost and terribly forlorn.

'Who's that, Dosu!' she whispered in Nyasanu's ear.

'Dangbevi, poor thing,' Nyasanu said. 'She's Kpadunu's first wife. But she hasn't any friends. And she won't have, I'm sure of that! The girls are afraid of her. They say she isn't human. I'll tell you the story of how they came to marry later on, when we're alone. . . .'

'I've heard it already,' Agbale said. 'And it's a lot of nonsense! The poor thing was probably hit on the head or had some other kind of accident that made her lose her memory, that's all. Child of the Serpent Dangbe, my foot! Snakes have snakes, Dosu, and women—daughters. Now send someone to call her. . . .'

'Send someone to. . . .'

'Call her. You heard me, Dosu! Don't make me mad today, or so help me, I'll go back to my father!'

Nyasanu stared at his bride. Then he grinned. Agbale was Agbale and what she was, all the *vudun* of earth, sky, sea, and thunder weren't going to change. Besides, he loved her as she was, full of fire and spirit and will and tenderness.

'All right, Hwesidaxo!' he said, a little mockingly. The word meant 'housewife eldest', and a husband never calls his bride that except upon occasions of great ceremony, or when he is a little angry with her, as Nyasanu was now.

'Well, I *am* your number one wife,' Agbale said, 'and don't you ever forget it, Dosu! 'Cause if you ever do, I'll give you such a life as to make you pray to the ancestors to come and take me away. Now do as I say! Send someone to call Dangbevi to me. . . .'

Nyasanu beckoned a slave to his side and whispered something in his ear. When all the people saw the man approach Dangbevi they stared open-mouthed a long moment before the

103

rippling tide of whispers began.

Shyly, the beautiful, strange girl came back with the Maxi slave to where headstrong Agbale had brought the whole wedding procession to a halt. The new bride clung to her young husband's arm and stared at Dangbevi.

'Oh, Mawu-Lisa, but you're pretty!' she said. 'No, you're beautiful!' Then suddenly, impulsively, she leaned forward and kissed Dangbevi's cheek.

'I like you, Dangbevi,' she said simply, 'and I want you to join my bridesmaids in this procession. That's where you should be. Among my friends, I mean.'

Dangbevi stood there, and her eyes filled with tears.

'Why do you weep, new sister mine?' Agbale said.

'From happiness, my lady,' Dangbevi said. 'I—I was so lonely! Of course, I have my husband but——'

'A woman needs woman friends, too. Good. Now you go join the others.'

There was nothing for the others to do then but to accept the Serpent's Child. And once they had, they soon lost their fear of her. Long before the wedding procession had reached Gudjo's house, they were all laughing and chatting with her and asking her questions about her past life. Questions that she couldn't answer, for the very simple reason that her amnesia was not feigned, but real.

But seeing how friendly they were towards her now, Kpadunu blessed Agbale in his heart.

When they got to Gudjo's house, Nyasanu's mother was already there, having rushed home by a shorter route, and already had the ceremonial dish of hot beans prepared for her new daughter-in-law's wedding supper.

'Go to thy house, foolish son of mine!' she said sternly to Nyasanu. 'I will bring thee thy bride tomorrow!'

There was nothing for Nyasanu to do but obey. In Dahomey, it was held the worst of bad taste, and an ugly display of lust and unseemly haste, for a husband to possess his bride upon the first night of their wedding. Even consummation was a high and holy rite, closely supervised by the mothers of the bride and bridegroom alike. But truth, said truth to tell, what the young husband felt at the delay was pure, blessed relief; at the state his nerves were in then, he had no confidence at all in his manly powers.

104

When he got to his house, he found all three of his friends awaiting him. Dangbevi was with her husband, and she and Nyasanu's own sister Axisi were laying dishes on the table while the savoury aroma of a stew rose from the cooking fire. There was a good bit of outrageously obscene jesting, in which be it said, neither Kpadunu nor Dangbevi joined. They both knew that marriage was too great and fine and holy a thing to be so mocked.

'It's not so much what you do,' Kpadunu reasoned in his mind, 'but how and especially *why* you do it. I've lain with whores in Whydah. I performed like a billygoat upon the poor helpless *tasino* who cooled the heat of my circumcisional knife. But with Dangbevi it was not the same from the first, and it will never be. The *gbo* that transforms the act we're all born to into a thing of mystery and magic is—love. Poor devils, they don't understand that. Not even Axisi, and she's a girl. I pray to Minona that they have the good fortune I have had to learn what the difference is——'

'Eat, brother!' Axisi mocked, 'I've put plenty of ataxi pepper and afiti mustard in it to set your blood afire and heat the iron in your weapon so that it won't hang down like a *gbe* banner does when there's not a whisper of a breeze astirring! My *gbo*, a real charm that works instead of all that muck of feathers and mud and thorns and dead frogs that this faker Kpad and his charlatan uncle make! So I can be sure you won't shame me tomorrow night and give that little black witch you're marrying the chance to whisper all over the village that Axisi's brother is no man!'

'Axisi, will you shut your foul mouth?' Nyasanu said.

'No. Besides, why should you care what I say? So long as Agbale doesn't clap her black and rusty knees together so tight that you can't pry them apart, you have nothing to worry about, Nya!' Axisi said.

Nyasanu got up and tried to clamp his hand over her mouth, but she skipped merrily out of the way.

'Axisi,' Dangbevi whispered.

'Yes, O Serpent's Child, who wiggles so seductively that poor Kpad is already down to skin and bones,' Axisi laughed, 'what would you say to me?'

'That you—shouldn't. That you make an ugliness of what is—beautiful. That when you hold your first babe to your breasts you will no longer see—the means by which you and

105

your husband gave him life—as a filthiness. That's what I want to say....'

'Oh Legba God of Lust!' Axisi said, 'let me out of here! This is much too solemn for my taste!'

'Not until you give me something to eat, Sister!' Nyasanu said sternly.

When, somewhat subdued at last, Axisi heaped his plate, Nyasanu found his appetite was gone. Still, politeness demanded that he eat at least a little of the stew. But the moment he put the first spoonful in his mouth, he bolted from the house and spat the stew out on the ground.

All of them, Amosu, Taugbadji, Kpadunu, Dangbevi, and Axisi stared at him in utter astonishment. But Nyasanu was glaring at his sister, a great and terrible anger in his eyes.

'Wouldst poison me, Sister?' he said.

'Nya!' Axisi wailed, 'don't look at me like that. What did I do? I made you the best stew I ever cooked in my whole life and you——'

'Axisi,' Nyasanu said slowly, 'what are the *su dudu* of our clan?'

'We mustn't work on Lamisi Day,' Axisi said, 'nor eat nyatoto lettuce nor the flesh of the ram—Nya! I didn't! There's neither nyatoto nor mutton in that stew! I swear I——'

'Taste it,' Nyasanu said, and dipping a spoon in the plate, held it out to her.

Axisi tasted the stew, gingerly; then she, too, bolted to the door and spat it out. When she turned, there were tears in her eyes.

'Nya, listen to me!' she said. 'I cooked you a stew all right, but Legba eat my breath if it was this one! Mine was made of pork and brushhen and boiled yams. And—and afiti mustard and ataki peppers just like I said! So stop looking at me just like Da does when he's mad enough to take all my skin off with a baobab rod! I didn't make this stew!'

She wasn't lying. All of them could see that.

'Somebody changed the pots once they were on the fire,' Kpadunu reasoned slowly. 'Now, who had reasons for doing that? Your Granduncle Hwegbe? If so, he's got more nerve than I'd given him credit for.'

At this point, Kpadunu stopped short. He'd remembered just in time that Nyasanu knew nothing of the beating that he and

106

his *gbe* of apprentice sorcerers and diviners had laid upon the old man. And he realised that same instant that it wasn't wise to tell his first friend that particular truth. For Nyasanu loved his granduncle, despite that malicious old man's many sins. Kpadunu knew that very well.

'No,' Nyasanu said quietly. 'What man could walk through the compound with a cooking pot dangling from his hands?'

'No man,' Taugbadji said slowly. 'But—a woman could.' Then they all said it, except Dangbevi, who didn't even know her: 'A woman! Yu! Who else but Yu!'

'After the display of his favour your father made today,' Amosu groaned, 'she's lost all hope of seeing that womanish swine Gbochi succeed him as chief. Look to what you eat from now on, Nya! And what you drink as well! I wouldn't put it past Yu to——'

'Murder him?' Dangbevi whispered.

'Even that,' Kpadunu her husband said.

That was the first warning Nyasanu had of impending trouble. But the second only confused the issue, because it came from quite another source. And before that year had run its course, the signs of trouble were like vultures circling about his helpless head.

All the next day Gbenu's compound was loud with talk and laughter, for all the people of Nwesa's clan who could came to visit Agbale in her new home. There was much eating and drinking, and some enthusiastic guests danced; but this was not considered Nyasanu's and Agbale's wedding feast, nor the day their wedding day.

That night, trembling like a loko sapling in a high wind, Nyasanu waited for his mother and Agbale's to bring his bride to his newly built wedding house. He had bathed all over, not once but several times, and perfumed his body; but despite all his efforts he smelled of sweat—the ice-cold sweat of nervousness, of fear.

They were long in coming. So long, in fact, that he was beginning to despair, to wonder if Agbale, who was capable of it, he knew, had not changed her mind, and fled his mother's house. Then he heard the knocking on his door, and sat there a long, long moment before he gathered his souls to him enough to open it.

But it was only his first friend, Kpadunu. He had a large clay flask in his hand.

'Here,' he said, 'drink this, my brother! Or else in the state you're in, you'll only disappoint your woman—and that's no way to start your married life.'

'What is it?' Nyasanu whispered.

'A *gbo*,' Kpadunu said, 'prepared by me. Strong magic against the little evil ones who race up and down one's spine with feet cold as the snows atop the eastern mountains. A charm against down-droop and dangle which is one of their manifestations, and also against the unseemly haste and un-skilled clumsiness that, though seemingly an opposite effect, is also their work. In short, brother mine, insurance that this night you play the man, and that in the morning thy bride awakes with stars in her eyes and singing like all the birds of heaven. Go on, Nya, drink it!'

Gingerly Nyasanu sipped the foaming drink. It had a pleasant taste, rather like palm wine to which something else had been added.

Only after he had drained the flask to the last drop did he notice the scalding bite of it. But that soon passed and he felt warmth invade him. He was quite suddenly surrounded by a vast and rosy calm. He looked at his first friend with eyes bemused and a little sleepy.

'And now?' he said.

'I go,' Kpadunu said, 'because when I passed your mother's house, the bridal procession was already leaving.'

But just before his mother and his mother-in-law arrived leading Agbale by the hand, Nyasanu had one more visitor—a boy bearing on his head a package from his Granduncle Hwegbe. He knew what it was before he even opened the pack-age: the *agbadome*, the guardian spirits that one places before one's door to keep all evil out. But when he did open it, he was surprised: the figures were not the same ones he had seen his *taugbochinovi* carve. Instead they were almost as slender as cast-brass figures and curved with willowy grace. Nothing about them was exaggerated except their slenderness; their male and female bodies were beautifully proportioned, with their respective genitalia represented, of course, but with a strangely becoming modesty; the male did not sport a huge and offensively erect phallus; nor was the pudenda of the fe-male *bauchie* shown enormously swollen and agape. These guardian spirits were, in fact, lovely.

'I pricked his pride,' Nyasanu laughed to himself, 'by comparing the ugliness of the figures woodcarvers make to the beauty of those that brassworkers cast! So now he has to show me. And he has. I thank you, Taugbochinovi! But you should also thank me in your turn, for I have angered thee into producing great art!'

Then very carefully, he placed them just outside his door. As he did so, he had a sudden feeling that there was something else odd about them, something he had only half noticed; but he couldn't for the life of him call to mind what it was, so he turned away and left them there. He had no sooner done that, than he heard the footsteps of the women.

It was, he soon realised, a very good thing that Kpadunu had prepared him that foaming drink, for what followed was calculated to test the nerves of Gu, the God of Iron, himself. He found himself surrounded by a host of laughing girls, most of them his sisters and half-sisters, and the rest Agbale's. The one exception was Dangbevi, who stood there smiling at him with a strange grave tenderness that was somehow comforting. But all the rest proceeded to tickle and kiss him and tug at his toga in the pretence of taking it off him. He clung to it desperately, for although he knew this was only a charade and that the girls had no intention of stripping him naked, he didn't put it past the devilry of Axisi, nor—he realised with a sudden chilling horror—the plain lust showing in Alogba's eyes, to cause the two of them to go too far. Of course Alogba was Yu's daughter, Gbochi's full sister and hence only half-sister to him; but what her little pig's eyes and gross mouth with a slime of saliva in its corners were showing then was the most terrible of all tabus. In Dahomey incest was punishable by death, except among the members of the royal family, who were permitted to, and therefore did, indulge in it to their licentious hearts' content.

So he felt a great relief when Gudjo and Adje came into his house and drove the laughing girls out of it with many blows. But what followed was even worse: for Adje and Gudjo between them stretched out a new sleeping mat upon the floor and covered it with white cloth. Then they placed the lovely appliqué work pillows that his third friend Taugbadji had made at the head of it.

After that they went out and came back leading Agbale by the hand. She was trembling so she could hardly walk and the 'head word' scars at her temples, and the 'kiss me' circular scar on her cheek stood up and jerked like living things. But her mother, Adje, paid no attention to her embarrassment. Briskly, matter of factly, Adje stripped her daughter naked before his eyes. Now Nyasanu, son of a tropical land, had seen his beloved naked to the waist most of the time, and entirely nude except for a loincloth upon several occasions. So what there was left for him to see was very little and that little shadowed, obscured by the dim flickering of the lighted bamboo slivers floating in little cups of palm oil. He was not moved to desire; what he felt was pity at her distress, her shame.

Which both in minutes he fully shared, for Gudjo, his mother, immediately proceeded to strip him, in his turn.

'Nochi!' he got out. 'Little mother——'

'Don't be a fool, boy!' Gudjo said in a voice whose gruffness was designed to hide the tears that were almost drowning it. 'Lie down!'

He sank down on the mat, and Adje caught her trembling, sobbing daughter by the shoulders and forced her down beside him. Then the two mothers of the newlyweds marched through the door and shut it behind them.

But, Nyasanu knew, they both sat down just outside of it on cushions they had brought, until they were assured that the marriage had been consummated.

'How in the name of even Legba, Lord of Lust,' he wailed inside his mind, 'is a man supposed to perform the act of love with his own mother listening outside the door?'

'I'm scared!' Agbale whimpered. 'Oh, Dosu, I'm so scared!'

'Don't be, Nyaunu wi,' he said gently, and took the trembling girl in his arms. She lay there against him and shook all over, drenching that part of his neck where she had hid her face with an endless flow of tears. He did not move or caress her or even speak. He simply lay there holding her until she quieted.

She came up on one elbow and stared at him.

'All right,' she said harshly, angrily, 'do it! Make me thy wife!'

'No,' he said, a warmth upon him then, a lassitude, a peace, born only in part from the drugged wine Kpadunu had given him, 'not like that, little black woman. . . .'

110

'Then—how?' Agbale whispered.

'Like this,' he said, and kissed her mouth so slowly, softly, sweetly, that the feel of his lips upon hers was a warmth and a benediction and a prayer, all at the same time.

She drew back and stared at him, and the stars Kpadunu had spoken of were already in her eyes.

'Now,' she said, 'please now, Dosu.'

'Not even yet,' he said.

'Then—when?' she whispered.

'Not until you are ready for my love,' he said quietly.

'And when will that be, Dosu?' she said.

'You'll know, Nyaunu wi,' he said, 'you'll know. . . .'

And a little later she did know, and a slow, tender, miraculously prolonged time after that, their mothers knew it, too, jerked awake from where they dozed before the door by the high, bright, trilling sweetness of her cry.

The two women waited, trembling a little, until Nyasanu, his green toga draped about his slender hips out of respect for them, came through the door with the white cloth they had draped over his sleeping mat in his hand.

'Here,' he said to Adje, his voice big with pride. 'Take this to my wife's father, woman!'

The two women took the sheet between them and spread it out in the moonlight to examine it. Then both of them rent the night with both laughter and sobbing, for on the white cloth the proof that Agbale had been virgin until this very hour was clear.

The next morning Gbenu gave such a feast as in Dahomey can be given only to honour a maid who came demonstrably virgin to her wedding mat. But what the chief of Alladah did not know was that the mighty feast with which he honoured his son and his bride came close to not being held at all for lack of the very presence of Agbale herself.

Earlier in the morning Nyasanu had brought the beautiful *agbadome* his Granduncle Hwegbe had carved to protect their house inside to show them to Agbale. They then both became aware at the same moment that the figures had no eyes.

'I won't stay here, Dosu!' Agbale stormed. 'I won't! This house is evil! Mawu herself doesn't know how many wicked spirits entered it during the night! *Bauchie* without eyes! So how can they see what comes stealing through the gate? Oh,

111

what an old fool thy *taugbochinovi* is—to have forgot the eyes!'

'Forgot—or deliberately did not carve them?' Nyasanu thought. 'But why? Because I rated the brassworkers' art above his own? Is this his answer to so small an offence? It could be. Oh Gu, I——'

Then he saw how great the horror was in Agbale's eyes. He didn't know the reason for it, not all the reason at any event. And it wasn't until long afterwards that she told him. His bride had remembered once again that she had killed her own *fa*; and now, on top of that, was this!

'Come, Nyaunu,' he said, 'come little love. Get up. We must go to the feast and——'

'No!' she shrilled. 'I won't! I—I'll run away! I'll go to the forest, Dosu! Before something else happens, and Legba eats my brains.'

Then, as it usually did in times of stress, what must be done came to Nyasanu. He opened a great basket in which he kept his personal effects and took out a small, razor-sharp knife. Then he sat down, and taking up the *agbadme*, he proceeded to carve in the eyes. And since, like the majority of Dahomeans, he was an artist to his fingertips, he carved them very well indeed.

He sat there, studying the effect.

'Let me see,' Agbale whispered.

'Not yet,' he said. Then he went to work on the mouths of the figures extending them out and upward on the cheeks, carving them into happy grins. Last of all, he cut the crinkles of laughter about the new-carved eyes.

'Please, Dosu,' Agbale wheedled, 'let me see!'

'All right then,' Nyasanu said, and held them out to her.

By then Agbale was supposed to be both woman and wife; but at heart she remained a child. She looked at the happy faces her Dosu had given the *bauchie* and laughter shook her.

'Oh, Dosu!' she said. 'How funny! Oh, I like them! Oh, now they're sweet!'

'Then will you get up, *asicki*?' Nyasanu said. 'Wilt thou arise, little wife?'

Agbale pouted, made an impish face.

'No, Medaxochi, No, older person mine,' she said, using the term a wife always calls her husband at the beginning of their married life.

'Why not?' Nyasanu said.

'Because—because'—Agbale giggled, and hid her face behind her hand—'I am not yet fully your wife—at least not so fully as I want to be, so——'

'So?' Nyasanu said.

'So thou must do again that which thou hast already done, now that I do not hurt so much! For, before, even hurting, it was—very fine. And now—not hurting, at least not very much, it should be—finer still. Is this not so, older person?'

'Yes,' Nyasanu said, 'truly it is so, little wife——'

So it was that they arrived one full hour late at their own wedding feast. And though all the people laughed and snapped their fingers at them and called them 'lusty ones', Agbale found she did not mind their gibes at all. To one so armoured and girded with happiness as she, what could mere words do to harm her?

Nyasanu stood before the assembled guests, who, since he was a chief's son, numbered in the hundreds, and made a speech. It wasn't a very good speech but nobody minded that.

'What, venerable elders and honoured guests,' he began, 'is the difference between the day and the night? Wait! I myself will answer the question that I put to you——

'In the daytime the sun bakes one's bones, and the work one has to do makes all the body ache. In the day one sweats and suffers thirst; and the greatest of all pleasures can not be practised for fear of prying eyes.'

All the assembled company roared at that.

'But night is truly the friend of man. At night one sleeps and dreams sweet dreams. The night is cool and one can rest. Night is the time of love. And the colour of night is black, which is the colour of beauty. Therefore I have named my bride after night's colour, and beauty's. Henceforth, let her be known as Nyaunu wi! Black woman. As beautiful as night, and all my own!'

Everybody snapped their fingers at that and laughed and cheered. And from that moment no one would ever pronounce the name Agbale again. She had become Nyaunu wi, now, henceforth, and forever more.

And then the drums began to thump and thunder all around the square. And Nyasanu danced alone, a dance of his own invention. It was very slow and stately and soft-weaving and beautiful. And as he danced the newly named Nyaunu wi

113

walked beside him and wiped the sweat from his face with a silk handkerchief.

When he was done with dancing, he turned to the members of his *gbe* and cried out.

'Push me!'

And all his fellow society members showered Nyaunu wi with gifts, which was a tribute to her virtue. For had she not proved virgin on her nuptial bed, the *gbe* members would not have come at all.

The rest of the celebration was feasting and laughter and many coarse jests and everyone, men and women alike, vied with one another to demonstrate that he or she was the best dancer of them all. Of course Kpadunu won the dancing contest with the greatest of ease. Or so everyone thought until that new and terrible dancer appeared.

Nobody, of course, noticed that Gbochi went strolling by the cooking fires a moment before, with that exaggerated and offensive way he had of moving his fat buttocks like a woman as he walked. It wasn't until he had gone by and had calmly taken his place behind the long rows of bamboo fronds laid edgewise on the ground to mark off the dancing square from the place of the spectators that a thick and choking cloud of smoke rose up from the cook fires and rolled across the square, in which Kpadunu, sweating rivers, was acknowledging the applause of those who had seen his all but incredible performance.

For a long moment everyone choked and gasped and wept great stinging tears; then the smoke thinned, and in it, or rather above it, that figure appeared. He was, without exaggerating even slightly, three rods, or more than nine feet, tall; and he was dancing on his head the way that ghosts dance. They could see his long, muscular black legs making unbelievably graceful kicks and scissorings and weavings towards the sky; and though every drummer had stopped his beat in petrified horror, the sounds of *zele*, funeral drums, rolled in upon them from everywhere.

Nyauni wi as clinging to Nyasanu and screaming like a demented thing by then, and all the women joined her, their shrieks tearing apart the very texture of sound, slivering the sky with the jagged edges of pure anguish, but still that figure danced head on the ground, feet in the air.

And now in a series of swooping rushes he dived towards

114

the screaming women. And as he came close, the shrieks died into a silence more profound than the echoes after a stopped heartbeat. For by then everyone had seen that his inverted face was no face at all, but the yellowish, polished old ivory of a human skull.

Nobody could recall afterwards who said it first, though, investigating the matter, Kpadunu reached the not unreasonable conclusion that it had been Gbochi. In any event, someone voiced the word, and then it was afloat, borne aloft on a current of whimpers, whispers, moans, until at last someone screamed it out:

'Ku! It's Ku! It is Ku, Lord of Death!'

By then Nyaunu wi was a senseless burden in Nyasanu's arms, so he laid her gently down, and stood up. He was afraid, so afraid that his fear was a sickness in him; but he knew that he had to end the horror or his married, and perhaps his own life, would be over for all time. So he gathered all his souls into his belly, lifted up his voice in a roar like unto that of a pride of lions, and rushed bare-handed upon that ghostly figure.

What happened next was a broil of confusion amid the smoke. Arms and legs twisted, entwined. There was a hoarse, voiced groan, the sodden sound of blows raining upon flesh: then a figure was seen bounding in enormous leaps out of the smoke and towards the forest but upon his feet this time, while Nyasanu leaped after him like a famished leopard. Two seconds later, Nyasanu's first, second, and third friends had joined the chase, then every young man present, the whole troop of them giving tongue like a band of jackals after a dik dik antelope, streaking across the vast African landscape, dwarfed figures half lost under that huge and brooding sky.

Then they came back again, leading their prisoner. In his hands Nyasanu bore the clever hand-stilts upon which the acrobat had danced upside down, thus increasing his normal height to gigantic size. Kpadunu carried the mask, fashioned out of the frontal portion of a human skull which had been sawn in half. And Amosu and Taugbadji held spread out the costume of reeds and net that had covered his upper body.

They led their prisoner before the chief who, clapping his hands and enstooling himself at once, established a court of the assembled elders.

But when Gbenu began to question the prisoner as to who had sent him to work his obscene mischief, and why, the man

115

did not answer him. So the chief, angered, roared out his questions louder than before, and still getting no response was about to order that the prisoner be put to the ordeal, when something about the man reached out and seized his attention, stopping in that instant both his heart and breath.

There was no light behind the prisoner's eyes.

Turning, Gbenu cried out, his big voice shaking:

'Call Zezu to me! And Mauchau!'

Both the *bokono* and the *azaundato* were brought, the worker of benevolent magic, the diviner, and of evil magic, the sorcerer.

Between them, they examined the prisoner, and pronounced sentence:

'My Lord Toxausu, he is one of the soulless ones!'

Everyone gasped at that, for well did the people know that an *azaundato* could bring upon one who had offended him a semblance of death so real that no ordinary man could distinguish the difference. Once the 'body' had been buried, the sorcerer came in the night and dug up the supposedly dead man and sold him secretly into a distant clan whom the said sorcerer wished to watch or control.

For, when removed from his premature grave, the victim became one of the soulless ones, the living dead, all three of his souls, his mind, his will came under the sorcerer's control.

So now, Gbenu could only stare at his newly married son with sick and troubled eyes. For they would never know now who had sent the soulless one to dance as Ku, Death, at the wedding feast.

Unless it were Ku, himself.

Which within a little year or two men would begin to think, and afterwards, to say.

NINE

Sitting before the king's compound at Abomey with all the rest of his fellow recruits from Alladah, Nyasanu shivered despite the heat of that early summer day in the first week in November. Beside him, his first friend Kpadunu laid a comforting hand on his arm. But neither of them said anything. They—

and all the rest of the army—crouched there on their buttocks, gripping their long, Danish-made muskets by the barrels with both hands. They pointed the muzzles skyward, pressed the stocks against the ground, and waited quietly for King Gezo to tell them against which of their enemies they must march out to war.

To their left, among the *ahosi*, the women soldiers, there was a stirring. Nyasanu looked in their direction, trying to see if he could make out the face or the form of his half-sister, Alogba, among them. Then he did see her, and gave a little gasp of astonishment. She was among the *gohento*, the archeresses, and like all the other bow and arrow women, she was naked except for a wisp of a loincloth.

'How in the name of Legba the Trickster,' Nyasanu whispered to Kpadunu, 'did she *ever* work her way into the *gohento* corps?'

'How did *who* work her way into the *gohento*?' Kpadunu said.

'Alogba,' Nyasanu said. 'Everyone says that the *gohento* are selected for their skill at dancing and their beauty, because nobody depends upon so primitive a weapon as the bow any more. They're parade troops, that's all. And Legba eat my breath if Alogba's pretty! Why she looks more like a sow with that face of hers than even Yu does. . . .'

'Look again,' Kpadunu said drily, 'only not at her *face* this time. . . .'

Nyasanu looked at his half-sister. Then he loosed a long, soulful, almost soundless whistle.

'Yalode, Goddess of Women,' he whispered. 'Tell me how I could have lived in the same compound with her all my life and never noticed——'

'That though she has the face of a slobbering pig, she also has the body of a goddess?' Kpadunu said. 'Simple. You never looked at her. You, first friend mine, are much too orderly, dutiful, and restrained for your own good. Your father gave you Nyaunu wi, and that was that. I'll bet your *tasino* had to rape you on the night she cooled the circumcisional knife. Even yet, though your woman is already great with child, you haven't even sought a substitute. I love Dangbevi, too—as much as you love Nyaunu wi, or more. But I have taken two other wives since, as a man ought. While you——'

'Let's not talk about that,' Nyasanu said morosely. 'And,

117

besides, Alogba's my sister—half anyhow—so it wouldn't have been seemly for me to——'

Kpadunu looked at him out of the corner of one eye and smiled in a way that was infinitely mocking, but he didn't say anything.

'You don't need to,' Nyasanu thought bitterly. 'Why repeat what you think, what every living soul in Alladah thinks what even I think—and possibly even my father *knows*: that of Yu's children, only little Chiwayi is *his*. But since Yu was an *avaunusi* bride given to him—No! Legba take it, no! Not given! Forced upon him by Princess Fedime, he couldn't, and still can't, do anything about the provable fact that Yu opens her legs to everything with a penis attached to its belly, down to the monkeys in the forest, to judge by the way some of my so-called half-brothers and sisters look! And Alogba takes after her in *that*, anyhow! Always rubbing up against me whenever she catches me alone. Well, as long as father acknowledges her as his daughter, it's still incest, the worst of all *su dudus*, as far as the law's concerned, and punishable by death. Oh, evil spirits take Gbochi, anyhow! For if he hadn't run away, Alogba wouldn't be here now to torment me all through the campaign. And if we march against the Maxi, as everybody thinks—that might be a half a year!'

Kpadunu smiled at him and whispered:

'What your little black one doesn't know can't hurt her. And it'll be all of three *years* before you can be with her again.'

Nyasanu stared at his first friend. What Kpadunu had said was true. He had abstained from sexual intercourse with his bride from the day he'd found out she was pregnant. And there were still months to go before she'd give birth to his child. Thereafter, he could not lie with her—by age-old law—until the child was weaned. And Dahomean women suckle their babies for two whole years.

He turned once more and stared at Alogba long and thoughtfully, confining his gaze to the lissome areas between her porcine face and her splayed and rusty feet. Immediately, he found it necessary to arm all three of his souls against temptation. The *ahosi*, the women soldiers, for all their enforced celibacy, were, by law, he reminded himself, wives of the king. To touch one was to invite certain decapitation. What's more, it was well within the realm of possibility that Alogba could be his half-sister, despite the fact that she re-

118

sembled his father not at all. And even if she weren't, if he got involved with her, getting disinvolved from a girl of her stubbornness would be difficult indeed. Worst of all, Nyaunu wi would never forgive so cheap and insulting a sin. But—three years! Legba would eat his brains long before then! Why, he thought, I'm about to burst now and——

At that moment, the *khetunga*, the *she-gao* or commander-in-chief of the Women's Corps, got up and began to make a speech. She started off in a hoarse imitation of a man's voice that gradually climbed up the scale into female shrillness as she became more and more excited.

'As the blacksmith takes an iron bar and by fire changes its fashion, so we have changed our nature. We are no longer women, we are men!'

Nyasanu looked at his half-sister at that, Alogba grinned at him, and made an exceedingly obscene gesture, the import of which was that he need only approach her, and she'd gladly demonstrate to him the falsity of her leader's words. He jerked his gaze away from her ugly, porcine face, from her astonishingly perfect body.

'Xevioso, God of Thunder, blast Gbochi anyhow!' he said.

Kpadunu threw back his head, and laughed aloud.

'That's one time Dada Gezo outsmarted himself!' he said. 'Remember your Taugbochinovi Hwegbe's theory as to why the king's men take a *woman* to replace a man too cowardly to fight?'

'Yes,' Nyasanu said. 'Granduncle Hwegbe says that a good many men couldn't care less if the king's men take their brothers to replace them when they run off or maim themselves to avoid being called up for war. But to take their *sisters* is another matter: shames them, makes them seem effeminate, hiding behind a woman's skirts. Only in this case——'

'Gbochi *is* an effeminate and was delighted at the news that the recruiters would take Alogba in his stead. So now all you've got to do is to see that Dada Gezo doesn't separate your head from your neck because one certain *ahosi*, reputed to be your half-sister, is all set to crawl into your hut on the *first* night of the march. Which is why she volunteered to take Gbochi's place in the first instance—to get a chance at you, first friend! As your Granduncle Hwegbe says——'

'Will you shut up, Kpad!' Nyasanu said and sat there shivering, not listening to the she-general's speech at all, for the

119

mention of the woodcarver brought another ugly memory jarring back into his mind.

For though Hwegbe had left Gbenu's compound the day after the wedding feast, and no one had seen him since, the fact remained that two days later, picking up the figure of the male *bauchie* before his door, Nyasanu had discovered that its eyes were gone again, carved out of its head by a hand of matchless skill. The female *bauchie* was likewise once more blind. So, without saying anything to his bride Nyasanu had taken both of the *abadome,* the guardian spirits, and thrown them into the brush. Better that his house go unprotected against evil, than be guarded by figures made by a hand that wished him ill. . . .

Thinking about these things was no good, so he opened his ears and his mind to the female general's speech.

'By fire we will change Abeokuta!' she was shrieking. And at that word the men in the ranks turned to one another, their black faces greying with undisguised fear. For Abeokuta was the capital of the Auyo who went to war on horseback. During nearly two hundred years the kings of Dahomey had kept their country alive by paying tribute to the fierce black horsemen to the north. Nine years after the beginning of his reign,* Gezo had finally fought the Auyo to a standstill, inflicting such losses upon them that the Auyo king had sued for peace and voluntarily given up the tribute. But in their own country the Auyo were still invincible, and for an army of footsoldiers, nearly half of which were women, to attack them and thus call down upon itself their wild cavalry charges was suicide, or something very close to it.

Another thing Gezo had done was to make a treaty of eternal peace and friendship with the Ashanti, which was why their kings lent him a whole army corps when he went to war, just as Gezo lent his troops for the Ashanti's battles. But, Nyasanu reasoned, if word gets back to Kumassi that the Auyo have decimated us, how long will it take the Ashanti to forget the treaty, and come howling out of the West, to wipe us from the face of the earth, thus removing the only serious rivals to their power?

'She's only talking,' Kpadunu whispered. 'You don't think Dada Gezo's informed *her* whom we're going to attack before he has told either the prime minister, or the chief justice?'

* i.e. 1827 by English reckoning.

'I don't know,' Nyasanu said. But the *khetunga*, the female general, was shrieking louder than ever:

'The king gives us cloth, but without thread it cannot be fashioned: we are the thread! If corn is put in the sun to dry and not looked after, will not the goats eat it? If Abeokuta be left too long, some other nation will spoil it! A case of rum cannot roll itself. A table in a house becomes useful when something is placed thereon. The army of Da's Belly without the *ahosi* are as both, unassisted. Spitting makes the belly more comfortable, and the outstretched hand will be the receiving one: so we ask you for war, that our bellies may have their desire and our hands be filled!'

There was a silence. Then the *gao*—or commander-in-chief —got up and said:

The king's house wants thatch!'

Nyasanu shuddered at those words, for raising his eyes he could see what they meant: every roof and sentry box and the two towers beside the gates were covered with the bleached skulls of enemies slain in battle.

Again they waited. Then the gates opened and Gbenu came out, regally clad in his uniform as *kposu*, or commander of the second section of the left wing, which meant that he was out-ranked in actual military power by only the *gao* himself, des-pite whatever ostentatious courtesy titles that the *minga* and the *meu* might hold.

Seeing his father striding through the gate like the *vudu* Gu himself, the hammering of Nyasanu's heart almost burst his chest. What a soldier his father was! What a hero! What a man!

Then he saw that his father bore the small leather case con-taining the war-rum, which meant that all hopes of peace must be buried. They were at war. But with whom?

Gbenu bowed and gave the rum to the *gao*.

The *gao* drank a sip and at once launched into a war speech, exhorting them all to fury, demanding that each of them take at least ten heads, bring back twenty captives each, leave the cities of their enemy levelled to the ground. But he still didn't say *who* the enemy was.

So all the army set up a shout:

'Dada come! Father ours, show thyself!'

Then for the first time, Nyasanu saw his king. Gezo was tall and surprisingly light in colour, being coffee brown rather than

121

black. Nyasanu stared at his first friend.

'His mother was half Furtoo,' Kpadunu whispered. 'Daughter of a Portuguese slaver. That's why he has no true colour. . . .'

And now, as the king began to speak, Nyasanu saw he had a cast in his right eye. But his voice was deep and rich. He spoke in Fanti, rather than in Fau.

'*Maheeyu mak'yo!*' he said, and all the soldiers, male and female alike, roared with joy. For those words meant: 'Maxi, good morning!' And they knew at last who their foes were to be.

Then the king began to perform the decapitation dances, which he did with great grace and skill. After he'd done, the prime minister, the chief justice, the commander-in-chief, and the general of the left wing danced in their turn. Nyasanu was sure that the commander of the left wing, Gbenu, chief of Alladah, was the best dancer of them all.

But all the same, he was aware of a sensation of disquietude crawling through his middle with the slow, sensuous coiling and uncoiling of a snake. All his life he'd dreamed of this day, or rather of another, subsequent to it: the day on which he, Nyasanu, man among men, his chest adorned with necklaces made of the teeth of the enemies he had slain, strode forward to offer the huge pile of heads that he, personally, had taken to the king. But now that that day was almost here at last, he found he didn't like it.

For one thing, he couldn't get out of his mind the image of Nyaunu wi, lying on her swollen belly like a stricken animal, her two arms wrapped about his ankles with so desperate a clasp that he had been unable to move, on the day he had told her the news his father had brought back from Abomey: this year, almost certainly, there would be war. It had been bad, very bad, to see her like that, with her eyes so swollen by the endless scald of her tears that she could no longer open them; but listening to her had been far worse, hearing the things she said, straining to catch her words, slowly murmured through the grate and scrape of a voice reduced not so much to the absence of sound by hours of unceasing sobbing, as to its negation, its denial: 'I'll die: I won't be here when you come back. Even if the Maxi don't take you prisoner and sell you to the Furtoo. Just waiting will be enough to send me to the ancestors. Just being without you. Long before you ever start

122

home, Legba will have eaten my brains and my breath both!'

And now, he thought miserably, a scant four days after leaving her, here I am, looking at that ugly, pig-faced Alogba with desire!

But another thing was that he was no longer sure he had in his belly what it took to become the kind of warrior his father was. For yesterday, he had actually, for the first time in his life, seen men decapitated. King Gezo, as custom demanded, had sent five slaves to his ancestors to ask their protection for his royal self, and for 'the Things of the Leopard', as, with bitter truth, the people of Dahomey were called, as they marched off to war.

With a chorus of hideous yells the king's club wielders had rushed through the gate into the slave pen and dragged the five men—selected, as far as Nyasanu had been able to see, by pure chance—out into the great square before the royal residence. There they had been gagged by thrusting one branch of a Y-shaped stick down their throats, with the other two prongs protruding from the corners of their mouths, which forced their lips—though this effect, Nyasanu was sure, was not intentional—into a macabre grin. Thongs of leather lashed around these two prongs and tied behind their necks held the effective and painful gag in place. This was done to prevent them from cursing the king, for, since they were about to die, their curses, according to the Dahomean belief, would have been terribly effective.

Then with great care they were dressed in long white robes of the finest cotton cloth; and the king's second guards—for the first royal guards were all women of the *Ahosi* Corps—placed the tall, curved, conical red caps, shaped like one of the two horns of a half-moon, on their heads.

Nyasanu had stood there, watching that. Not one of the slaves, all Jacquin, or Tuffoe or Maxi captives, showed the slightest trace of fear. But he, Nyasanu, man among men, had hung there, his black face going greyish, his stomach invaded by a host of loathsome crawling things, a knot of coldness in his throat, a taste of utter vileness in his mouth, watching as the slaves were placed in the canoe-shaped wicker baskets and then hoisted upon the heads of the king's guffawing, prancing, ape-like club men. The captives were paraded three times around the square, the whole procession led by the *tauvuduno* of the royal ancestral cult, dressed in his most impressive robes, with the most hideous of all his many appallingly hideous masks upon his face, waving his walking stick, which had a bleached human skull affixed to the top of it, and chanting gibberish at the top of his lungs.

When they came to the place where King Gezo was enstooled, Nyasanu saw a curious thing: just for a moment an expression of acute distaste distorted the king's mouth. The boy remembered then what Gbenu his father had told him:

'He makes fewer sacrifices than any king we've had. Certainly, he isn't the monster that his half-brother Adanzan was. When he makes a custom he kills at the most five or six. All the other kings gave the ancestors upwards of thirty. I think he'd do away with the annual customs if he could. . . .'

But the howling, dancing high priest of the *tauvudun*, or ancestors-become-gods, stood before the king and waved his skull-headed walking stick. To Nyasanu the gesture seemed almost threatening. Perhaps there was something after all in the rumours that the *tauvudunoe*, the priests of the royal ancestor cult, were angered by the moderation of the king, by his reluctance to give the ancestor gods all the blood they desired.

Wearily Gezo nodded. At once, everyone rushed forward to get a better view. Nyasanu and Kpadunu were swept forward by the wild surge of shouting, laughing, finger-snapping black humanity like ships upon a wave. In fact, if they hadn't caught and held each other's arms, dug their heels into the turf, they'd have been pushed over the edge into the execution pit itself.

Down below, the executioner waited. He, too, was robed and masked, but his robe was blackened with many years' accumulation of dried blood. In his hand he held not a sword, but a sort of butcher's knife. And, then, as the priest of the ancestors split the sky apart with a shriek of pure, murderous fury, the men bearing the basket boats tilted the first one so that the bound, gagged, robed, red-hatted slave who rode in it was spilled out of it and fell head first into the pit, where he lay stunned into unconsciousness.

At once the executioner caught him by the hair of his head, allowed to grow long just for this purpose, and jerking him into a sitting position, ringed his neck with a series of deep cuts, sawing away lustily until the dying man's blood was a spray, a spurting, a flood; then catching him by the ears he twisted the slave's neck until the head tore free. With a great shout the executioner hurled the bloody head high into the air, whereupon a fiendish din arose, and men fought like savage dogs for the honour of bearing this trophy to the royal presence.

Kpadunu touched Nyasanu's arm.

'Come, Brother,' he whispered, 'I will help you. Can you walk? If you let one of your souls leave your body so that you fall to the ground, you'll be in trouble. Even if you give back your breakfast to the earth, they'll see it and tell the *adanejon* and you'll be disgraced. . . .'

Nyasanu straightened up then, and shook his head to clear it—a gesture similar to the one a lion makes when, having caught a zebra by the back of the neck, he shakes his prey to break its spinal column. As proud as that. As fierce. 'No,' he said, 'I'll stay. This is a thing of men—and I am a man.'

So he stood there, crowding all three of his souls down into the pit of his belly and watched that gory butchery repeated four more times. But when he walked away at last with his first friend, he saw to his astonishment that Kpadunu had tears in his eyes.

'What ails you my brother?' he said.

'Disgust,' Kpadunu said, 'and a great envy of that simplicity of soul that thou hast. You were like to die of—of horror, pity, shame—I know not, but you shook your head, roared lion-mouthed, and thy souls came back to thee. I, Nya, am not thus. Mine, I fear me, have fled me long ago, and much too far. I live by a profession in which I do not believe at all, which even my Uncle Mauchau, when he's drunk, admits is pure mummery. . . .'

'Kpad!' Nyasanu said.

'Aye, my bother! I do not like being a member of a race of blood-swilling savages, which is all we children of Da's Belly are, and I wonder if there isn't a place somewhere on the face of the earth where people don't kill each other in the name of nonexistent gods or for any reason whatsoever. Where kings rule by love. Where we don't march out to lay siege to and starve and hack to death their brothers. . . .'

'Their brothers?' Nyasansu said. 'The Maxi?'

'And the Auyo. And the Hausa. And the Fanti. Maybe even the Furtoo, for all their purplish-pink flayed bodies that some-how live on, though men say they're more cruel than even the Ashanti because their blood lust is cold. I don't know. We cast the *du* to determine our fates then make sacrifices to the *vudun* to change these fates in a manner pleasing to us. Is this not

125

madness? What sort of gods are *vudun* you can bargain with? What kind of life have we when one god who favours us can always be overcome by another summoned up by an *azaundato* at the behest of any man who hates us?'

Nyasanu looked at his first friend with troubled eyes.

'The *vudun* you now say you don't believe in gave you—Dangbevi. Who told me that the Serpent Dangbe spoke to thee and offered thee his daughter?'

Kpadunu bowed his head. Looked up again. Faced Nyasanu.

'I did,' he said. 'But when that happened, I was *very* drunk, Nya. Perhaps I dreamed the whole thing. . . .'

'As you dreamed Dangbevi—and the child who swells her belly now?' Nyasanu said.

'No,' Kpadunu whispered. 'Dangbevi is real. For which Fa be praised! But, brother mine, beneath the hair of her head she hath a scar fully as long as my hand. A newly healed scar. That is why she cannot remember her tribe, her clan, her family, her fathers. Do serpents speak Ewe, Nya? Do snakes give birth to girl children?'

Nyasanu looked at Kpadunu.

'You'd empty the sky, Brother,' he said, 'rob life of magic and of meaning, make us small. . . .'

'No!' Kpadunu said. 'I'd make us men, Nya! You said—ha! —that you must watch that ugly slaughter of bound, gagged, trussed-up captives, because it was a thing of men! Is it? I ask you, Brother, is it? No beast of the forest, not even the cruel leopard, kills for pleasure! All the victims of the great flesh-eaters have defences: speed, cunning skill, horns, tusks! No lion, leopard, hyena, jackal keeps dik diks, or gnu, or zebras shut up in little houses to drag them forth on certain occasions for a killing that doesn't even serve to fill their bellies. . . .'

Nyasanu stared at his friend in horror. 'You'd have us *eat* them?' he whispered.

'Like those dirty, degenerate tribes from the Congo regions? No, my brother. I'd have us let them live, eat, drink, love their wives, beget children—and be free. Is this too much to ask?'

Nyasanu bowed his head. Looked up again.

'Yes,' he said, 'it is. For it is more than the gods grant us.'

Kpadunu looked at his friend in a new way. The look had a strange quality in it, the quality of recognition, perhaps.

'I have wronged thee in my thoughts,' he said at last. 'Thou'rt *not* simple, Nya. Oh no. Thou'rt not simple at all!'

126

In the morning, they marched out of Abomey, heading northward towards the mountains where the Maxi lived. And waiting with their fellow members of the *Hastati* Company for their turn to fall into line, Nyasanu and his first friend Kpadunu saw the first half of the parade.

The *gao*, the commander-in-chief, led the troops mounted on a magnificent grey horse. Nyasanu wondered where he'd got a horse like that in a country where the few horses and cattle that survived the sickness caused by the bite of tsetse fly were left miserable racks of bones all their lives. The only other exception he knew of was his father's white stallion N'yoh; and Gbenu knew better than to ride so fine a mount upon public occasion, for the king would have confiscated the beautiful animal on sight.

The *gao* wore a splendid uniform: blue toga over white trousers, a great Spanish hat, ropes of teeth necklaces, bracelets of silver and brass. Attached to the bracelets were a host of *gbo*, to ward off all evil and danger from his imposing person. A slave held a gaudy umbrella, decorated with appliqué-cloth representations of his heroic deeds, over his head. Behind him came the *minga*, or prime minister, with his assistant, the *biwanton*, or political commissioner. On the left wing, Nyasanu knew, the *meu*, or chief justice, and his assistant political commissioner, the *adanejon*, would follow Gbenu, who was the *kposu*, or commander of the left, in much the same way. Both of these officials were dressed in different uniforms, as grand as that of the *gao*, and shaded by parasols only a little less fine than the commander-in-chief's.

'But you'll see how fast they'll skip out of the way and let the *gao* and your father take over once the fighting starts!' Kpadunu whispered in Nyasanu's ear. 'Look! Here comes the king!'

Nyasanu craned his neck a little and saw King Gezo. But, after he'd gazed at the royal personage for half a minute, he turned back to Kpadunu, astonishment in his eyes. For Dada Gezo rode a nag that even in a country where nearly all horses were poor specimens set new records for equine poverty. Besides which, the king's dress wasn't even as good as that of a common soldier. He had drawn war markings on his face with gunpowder; but then, all the officers did that. He wore a short, kilt-like toga of indigo colour over short drawers. The toga bore no insignia. Nor did the chocolate-brown umbrella a slave held over him. He wore a horse-tail fly whisk around his neck on a leather cord, but no teeth necklace. His toga had splotches of goat blood on it, and *gbo* sewn to it—but then so did the uniforms of most of the foot soldiers. He had a pistol of ancient make stuck through his belt, and a war club spiked plentifully with nails rested on his shoulder. There were anklets of black seeds about his legs, and his feet were clad in sandals. All in all, he looked like a competent and fierce warrior, but he did not even look like a high officer, much less a king. Even the pipe he was smoking was smaller than those of the *biwanton* and *adanejon*, whose importance in wartime, at least, was open to serious doubt.

Seeing Nyasanu's look Kpadunu grinned at him.

'Looks like a beggar, doesn't he?' he whispered. 'That's smart, Nya! Can't afford to make our king the target for every spear, arrow, or stone the Maxi have got, can we? He doesn't even command. The *gao* and the *kposu*, your father, do that. So if we lose, it's them the enemy take, sure that least one of such imposing men must be the king. Besides, not being responsible for waging the war, the ghosts of his dead enemies plague the *gao* and *kposu*, not him. You'll see, tonight when we make camp, he'll sit on a stool much lower than your father's and the *gao*'s. And they can smoke in his presence. In peacetime such a want of respect would cost them their heads. But the farce must be kept up every minute; because some of the tradesmen who come into our camps to sell us food and drink are sure to be enemy spies. This way they can't pick out *who* the king is, and have their soldiers prepared to seize him from the outset, which is the surest way of winning a war at almost no cost in blood. . . .'

'He ought to rub soot on his face,' Nyasanu said judiciously. 'He has no true colour. They could still pick him out. . . .'

'But not, necessarily, as king,' Kpadunu said. 'In fact the Maxi would never believe that a man who looks almost like one of the mulattos the Portuguese get on slave women would be king of Dahomey. . . .'

'That's true,' Nyasanu conceded and stood, then, watching the troops march by. First came the Blue Company, whose uniform was the indigo-coloured one with white crossbelt. Their heads were covered with a kind of beret or tam-o'-shanter with alligators embroidered on the side. Afterwards came the *achi*, the bayonet men, who wore much the same

128

uniform, but whose berets bore a trefoil instead of the alligator. Next came the *agbaroya*, named for their weapon, which was a short, bell-mouthed blunderbuss that couldn't be aimed with any accuracy but did at least make enough noise to stampede the enemy's horses, and in the mountains, where tsetse flies were few, they might run into Auyo cavalry, come to aid the Maxi. It's a tribute to Dahomean subtlety, and our sense of humour, Nyasanu reflected, that we put the Blunderbuss Company under the *kpofensu*, the court jester. Because no joke the king's fool could ever invent would be a bigger one than the *agbaroya* are in battle! Half the time those brass cannons kick so hard the *agbaroya* are knocked back on their own buttocks with their feet in the air and bring down only a shower of leaves from the trees. . . .

But the *ganu'nlan*, the royal hunters, were passing now, and, watching them, Nyasanu fell silent. They were all Ashantis, warriors loaned the Gezo by the Ashanti's queen mother. And a feeling of being reduced, of being made small, came over him. For although he stood six feet fives inches tall and was beginning to fill out now to approach the imposing size and weight he'd have as a man, the shortest of the Ashanti topped him by a full inch. Of course, they were slenderer than he; but that meant nothing. The Ashanti were born to war. He'd never heard of one of them running away from a battle or hiding or maiming himself to avoid conscription the way many Dahomeans did. And the lean, elongated black faces were so—intelligent. 'The dullest Ashanti born,' his father had said, 'is a military genius—that is, if they aren't geniuses in all ways, which is what I sometimes think. . . .'

They wore ornaments not of brass but of gold, for the lands around Kumassi are rich in that precious metal. And man for man they were handsomer far than nearly all the Dahomeans, except, perhaps, a few upper-class youths such as Kpadunu and he, Nyasanu himself.

But after that, it was the turn of the *hastatis* or carbineers, to fall into line, so Nyasanu couldn't see any more of the parade, having joined it. He knew, however, what companies came behind his: the madcaps, or *mnau*, and the *aro*, who are archers.

Each of the companies had its complement, with the same uniforms, weapons, insignia in the left wing, which Nyasanu's father led, and the two phalanxes were separated by the right wing's division of *ahosi*, women soldiers. They were led by the *gundeme*, or she-prime minister, who was the equivalent of the *minga*, and by the *khetunga*, or female *gao*. And the companies were exactly the same as the men's except their *gun'-unlon* weren't Ashanti women, but Dahomeans, since the Ashanti didn't have women soldiers. There were other differences. Alogba's corps, the archeresses, were called *gohento*, instead of *aro*, the name of their male counterparts, and their bows were much smaller and lighter; the fact that their arrows, like those of the men, were poisoned was held sufficient to make up for the lesser strength of their weapons. Also, the *ahosi* had three companies that the male army didn't have: the elephant huntresses, the bravest of the brave, who in the last hunt, had brought down no less than seven elephants with one well-aimed volley; then there were the *nyekplo'honto*, the razor women, who were scouts; and, last of all, there were the infantry troops, armed with tower muskets, who were to hold the centre against all attacks.

The left wing also had a division of *ahosi*, whose officers were called the *yewe,* the female *meu* and the *akpadume*, who was the she *kposu*.

So marched out King Gezo's army to make war in that twentieth year of his reign, 1838.

Among King Gezo's many thousands of soldiers were two unknown, recently married eighteen-year-olds, Nyasanu and Kpadunu, who between them were going to win the war. But at so great cost to them both, that Nyasanu afterwards swore it would have been better to have lost it.

TEN

As they sat by the fire at night in the intervals of rest during that long march northward to the country of the Maxi, Nyasanu and Kpadunu had time for talk. Occasionally Taugbadji, Nyasanu's third friend, joined them, but these occasions were few, for Taugbadji was not of the *hastati* or *zohunan*, as the carbineers to which Nyasanu and Kpadunu belonged were called, but a member of the *Aro* corps, the company of archers. And the officers of the various corps discouraged fraternisation among them; probably, Nyasanu thought, in order not to diminish the rivalry that was one of the incentives to valour. To make matters worse for Taugbadji, the bowmen were looked down upon by the gun bearers. Every time he crossed the camp to visit Nyasanu and Kpadunu, he had to endure the gibes of the soldiers of the other companies who called him a 'partridge-chaser-person playing with toys'. The truth of the matter, Taugbadji knew, was that the Archer Corps should have been abolished long ago when the sale of war captives, criminals, and even politically troublesome high-born Dahomeans to European slavers first made it possible for the Leopard Clan to procure guns, and gunpowder. Yet, for some reason, out of innate conservatism, perhaps, or maybe out of a quasisentimental memory of the *aro* corps' former glory, the Aladaxonu kings had kept the bowmen in the army. But despite this clear evidence of royal favour, the archers, formerly the flower of the army, had fallen into disrepute. Nowadays only the less desirable recruits, the short, the fat, the slightly lame, were placed in the Archer Corps. Of this fact, Taugbadji was painfully aware. Being of less than average height, and having his natural tendency to corpulence increased by the sedentary nature of his craft—sewing appliqué figures on fine cloth—poor Taugbadji tried to compensate for his inferiority feelings by practising with the peculiar Dahomean bow until he fully mastered it. Which meant, as Nyasanu pointed out, in an effort to comfort him, that he was a more effective soldier than ninety per cent of the gun-bearing troops, who were surely the greatest wasters of ammunition in all the world.

'Besides,' Kpadunu added, in his dry, sardonic fashion, 'you don't actually believe that the purpose of the campaign is to kill people, do you, Badji?'

'If it isn't, why does the king pay us for the heads we bring back?' Taugbadji asked.

'A pittance,' Kpadunu answered him, 'and that pittance for show. What he wants is slaves. To sell to the Furtoo for more gunpowder, cloths, rum, gold. So that he can procure more wives than the number he has now. So many it is impossible for him to mount them all, even if he assigns each wife only one night in a whole year. So that his princess daughters may have many silks, many beads, much perfume—so that they will be beautiful and smell nice as they lie with their own brothers.'

'Kpad!' Taugbadji and Nyasanu exclaimed together.

'They do,' Kpadunu said serenely. 'Incest is not a *su dudu* among the Leopard Clan. In fact, they haven't any tabus—except chastity, perhaps. If a princess reaches thirteen, and is found to be still a virgin, they beat her half to death. Then they call in her uncles, and her brothers, and her cousins to line up and——'

'Oh come off it, Kpad!' Nyasanu said.

'All right,' Kpadunu laughed, 'but I'm not lying—only exaggerating a little. Seriously Badji, our friend Amosu was the lucky one——'

'I shall miss him,' Nyasanu said. 'Still, it was a great honour for him, I suppose, to have been called to Abomey to serve as silversmith to the king. . . .'

'If he has any sense,' Kpadunu said seriously, 'he'll make his figures badly, so that they'll give him a beating and send him home again. Else he might end up married to a princess, and elevated to nobility. Than which, Legba witness it, there is no worse fate!'

But most of the time, the two of them were alone after the day's march was over. They lay on their backs and stared up at the stars, lost in the immensity of an African night. The thoughts that came unbidden to them were long, long ones, difficult to contemplate or even bear.

'Nya,' Kpadunu said. 'Promise me something.'

'Promise you what?' Nyasanu said.

'That if—if I'm killed in battle, you'll marry Dangbevi. The other two, I don't care about. But Dangbevi is strange. She's timid. Shy. Tender. She hasn't the defences that most women have. I've never heard her speak badly of anyone. I don't think she could live alone. She's neither tough enough nor mean enough to—to survive. Promise me?'

Nyasanu thought about that.

'All right,' he said at last, 'if you'll promise me to take Nyauni wi, if I die. But one thing more, Kpad: what of our sons? Both our wives—and probably all three of yours—are with child. What status would the sons have?'

Kpadunu looked at his friend, and his eyes glowed in the firelight.

'Should you die, your son will be my son,' he said quietly, 'and if firstborn among all the children of my house, he shall

132

inherit. By Fa, who is Fate, I swear it!'

'And I, also, take the same oath,' Nyasanu said, 'and here's my hand upon it!'

Legba, the Linguist or Messenger of the Gods, is a great trickster and lover of mischief. Besides which, in a certain sense, he is the God of Sex. When he was discovered in flagrante delicto with his own daughter Minona, the Goddess of Women, his mother Mawu punished him with the torture of a constant and perpetual erection and unappeasable desire. So there is no doubt that it was he who put mischief into Alogba's mind that same night. The question is whether he chose well or ill the time to work out his ribald designs, for having sworn so high and holy an oath, Nyasanu lay upon his sleeping mat thinking of his Nyaunu wi with great and reverent tenderness.

He was still thinking of her when the weariness bred in his limbs by a whole day's marching overcame him. And even after that he dreamed of her. It did not surprise him that she swayed towards him as slender as a loko sapling with no signs of her five-months pregnancy visible at all. In dreams the elements of surprise, of astonishment even, are forever missing. Instead gently, slowly, he doubled his great length almost in half—for in sober truth he was almost twice as tall as she—and bent to kiss her mouth.

Then the dream went wrong. Nyaunu wi behaved in a manner uncharacteristic of her, in a way he knew from experience she was incapable of: she drove her nails, ten widely separated fine points into the flesh of his back, ground a mouth whose lips had grown to an astonishing width and thickness into his own so hard that he was forced to open it to gasp for air, whereupon she thrust a tongue the size of a full-grown cow's halfway down his throat, while her smell, a combination of unwashed armpits, body sweat, and female genitalia in heat, rose up around his head, threatening with every passing moment to complete the process of death by asphyxia.

It was that smell, more than anything else, that convinced him he was inhabiting the wrong dream. Nyaunu wi, like most upper-class Dahomean women, was clean to a fault. She spent hours of every day bathing and perfuming herself to make sure that even in the intense African heat she would never offend. So he knew she didn't smell like this. And as if to confirm the fact that his dream had turned nightmare, she tore her mouth

133

away from his and began to chant the *agu gbe* words, the 'adultery language', into his ear, thrusting each moaning, keening, prayerful obscenity against his eardrums upon a rusty spear of breath, begging him to do this to her, with that, in such a manner, with a monkey's lasciviousness, and a bullock's force. And all the time she was writhing against him, scalding him with her sweat, grinding her pelvis into his so furiously that the stiff crisping of her pubic hair actually lacerated him, brought blood.

He opened his eyes. It was dark in the little hut of branches that Dahomean soldiers construct for shelter every night when they make camp. The smell of ruttish female was overpowering. So he didn't need to see. All three of his souls came jarring back into his belly from wherever it is a man's souls go during the night. His mind, his eyes came clear.

'Get out of here, Alogba!' he said.

But she was not to be put off so easily. She climbed all over him, panting, wild. She clutched the most delicate parts of his body with frenzied fingers. She said words to him that he had never before heard upon a woman's lips, and seldom upon men's, and thereby defeated her own purpose; for if sexual desire is the strongest of all emotions, easily vanquishing sense, caution, prudence, fear, there is one feeling that conquers it effortlessly. And the name of that feeling is—disgust.

He did what he had to do: caught her by the shoulders and whirled her about until she was facing the opening of his hut; then planting his right foot upon her soft, rounded, utterly delectable little behind, he propelled her out into the night.

Reeling away from his hut, burning with a double fire—unappeased lust and the fury of a woman scorned—Alogba encountered, by purest chance, a man whom ordinarily she wouldn't have looked at, whom actually she despised: Taugbadji, Nyasanu's third friend.

The reason Taugbadji was there at such an unlikely hour was very simple: people like him, the gentle, the dreamers, the imaginative are, more often than not, victims of their own too keenly visualised fears. He had realised suddenly that by tomorrow or the day after, they would cross the River Tevi and enter Maxi territory. And terror had hit him in his fat belly like an Ashanti warclub, had pierced his breath like a razor-edged *assegai*. He found it impossible to remain in his hut: the fresh, still-wet mud and wattle walls curved in upon him with

134

claustrophobic fury. His own smell became insupportable, he stank of anticipated terror. So he'd got out of there, eluded easily enough the sleepy *Aro* sentries, and come in search of Nyasanu, despite the lateness of the hour, knowing that his big, strong, manly, heroic friend was at heart as tender as a woman, and could and would forgive this breaking of his sleep when he found out how badly poor Badji needed reassurance, even comforting.

And crossing the whole camp in the darkness, Taugbadji arrived just in time to meet Alogba as, head down, and weeping the hot tears of frustrated desire, of humiliation, of rage she raced away from Nyasanu's hut.

Seeing a stark-naked girl coming towards him through the soft whiteness of a moonwashed night, Taugbadji's first impulse was to run away. But something else held him : the girl who moved towards him had the very body of Minona, Goddess of Women—night-made, singing flesh, beauty's own blackness aureoled in silver. He hung there trembling until he could discern her face; and by the time he did, even its porcine ugliness made no difference, he was already lost.

'Alogba!' he said, 'what in Xevioso's name are you doing in the men's camp? Don't you know——'

'That I'll get in trouble?' she said in a strangled voice. 'Yes, I know that, Badji! What difference does it make? When a girl gets as lonesome as I am tonight, she'll try anything, risk anything to hear a kind word from somebody. So I came to visit Nya. Seeing that he's my brother, I thought he'd—talk to me—be—kind. But——'

'But what?' Taugbadji said. It was characteristic of him that the right question didn't even occur to him : that he didn't think to ask why a sister visiting her brother walked mothernaked through the night wearing not even the wispy loincloth of the *Gohento* corps.

'He got angry with me,' Alogba whimpered, lying now, not with any conscious intention to take whatever profit there might be available from her situation, but out of pure, unpremeditated feminine instinct. 'Said I'd cost him his head with my thoughtlessness. That the king would never stop to think that we're brother and sister and therefore wouldn't—couldn't —do anything bad, but only that he's a man, and I'm an *ahosi*. So he put me out. And now——'

She stopped short, peering at Taugbadji. Her Stubborn Pig

135

Person's mind worked hotly, meanly inside the convoluted darkness of her head. She thought: 'Why not? He's Nya's friend, which makes him good enough to use to get even with old long tall chaste'n pure! Besides, he's not bad looking. Just— too fat. Fat boys usually aren't worth anything on a sleeping mat, but by Legba, tonight I'll try even him! Oh, Danh and Dangbe both, I want, I need——'

'And now?' Taugbadji whispered.

'Haven't *you* a kind word for me, Badji?' Alogba said.

'There is,' Mauchau the Sorcerer was fond of saying to Kpadunu, 'no evil that is pure. Always, the very worst things we do carry some good along with them, whether we want them to or no. Good and evil, Nephew, are but two faces of the same god, so therefore——'

So therefore, in spite of herself, Alogba performed an act of charity that night. Perhaps even of grace. For at eighteen years of age, Taugbadji was still innocent of women except for the poor old *tasino* who had cooled the heat of his circumcisional knife. And his performance upon her had been of such a nature as to deepen his already profound doubts as to the extent and completeness of his own virility.

By morning Alogba had ridded him of his doubts forever. That and something more; by climbing all over him in a fine excess of the *furor uterinus*, oestrual rage, she had unfortunately inherited from her black maenad of a mother, Alogba awakened in poor, timid Taugbadji so great an answering rage of desire that his alter ego, his opposite, the chained-up, unacknowledged ancestor beast that the slow, imperfect workings of evolution has left sleeping within the blood and nerves of every man, awoke, reared up, and shattered the night with roarings.

Together they set the night afire; blazed in the dawn. And lying there beside him finally, too spent to move, Alogba whispered to herself in amazement.

'Why—I—I *love* him. I must. I have to! Or else how could I have felt—what he made me feel? But anyhow, little fat fool that he is, he's a man. And I'm not even starting to turn him loose now 'cause——'

She bent slowly and kissed Taugbadji's mouth.

'Magic,' Kpadunu said, 'is the art of guessing at unknown

136

causes in order to try to determine why a thing has happened. And since we don't know the "why" of anything, we apply *gbo*—a whole crazy collection of assorted garbage in the hope they might have some relationship, some influence upon the workings of cause and effect that we don't know either——'

'You're saying,' Nyasanu said, 'that you and your Uncle Mauchau both are a couple of fakers——'

'I'm saying that people are—lonely, desperate, hurt, afraid, and that we, the sorcerers, and the diviners, and the priests of all the various cults, give them hope. And by the same method, we speak loudly and confidentially about things which by their very nature mankind does not nor cannot know. Repeating over and over again words like magic, charms, *su dudus* tabu, spirits, ghosts, gods, until almost we convince ourselves that they mean something, which they don't——'

'You mean that you——'

'Deceive out of pity. Fake out of love. Say the ritual words, intone the formulae until I find myself having to hold hard on to my reason, because the hunger for hope, the need to believe in something, is so seductive, Nya. And also because, strange as that may seem, it quite often works——'

'If it works,' Nyasanu said judiciously, 'it can't all be fakery, Kpad. . . .'

'Not all of it is,' Kpadunu whispered, 'and that's what makes it so—disturbing, Nya! Zezu, now, your father's *bokono*; men say he's *never* wrong in his predictions about the future. I've investigated that—and they're mostly right. He very, very seldom is——'

'So?' Nyasanu said.

'So men when they consult him give him an advantage they give no other. They tell him the truth, Nya! Naked, pure, and whole. And he's been in this business a long time. Long enough to have stored in his woolly black head many, many facts, many, many memories. So when you bring him a problem, he thinks back until he recalls a similar problem. Human problems, after all, are not very diverse, first friend eldest! How can I get Tondose to lie with me? Or marry, you can put it, but the problem's essentially the same. How can I gain my father's favour so that he will leave me the inheritance and not my brother? How can I cure my wife's barrenness since I can't afford to take another? How can I make my fields more fertile, my wife's mercantile business more profitable? How can I appease the *vudun* who've brought me so much bad luck? And a few more, but very few, Nya. So Zezu remembers a former problem, very like the present one, which time itself has already solved or cured. Then he suggests a remedy he knows has already worked and hence probably will again. Thus he applies experience, gained wisdom, to the present problem. So how *can* he go wrong?'

'I see,' Nyasanu said. 'That takes care of the *bokonoe*, the diviners. And my father brought me up to have very little faith in priests, who're mostly, according to him, indirect agents of the king in fiscal matters and enforcing the law.... But you chose to be an *azaundato* of your own free will, Kpad. And now you say you don't believe——'

'In sorcery? That's not entirely true, Nya. I don't believe in it, and I do. The feelings I have about it alternate—according to the mood I'm in, I suppose. Most of it—nearly all of it—*is* fakery, Brother. I don't believe in *gbo* at all, useful as they are——'

'Useful?' Nyasanu said. 'If you don't believe in them, how can they be useful?'

'Because other people do. Therefore they work. If a man *believes* a certain *gbo* will kill him, he will die out of his own fear. What matters if the reasoning's wrong when the result is the desired one, Nya? The sorcerer's art is that of controlling people, which is why I propose to teach it to you. As future chief of Alladah, you're going to need to know how to manage your subjects——'

'My *du* says my life will end in Dahomey,' Nyasanu said, 'to begin anew in another land——'

Kpadunu bowed his head. Looked up again.

'And mine say I shall not survive the campaign,' he said quietly. 'No matter how many times I cast them, they always say that....'

'Kpad!' Nyasanu got out. 'Brother mine! I...'

'Don't worry about it, Nya,' Kpadunu said mockingly. 'The *du* are pure nonsense, as I propose to prove by going back home, marrying ten more wives, and siring two hundred children!'

'You mock everything!' Nyasanu said a little angrily, 'and yet you propose to teach me things, you, yourself, don't believe....'

'Because they're *useful* things, my brother. Whether you be-

138

lieve your hoe is a *gbo* sent by Gu, God of Iron, or not, it still wounds the earth, doesn't it? And if men are willing to put into your hands their ignorance, superstitions, and fears, why not use these tools they give you? Tell me, why not, Nya?'

'Because,' Nyasanu said slowly, 'it's—dishonourable, Kpad. I wouldn't like to live by fakery——'

Kpadunu threw back his head and laughed aloud.

'Whoever told you life was honourable, Nya?' he said. 'Your father is one of the most honourable men I know. And you take after him. And yet even he has had to make his compromises with life, with the way things actually are. I'm not telling you anything you don't know when I say that his first wife eldest, Yu, is the biggest whore in Alladah, if not in all Dahomey. Yet he has not put her by. Why not, Nya?'

'She was *avaunusi*,' Nyasanu said gruffly. 'The Princess Fedime commanded my father to take Yu to wife——'

'And since he did not, and does not, love her, wouldn't it have been the honourable thing to refuse to obey the princess? To refuse at any cost?'

'Oh plague take you, Kpad!' Nyasanu shouted. 'You twist life to shreds! You know well that father couldn't——'

'*I* know it. But do you? It was you who were defending honour, Nya, not me.'

'All right,' Nyasanu said. 'You win; but then you always do. Your mind is keener than mine, I'm afraid. Still, I don't like the idea of using sorcery to gain my ends. If you believed in it, I might accept it, but since you admit you don't——'

'I admit no such thing!' Kpadunu said. 'I dislike the part of it—the very large part that is fakery—but the true part of it I *hate*, Nya. Because it frightens me, and I don't like being afraid——'

Nyasanu looked at his first friend, studied his eyes, his face. He had no difficulty at all doing that, because since they were already in Maxi territory, they camped in the dense woodlands by day, and marched only by night. Surprise attacks were one of the best and most brilliantly employed Dahomean tactics.

'Of what, precisely, are you afraid?' he asked.

'Remember the soulless one who danced upside down at your wedding?' Kpadunu whispered. 'Of that. Of the ways—the mysterious ways we don't understand ourselves—that we can put a man's souls in our power. Wait! I'll prove it to you. Would you like to pay a visit to Nyaunu wi right now, without

139

moving from this spot?'

Nyasanu stared at Kpadunu.

'Now you're *really* talking nonsense!' he said.

'Am I? Just wait. I'm going to send all three of your souls to visit her. Your body will stay here, fast asleep, until they come back. Of course I can't promise you that she'll see *you*, because the *djautaux*, the *semedo*, and the *selido*, by which I mean: thy guardian soul, who pleads for thee before the gods; thy speaking soul, or voice which forms thy individuality, thy identity; and thy thinking soul, or intellect, are usually invisible. She might of course; that depends upon how strong the affinity beween the two of you is. But through the eyes of your souls, you *will* see her; and you'll tell me so when you come back, I mean, wake up. . . .'

'Kpad, I don't believe . . .' Nyasanu began, but Kpadunu stopped him with a lifted hand.

'Wait!' he said and began digging in the bag in which he kept his *gbo*, or charms. A few seconds later he came up with a Portuguese doubloon, polished until it shone. A hole had been bored through the coin near one rim and a cord passed through the hole and tied in a knot thick enough to keep the silver piece from slipping off the end of the cord.

Now Kpadunu looked around until he found a little patch of sunlight unfiltered by the leaves and vines of the tropical rain forest in which they were encamped.

'Come, my brother,' he said and moved over into that patch of sun. Nyasanu followed him.

'Sit down,' Kpadunu said. 'No; not there; here—with your back to the sun. That's it. Now look at this silver *gbo*. It is a very powerful *gbo*, the most powerful *gbo* in all the world——'

'Kpad, I don't think——'

'Silence! See it move. It moves slowly, slowly. The light it makes is starlight, sent by Mawu to light the way for your souls upon their journey. . . . It moves—it moves—it moves. . . . Towards Alladah—towards thy woman's house— and thy souls—thy souls—they follow it——'

'Kpad,' Nyasanu whispered, 'it grows dark—I—I——'

'Thou'rt asleep, my brother! Thou'rt asleep! But thy three souls are awake. Now they steal forth from thy nostrils upon thy breath. . . . They drift upward like smoke. They fly! They fly! Swift as the otutu through the air. Now—even now— they've reached Alladah. They stand like shadows at the door

140

of thy woman's house. . . .

'We'll leave them there a while—and then I'll call them back. No, wait! Before they return they must visit Dangbevi as well to—to see how she fares—and report this to me. . . . So sleep now, Brother. Soulless Brother, sleep!'

Kpadunu crouched there looking at the prone, relaxed figure of his first friend. 'Now why did I say that?' he thought angrily, 'I *know* how this business works. Being the stronger mind, I bring sleep upon him. I think it's the movement of the coin flashing in the sun that tires the eyes and the mind very quickly. And the tone of voice we use, crooning the words the way a mother croons to a child to put it to sleep. Then when he's half asleep and his *selido*, his intellect, is almost dormant, I instruct his mind to dream what I want it to. To dream, that's all! For Legba eat my brains if I believe that we have souls at all, much less that they can fly through the air to Alladah!

'And yet—and yet—I asked his souls, or his dreaming mind —to do what I cannot do: visit her. See her whom I love. Thus doth longing unman me. Thus my love—pushes me— even me!—into caves of unreason to bow down before the ugly, blood-smeared idols we erect to our own littleness and our fears. . . .'

He knelt there beside Nyasanu, studying his first friend's sleeping face with great care as though he were searching for a sign.

Nyaunu wi lay on her sleeping mat. She felt very heavy and tired and uncomfortable and afraid. She was still sick most of the time; not only in the mornings but also at night, which worried her, for both her mother and her mother-in-law had told her with real concern in their voices that her morning sickness should have disappeared long ago.

Only it hadn't. In fact, it seemed to be getting worse. She had to be attended most of the time now, even though it was still four months to the day when she should give birth to Nyasanu's son. That it would be a son, and a young lion of a manchild, she was absolutely sure.

At the moment, Nyasanu's Aunt Chadasi, who, having no children of her own, had more leisure time than most of either Nyasanu's or Nyaunu wi's female relatives, was with her. At other times her own mother, Adje, or Nyasanu's mother, Gudjo, watched over her, or even Dangbevi—for since their husbands had marched off to war, the friendship between the two young wives had grown until they were closer in their mutual sisterly love than most sisters ever get to be.

But now, suddenly, Nyaunu wi sat up on her sleeping mat and peered towards the door. Then she turned her head a little to one side and listened hard, her slim neck stretched upward with a taut grace until it resembled a black swan's, her wide, soft, heavily-lipped mouth trembling a little.

'What ails you, child?' Nyasanu's Aunt Chadasi said.

'Nothing,' Nyaunu wi muttered irritably. 'Just the heat—I guess, I thought——'

'What did you think, daughter?' Chadasi said.

'That I—that I—heard somebody—calling me. Saying my name. And oh Aunt Chadasi!'

'Now what, Nyaunu?' Chadasi said soothingly.

'It sounded like—like Nyasanu! Do you think that—that——'

'He's in trouble, or hurt, and calling to you?' Chadasi said. 'No, child. They haven't had time to reach the mountains yet. Why surely they're still in our territory. It's your state, baby girl. I—I never had a child, but all the women who have tell that while like that, they suddenly had overwhelming desires to eat—the strangest things: all the *su dudus*: monkey flesh and broiled snake and—and locusts! And they were *always* imagining things. So lie back down, little black one. You need to rest. . . .'

Nyaunu wi sat there straining her ears a moment longer. Then she bent her head listlessly.

'All right, Aunt Chadasi,' she said.

It was no more than five minutes after that that Chadasi saw Dangbevi come flying up the road under the loko trees.

'She's as graceful as an antelope,' Chadasi thought. 'She moves as though she has no bones. Well, she can run again now, more's the pity. . . .'

'What's the matter, Aunt Chadasi?' Nyaunu wi said.

'It's your friend Dangbevi,' Chadasi said. 'Looks like she's coming here. And she must have news of some kind, because she's running like a dik dik!'

'She shouldn't run!' Nyaunu wi said worriedly, 'she'll start haemorrhaging again! When she gets here, scold her, Aunt Chadasi, do! Oh, Mawu save her, she has no sense at all!'

'She is—strange. The poor little thing,' Chadasi said. 'How was it that——'

'She lost her child?' Nyaunu wi said, real anger shaking her voice. 'By being a fool! She didn't eat or even drink water for two whole days and nights after Kpadunu left for the fighting. So naturally she fainted. And because her belly was the heaviest part of her by then—she was a whole month ahead of me, Aunt Chadasi!—she landed on it. When Kolo, Kpad's mother, found her, she'd almost bled to death. And—what would have been a man-child had she given it time to grow was lying dead between her legs. I—I love Nya more than she can possibly love Kpad; but I've got sense enough to——'

But then, Dangbevi was there. Nyaunu wi got slowly up from her sleeping mat and came towards the doorway where the serpent's child swayed, still fighting for breath. Dangbevi was very thin and drawn. Her lovely, brownish black complexion, with a hint of her remote Arabic ancestor's ruddy colouring beneath its soft, velvety midnight surface, had gone bluish, greyish, and her dark eyes were abject.

'What ails you, Dangbevi?' Nyaunu wi said worriedly. 'Are you sick? Have you started bleeding again? Here, let me see! Are you wearing many cloths the way my mother told you to? And running! Oh Dangbevi, Dangbevi, haven't you any sense at all?'

'No, none,' Dangbevi said, forcing the words out on ragged spurts of breath. 'I think—your god Legba has eaten my brains. Or—in words that come to me from long ago—from another time I don't, I can't remember!—the finger of Allah the compassionate, hath touched me—and left me, mad. In any event——'

'In any event what?' Nyaunu wi said.

'I come to ask thy pardon, sister, for I have sinned against thee!' Dangbevi said.

Nyaunu wi stared at her, then glanced at Aunt Chadasi. Chadasi raised her index finger to her own temple and made a swift circle with it, thus indicating that she thought Dangbevi insane.

'Sinned against me, how?' Nyaunu wi said.

'Against thee—and against my husband!' Dangbevi wailed. 'With—thine. With Nyasanu!'

Nyaunu wi stared at her friend with pity in her eyes. Then they changed. Suspicion narrowed them. A warlike glint glowed in their depth.

'Dangbevi,' she said evenly, 'you're trying to tell me that the child you lost was—my husband's?'

Dangbevi stiffened then; her lovely eyes flared in pure astonishment, then darkened with hurt.

'Oh, Nyaunu!' she said. 'Oh no! You *couldn't* believe that!'

'Then just what are you trying to tell me?' Nyaunu wi said.

'That I sinned against thee. In my mind. Maybe even in my heart. But not with my body! Oh no!'

'Not *yet*,' Nyaunu wi said grimly.

'Let her speak, child,' Aunt Chadasi said. 'Can't you see she's suffering?'

'All right,' Nyaunu wi said, 'I'm listening, Dangbevi!'

'Just now,' Serpent's Child whispered, 'I was in my house. And I—I *think* I was awake. Of course I could have dozed off—it was so hot, and . . .'

'Get to the point, Daughter of the Python!' Nyaunu wi said.

'And all of a sudden—*he* was standing there, looking at me—and his face—his—his face——'

'What about his face?' Nyaunu wi said.

'It was—so tired. So completely weary. As though he'd come a long, long way. And it was sad—very sad. So I——'

'So you?' Nyaunu wi prompted.

'So I got up, like a sleepwalker, and went to him. And then —he—he bent down and kissed me——'

'And this is your sin, child,' Aunt Chadasi laughed, a little shakily, 'that you dreamt that my nephew—who is eight or ten days' journey from here by now in the country of the Maxi—kissed you?'

'I did not dream it!' Dangbevi said hotly. 'He was *there* I tell you! Just for a moment, Nyasanu was there. I could feel his lips on mine—and—and, oh, Allah the Compassionate forgive me—but they were sweet! And I——'

'And you,' Nyaunu wi's voice was strangling, 'you——'

'I kissed him back. *That* was my sin. Against you, my sister —and against my husband. Then all of a sudden, he grew dim before my eyes, became smoke drifting up and away from me. That's all. So now——'

Her voice died. Her face changed; the colour came flooding back into it, a tide of rich, red warmth beneath the nightshade velvet. Her hand came up, and her fingertips strayed lightly,

144

lightly over lips as thin as those of the white races, and they, gone beyond her will, shaped themselves into the form, the texture, and the warmth of a well-remembered kiss.

It was then that Nyaunu wi slapped her across the mouth. Hard.

Kpadunu snapped his fingers under Nyasanu's nose.

'Wake up, my brother!' he said in a loud voice. 'Thy souls have come back to thee!'

Nyasanu blinked once or twice, then opened his eyes. They were blank, glazed, unfocused; but almost immediately, they cleared.

'Kpad!' he whispered. 'Oh, Kpad!'

After that, he bent his head and cried. Noisily, with great strangled sobs like a whipped child. It was, Kpadunu found, very bad to listen to.

It was almost night and time to march again before Kpadunu got the story out of him:

'She didn't see me!' he moaned, 'she couldn't, Kpad! She didn't know I was there! She was—very big. Very heavy. She looked—awful. She was all alone. There wasn't anyone with her. I called to her and called to her and said her name a thousand times, but she couldn't hear me, either. Once she almost did, but then somebody spoke to her—somebody I couldn't see or hear—and she stopped listening——'

'Then?' Kpadunu said.

'My souls—or I—went to your woman's house. Just as you'd told them to. But as they were—or I was—leaving Nyaunu wi's, I looked back and saw him again——'

'Saw *who* again?' Kpadunu said.

'Ku. Death. He was dancing upside down before her door. . . .'

'It means nothing!' Kpadunu said. 'It's only a dream. I forced you to dream it! I put it all in your mind so that——'

But Nyasanu shook his head.

'You did *not* put Ku into my head. You wouldn't do that. Nor would you make me dream——'

'What?' Kpadunu said.

'That I kissed your woman. On the mouth. Hard. With passion. I went to her house. She was there. She was very slim. She didn't look pregnant at all. And *she* saw me. She cried out my name and came to me. And I—and I——'

145

'You kissed her,' Kpadunu said.

'Yes. I don't know why. It just seemed the thing to do. Do you forgive me, my brother? I—I meant no harm.'

Kpadunu stood there staring at his first friend eldest.... A long time. A very long time. When he spoke at last, his voice was infinitely weary.

'Of course. *Now* do you see why I hate this business of sorcery, Nya?' he said.

'Yes,' Nyasanu said, looking at him, 'because you have no true control over its effects. To juggle the souls of men—and of women—about, is a dangerous business, my brother! Still. . . .'

'Still, what?' Kpadunu said, shortly.

'Still, you have convinced me, and I would learn it. Will you teach me to juggle souls, my brother?'

Kpadunu stood there. Then he sighed.

'Yes,' he said. Then, 'And I wish you joy of the knowledge! For perhaps the *du* have it right. Perhaps you'll kiss Dangbevi again—as her husband. Perhaps . . .'

Nyasanu smiled at him then, and laid a powerful hand on his shoulder.

'That, no,' he said, 'because if the *du* are right, I shall be—a slave in some Furtoo's fields, labouring under the whip. So do not——'

He stopped short, appalled by his own words. It was the first time he had spoken them aloud, after all those months of thinking them. He was sorry he'd said them. It seemed to give them peculiar force.

But he was saved from the labour of thinking up something else, something more to say that would lend some comfort to them both, for at that moment the great conch shell of the war leader sounded, summoning them to march again. By daylight tomorrow, they'd reach the plains that the Maxi cultivated at the foot of the mountains upon whose crags they perched their towns.

And then? That was the question. And it echoed like death through both their hearts.

ELEVEN

From where they were, in brush and scrub on the southern slopes of the valley, they could see the Maxi. The mountain people moved out in long lines, their hoes flashing in perfect rhythm as they worked the long, narrow strips of fields, which were the only source of sustenance they had, aside from the birds they snared and an occasional small beast who fell into their traps.

Nyasanu crouched there, gripping his musket until the knuckles of his black fingers whitened from the strain. He turned his face towards his first friend, and now Kpadunu could see how sick his eyes were, how his mouth trembled. The young sorcerer leaned close to his first friend's ear.

'Wanted to be a hero, didn't you?' he whispered. 'Well, here's your chance, Nya! Dahomean fashion! Against those grubbing little beggars armed with hoes. It's easy. You shoot them in the back as they run away. Then you sit on their stinking corpses and saw and saw at their tough necks until——'

'Oh, for Legba's sake, be quiet, will you?' Nyasanu said but at that moment, the whole left wing, under his father's command, loosed a singularly ragged volley. The smoke from it drifted down upon him, blinding him. When it cleared he saw three Maxi farmers lying grotesquely amid their rows while the rest were running like antelopes towards the foothills of their mountains.

'Dahomean marksmanship!' Kpadunu laughed. 'The whole Left—two thousand men, Nya! All shooting at once—to kill three unarmed farmers. How many balls does that make per corpse? Let me see—seven hundred? No, not quite.'

'Oh shut up, will you? Nyasanu said, but just then their corps leader screamed out, 'Fire!'

Coolly, insolently, Kpadunu lifted his musket until it was pointing at the sky, jerked the trigger. Nyasanu imitated him.

'Charge!' the leader shrieked.

They poured out of the brush in a formation that would have, Nyasanu thought bitterly, disgraced a herd of sheep and charged after the fleeing Maxi. And since they were running downhill, while the Maxi were beginning to climb the hills on the other side of the narrow valley that was the only land they had flat enough for cultivation, they easily came in range again. What saved the Maxi from a massacre was the fact that ninety-seven per cent of the Dahomeans had forgotten, or hadn't time, to reload their muskets after the first volley.

Still they killed two farmers and wounded seven or eight more. And again the Maxi fled.

But a group of twenty or more, blinded by their terror, dashed up a ravine that turned out to be no more than a cul-de-sac with no way out at all. Nyasanu and Kpadunu watched with the sick certainty that there was going to be a slaughter. Then Nyasanu heard his first friend's voice go shrill with astonishment.

'Xevioso blast me, Nya! Look at that!'

Nyasanu turned and saw little fat Taugbadji charging up that ravine alone. He was pumping arrows from his crooked Dahomean bow in a steady stream, far faster than any gun-fighter could have shot, since at that time the Dahomeans had only single-shot weapons. The trouble was that he had far out-distanced any other Dahomean of any corps, and to make matters worse, killing a foe with a Dahomean bow and arrow was too slow a process. For, Nyasanu knew, while the barbed arrow points were poisoned and *always* killed whatever foe they hit, even if the bowman shot him in his big toe, it was just as true that the bow itself was so weak, had so little pull, that the wounds the arrows made served only to madden the enemy and left him quite capable of killing since the poison didn't even begin to make him sick for some hours, and it usually took him days to die.

But what was evident was that their gentle, dreamy, slightly effeminate little friend was going to find himself entirely alone, facing twenty Maxi farmers armed with hoes, to whom, more-over, his own inexplicable intrepidity, his new-found insane valour had already granted time to spare for the slight labour of chopping him into bloody bits long before any member of his corps could even get within bow shot of where he was, not to mention coming close enough to really help him.

'By Danh and Dangbe both, come on!' Nyasanu roared.

'No,' Kpadunu said coolly, 'first we reload, Brother. An un-loaded musket is no better than a hoe. No, not even as good.'

'There's no time!' Nyasanu said. 'Look at him, Kpad! Gu, himself, must have got into him!'

'Reload, Nya,' Kpad said. 'If you don't we'll never save him!'

They reloaded their muskets with trembling hands. That took them far too much time. First they had to pour black powder down the muzzle, ram a patch of cloth down on top of it to hold it in, and compress it into a compactness that would explode instead of burning slowly; ram the ball down on top of that; lift the striking plate and pour fine white powder into the primer, drag the big flint-tipped hammer back—all this before they were ready to fire one lone shot, which as often as not, considering the exceedingly dubious accuracy of a smooth-bore musket, missed their foe entirely.

When they got there, the farmers had Badji surrounded. But the fat little clothworker was fighting like a whole pride of lions. He wasn't shooting any more but had drawn an Ashanti-made *assegai*, and even as they watched, went under the swing of a Maxi's hoe, and buried his blade to the hilt in the man's belly. He jerked it out and whirled, slashing, opening a second mouth in another Maxi's throat; but at that moment a hoe crashed down on his sword arm, breaking it very cleanly; and heroic little Badji was done.

Kpadunu fell to his knees and aimed slowly, coolly. His big Danish musket jumped and thundered and the Maxi whose hoe was about to cleave Badji's skull fell over backwards. Then Nyasanu, firing from a standing position, shot another Maxi through the chest and the fight went out of them. Sullenly, they threw down their hoes.

'Keep your musket pointed at them while I reload!' Kpadunu hissed. 'They don't know anything about guns!'

That, Nyasanu reflected, was true. Since the Maxis had no access to the sea, to even attempt to sell them firearms, powder, and ball, a trader would have to cross Dahomean territory. Even if the guns were brought ashore at Lagos, at Benin, or at any other seaport outside of the realm, traders would still have to cross Dahomey to reach the Maxi. And he knew what would happen to any trader who attempted that; his head would decorate the roof of the first sentry post he tried to pass. The only other possibility would be for the Fanti, the Nupe, or some other Moslem tribe to the north to bring in arms across the vast desert. But the Mohammedan blacks were themselves great slavers. And the Maxi, a poor mountain folk, were far more valuable as slaves than as customers. No, the Maxi would have to go on fighting with the bow, the brush knife, and the spear, as their ancestors had for the past two thousand years. . . .

'Now you!' "Kpad said. 'While I keep them covered . . .'

Nyasanu reloaded his musket. The battle drunkenness, blood-lust that had invaded him at the sight of his little friend's danger drained out of him through his toes. He felt sick; he'd killed a man. He had—murdered a farmer with a hoe in his hands—from twenty rods away, using a musket.

'Pick him up!' Kpadunu said in Ewe to the Maxi. 'Gently, you swine! Or by Xevioso, God of Thunder, I'll blast the lot of you!'

'The heads, Kpad, Nya!' Taugbadji groaned. 'Get the heads!'

Nyasanu stared at his third friend. What in the name of Sagbata, God of Earth, he thought, *ever* got into him? Then he picked up Taugbadji's *assegai*, and began to saw at the neck of the first of the four dead men. The Maxi captives watched him impassively. Even though he could have shaved with that *assegai,* he had to saw and saw and the blood got all over his hands and still the dead man's head wouldn't come free until Kpadunu said pityingly:

'Catch him by the hair and twist.'

He did that and the head came free. He stood up then and vomited on the ground.

'Thou'lt *never* make a soldier, Nya!' Taugbadji crowed, sick as he was from the terrible pain of his broken arm. 'Art tender as a woman, Brother!'

By then, a troop of their own corps, the *zohunan,* or car-bineers, were there.

'Take the heads!' Kpadunu ordered them sharply. 'Bring them along!'

They moved out then, guarding the sixteen Maxi captives taken by two lone heroes and bearing the four dripping heads taken by them. Two of the Maxi bore Taugbadji between them, and they were followed by three more who had been wounded by the fat little archer's arrows and hence were walking dead men. One of them groaned aloud, and Taugbadji heard him.

Nya! he said excitedly, for he was already a little delirious from pain; 'the—the ones I shot! Did you bring them along, too?'

'Yes, Badji,' Nyasanu said.

'Take their heads!' Taugbadji shouted.

Nyasanu looked at Kpadunu.

'He's right, Nya,' Kpadunu said tiredly. 'Those arrows are poisoned. Tomorrow they're going to die—horribly. On the next day at the most. It's kinder to kill them now.'

Nyasanu felt the green tide of nausea rising in his throat. 'Badji's right,' he thought despairingly, 'I am more woman than man....' Then, as always, when confronted with the natural, human tendency towards compassion, pity, with his own kindly disinclination to give hurt, deal pain, an answering fury, directed mostly against himself, rose to save him. He turned to the *zohunan*, his handsome young face twisted into a savage scowl.

'Those three!' he said and pointed to the wounded Maxi. 'Brain them with your musket butts, then take their heads!'

'So it was done. He heard the gun butts thud woodenly against the Maxi skulls and turned away his eyes from the butchery, only to have them fall on something worse:

The *ahosi*, the women soldiers, were swarming out upon the field. Not the gun-bearing troops. Just the *gohento*, the archeresses, and the *nyekplo'hento*, the razor women. And now the first of the *nyekplo'hento* reached one of the wounded Maxi where he lay groaning in the field he'd come to that morning with the intention of clearing weeds, hoeing brush. She bent above him, tearing at his loincloth with frenzied fingers. A moment later Nyasanu heard the man start to scream, hoarse voiced, in pure animal terror. Then the screaming changed, went up the scale, rising from drum bass to flute note, to hold on a shriek that was pure soprano, except that it had no music in it, was in fact the sound sand makes scraping over glass. Then that stopped, too, on a choking note. As the razor woman straightened up, Nyasanu saw why; she'd rammed what she'd cut off him into his opened mouth.

He turned to Kpadunu, the rage in him a sickness nearly mortal; he saw his half-sister Alogba straddle another wounded man. She had the little scythe-shaped knife that the *gohento* wear on lanyards from their wrists. And even as he watched she began to cut the dying man, light, almost playful cuts; once, twice, then ten times, thirty, until the poor devil was tearing the day apart with his screams and twisting so that he splattered her naked, magnificent body with blood, so that her throat, her breasts were dyed with it, so that it dripped off

151

nipples erect and quivering with an emotion that Nyasanu was suddenly sure was sexual, and seeing the slack-lipped, saliva-foamed mouth, the eyes rolling back in her head, knew with horror that in this sister of his cruelty was but another form of sensuality, a lust so deep and so perverted that she could and did reach orgasm through it.

The horror that had held him frozen was shattered suddenly by an explosion of rage that was like the blow of a brass-bound fist to the roots of his manhood. But it released him from horror's grip, drove the sickness from him. He got to where Alogba sat across the dying Maxi in two long bounds. He tore off his cartridge belt, a huge broad piece of buffalo hide, onto which the little leather boxes holding the musket balls and the powder patches were sewn, and swung it with all his force. It broke the skin on her back open like a ripe plum. Then he was beating her, beating her, and her screams were floating up around his ears in a note so musical that it should have told him something else about her, but it didn't; so he went on reducing her back from shoulder to knee-bend into so much ground meat, until he felt a sharp sting low in his left side, and turning saw Taugbadji; swaying there before him, the *assegai* he'd used to stab Nyasanu trembling in his left hand, his round, ordinarily gentle face twisted into a rage that was murderous.

Nyasanu did what he had to then, which was bring the gun belt down across Taugbadji's left hand and knock the *assegai* from it.

'I'll kill you!' Taugbadji wept, 'even though you're my friend! Touch her again and I'll——'

Then he stopped short, and what got into his eyes was a kind of death. Looking down, Nyasanu saw why: Alogba had both her arms wrapped around Nyasanu's ankles and she was kissing his feet over and over again, great hot, wet, slobbering kisses that made his gut churn within him.

He looked up at Taugbadji with real pity in his eyes.

'Don't Badji,' he said gently, 'don't love her. Can't you see what kind of a thing she is? Worse than Gbochi, because he's only twisted in one direction. While she——'

'While she?' Taugbadji echoed.

'Is wracked two ways at once. Two opposite ways. All variations in between,' Nyasanu said.

Then he kicked Alogba in the face, just hard enough to

152

make her turn him loose, and walked over to where Taugbadji hung trembling, his eyes full of tears, his right arm dangling, already beginning to puff obscenely, and put his own arm about his third friend's shoulder.

'Come, Badji,' he began, but Alogba's voice cut him off.

'*Gagloe!*' she screamed. 'Homosexuals!'

Nyasanu turned towards where she lay on her belly like a whipped *se*—like a wounded jackal bitch. Then he smiled at her, very slowly.

'If thou'rt a woman, my sister,' he said, 'I might turn *gaglo* at that!'

That same night, Nyasanu was summoned to appear before the *kposu*, the commander-in-chief of the left wing of the army. And though the *zohunan* of which he was a member belonged to the right wing, no one was surprised at that, for by then all the world knew that Kposu Gbenu, commander of the left, was his father.

Gbenu looked at his beloved son sternly.

'I've had—disquieting news of you, Vi,' he said. 'But first— where are the heads I heard you took today?'

'Head, Da—not heads,' Nyasanu said. 'Just one. I—I gave it to Badji to add to his store. . . .'

'You did what!' Gbenu said.

'I—I gave it to Taugbadji, Father. He's my third friend. He was very brave today. He took two heads. No, five——'

'Make up your mind,' Gbenu said. 'Two heads or five.'

'Five, really. He killed two Mahees outright,' Nyasanu said —pronouncing the name of the Maxi as they themselves did in their Ewe dialect, 'and wounded three others with arrows. And since people with arrow wounds always die, because the points are poisoned, I ordered them killed and their heads taken for him. . . .'

'I see,' Gbenu said. 'Not only does your friend take five heads singlehandedly in one fight, a feat unheard of in Daho-mean history, but you must make it six, by giving him the one you took. Mind telling me why, son?'

'They—they broke his right arm with their hoes,' Nyasanu said. 'The bone-setter says he'll never lift it again. So since he can never again fight or take any other head I thought——'

'Generous of you,' Gbenu said drily. 'And that bandage on your side?'

153

'A little cut. A scratch really—doesn't amount to anything, Da——'

'Which your friend Taugbadji gave you to keep you from beating your half-sister to death!' Gbenu said grimly. 'I have a formal complaint against you from no less than the *khetunga* of the *ahosi* Right, herself. Fortunately, she knew you are my son and directed the complaint to me instead of the *gao*, your own commander-in-chief. Or else you'd be facing decapitation right now! No one is permitted to touch the *ahosi*, whether they be kindred or not!'

Nyasanu bowed his head.

'What do you have to say for yourself, Nyasanu?' Gbenu roared. 'If they had not told me how bravely you bore yourself today, I'd order twenty rods laid on you, so help me!'

In spite of himself, Nyasanu shuddered a little at that. In the Dahomean army, the administration of corporal punishment was not measured by the number of individual whiplashes dealt the culprit, but rather by the number of rods broken over his back. And since one rod might last for twenty strokes, or a hundred, many a man had died for less than twenty rods.

'She—was torturing a wounded Maxi,' he whispered. 'Somehow I couldn't stand—seeing a daughter of *yours,* doing that. It—it's ugly, Da! Hateful! I——'

Gbenu's broad face softened.

'I agree with you, son,' he said, 'but that has been the *ahosi*'s privilege for many years. Still you had no right to interfere——'

'Not even when I saw she was getting the—the kind of pleasure out of it that a woman should only get—on her sleeping mat—with her own husband?' Nyasanu said. '*That* was what enraged me, Father!'

Gbenu stared at his son.

'Thou'rt too intelligent for thine own good, Vi,' he said softly. 'I've often thought that, myself. No, to tell the truth, I've long been sure that what makes the *ahosi* more ferocious than a herd of wounded gorillas is their enforced celibacy. So in them, cruelty—becomes a perversion. Minona, Goddess of Women and Sorcerers! Tell me, what should I do with you?'

'Don't know,' Nyasanu said morosely. 'But what I do know, Tauchi, my father, is that I didn't march twelve days to murder peasants armed with hoes and working in their fields! I came to face men and warriors, not poor country louts who

154

run like sheep! Why——'

'You expected war to be glorious, my son?' Gbenu said, his big voice vibrant with sadness. 'It isn't—any more than life is. I've often thought that nothing degrades a man more than the nasty stinking business of man killing. We, Vi,' he went on, his voice sinking, deepening, becoming the echoes of thunder far away, on the edge of whatever horizon it was where he had left both his illusions and his youth, 'are the cruellest beasts who walk earth. No other creature the *vudun* have made, no lion, leopard, crocodile, snake, kills except out of hunger or to feed his young, While we kill out of pleasure. Out of blood lust, making the excuse that the gods demand sacrifices of us. I do not, cannot believe that. For if the *vudun* be less, be crueller than man, why worship them?'

'Because we fear them, Father!' Nyasanu said.

'Aye! That's reason enough, isn't it? That's the reason we give for everything! Accepted dishonour—the burden of a wife we hate—children who have other men's faces! I—I've lived a long time, Nyasanu, in the belief that riches, power, influence, fame compensates a man for the slow thoughts that crawl through his head and his belly in the dark, sickening both. Even for the knowledge that there're many ways of being a coward and that the battlefield's the easiest place of all to be brave. And the older I grow the more I wonder, what is life when it hath lost all savour? What is wealth gained by selling our brothers to creatures, but dubiously human beings, into a slavery that's a total horror? Is there such a thing called honour, Son? Tell me, I'm sure I don't know. . . .'

'Da,' Nyasanu whispered. 'Father mine, I——'

'No matter! I am become an old fool who talks too much! In any event, I shall have you transferred to my corps where I can keep an eye on you. Or where you can keep an eye on me. Or we two on each other! What say you to that, Vi?'

'Only—can Kpad come with me? He—he thinks he's going to be killed in this campaign. His—his *du* told him that. So I'd like to be near him to—to prevent——'

'What can never be prevented, but only postponed,' Gbenu sighed. 'Of course, Vi. I'll give the orders this very night.

'Now come, let us sup together—and talk of only such light and pleasant things as will add no more aches to those my head is burdened with already!'

'I can't eat, Da!' Nyasanu burst out. 'I couldn't! For——'

'Oh yes, you can, young lion with a heart more tender than a maid's. Do not gainsay me. Do as I tell you: come!'

TWELVE

'By Aido Hwedo, who holds up the world!' Nyasanu said. 'This is supposed to be a *war*, Kpad?'

Kpadunu looked out to where the *ahosi*, the female soldiers, were busily engaged in harvesting the crops the Maxi had planted.

'Yes,' he said, 'and as far as I've been able to find out, just like every other war in the memory of the oldest clan head I know, except when we fought the Auyo, Nya. We march out against a peaceful mountain people like the Maxi, and capture the only fields they have, killing in the process eight or ten men. Then we camp down here at the foot of their mountains and wait for them to consider whether it makes more sense to starve to death or to surrender to us, knowing all the time which choice they're going to make, the choice they've always made every time we've attacked them, just as we know it's never going to occur to them to store up some food against our coming.

'A man's *fa* is what that man is. So is a tribe's. A nation's. A race's.'

'Kpad,' Nyasanu said, 'that's a hard saying.'

'But a true one. The Maxi are born slaves, Nya——'

'No man is born a slave!' Nyasanu flared.

Kpadunu looked at his first friend sadly, pityingly.

'A man who can be enslaved,' he said, without even raising his voice, 'is a born slave. Remember that. Oh, I won't insist that a man should always die first——'

'I do!' Nyasanu said.

'But you're very simple, very noble, and very pure—which are nice-sounding ways of saying you're a fool. Wait! Don't rear up at me. Half of all our battles have been won, and Dahomey repeatedly saved, the elders say, by noble fools. Only they don't call them that. They call them heroes. Like you, Like Taugbadji . . .'

156

'Legba eat my brains if I can figure what got into him!'
Nyasanu said. 'You don't think he did that to play the hero in
front of Alogba, do you?'

'No. She wasn't anywhere around when he did it—and besides she'd never be interested in a little fat fellow like Badji.
You're more her style.'

'And I'm also her brother, which she conveniently forgets,'
Nyasanu said. 'Anyhow, even if she weren't my half-sister, she
still wouldn't interest me. Sorry I even brought the subject up.
Tell me—what *were* we talking about?'

'Slaves. Whether they're born or made.'

'All right. You were saying . . .'

'That they're born. That even if the slavers do capture a
man, they have to kill him or let him go. Because keeping him
is too much trouble. I found that out when I visited Whydah.
Some of the Furtoo—the darker ones, the ones who look almost human, and speak tongues that sound pleasant on the
ear—will take a Dahomean or an Ashanti if he's offered to
them as a slave. But the really flayed ones, the ones who have
ghosts' eyes and dried-grass-coloured hair and whose lan-
guages are like the barking of jackals, refuse to buy slaves from
either one of the warrior nations. So much so that to dispose
of our political prisoners, our dealers in Whydah have to lie
about their origins. And since the Furtoo are exceedingly
stupid and can't tell a Tuffoe from a Fulani, or *us* from the
Maxi, they buy. But they don't want *men*. And since men
seldom get taken anyhow, they mostly get what they want,
which is born slaves—like the Maxi, the Ibos, the Tuffoe,
the——'

'I know, I know,' Nyasanu said. 'But you can be sure of one
thing, Kpad: if I am ever taken they'd have to kill me because
I——'

'Because you're a fool,' Kpadunu said, 'a noble fool, but still
a fool. If I were ever enslaved, I'd make sure they turned me
loose—to live, eat and get fat, love women and beget sons.'

'How would you do that, Kpad?' Nya said.

Kpad smiled.

Oh, things would happen, he said. 'My master's horse would
go lame or break his leg. His crops wouldn't grow. His pigs
would get sick. His people would chop the maize instead of the
weeds. His house would catch afire——'

'Sorcery,' Nyasanu said. 'But I don't know enough even yet

to do all those things, in spite of all you've taught me. How could I? I've only been at it less than three months. And you yourself say it takes seven years——'

'Yes, you do. The basic principle anyhow, which is to make simple things *seem* imposing, mysterious, magical. What would happen to a field if salt somehow got mixed in the manure used to enrich it? If the pigs ate something they shouldn't? If a blacksmith, say, drove in a nail too far while shoeing a horse, wouldn't the beast go lame? But what I'd do would be to control the other slaves—make them fear me, believe in my powers, until I became master in fact. That done, nothing would ever go right for the man who'd bought me until I'd be able to convince him it would be smart to turn me loose——'

'*Sounds* all right,' Nyasanu said, then, 'in the name of the Earth Gods, how long do you think it's going to take these stubborn Maxi fools to give in? We've been here over three months. By now, Nyaunu wi should be close to her time, and you should already have a son. . . .'

'I know,' Kpadunu said sadly.

'Kpad——'

'No, Nya. I've told you twenty times now that I won't send your souls on that journey again. And not because your disembodied soul kissed my woman, which was a small thing and of no importance at all. But because I found then that I really can't control them once they've left you. What if they didn't come back, Nya? You'd be one of the soulless ones then, and —by Xevioso, look who's coming——'

'Badji!' Nyasanu said. 'That's strange! He hasn't been near me since I whipped Alogba's tail for her. I wonder . . .'

The little ex-archer, ex-clothworker came over to where they sat. His right arm was no longer bound up in splints now. But he couldn't move it; he couldn't move it at all.

'I give you greetings, my brother,' he said sadly.

'Badji!' Nyasanu said. 'I'm glad to see you. I thought you were mad at me because . . .'

'You beat Alogba bloody? I was. But I'm not any more. She convinced me I shouldn't be . . .'

'Look, Badji,' Kpadunu said, 'you shouldn't talk to Alogba. You may have known her all her life, but she's still an *ahosi*. And you know the saying: "More men have lost their lives going over the walls into the *ahosi* camp than have been killed

158

in all Dahomey's wars put together!" '

'I know that,' Taugbadji said. 'The *ahosi* are the king's wives even though he doesn't lie with them. If a man is caught with one, off goes his head. But, in my case, there's little or no danger. I'm a cripple. And I've been a cripple long enough for men to have forgotten *how* I got hurt. . . .'

'Badji!' Nyasanu said reproachfully.

'I speak truly, Nya! I'm little and fat and short and crippled. So nobody cares enough to watch me where I go. So I stroll into the wood—and meet Alogba. We talk—that's all. Mostly about *you*, 'cause that's the one subject that really interests her. Which is why I'm here. She wants to see you.'

'She might as well forget it!' Nyasanu said. 'This is the only head I've got, Badji. And, as you can see, it's sitting atop of just one rusty black neck. I'd prefer to keep the two together, third friend! And talking to an *ahosi*—sister or not—isn't the best way I can figure on staying alive——'

'She says—it's important, Nya. A matter of life and death. She's begging you to help her. To save her life. So am I. See her, please.'

Kpadunu leaned close, peering into Taugbadji's face. When he spoke at last, he was so sure that the question had become rhetorical:

'Badji,' he said quietly, 'have you been lying with Alogba?'

Taugbadji straightened up, cloaked his short, fat, black all but naked form in dignity: sad, ineffectual, comical, but none the less real.

'That's my business, Kpad,' he bristled. 'And even if I had, d'you think I'd tell you? A man who spreads tales——'

'Even if those tales be true,' Nyasanu said, as sure as Kpadunu now. No, surer, because he knew Alogba better.

'Even if those tales be true,' Taugbadji echoed. 'Not that I admit they are, mind you, Nya! I say only that a man who spreads tales about an unmarried girl is no man at all. You're Alogba's brother—father's child—male, anyhow; so it seems to me you owe her——'

'I owe her nothing!' Nyasanu said. 'But since it's very clear that you, third friend mine, are involved in a thing that, sure as Legba is Lord of Lust, is likely to earn you the red cap and a basket ride around the king's square to the pit, I'll come——'

'Nya——' Kpadunu said warningly.

'You come, too, Kpad,' Taugbadji said. 'You and I can keep

watch while they talk. Make sure that nobody sneaks up on them and accuses them. . . .'

'All right,' Kpad said. Then he bent and picked up his *assegai* and Nyasanu's.

'Here,' he said to his first friend, 'take this. Guns make too much noise. . . .'

Nyasanu stood in the little clearing high on the far side of the valley, the side closer to the Maxi's largest town, and looked at his half-sister. Specifically, he looked at her belly in the general area of her navel; but he couldn't be sure. She did seem a little plumper, at that, still——

'All right,' she said morosely, 'I am. So stop staring at my belly and look at my face. I don't think you can tell yet, by looking at me. Can you?'

'No,' Nyasanu said.

'Good, that means I—we—still have time. . . .'

'Who's the father?' Nyasanu said.

'Badji, I think——'

Nyasanu stared at her.

'You *think*?' he said. 'Don't you *know*?'

'No,' Alogba said. 'I don't know. Him more often than anybody else; but that doesn't matter, does it?'

'Legba, Lord of Lust!' Nyasanu said.

'Your fault,' Alogba said. 'If *you'd* obliged me there wouldn't have been anybody else. Ran into Badji the night you kicked me out of your hut. That was when it started.'

'Alogba, I'm your *brother*!' Nyasanu said.

'No, you're not. Mother says you aren't, and she should know, shouldn't she?'

'I doubt it. For the same reason that you don't know whether the child you're carrying is Badji's or not. . . .'

'I think it *is*,' Alogba said. 'In fact, I'm almost sure it is. I—I only did *that*, with three other fellows——'

'May Chaunu strike them!' Nyasanu said.

'No, Nya. That's unfair. Why should you make them useless to all other women simply because I let them lie with me? That's what Chaunu does, doesn't he?'

'Yes,' Nyasanu said. Chaunu, 'Hold-Back-Thing', was one of the Earth Gods. His speciality was rendering impotent those who broke the sexual tabus. A punishment most aply fitted to the crime, Nyasanu thought.

'And I was only bad those three times because Badji was laid up with his arm broken and couldn't, I had to have *somebody*, so——'

'So get to the point, Alogba,' Nyasanu said wearily. 'What do you want of me?'

'That you and Kpad help me take Agwe. Just the three of us. And Badji. He can't *do* anything with his arm like that, but we'll let him take credit too, so that——'

'By the time your belly begins to swell so much you can't hide your sins, your "husband", the king, will have been so impressed by your heroism that he'll forgive you your adulteries. That's it, isn't it, sister mine?'

'Yes, Nya. Isn't it a good plan?'

'Excellent. Except for one thing: Agwe, up there, is the capital of the Maxi. How in the name of Legba, who eats the brains of idiots, do you propose that two men, one cripple, and a pregnant girl shall take a city almost the size of Alladah?'

'Easily, they—they're awful sick up there. I've sneaked into the city several times, wearing a skirt belonging to a woman of theirs I killed. She got too hungry and came down too far in search of food. And I know a little Ewe. Enough to get by, anyhow they—they're dying of hunger up there, Nya! They've eaten all their animals—even the dogs. I think they're even beginning to eat each other——'

Nyasanu considered that.

'Yet, two days ago when Father sent me out to lead a scouting raid against them,' he said, 'to sort of test their defences, they showered more arrows, spears and rocks down on us than anybody would have believed there were in this world. . . .'

'That's because in spite of being tall and strong and good looking, you really aren't smart, Nya. I mean the way Kpad is. You attacked them from the front, now didn't you?'

'Yes. But sister mine, there isn't any *back*—Agwe sits on the edge of a precipice and behind it are some peaks that not even a goat could climb and——'

'I'm not a goat. I climbed them. Besides, the way I know into Agwe isn't very hard,' Alogba said.

Nyasanu stared at her.

'All right,' he said at last. 'I won't argue that point, or even mention that judging from the way you act, you *are* maybe more of a she-goat than a woman. All I'll say is this: if there're even fifty men up there still on their feet, and with strength enough to draw a bow or throw a spear, the three of us can't take them. It's not a matter of bravery Alogba, but of tactics. We might be able to manage to keep ten warriors so busy that none of them could sneak around the back of us or some in at us on a slant or——'

'Nya,' Alogba said patiently, 'you just aren't smart. That's not the way to do it at all.'

'Then what *is* the way to do it, my lady general?' Nyasanu said.

'We go to the house of the chief—I know where it is. Then *I* go up to it alone. And although you never bothered to take notice, I've got a nice shape. My face is kind of ugly; I know that. But, apart from you, who ever heard of a man who pays much attention to a girl's face, especially when she's wiggling the rest of herself at him?'

Nya threw back his head and laughed aloud. Alogba giggled a little, too, in appreciation of her own wit.

'Go on,' he said, 'this is beginning to sound a little better! You think that after we've killed the chief, the rest of them will surrender?'

'Yalode give me patience!' Alogba said. 'Haven't you any brains at all, Nya? We kill the chief, and they'll simply choose a new one and go right on fighting. No. What we do is to take him *alive*. Him and the high priest of their ancestor cult, too, if we can catch them both. Then we threaten to kill them by inches. . . .'

'Alogba!' Nyasanu said.

'I know! I know! So I'm cruel. We *ahosi* are trained to be. I said "threaten". That doesn't mean we really have to do it, Nya. But I'm almost sure that if we take their leaders prisoner, they'll give in. And the war will be over. And we'll be heroes, all of us. And the king——'

'Will forgive you for opening your thighs to half the army,' Nyasanu said.

'Nya! That's unfair! There was only Badji—and——'

'Three others. Or four. Or five. Or six—or——'

'No! just three. Well—maybe four——'

'Legba, Lord of Lust!' Nyasanu said.

Alogba came up close to him. So close that he could smell her. She had bathed and perfumed herself, which helped. But not enough. He took a backward step.

'Oh don't be like that!' she said. 'I can't help loving you.

And you're not my brother, for the very simple reason that Gbenu isn't my father, the old fool! We could even marry. Mother says that if I really want you that much—and I do—she'll tell the truth to the *vuduno* and——'

'Alogba,' Nyasanu said quietly, 'forget it. You are in trouble enough, without asking for more. Now come on——'

'Come on where?' Alogba said.

'Down there. Where Kpadunu and Taugbadji are—I want to talk this over with Kpad. As you said, he's smart. If he thinks your plan will work, the chances are it really will. So just don't stand like a ruttish she-goat, sister mine, come on!'

They came up to Agwe just before dawn. Nyasanu and Kpadunu each carried four muskets—stolen from their comrades-in-arms. Alogba bore another two, and Taugbadji one. All the muskets were loaded, but only Nyasanu and Kpadunu were to shoot if they had to stand and fight. Alogba and Taugbadji were to pass them a loaded musket each time they fired. And, if the fight became prolonged, Taugbadji was to pass them the muskets, which he could do with his one uncrippled hand, while Alogba reloaded.

Alogba also had her bow and arrows, and one more weapon, or rather two: a long semi-transparent silk woman's cloth and a flask of almond blossom perfume.

They stopped to rest beside a little waterfall, because in spite of what Alogba had said, the climb had been both long and hard.

'Here,' Nyasanu said to her. 'Take this soap and wash yourself. All over. Then stand under the waterfall——'

'Nya!' Alogba said.

'We won't look at you. The point is, Sister, if you're going to tempt the *toxausu* of Agwe with your feminine charms you'll do a lot better job of it smelling of almond blossom than of she-goat. That's one thing. Another is, you must put on that cloth you've brought. Really cover yourself up—even your breasts. Clear?'

'Yes,' Alogba said, 'the first part anyhow. Climbing up this trail has got me all sweaty. But if the chief can't see what a nice shape I've got, why should he be——'

'Tempted? Precisely because you're covered up, Sister! The Maxi woman goes stark naked most of the time, except during the rainy seasons, when it gets too cold up here. So another

163

naked woman would make him yawn. Covered up, you'll excite his curiosity, make him wonder——'

Kpadunu threw back his head and laughed aloud.

'You see, first friend mine, you *are* learning, after all!' he said. 'Nya's right, Alogba. Another thing: when you talk to the chief, be coy. Cast down your eyes. *Don't* wiggle your anatomy at him. Let him make the first moves and——'

Then the three of them heard the strangling sounds come from Taugbadji's mouth.

'No!' the fat little ex-archer got out. 'No, by Xevioso, no! Alogba, I won't permit——'

Alogba turned to him then and kissed him, full on the mouth, winking one eye merrily at Nyasanu and Kpadunu as she did so.

'Now just you be a sweet little old fat piggy,' she giggled, 'and help me stay alive so that you *can* marry me. Then you give me orders; but not now. Badji, love, I don't think either one of us will do the other much good without a head, and that's what'll happen to both of us if we don't give Dada some reason to forgive us for making babies out of season.'

She stopped short, and shivered as from sudden cold.

'Kpad,' she whispered, 'if—if this doesn't work—will you—will you kill me, please? Shoot me from behind while I'm not looking, so I won't know it's coming. When I'm not expecting it. Will you, huh, please?'

'But Alogba,' Kpadunu said. 'Why in the name of . . .'

' 'Cause you men are lucky,' Alogba said. 'Do something wrong, and you're killed by an expert. The royal executioner does a good job, Kpad. But when an *ahosi* is condemned to death—mostly for letting some man push her knees apart one time too many—our own officers do it. Women, Kpad. And they're messy. I've seen it done, so I know. I think they choose a dull knife on purpose so's to make it last longer. They saw'n saw'n saw, ugh! Please, Kpad?'

'But—but,' Kpadunu whispered, 'why *me*?'

'Because Badji can't,' Alogba said, 'and Nya won't. You know him, Kpad. Big as he is, he's got a woman's heart. He couldn't do it. He'll remember all the happy times we had together as children and his fingers'll turn to stone on the trigger. And I'll be left to be thrown head first into the pit and some fat old sow of an officer who is broiling mad 'cause nobody even *wants* to shove a good one up her will mess

164

around with my neck for half an hour, saving my windpipe for the last so she can enjoy hearing me scream. That's why. So if I'm hurt up there—or taken by the Maxi—kill me. Even if—if it doesn't work, do it on the way back down to camp. While we're talking about something else. While—promise me, Kpad?'

Slowly Kpadunu shook his head.

'I've three wives and maybe a son by now,' he said, 'waiting for me when I get back home. A man can be executed for merely pinching an *ahosi*'s behind, Alogba. What d'you think they'd do to a fellow who *killed* one?'

'They wouldn't know!' Alogba said. 'You can say it was the Maxi and——'

'Alogba,' Nyasanu said sternly, 'shut up and go bathe!'

The three of them lay there hidden just behind the thorn thicket that blocked the narrow trail which wound down from the peaks of the mountains, the same trail Alogba had shown them, this making it possible to come up to the city of Agwe by its almost unguarded back entrance. But Alogba herself wasn't with them any more. She had already entered Agwe on her mission of seducing the *toxausu*, or chief, of the Maxi capital into the folly of walking in this direction with her, in order to bargain with her 'father' over the price to be paid for her ebony charms.

And she had been gone a long time. So long that neither Nyasanu nor Kpadunu could bear looking at Taugbadji any more. The worst of it was they could easily put themselves in his place, imagine all too vividly how he felt having left achingly beloved women of their own behind in Alladah.

'Now, Badji,' Nyasanu began; but that was all he had time for, because it was then that they heard Alogba scream.

Looking up, they saw her. She came bounding towards them like an antelope followed by a band of Maxi archers. The Maxi were living skeletons, who skipped, hopped, and gibbered over the ground. From the looks of them, Nyasanu wondered whether they meant to rape Alogba or eat her; but whatever their intentions were, they pursued her with a speed astonishing in men clearly dying of famine. So fast did they come that even as the three Dahomeans watched, one of them put out a skeletal hand and caught Alogba's cloth. Which did him no good; she simply wiggled out of it, and came on, running

165

faster than ever, now that her really fine body was no longer hampered by clothing. Another clapped his ravenous claw of a hand onto her sweat-glistened shoulder; but then all the world rocked with flame and smoke and thunder, for Taugbadji laid the barrel of the musket he was holding across Nyasanu's shoulder and, using his friend's body as a tripod, jerked the trigger of the gun, and shot the Maxi dead.

That stopped them in their tracks, but only for the brief instant it took them to jerk a hand backwards over their shoulders, claw out arrows from their quivers, and fit them to their bowstrings. A second later, the very air was black with the whining shafts. Nyasanu felt something sting his left arm, and, looking down saw a Maxi arrow hanging from it. The barbed point wasn't in him deep, but only slanting diagonally just beneath his skin a little way, so he jerked it free and began to shoot at the Maxi, firing slowly, coolly, and with deadly aim.

And now the Maxi were so close that even the worst marksman in the Dahomean army couldn't have missed, and both Nyasanu and Kpadunu had become fairly good with guns by then. But they were also close enough for the four Dahomeans to see what a sixty-calibre Danish musket ball did when it hits a man, which was to tear a hole in the softer parts of his body big enough to shove your fist into. Or to dissolve his face into a bloody mess. Or to lift a slab of bone out of his skull and splatter his brains into the faces of his comrades.

Nyasanu saw that. His finger froze on the trigger of the third musket. Somebody, Sagbata, maybe, King of the Earth Gods, and Lord of Plagues, poured a sickness, green as swamp slime, and utterly vile into his belly until it pooled there and rose into his throat; somebody else, Legba, likely, the Messenger of the *Vudun*, that infernal trickster who eats his victims' brains, gibbered and mocked and laughed inside his head. And Ku, surely Ku, God of Death, caught his heart, his lungs, his guts, his testicles, in one immense and ice-cold grip and squeezed them, slowly.

'Shoot, Nya,' Kpadunu said, 'shoot, Brother! If you don't, we're done!'

Then Nyasanu felt the butt of his musket slam into his shoulder, heard the splat and thunder, saw the orange flames stab through the grey-white smoke. A Maxi archer dropped his bow, and sat down abruptly, clutching his middle. His black face, above his scraggly, kinky beard, showed no signs of either

166

shock or pain, surely because neither had had time to reach him yet, but only astonishment. Then very quickly, without a word or groan, he died.

But now Taugbadji passed Nyasanu another musket, reloaded by Alogba, and Nya shot and shot again, the tears streaming down his face, pencilling tracks through the powder soot on his cheeks, watching those huge sixty-calibre, ill-shaped musket balls tear the guts out of the howling, dancing, hunger-maddened, suffering scarecrows before them, until it finally occurred to the two or three Maxi who were left that their pitifully primitive bows and arrows were no match for the musket fire, and they turned and ran.

Even after that, Nyasanu hung there, staring at the scattered heaps of black carrion, at the boneless sprawl of man-meat, at the slow seep that the thirsty earth drank at once, making rusty mud of what had been life, at the green-blue metallic clouds of the already gathering flies, until Ku turned his vitals loose, allowing feeling, recognition, even thought to come shuddering back again, and he opened his mouth and gave back to earth in one great foaming rush all his horror, sickness, shame.

When he straightened up at last, he saw Alogba staring at him. And what was in her eyes was very bad. Compassion, maybe—pity. He couldn't stand that look.

'Yes!' he grated, 'I *hate* killing people, Sister! Even Maxi. So if that makes me no man, I——'

'No,' she whispered. 'You—you don't understand—that—that—wound in your arm, Nya. Did—did—one of their *arrows* do that?'

'Yes,' he said; then, looking at her, 'So it was—poisoned. So they've learned that much. Kpad, my brother, what think you of your *du*'s predictions now?'

'Nya,' Kpad groaned; but before he could say anything else or any of them could move, Alogba was upon Nyasanu. She clamped her big, fleshy mouth down over the wound and began to suck at it with terrible force. They could see her throat jerking and quivering as though all her life was concentrated there.

'Alogba!' Taugbadji screamed, his voice high, wailing, woman shrill, 'Alogba, no! Oh, Yalode, Goddess of Women, I——'

'Leave her alone, Badji,' Kpadunu said. 'Most of the poisons

167

people put on arrowheads don't kill you if you swallow them. They only make you sick. They have to get into the blood to kill, so if she——'

He stopped then. His hand shot out and clamped into Alogba's woolly hair. He jerked her head back, and bent down staring at her mouth.

'Let me alone!' she shrilled. 'Let me at least *try* to save him, Kpad! I'm going to die anyhow since this didn't work. Since we've failed. So let me——'

Kpadunu turned her loose.

'She hasn't any cuts or cracks in her lips, Badji,' he said, 'so she's safe enough. She'll probably have a terrible gut-ache tomorrow, and may have to spend three days squatting over a latrine, but that's about all. Alogba, when you get tired, I'll——'

She straightened up then and smiled at Nyasanu. She had blood all over her mouth, but her smile was very tender.

'No,' she said. 'No, Kpad. I—I think I got it all. Now lend me your *assegai*, will you?'

'Lend you my *assegai*?' Kpadunu said.

'Or hold it straight out so I can run up against it. I'm going to die now, anyhow; and even if I'm not pretty like Dangbevi and Nyaunu wi are, I want to be buried looking the best I can. I don't want to be laid out with my face and—and my whole body covered with sores and dripping pus—'cause——'

'Now wait a minute, Alogba,' Kpadunu said. 'In the first place, arrow poison doesn't kill you if you swallow it. In the second, even if it did get into your blood through a crack in your lip say, you'd be already dead by now, because the Maxi use snake venom, not that slow stuff our *azaundatoe* brew. And in the third, no kind of poison I know makes sores on the skin, or pus, or——'

But Alogba was still holding her hand out for him to give her the Ashanti sword. And she was still smiling.

'Not a *poison*,' Kpad,' she said. 'You see, I never even got a chance to tempt their chief. He was dead. Sagbata had struck him. And they—they were dipping their arrows into his sores. . . .'

Nobody said anything then. None of them moved. None of them even breathed. Then Taugbadji let his breath out on a note halfway between a whimper and a sob.

'Give her thy assegai, Kpad,' he said almost gently, 'and thou, Nya, give me thine. For I won't live without her. I can't.'

168

Nyasanu didn't answer him. He stood there, staring at Alogba, and very slowly the tears pooled his eyes, and spilled down his black cheeks. Then, even more slowly, he bent his immense height in half, going down on his knees before Alogba, pressing his forehead to the ground, and clawing up a handful of earth, poured it over his head.

A moment later, both of his friends imitated his gesture of self-humiliation, of grief. And Alogba stood there above them proudly, smiling down upon her worshippers like a queen.

'Oh no!' Taugbadji moaned, 'not the plague that Da Zodji sends! Not the smallpox! Not even that! Sagbata save her! She is so beautiful and her skin—her skin——'

Kpadunu straightened up.

'Come, my brother,' he said, 'let us take counsel together. For if they have Sagbata's disease among them, that hideous death his son Da Zodji sends, we'd best get word of it to the king. . . .'

The four of them stared at one another. Their eyes widened then darkened, turned inward with thought, with disquietude.

'I'll do it,' Alogba said.

'No,' Taugbadji said. 'I'll——'

'Badji,' Alogba said, 'you know what Dada Gezo's going to do to the person who brings him the news that after all these months, we're going to have to run back home like a pack of jackals with our tails 'twixt our legs because——'

'We can't take the slaves we came after,' Kpadunu sighed. 'We can't because if we do, we'll only spread the plague throughout our own ranks, making the grains that Sagbata gave us to eat come out on our skins, and turn into pus, until our bodies are living rot, and we die. I've heard that the Furtoo in Whydah have a *gbo** against it, a means of giving one a little of the disease—they call it *akpotin kpevi,* or smallpox, Legba himself couldn't explain why—in only one place, which according to *their* sorcerers keeps you from getting it all over, or from dying from it not only then, but ever. But we aren't in Whydah. And the king is going to have the head of whoever brings him the news that his second campaign in a row has to be a flat failure, not from lack of valour, but because the gods——'

'I,' Alogba pointed out, 'drew the plague from Nya's blood.

* Edward Jenner had introduced vaccination against smallpox into Europe many years before this time.

169

So I'm already dead. Let me tell Dada Gezo that——'

'And I,' Nyasanu said, 'am dead, too, if you didn't get it all, Sister. Besides, it had been in my blood a long time before you did that. So it seems to me——'

'I'm a cripple,' Taugbadji whispered, 'useless forever now. In love with a woman who loves somebody else and——'

'Wait!' Kpadunu said. 'Alogba, let us, you and I, take the Maxi's heads.'

'What!' Nyasanu said.

'Let us take their heads, which are many,' Kpadunu said calmly. 'Then you, Nya, take *all* the heads to the king. Pile them in a heap some distance away from him. If he or some officers try to touch them, warn them away—and tell them why. If he orders you too close to his presence, refuse to go, and tell him that you fear that you're infected. Under those circumstances, he will banish you from the camp; but he won't dare order you killed, who will have displayed your heroism before his hosts. *That's* the way to do it. Now Alogba, of the ever-parted knees, come on!'

So it was done. They started the long descent towards their camps, bearing the Maxi's heads. But they went in silence, exchanging no single word among themselves.

They were part of a defeated army and they knew it; their conquerors no human foes, but the very gods themselves; two of them bearing in their veins, perhaps the deadly seeds of Sagbata's scourge, which their lightest, almost accidental touch could spread like a brush fire through the ranks of their comrades in arms.

They had gone up to Agwe seeking glory. And what had they found?

Death. Almost surely, death.

THIRTEEN

From where he crouched on his hands and knees, with his forehead pressed against the ground before His Royal Majesty Gezo, tenth *dada*, or king, of Dahomey, Nyasanu couldn't see the *khetunga*, female commander of the *ahosi* right wing. But he could hear her, all right. Not being deaf, he couldn't avoid that. And, from the way she was shrieking, he suspected that everybody between the kingdoms of the Nupe and the Fulani far to the north, and Kumassi, the Ashanti capital three weeks' journey to the south, could too.

'He's lying, Great Father of us all!' the she-general howled. 'I, your wife, and commander of your soldier-wives, the *ahosi*, tell you that! Look at him! Where are his sores? Where do you see the grains of Sagbata's scourge upon him? A bandage around his arm, that's all! Plain trickery! Can't you see, sire, that he's only trying to keep his head connected to his neck in spite of his having betrayed you?'

Gezo's voice came over to Nyasanu now. It was grave and slow and infinitely weary.

'Betrayed me how, O Khetunga?' the king said.

'With one of your *ahosi*, a foolish girl named Alogba. I first suspected it when he whipped her with his gunbelt out of jealousy because——'

'O father of us all,' Gbenu's big voice cut in then, 'will you allow me to say something about all this hysterical female nonsense?'

Gezo smiled.

'Of course, My *kposu*!' he said.

'The boy is my son,' Gbenu said quietly. 'All his life he has been brave and honourable and very largely free from fault. Of course, once he *is* a man, I wouldn't go so far as to claim that he is less given than other men to the lusts of the flesh. But I do say that it doesn't seem to me likely that a young fellow who's just got married—and happily at that—would indulge whatever vagrant desire he might feel upon the person of his own sister——'

'Sister!' the *khetunga* gasped. 'Impossible, O Great Father! I know the archeress Alogba well, and you can take my word for it that they don't look alike at all! Believe me, sire, there's not the slightest resemblance between them!'

'His sister, O father of us all,' Gbenu said quietly, 'and my daughter, as he is my son. By different mothers, of course, which accounts for the fact that my lady Khetunga is telling the truth when she says the resemblance between them is slight, if any resemblance exists at all. Alogba's mother, the Lady Yu, was given to me by your eldest daughter, her Highness, the Princess Fedime. And I would stake my head upon my honest belief that my son Nyasanu, here, is incapable of even the

171

thought of incest, the sternest *su dudu* among us. . . .'

Nyasanu raised his head a little so that he could see the king's face. And, just as he had expected, Gezo winced a little at Gbenu's last remark. All the world knew how little attention the members of the Leopard Clan paid to that particular prohibition.

'Nyasanu, son of Gbenu,' the king said then, 'get up from there. You have my permission to stand in my presence. . . .'

'I thank you, father of us all,' Nyasanu said, and got to his feet.

The king's gaze flew upwards, following, with evident astonishment, the towering of the boy's great height.

'A giant,' he said. 'Even bigger than you are, Kposu! I hope he knows how to defend himself for we need men like this in Dahomey——'

'Ask him whatever you want to, O Father,' Gbenu said serenely.

'On pain of death, for you can be sure your head and shoulders will part company the instant I find out you've lied to me, I ask you, son of Gbenu: have you played the man with your sister? Have you crawled into the hurt of this archeress—what's her name again, Khetunga?'

'Alogba,' the *khetunga* said.

'Alogba. Have you done this stupid thing, my son?' Gezo said.

There was a stirring among the spectators at this. For the king to call the boy 'vi', my son, was a clear, if unintentional, sign of royal favour.

'No, Great Father of us all,' Nyasanu said, 'I haven't. And though my sinful parts have ached me much in consequence, I have been faithful to the vow I made my lady wife, when I joined your hosts, Great Father: I have known no other woman except my own since the day I wedded her!'

Hearing the calm sincerity of his son's voice, Gbenu was sure, made it impossible for any rational man to doubt him.

But the Khetunga, despite the standard boast of the *ahosi* that they'd unsexed themselves, that they had become men, was not a man. What's more, it was evident that she had even less than her own sex's somewhat dubious claim to rationality.

'Put him to the ordeal!' she shrieked.

The king bowed his head, looked up again.

'Very well,' he sighed. 'Let the knife be heated.' Nyasanu

172

stiffened hearing that. It was, he realised, one of the simplest, least painful of the ordeals. But it was also one of the most dangerous. A red-hot knife blade was held before the suspect's mouth. He was then supposed to touch his tongue tip to it, as lightly and as quickly as he could. The theory was that Legba would dry the saliva in a liar's mouth so that his tongue would be blistered by the heat.

But, Nyasanu wailed inside his mind, isn't fear alone enough to do that without the help of the Trickster or any other *vudun*? Just thinking about the heat, imagining how a red-hot blade will feel, will make my mouth go drier than a water-hole at the end of the big dry season when even the mud at the bottom of it has turned to stone, and you can smell the bodies of the animals who've died of thirst all around it from very far away. It's just like Kpad says, 'A brazen liar can pass this ordeal ten times out of ten, while a nervous honest man will fail it. . . .'

Then, even as he thought his first friend's name, he saw Kpadunu. The young sorcerer held him with his eyes. Nyasanu could feel that dark and brooding gaze boring into his brain. Thought formed inside his head, as clear as sound, making a chant: 'You'll feel no pain my brother! The knife will not burn thee! You'll feel no pain, you'll——'

Suddenly, Kpadunu stooped and picked up a small stone and put it in his mouth.

Nyasanu knew what that was for: any smooth object placed in the mouth stimulated the flow of saliva. Still, he had to wait a long time, until every eye was fixed upon the beginning glow of the blade, before surreptitiously he was able, upon the pretext of scratching his left foot, to seize a pebble in his turn, and put it in his mouth. Almost at once he felt the comforting moisture gathering in his cheeks. He rolled his tongue around in his mouth until he was sure it was wet enough——

The king's *bokono* approached holding the glowing knife.

'Touch it with thy tongue, son of the *kposi*!' he said.

Nyasanu thrust out his tongue. It made a sizzling sound. Quickly he jerked it back before the heat could dry the protective saliva and blister it. The *bokono* took the knife away.

'Let me see thy tongue, son of Gbenu!' he said.

Nyasanu stuck out his tongue again. The king's diviner examined it carefully.

'The boy speaks truth,' he pronounced. 'His tongue is not

173

blistered.'

'Trickery,' the *khetunga* cried. 'Just because he's the *kposu*'s son, you've arranged it so that he can escape the punishment for his terrible sin! I say unto you present here that he——'
Nyasanu stared at her. 'Has my father refused to lie with her, thus earning her hatred?' he thought. But then he stared at her more closely and his gaze narrowed. No, that was not the reason. He groped for words to form his thought, but it was a long time before they came.

They, who for any cause outraged nature—be that cause a coldness of heart, or the king's command, even a singleminded worship of the gods—are punished for their neglect of life. In the eyes of the *vudun* of earth, the children of Sagbata who grant us the divine gift of fertility, lifelong chastity is itself a deadly sin. Women and men were *meant* to lie together, to delight each other with their bodies, to get children. When they don't, or won't, the price is fearful: they turn into such twisted things as this commander of the *ahosi* is. No, 'tis not my father she loves, but Alogba herself! Don't they see it! Cannot they tell by looking at her that she's more *gaglo* than even Gbochi is?

But they were all watching the howling, dancing, completely hysterical *khetunga*. So intent were they that no one noticed that Kpadunu had moved from where he stood. Then the chief's son felt something touch his hand, and, and, and looking down, saw it was a leather flask; he raised his eyes to his first friend's face.

Kpadunu smiled at him.

'A *gbo*,' he whispered, and moved away, leaving the flask in Nyasanu's hand.

At once, Nyasanu realised his friend's intent. It was a trick they'd often practised during the lessons in sorcery that Kpadunu had given him. So now, holding the flask pressed tight against his side to keep it hid, the young Dahomean called out:

'Heat your knife again, O *bokono*! For I'm going to convince the august lady general beyond all doubt!'

He saw his father staring at him with anguish in his eyes and smiled reassuringly. All fear had gone from him. At this sort of contest, which did not involve his having to hurt or kill anyone else, he was at his best. Just as he had held the bowl of water on his head without spilling a drop while undergoing the really dreadful pain of circumcision, he was fully prepared for the new and dangerous ordeal Kpadunu had silently suggested; for, once his pride was up, he could force his nerves to obey his will to a degree little short of astonishing. . . .

The diviner turned a questioning, troubled gaze to the king; slowly, Gezo nodded.

And now all the spectators in that little clearing where Gezo had enstooled himself before his hosts had quite literally ceased to breathe. The *khetunga*, herself, no longer howled and danced, but with her eyes and mouth both stretched wide, she stood there watching as the *bokono* quickly brought the still hot blade to glowing redness again.

The diviner turned towards Nyasanu. Silently, the young Dahomean put out his hand. Of them all, only Kpadunu knew why Nyasanu did not speak. He couldn't. When one holds half a flask of palm wine in one's mouth, speech becomes an impossibility.

The *bokono* gingerly—and with some difficulty, because it was hard to do so without burning himself and Nyasanu both —gave the tall youth the red-hot blade. Then, so fast that his hand blurred sight, Gbenu's son plunged the knife down his throat. A cloud of steam-like smoke came out of both his nostrils and his mouth; then very slowly, and with an impressive calm, Nyasanu took the knife out of his mouth. The red glow was gone; the knife was dull blue-grey again. Smiling, the youth walked towards where the *khetunga* stood, and held the knife out, hilt first, to her.

'You see, my lady Khetunga,' he said, almost gently, 'in this, as in all other things I have no need to lie. . . .'

When the resulting uproar had quieted, the king called Nyasanu to his side.

'Sit here before me, my son,' he said, 'and explain in clear, untwisted words, this business of your visit to Agwe——'

At once Nyasanu prostrated himself again before the king, as age-old custom demanded, and threw dust upon his head. At this, the *dada* sighed deeply and audibly. It was here, he suspected, that men most grossly mistook the nature of true kings —and of gods, if there were gods; for the intelligent, worship is almost impossible to bear.

'Get up from there, my boy,' he said, 'and sit here before me. Give him your stool, O Gao!'

Sullenly, the great commander did so, and Nyasanu en-

175

stooled himself before the king. At once, an ill, surprised titter of laughter broke out among the ranks. In wartime, as Kpadunu had already pointed out to Nyasanu, for reason of policy, a desire to free the throne of moral responsibility in so many deaths, and the shrewd strategy of concealing the monarch's identity so far as it was possible from enemy spies, in order that their foe be given no chance to end the war at one bold stroke by taking him alive, the *dada* sat upon a lower stool than those of his officers. And now, when Nyasanu's immense height was added to that fact, the result was more than a little ridiculous: Gezo's head was on a line with the youth's navel.

At the sound of the soldiers' laughter, Nyasanu jumped to his feet and kicked the *gao's* stool aside. Then he squatted on his own heels before the king. Even like that he stared the monarch full in the eyes.

Gezo smiled.

'I can see your father, my *kposu*, has brought you up strictly,' he said, 'for you don't even have to be reminded to be polite, do you, my son? And now, tell me: what made you do something so foolish as to enter the city of our enemies alone?'

'Because, O father of us all,' Nyasanu said, 'my sister, the archeress Alogba, told me how badly off they were. You see, sire, it never occurred to me that people were going to think such ugly things of us because we talked to each other occasionally. I knew that as an *ahosi*, she was one of your wives, Great Father; but in Alladah, brothers talk to their married sisters and nobody thinks anything of it. I thought the command against having anything to do with the *ahosi* didn't apply to their blood kindred, but only to men who might *want* to do something bad with them. So, if I've sinned, I ask only that you remember I did so through ignorance and grant me what mercy you can by making my punishment light. . . .'

'For that, you have my pardon, freely given,' Gezo said. 'Go on, my son. . . .'

'Only,' Nyasanu continued, couching his speech in the most courtly and eloquent terms of the Fau language, which, since Fau ise truly a tongue designed for orators, was courtly and eloquent indeed, 'she did not know that the rod of Sagbata had struck them, attributing their weakness, their lassitude, to hunger only. So I, and two friends of mine—my first friend and my third——'

176

'And your second?' the king interrupted at once. 'Why not he as well?'

'Because he is already in your service, O father of us all,' Nyasanu said. 'Some castings of his were brought to your attention, and, seeing his great skill, you had him called to Dahomey to serve you as royal silversmith. Amosu is his name. . . .'

'And well have I marked it, for truly his skill is great,' the king said. 'Say on, my son.'

'The three of us went up to Agwe,' Nyasanu said, concealing the fact out of pure Dahomean instinct that Alogba had spent many hours in the company of two men who were not only not her brothers, but friends of her childhood, and even, in the case of one of them, her lover, guilty of the crime that the *khetunga* had accused Nyasanu of. 'We thought, O great King, that we might win you praise, and spare your army many deaths by taking the city alone. . . .'

'Alone?' Gezo said. 'Just the three of you?'

'Just the two of us, father of us all,' Nyasanu said, 'since my third friend, the archer Taugbadji, is an invalid, having lost the use of his right arm in the first battle, on which occasion he took singlehandedly no less than six heads.'

'For which he'll be rewarded in due time,' the king said. 'But since he was crippled, why did you take him with you?'

'To bear the extra guns, O King,' Nyasanu said. 'So that by rapid fire, my first friend eldest, Kpadunu, and I might trick the Maxi into thinking us an army. The ruse worked, as you can see, father of the nation, for in each of these baskets there is a Maxi's head. . . .'

'Make him show them!' the *khetunga* said. 'I do not trust this black giraffe!'

'Later, my lady Khetunga,' the king said tiredly. 'But now——'

'The great she-general,' Nyasanu said then quietly, 'can, if my lord, the father of all who dwell in the Belly of Da, permits, take out the heads herself. One by one, and count them——'

'I'll do it!' the *khetunga* said. 'For it is my duty to protect thee, my lord husband, from trickery!'

'Do so, then,' the king said, but at once Nyasanu lifted his hand.

'What my lady forgets,' he said smoothly, 'is that though she, like us all, is but a thing of the Leopard, nevertheless she is one of the commanders of our father's female hosts. Therefore, out of respect for her rank, I'd like to remind her that the Maxi have Sagbata's scourge among them. And though, out of loyalty to your royal person, she has foresworn feminine vanity, I hold it unkind of me to expose her skin to the ravages of the pox....'

The *khetunga* reeled away from the first basket, whose lid she had been tugging at, as though Legba had struck her blind. She whirled then, snarling:

'How then are we to know it's not a trick?'

'Because I will open them,' Nyasanu said quietly. And unwinding the cloth he had bound about his upper left arm, showed them the great ugly cut, already yellow with pus, that scarred his smooth black flesh. 'Since it is likely that all three of my souls stand trembling at the brink of the final river,' he went on in the same quiet, utterly calm tone of voice, 'for me the risk is as nothing....'

The king leaned forward, his strangely light-coloured face troubled.

'You mean to say——' he began.

'That the wound is infected with the scourge of Sagbata?' Nyasanu said. 'Yes, sire. For when my sister, Alogba, entered the city to spy out the way for us, she found them dipping the points of the arrows in the sores of their dead chief. And though she tried to cleanse this wound—made by one of those self-same arrows—for me, it is evident from the looks of it that she failed. So since I have already become a ghost, allow me at least to show you your enemies' heads, Great Father——'

'Do so then,' the *dada* said, but his voice was very soft and sad.

Nyasanu took the heads out of the baskets, trying not to shudder as he did so. There were twelve of them. He piled them up in a neat, triangular heap, the way the Furtoo did their cannon balls. The king sat there staring at him, his light-brown face working with emotion.

'*Vudun* of Earth!' he cried out suddenly. 'Gods of fertility! Why didn't you grant me such a son as this, instead of the idle, lecherous jackals I have sired?'

'But they did, Great Father,' Gbenu said in his great voice, though Nyasanu, who knew how his sire loved him, could hear

178

the grief moving through it like a rusty blade, 'since you are father of us all, my son is likewise yours. Is he not a thing of the Leopard, like all who dwell in the Belly of Da?'

'He isn't a thing of anybody, but a man,' Gezo said simply. 'Though now he belongs to Ku, much do I fear. Call me my *azaundato*, someone!'

The king's sorcerer came and examined Nyasanu's wound by touching the flesh all around it with a wand more than a rod long. After he'd finished that, he threw the wand into the camp fire.

'I don't think he'll die, sire,' he said. 'The flesh about the wound is firm and sound. I'd suggest that you have your work troops build him a hut some distance from the camp and provide it with enough food to last five days. If, in that time, the scourge hasn't broken out all over him, he'll get well. And once he has the scourge it will never touch him again. This wound could prove to be the kind of *gbo* the Furtoo in Whydah use. They give themselves a little of the scourge to prevent getting a fatal dose of it. But for your own safety, and of those of your soldiers who haven't already had Sagbata's skin grains break out all over them, the boy, hero or not, must be banished from the camp. . . .'

'Very well,' Gezo sighed. 'I do so order it. . . .'

Six days later, Nyasanu stood once more before his king. The wound in his left arm had almost healed, for though it showed raw and red, it was entirely free of pus; and all the rest of his remarkably long, lean and fine body glistened with ebony health.

'So now, son of Gbenu,' the king said, 'what shall I do with you? You've played the hero and the man: you've taken many heads. For that I should reward you. But, on the other hand, you've been the bearer of bad news. Because of the information you have brought, I have to go back to Dahomey without slaves whose sale would fill my treasury, which, Legba witness, is depleted after two unprofitable campaigns in a row. Generally speaking, he who brings ill tidings to the *dada* of Dahomey loses his head. Tell me, my son, which I do *first*, cut off your head or reward you?'

Nyasanu considered that, though less King Gezo's words than the tone of voice in which he'd said them. It was light, mocking; but, all the same, the young Dahomean thought he

179

detected a note of gruff fondness in it. He was already aware of the effect he generally had upon older men, which varied according to their natures: those who had been brave warriors in their youth looked upon him with a sort of paternal pride, as a reminder, a reflection of what they, themselves, had been, while those who'd been weaklings and cowards tended to resent him. . . . And Gezo, as all the world knew, had been exceedingly brave. Therefore, Nyasanu decided to take a chance upon the slight evidence of royal favour.

'Neither, O father of us all,' he said, 'for taking the heads of your enemies is no more than my duty and deserves no reward. On the other hand, since your justice is sung at every crossroad in Da's Belly, I throw myself upon your mercy; surely, sire, you will not separate this poor foolish head from this aching neck because I warned you that the Maxi had Sagbata's scourge among them, in time to prevent half your hosts from catching it?'

The king threw back his head and laughed aloud.

'A true diplomat and a courtier, this son of yours, Gbenu!' he said. 'Well have you taught him your subtlety and your wiles. But now, young man with wisdom far beyond your years, tell me this: what suggestion have you that I might escape the problem of a long and hard campaign which brings no profit— and an empty treasury to boot?'

Nyasanu thought quickly. That there really wasn't any answer to the king's question was evident at once; but it was equally evident that he'd better invent some kind of an answer quickly or he'd lose whatever degree of royal favour he had gained.

'Sire,' he said, 'the sorcerers say that a man who has had the sickness of Sagbata and didn't die of it is very unlikely to catch it again——'

'True,' the King said. 'Go on, my son.'

'So let me take such men as can be found among your hosts who have pockmarked faces and enter Agwe. Surely some of the Maxi survived the plague, and those that have——'

'Will be worthless as far as selling them is concerned,' Gezo said sadly. 'The Furtoo won't buy racks of bones with the scars of the pox still pink and fresh upon their skins. But, anyhow, do it, son of Gbenu. Perhaps we can put a few of them to work on my plantations and sweat some profit out of their miserable hides that way. Go. Gather up your troop of scoundrels whom even Ku didn't want. Then we'll see—we'll see——'

'I hear and obey, father of us all,' Nyasanu said, and prostrated himself once more before the King.

That it was no good, useless, dangerous, a near disaster, became clear even before Nyasanu and his little band entered Agwe. For from two hours' marching, or rather climbing, distance from the Maxi city, they could see that all the sky above it was black with kites and vultures. Half an hour's climb from the city gates, the wind, sweeping down from the peaks of the mountains, brought that smell with it. Within three minutes every man in the company had vomited up his morning's rations. Within ten, some of the younger, less experienced men had begun to faint; and even the faces of grizzled old warriors had gone as grey as death itself.

But Nyasanu kept them at it, roaring at them lion-mouthed, threatening to separate their cowardly heads from their spineless necks if they failed to follow him, obey the king's command.

What they saw, smelt, experienced once inside the capital of the Maxi could not, Nyasanu was sure, be told in any language spoken of man. Certainly his own native Fau had no words to describe it.

A long black hide, shrunk so tightly over a skeleton that every bone showed through it, dragged itself over the ground, leaving a smear of blood and pus and rotting flesh behind it as it went.

A thing that had been a woman once— perhaps even a pretty woman, though that was now impossible to tell—lay upon the hard earth with a vulture sitting on her belly; and two kites perched upon her forehead beaking out her eyes. Then Nyasanu saw that incredibly enough she was still alive, and dashed towards her to drive away her feathered tormentors. But the carrion birds stared at him with solemn insolence and would not move. He smashed one of the kites to a bloody pulp with his gun butt and the other rose slowly, heavily, flapping towards a nearby tree. And, as it went, he saw the woman's eyeball staring at him from its beak, trailing a long nerve cord behind it like a red wet string. . . .

He killed the woman then, with one sharp blow of his gun butt; whereupon the vulture cocked a baleful eye at him and proceeded to thrust his great beak into her mouth and tear out

181

her tongue by the roots.

Nyasanu reeled away from there, moving through air gone thick with a stench beyond any man's endurance, picking his way past corpses so covered with vultures, crows, and kites that they seemed to be mounds of moving feathers, stumbling over beaked and scattered skeletons to which here and there a black-red strand of sun-baked human flesh still clung.

It was no good. It was finally and completely no good. The cruel gods of the land, unkinder to her children than any other on the globe of the earth, had had their fill. He would have to go back to Dada Gezo without even one captive slave and take the consequences of his failure. For in Agwe, by that time, there were only the dying and the dead.

'Come,' he said then to his pockmarked band, 'let us go home. This place belongs to Ku himself. There is nothing else we can do here. . . .'

All the way back down to the Dahomean camp, Nyasanu tried to think of how he could appease the *dada*'s wrath, which, with this new failure added to the rest, was sure to be great.

'It's not my fault,' he thought worriedly, 'but what difference will that make to the king? I've failed him again. O Legba, lord of clever tricksters, help me! Send me some ruse, some wile to turn aside the *dada*'s anger so he won't be too tempted to separate my head from my neck. Oh Fa, who is fate! O Rainbow Snake who holds up the world, tell me how——'

And it was then that he saw the Auyo horsemen. There were, without exaggeration, more than a thousand of them. Perhaps there were as many as two thousand; but they rode so fast it was impossible to count them. And what those beturbaned black centaurs were doing to Gezo's hosts was very simple, very finally and completely simple: the black Mohammedan tribesmen, come down from the desert's edge, were making a slaughter. No, a massacre.

Even as he watched, the bulk of the Dahomean army whirled and began to run away in every direction. Which was folly. All they did by flight was to provide their hereditary enemies, the Auyo, with target practice. The black horsemen began to make lance charges, spitting as many as three Dahomeans at a time upon a single thrust of their long-bladed spears. Or they'd ride alongside a fleeing Dahomean and behead him with one slashing stroke of their curved scimitars, laughing uproariously at the fact that the running bodies continued to take from three to four additional steps before death finally convinced them they no longer had heads.

The air was grey with smoke. Even from where they were, Nyasanu and his little band could hear the coughing bark of the long, slim, highly ornamental Arabian muskets that the Auyo bore; and above even that the screams.

'Come,' Nyasanu said to his troop, 'we have to save the *dada*——'

'No!' one of the younger men cried. 'Let them kill him, for all I care! Those are Auyo, my lord! Mounted on those horses of theirs that breathe fire! Anybody can go down there who wants to, but I'm staying here! I'm too young to die! I——'

'I gave you an order,' Nyasanu said.

'And I refuse it!' the young soldier said, 'for I——'

Slowly, Nyasanu drew his *assegai* out of its sheath. With one smooth motion he brought the point of that Ashanti sword up until it was touching the soldier's throat just below his adam's apple.

'My orders are to be obeyed,' he said quietly, 'for, although you hear them from my mouth, they come from the king. So, before I repeat this order to you once more, I give you a choice: would you rather die as a coward at my hands or like a man facing the Auyo? Wait. Before you speak, remember this: you *might* come out of the battle down there alive; but you can't defy my orders and live. I won't let you.'

The young soldier hung there, his face gone grey with fear. But he didn't say anything. He kept his mouth clamped shut so long that Nyasanu could feel the cold green sickness rising in his own throat.

'Don't make me kill you,' he prayed silently. 'I hate it above all things, but now I'd have to. Because if I don't I'd lose control of my troops. So it's your life against—my father's. Against Kpad's. Against Badji's. Even against Alogba's. For this I'd do it, friend. It would melt my guts inside my belly, but——'

'Kill him!' a grizzled old veteran said.

'No,' Nyasanu said. 'I must give him another chance.' Then looking the frightened young soldier straight in the face, he said, without raising his voice, simply almost gently, 'I order you to join your comrades. Do you obey?'

Beyond speech, the young soldier nodded. Nyasanu took the

point of the *assegai* from his throat. The young soldier fell into line and all the company went down the long ravine behind their commander.

What gave them time were the Ashanti of the royal hunters, the *ganu'n lan*, whom not even such chroniclers as were the sons of men who'd fallen in the battles against that nation, and therefore hated them, ever dared accuse of having run from a fight. Those tall and magnificent warriors from Kumassi formed a hollow square around the king and his guard of female soldiers and sold their own lives to the last man at a terrible price.

But even so, they were all dead, lance spitted, shot torn, beheaded, before Nyasanu and his twenty pockmarked heroes got there. And, by one of those mocking ironies that Fa and Legba love, it was the fact that Gezo's guard were all women that gave Gbenu's young lion of a son the time he needed to do what had to be done.

The *ahosi*, of course, fight like wounded she-gorillas; but it was not their valour but their femininity that opened an instant's wedge between death on the one hand and disaster on the other, bought at the last that one priceless second that made whatever difference there was by then left to be made. For, even as Nyasanu watched, an Auyo horseman, his white teeth gleaming in his inky face, his snowy turban making his look even blacker than he already was, dashed in close, and leaning from the saddle, encircled a buxom she-soldier with one long arm. He lifted his clawing, spitting, shrieking prey from the ground and dashed back to his own company. At once four spears went whistling through the air to stand and quiver in the earth, marking off an almost perfect square. A flock of laughing, howling dancing Auyo, resembling in their turbans and burnooses some kind of great rapacious birds of prey, cut and ripped the *ahosi*'s uniform off her, then hurled her, naked, to the ground, staking her out, her arms and legs spread wide, her wrists and ankles bound with rawhide thongs to the four spears.

Then an Auyo horseman galloped towards the prone *ahosi* at breakneck speed, as if to trample her. But, at the last moment, he pulled up his mount and flew from the saddle like a great black and white bird, to land with perfect aim between the *ahosi*'s open thighs. Nyasanu heard her scream, terribly. There was a brief flurry of motion, a flopping about of a

184

loosened white burnoose upon black twisting flesh; then the Auyo got up, grinning broadly, and adjusted his baggy trousers. That done, he waved the next horseman, who, at his signal, came pounding towards the moaning, writhing girl.

'It,' Nyasanu thought bleakly, 'is going to take a good, long time for all of them to have their sport of her.... Time I can use, to get into position. Position to do what? To take whatever chance that comes our way, I suppose. I wonder why—*that* angers me so little? I guess it's because the *ahosi*'s training in—in obscene cruelty takes all female softness from them, making it hard to consider them real women, in the sense our mothers, our sisters, and our wives are. Only that one's a woman all right. Listen to her. Oh Legba, Lord of Lechery, hear her. Poor thing, poor lust-butchered thing!'

For the girl was screaming now. Her voice tore the day apart. But that didn't stop the Auyo horsemen. By then, nothing could.

'Come on,' Nyasanu whispered to his little troop, and led them, crawling on their bellies, through the brush, around to the far side of the *ahosi*'s defensive square. By the time they got there, the girl had stopped screaming. Nyasanu looked questioningly at the old veteran at his side.

'She's dead,' the old man said. 'They play too rough, those Auyo. So now they'll take another one....'

The old soldier was right. A cloud of horsemen bore down on the *ahosi* left flank, and though the she-soldiers fought so hard that the Auyo had to kill twelve of them to do it, the black horsemen took another three girls alive.

Nyasanu beckoned his troop forward. And then he saw a thing that caused him to lift his hand in a signal to his men, stopping them where they were.

The Auyo were not trying to capture the *dada*. They weren't because, very clearly Nyasanu saw, they thought they already had him. A group of their guards, dismounted, were laughing and jabbering away around the imposing figure of the *gao*. And what was more, they had taken the *meu* alive too. And——

And the *kposu*. Gbenu, his own father.

Nyasanu's breath turned to sand in his lungs at that sight. Gbenu sat there on a low stool, cradling his right arm against his body. It had been bandaged with the kind of white cloth the Auyo made their turbans out of, and great red splotches showed in four separate and distinct places through the ban-

dage. Seeing that, Nyasanu relaxed very slowly. Hope came
back to him. The Auyo were anything but tender with their
prisoners. The fact that they had dressed Gbenu's wounds
meant that they had no intention of killing him or any other of
their important captives. Alive, the *gao*, the *meu*, the *kposu*
were worth tons of cowries, hundreds of lissome Dahomean
maidens, thousands of slaves—anything, in fact, that the conquering Auyo wanted to demand.

He lay there watching the Auyo guards. It was absolutely
certain from their attitudes, their gestures, that they believed
the beautifully uniformed *gao* to be the king of Dahomey.
That this one last miserably clad beggar who still held out
against them had a corps of she-warriors to defend him, they
attributed to his being, probably, an official of special, even
priestly rank, in one of the many women's cults they knew the
Dahomeans had among them. All the other great captives—
'the prisoners with names' in the Dahomean Ffon phrase—had
likewise had their personal guards whom they, the Auyo
cavalry, had already slain, and with ludicrous ease at that. The
curious fact that this final defiant, valiant war chieftain had a
female guard struck them as odd, or funny, or both; but nothing more.

Then, raising his eyes, Nyasanu saw *why* the Auyo believed
the Dahomean *gao*, or prime minister, to be the king. For that
tall horseman riding there, clad in a snowy turban with an
ostrich plume rising above it, ropes of silver and gold and pearl
beads about his neck, jewellery flaming from every fold of his
burnoose, his weapons all having hilts and guards of gold, their
silver scabbards encrusted with red gems and blue and green,
half a score of bracelets encircling his arms, rings on all his
fingers including his thumbs, sandals, equally bejewelled, upon
his feet, his mount a snowy Arabian mare, her harness as
richly ornamented as her master's dress—surely, surely this
magnificent black rider was the Auyo's king!

A paean of exultation sang and laughed under Nyasanu's
breath. He had them! By their very pride, he had them! By
their vanity, their love of show, their lack of the Dahomean's
monumental guile.

He beckoned his pockmarked warriors to close ranks about
him, whispered his orders:

'You, M'bala, accompany me. And you, too, Nyakadja.
Nwesu, I leave you in command. First we move into five or six

186

rods of that one there, who is their king. Wait! No one is to
shoot *him*, do you hear? But those four guards of his must die
at once, at the same time, when I raise my hand like this,
understand?'

They nodded silently. But the young soldiers who had
played the coward before whispered fretfully:

'But if we killed their king, my lord, it seems to me they'd
lose heart and——'

'Shut up!' the old veteran Nwesu snarled. 'Kill him and they
butcher us like sheep. Take him alive, and what won't they
give for his freedom and his life? So keep your flap-lipped jaw
shut, oh fool and son of ninety generations of fools! Haven't
you yet seen that our young leader is the *kposu's* son in guile
as well as in valour?'

Nyasanu and his two companions, M'bala and Nyakadja,
moved through the brush on their bellies, as silent as serpents,
and as intent. When they were no more than five rods from the
magnificent horseman, Nyasanu studied the Auyo leader carefully. And the longer he studied this prancing peacock of a
rider, the surer his dismal conviction became that this one
could not possibly be the Auyo ruler. He was too young, far
too young. His unlined, glistening black face proclaimed that
he had not reached the third decade of his life. Twenty-two or
three, Nyasanu guessed, no more....

Not the king then. But—his son? That well could be! And
in any event, surely a personage with name. A most weighty
name, to judge by the looks of him. So now to toss our lives
into the balance to prove once and for all if that name hath
weight enough to unsettle Fa. To change Fate. To fall upon
Aido Hwedo's belly hard enough to make him take his tail of
his mouth and up-end the world....

With one stark jerk his black hand flew upward. Behind him
eighteen Danish muskets spoke, but with a single voice. The
four outriders accompanying the bejewelled horsemen reeled
from their saddles, dead before they struck the ground.

At once Nyasanu was up and off like a great black panther
bounding over ground; but out of one corner of his eye he saw
an Auyo horseman, levelled spear at rest, racing to cut him
off; and though the rider was some distance further away from
the young Dahomean's intended victim than Nyasanu was
himself, the fact that he was mounted more than made up the
difference. It was bitterly clear that the Auyo rider was going

187

to get there first.

And then, as, despairingly, Nyasanu turned to face his new foe, this embodiment of ill fortune, back luck, of all the evil mischief at Legba's command, a lead black figure rose up like a bird from the thick undergrowth, and fired the one shot he had time for at the rider thundering down upon him and Gbenu's son. Nyasanu saw the rider reel in the saddle; saw a great red flower bloom almost instantly upon his white burnoose at belly level, but in spite of the flooding of what was clearly a mortal wound the Auyo horseman came on, the hoofbeats of his mount drumming time into a total dichotomy—Ku at the Zeli; ghosts dancing upside down—so that there was no clarity any more; the world fragmenting into all the simultaneously contradictory images of confusion:

In his ear a voice familiar, known, loved, grating, 'Go on Nya! Take their king! I'll——'

And the dying horseman upon them, and the face of the one who had said that, who had shot the horseman, jarring into focus, exploding through time's, breath's, life's fractioning, splintering, halting, into recognition, becoming finally and terribly Kpadunu's face, changing, in that dead, stopped, no-time hiatus carved out of now into a mobile sculpturing of unbearable anguish, as the young sorcerer, lifting his useless musket to club the horseman from the saddle, took three feet of razor-edged spear point through his middle and died.

There was no time. Not even for Nyasanu to howl his grief against deaf heaven, to curse the invisible, absent, non-existent gods. No. What there was he felt as a stone in his guts, the breath-murdering, mind-crushing, awful weight of necessity: with one big fine splendid part of his life gone, lance spitted, dead, he still must do what had to be done to save his father, Taugbadji, Alogba—and the king.

Must—and did. He raced through the shower of Auyo spears, through the wall-solid whine, and splat of a thousand musket balls, seeing and not seeing—his conscious mind reflecting, refusing sight—M'bala and Nyakadja as they died beside him; M'bala with his two hands clawing at the flung lance now embedded in his throat, and Nyakadja dancing, hopping, jerking under the impact of the hundred musket balls that tore him, lifting huge slabs of bone out of his skull, splashing his brains in thick grey, red-pink globs onto Nyasanu's chest and neck and shoulders and even into his face, turning the dying

188

man's thickset black body into a fountain that sprayed red through a hundred jets long before Ku unlocked his limbs and let him fall, all of it drawn out, prolonged by utter horror's deliberate slowing of the stuff of time, through which Nyasanu's straining lungs, his pumping legs caught in the quagmire of that horror moved him already soundlessly silkensmoothly until he reached the gorgeously clad horseman.

Reached him, and soared, rejecting as irrelevant the whole ponderous downpull of the world, denying by sheer force of will gravity's existence, rising through the flame-stabbed white smoke puff of the horseman's pistol—this, too, soundless and unheard so that the ball's whistle, keening past his ear, was gone from now and a part of no time or memory as he settled to rest behind the horseman on the white mare and thrust the point of his *assegai* into the magnificent one's throat hard enough to draw blood and said, sighed, whispered:

'Their arms. Tell them to throw them down.'

And it was done. Nyasanu, man among men, Gbenu's young lion of a son, had won the war. Almost alone he had won it. Now all he had to do was to count the cost:

Kpadunu, lying there upon the hard-packed earth, his two hands cut to the bone, still clasped around the Auyo spearhead that had found his life, facing the foe with whom he had exchanged the mutual gift of death; the Auyo horseman's hands, too, locked in final, rigid rage about the lance shaft, his eyes and Kpadunu's both wide open, but, while the horseman's face was contorted with murderous fury, Kpad's was peaceful now, even smiling——

And he, Nyasanu, leaving that and going over to where Gbenu his father sat, his broad face grey with pain, his right arm dangling, broken in four places by as many musket balls, so that it was apparent at once the arm would have to come off at the shoulder if there were to be the slightest hope of saving his life, knelt there before that brave warrior, wily chieftain, gallant gentleman that Gbenu was and kissed his father's dusty, sweaty, bloodstained feet in an agony of grief, of tenderness of loss, until Gbenu caught him by the hair with his one good, left, hand and raised him up and wept aloud and kissed his face saying:

'My son, my son, in whom I am blessed! And for whom all the gods be praised!'

And even after that, going away from there and moving

down the rows of spread-eagled female carrion, staked out, x-shaped, each one with wrists and ankles lashed to four spears, staring into the faces twisted out of humanity into masks of unbelievable anguish, into mouths opened wide, seeming to scream still, at the shimmering bottle-green masses of flies, swarming the wound they were born with and had finally died of, until he came to where Alogba lay staked out like a sacrificial animal among the rest, equally lust-butchered, lying in a pool of her own blood, the flies at her, her sightless eyes accusing the eternally silent sky——

While poor Taugbadji sat there beside her not even crying, motionless, intent, until he looked up and saw Nyasanu's tall form bisecting the dying sunlight, and whispered:

'Your *assegai*, Nya. Please.'

And Nyasanu standing there thinking, not thinking, not feeling numb, saying, not saying, hearing unspoken the words, an interior whisper in his own blood:

'It is his right——'

And drawing the blade and handing it hilt first to Taugbadji and turning, moving away, not wanting to see it, having at least that much feeling left——

And it was then that the Half Heads, the royal messengers, who had been searching for him all over that manmade map of desolation, that slaughterhouse, that realistic imitation of hell, found him, and bowing low and reverently before him said:

'Come, young lord. We must take you to the king.'

FOURTEEN

'By what you've done,' Gezo, *dada* of Dahomey said, to Nyasanu, his tone of light and playful mockery betraying to those who knew him best how greatly moved he was, 'by this wild foolish, childish act of risking your own skin and the lives of your troops in order to take alive Subetzy, crown prince of the Auyo, heir to their saddle-throne, you have saved us, son of Gbenu! Which changes things a little, doesn't it? When utter idiocy succeeds, we call it heroism—and rightly, I suppose. But what is beyond supposition is the evident fact that Fa watches

190

over fools. For, having seen you run, without getting a scratch, through musket fire so thick it cut down even the savannah's grass like a mower's scythe, I can have no doubt but that Fata and Legba, and the Sky Gods love you. Or that Ku doesn't want you yet.

'And, though it pains me to admit it, today—cub of my bravest and best old lion—you've taught me something new: that even fools have their value. Greater, at a time like this, than that of all the wise men, prudent counsellors in my kingdom, piled one atop another to make grease for a funeral pyre! For truly must I marvel as I look upon the results of folly. The warriors of an all but victorious army compelled to throw down their arms and surrender themselves as captives to my officers to save the tender skin of a worthless pretty boy who happens to be a prince! Hundreds of battle-tested veterans converted into merchandise, into valuable slaves I can sell to those ugly, skinless people for gold, gunpowder, flint, balls, silk, rum! And the ransom I'll sweat out of that murderous old scoundrel, Ibrahim T'wala's hide, before I'll condescend to give him back his gaudy peacock of a son, will make up for all my losses, in the last campaign and in this!

'So now, what do I do with you, splendid young idiot? What reward is enough for your folly, madman? Or for your valour, hero? Legba eat my brains if I know! Therefore I'll have to order you to come back to Dahomey with me, there to live in the apartments of my sons, the Leopard princes at the Royal Palace, until I take counsel with the elders as to what under the Sky God's heaven recompense is great enough for this!'

'Make him ruler over a province!' the *meu* cried out.

'Elevate him to princely rank!' the *gao* shouted.

'Wed him to one of your daughters, sire!' the *khetunga* shrilled.

If he could have, if it had still been possible for him to, Nyasanu would have smiled then. In fact, his wide, heavy-lipped mouth twisted into a hurt, sick, painful-to-see grimace that was as close to a smile as the utter horror in him would let him get. For, as usual, human nature was being predictably human, which was to say, base. The *gao* and the *meu* had scarcely been aware of his existence before this one last battle; and the *khetunga*, out of jealousy, surely, over poor slaughtered Alogba, had actively hated him. But now they were vying with one another to do him honour, seeking thus to gain some hold

191

upon, some influence over, one now clearly favoured by the king.

'Reward?' he thought, and the word went screaming through his lungs in a burst of wild and bitter laughter: 'That you give me Kpaduna back again. And poor Badji. And Alogba. That you decree a miracle that will save my father's life, so that shattered arm of his will not rot him into a stinking corpse as such wounds usually do. Or that he won't bleed to death, if your surgeons decide to take it off. Can you do all that, little, vain, pompous, posturing man with skin the colour of the excreta of a sick child, who call yourself a king?'

But he did not say his thoughts. For to voice aloud such disrespect for the royal personage was to die bloodily and badly in the pit at the hands of the king's executioner, if not at once, then surely at the next 'Customs' honouring the Leopard's ancestors. 'And though,' Nyasanu added sadly in his mind, 'my days have lost all sweetness and all savour, yet must I live them out—for Nyaunu wi's sake, for the sake of our children; and to do what honour to my father's declining years —if Fa and Legba grant him any!—that I can, or to his cult as my ancestor if he dies. As he most likely will. Men have got over one gunshot wound; but four are far too many!'

He raised his eyes from where he knelt, and gazed upon the king.

'None of these, O father of us all,' he said quietly. 'What I have done is but one of the many duties that his "things" owe the Leopard. And who among all those present is more than that? But if my small efforts have found any favour in your sight, all I ask of you, O sire of all who dwell in the Belly of Da, is your permission to return to Alladah. My father, your *kposu,* is badly hurt—four terrible wounds got in your service, sire!—and I must watch over him until he's well again. That is, if he ever is. That's one thing——'

'And another?' the *dada* said. Nyasanu could hear a slight edge of annoyance or of disappointment in his voice. Very slight, but there. The kings of Dahomey were totally unaccustomed to being gainsaid.

'The time is near at hand—or perhaps it has even come, Great Father—for my housewife eldest to give birth to my first child. The birth of a man's eldest son is of no importance, I know—except to that man, himself. But to him, it is great. Mighty as the Leopard is, truly all-powerful, yet he retains

192

humanity, I think. I cannot bring myself to believe that our *dada*—the very emblem of fatherhood!—has forgotten how he felt when he held the first Leopard princeling in his arms. So, truly, if you'd reward me, sire: to grant me leave to know that joy and to do a son's simple duty towards my own father, to me would be compensation enough and to spare. . . .'

'No,' Gezo said shortly, 'it is far too little, son of the *kposu*! However, I grant you your request, on the condition that you present yourself before me at Abomey as soon as the birth of your child and my good *kposu*'s health permits. And, on that occasion, know all men present here, the world will see how great a thing is the gratitude of a king!'

Nyasanu trotted beside the great hammock in which his father lay. Without breaking his stride, he turned his head so that he could see into Gbenu's face. It was grey as ashes from a burnt-out fire. And the chief's arm was enormously swollen. The white bandages bit into it. Above and below and between them the flesh puffed, no longer black, but purple. A dark and ominous purple. The colour of the poisonous t'eekli berries the *azaundatoe,* the sorcerers, used to kill people. It seemed to Nyasanu that the wounds were beginning to stink. When that happened all hope was gone. For when Ku blew his fetid breath upon broken flesh, it rotted and you died.

He leaned closer, still keeping up his hopping, skipping step. Then he almost retched, so strong was the odour from his father's ball-shattered arm. Fear caught him by the throat and almost strangled him. He couldn't imagine a world without either Kpadunu or his father in it. Such a place would be—a desolation, a wasteland, empty, barren, poor, with no wisdom in it, no help, no comfort, and no joy.

He forced air through his constricted throat and screamed at the hammock bearers:

'Faster! Faster, or by Ku, I'll have your heads!'

Gbenu opened his eyes.

'No, my son,' he said, his great bass voice an echo, a reverberation beneath the surface of sound, 'the jogging hurts enough as it is. And . . .'

Nyasanu bent over him, straining to catch his words.

'I'd not have you—rule—by force or threats,' Gbenu whispered, 'since you are to succeed me—become *toxausu*—you——'

'No!' Nyasanu wept, 'no by Gu, who is our *vudun*, father! I renounce chieftainship! What comes to me by your—your...'

'By my death,' Gbenu said calmly, 'you don't want——'

'I don't want it!' Nyasanu said. 'I want nothing by such a curse! Hear me my father, I——'

'Stop the bearers, son,' Gbenu said.

Nyasanu lifted his hand. The hammock bearers stopped, gratefully. They were sweating rivers. Gbenu was a huge and heavy man.

'Bring the umbrella closer,' Nyasanu said to the royal umbrella bearer. For the *dada* had sent no less a personage than his own personal attendant to provide the wounded *kposu* with the comfort granted only to the highborn and the great, the protection of their faces from the murderous African sun. And the royal umbrella bearer's presence was only one of the two ways that Gezo publicly proclaimed that this house enjoyed his special favours; the other was the fact that both the hammock and the umbrella displayed in appliqué work royal standards that were, in sober fact, the king's.

'My son,' Gbenu said, and now his voice, though weak, was clear, 'I am going to die——'

'No!' Nyasanu all but screamed.

'Don't behave like a hysterical woman,' Gbenu said calmly. 'All men die. Some sooner, some later. What difference does it make, as long as one can do it well? So hear me, Nya. I have a duty towards our clan, our city, our people. It is my obligation to see that they're well governed, their affairs well managed, their happiness—as far as it lies in any man's power to do so—insured. You're my son. My only son. Though I have sired many. For among the yelping of jackals, it is easy to distinguish the voice of the lion——'

'Father,' Nyasanu wept, 'don't tire yourself! Don't waste the breath you need to tell me——'

'What you need to know. It is no waste, my son. Fa shares us out our measure of breath at the hour of our birth, and mine is all but used up, now. So——'

'Father, please!' Nyasanu said.

'So let me use the last of it as I will, cub lion! You will rule Alladah, not because I love you above all my other sons—I do, of course, but that's neither here nor there, now—but because by temperament, by inclination, by force of character, you are by far the best fitted to rule. Your only weakness is that you really are not very smart; not in the sense your friend Kpa-dunu is. But with him there to counsel you——'

'Father!' Nyasanu cried. 'He—he can't! He's—he's dead! He took an Auyo lance through the belly in order to save my life and——'

'So?' Gbenu whispered. 'A pity. A great pity. A fine boy. Too bad. So now you must find another counsellor—or learn wisdom, yourself. And here's a tiny store of it I'd offer you: all government must have the assent of those governed. The—the Leopard gains that assent through force—and fear—I know! I know! The umbrella bearer will report my words to the *dada*—but I will be beyond even the Leopard's reach by then, and when he hears them, I only hope he is wise enough to take some profit from the babble of a dying fool. Son, gain your people's love! That is the only way to rule them well and wisely. Treat all men as brothers—so love and judge that you can walk unguarded through the blackest night and fear no dagger lifted against your back—deal justly and——'

'Father,' Nyasanu moaned, 'I——'

'Hear me, my son. A harsh ruler is more a prisoner than the basest slave. Can the Leopard walk alone in the forest and listen to the voice of the otutu crying silver against the dawn? Can he stride the streets even of his own Dahomey and jest with passers-by? Can he enter a shop to buy a trinket for one of his wives, a toy for his youngest son? By Ku, Nya! What freedom hath a man who, when he goes to the latrine to re-lieve himself must be guarded by women, even as he squats? No, son of mine—deal justly, rule not by threats, but by love, by love——'

'As you have ruled, Father,' Nyasanu whispered.

'In so far as I was able,' Gbenu sighed. 'I have failed in the attempt many times, and so, my son, will you. But you must try again and again. Forgive those who will envy you all the things you have: your status, your commanding presence, your great beauty, your manhood, and your valour. . . . Deal even-handedly with your wives and show no son greater fav-our than his brothers. But select the best of them to follow you, as I have selected you to succeed me. The eldest, of course, if he is fit; but fitness before age, as I have done! So now——'

'Now?' Nyasanu got out, over the choking mountain of his grief, the steam scald of his tears.

'Tell the bearers to march. I'd like to see Alladah—and your mother's face—once more before I die. . . .'

And he did both, upon what Nyasanu afterwards realised was nothing more than the sheer force of his indomitable will. For as Alladah came in sight, Gbenu was still alive, still conscious. Hanging, as it were, on the bank of his final river, staring across it into the brooding faces of the ancestors, with great resignation and great calm.

Neither of which, be it said, did his son share. What was in Nyasanu's mind, his heart, was closer to rage than to any other emotion. He trotted at his father's side into the clearing before the village, not really seeing the shrine to Legba, the low thatched roof under which the Trickster sat, his huge, ever-erect phallus pointing mockingly skyward, a bowl at his feet to receive the offerings of the faithful, Kaunikauni, his wife at his side, her genitals hugely swollen, monstrously agape; and beyond them, the secondary shrine dedicated to the same god, uncovered mounds with pots on them, the smallest for the little children of the village, a larger one for the women, and bigger still, the one for the as yet uncircumcised boys, who had received their partial *fa*. Further off, near the village gate, was a mound of earth with a pot turned upside down on its summit and surrounded by a row of sticks between which palm fibres had been strung. This was the *aiza* of Gbenu's family, designed to protect every member from all harm. Next to it, under a baobab tree were two covered pots sacred to the male and female Danh. Then the cult house of the ancestors, with its iron altars, and next to it the individual house of the *tauhwiyo*, the founder of the clan. After that, the house of Dambaba Hwedo, the Serpent God. And finally, at the entrance itself, the two-faced wooden figure, a double figure really, the front half male, looking outward, the rear half female, looking inward, heads, trunks, limbs, joined back to back, gazing in two directions, this *bauchie* was supposed to prevent the evil from even entering Alladah. . . .

Then suddenly, Nyasanu did see them, and his breath knotted in his throat, choking him. Inside the village, he knew, there were many more *bauchie*, shrines, images, gods—the teeming, multiple polifaceted gods of Mother Africa, brooding and dark, who——

'Are garbage!' Nyasanu raged inside his mind. 'Oh you blind

196

pieces of mud and wood, can you see Ku as he dances before me, upside down? You *bauchie* who ward off evil—what evil is there greater than death? And this I bring with me! Sacrifices, rites, ceremonies, prayers—a good and noble life—for what in my father's case have any of these served? What in the life of any man? Kpadunu was wise, gay, fine, handsome, a good brother, a true friend. Did any of these things keep the Auyo iron from ripping his guts? Taugbadji was gentleness and innocence personified. And his gentleness and his innocence led him step by step to such a pass that only the *assegai* I loaned him, piercing an already thrice-pierced heart, could cure. . . .

'Alogba? A slut, I grant you. A prey to lust, which, by its rarity in woman, seems to us uglier when it does appear. But brave and gallant and gay, and no more carnal, after all, than most of the Leopard princesses are. So tell me you things of mud and bone and straw and wood made by our trembling hands in the image of our unreason and our fears, why should I worship you? Is it not better to stride through life head up and tall than to cower on my hands and knees muttering gibberish that does no good in any case? Monsters! Frauds! Rubbish! I tell you I——'

'Young lord,' the king's umbrella bearer said, 'we'd best bear him to his house. He grows very weak. I fear that——'

Slowly the hard glitter left Nyasanu's eyes; the snarl into which his heavy lips were twisted slackened, softened, disappeared.

'Aye,' he said, 'let us carry him to his house. . . .'

And now, as they wound through the narrow streets of the village, a crowd gathered, growing every moment as the whispers flew from mouth to mouth.

'Gbenu. Our *toxausu*. Dying. Nearly dead. His arm. Wounded in battle. A great feat of valour surely, for they have brought him upon the very hammock of the king!'

'And beneath the *dada*'s umbrella. See it—how it goes before the procession. And Nyasanu leads them! He goes like one crazed by grief! He——'

They reached the chief's bungalow. Four of his wifes were there. At once they began to shriek like madwomen, tearing their clothing and pouring dirt on their heads.

'Silence,' Nyasanu screamed at them. 'One of you go fetch my mother, the Lady Gudjo. . . .'

'My lord Axo,' the youngest of the four said, calling him

197

Axo, the Fau word for prince, both out of respect and out of a desire to flatter him who very soon, she hoped, was going to be her own husband under the sacred institution of *chiosi*, 'she cannot come. She is with your *hwesidaxo*, who has been these four days in labour trying to bring forth your child——'

Nyasanu stood there. Then he bent towards the royal hammock.

'Father,' he said.

'I heard,' Gbenu said tiredly, without opening his eyes. 'Go my son. Birth is more important than death. Far more important. Go. But Nya—Nya——'

'Yes, Da?' Nyasanu said.

'Send—thy mother—to me. Tell her—tell her——'

'Yes, Tauchi?' Nyasanu said. 'Yes, father mine?'

'That she has all my love. Has always had. No other woman ever——'

'Yes, Da!' Nyasanu said; 'I know! I know. And I will send her to you. Wait my father, wait! Hold on to your souls until she comes!'

Even before he reached his own house, Nyasanu heard his mother's voice. She was screaming at the top of her lungs, and her rage vibrated like a knife blade plunged into a baobab tree.

'Tell me!' she shrieked. 'Confess your sin, O faithless one! Speak the name of him with whom you have betrayed my son! Own your fault, whore! Or else you'll die! You'll die!'

Nyasanu stopped. All of him. His breath, his mind. His heart. He heard his mother, beside herself with fury, shriek:

'Whore! Whore! Whore!'

And then short and sharp the sound of a slap; and after that, Nyaunu wi's voice, moaning:

'I did not—you saw—the cloth from my sleeping mat—I've known—no other man——'

'Ants!' Gudjo yelled. 'You used night warrior ants! Or hid a flask of chicken's blood or——'

She stopped short, for Nyasanu had come inside the house. He stood there, staring at his mother, at Adje, his mother-in-law; at Dangbevi, who crouched beside Nyaunu wi's grossly, obscenely swollen body and raised her eyes to his face with such an expression that one might think she gazed upon the face of a god; at Nyaunu wi, herself, her face as grey as Gbenu's now, death seated upon her brow, her eyes veiled, gazing across the river in the same way that the chief's did, brooding, lost, resigned.

'Mother!' Nyasanu said. That was all. But he made of the word a whip-crack, and his voice was terrible. But Gudjo was too far gone in the emotion that drove her—that curious combination of pity, rage, and grief—to even notice her son's tone.

'She's dying,' she said flatly. 'She cannot give birth to your sons, *hohovi-twins*! The greatest honour the gods bestow upon a man! For I have heard their two heartbeats, drumming to different rhythms, separate and apart. And when a woman dies in childbirth, there's only one reason for it, my son: she has played the whore with another man! Then do the *vudun*, who know all things, punish her for it! So now, poor, foolish, deceived son of mine, get out of here and let me handle this! For, if she confesses her fault, the gods will relent and——'

Nyasanu looked at Adje, then; but his mother-in-law turned away her face, her eyes sick with acknowledged shame.

'Mother,' Nyasanu said. 'Get out of here! You, too, mother of my wife. And you, Dangbevi! Leave Nyaunu wi and me alone! You heard me, go! All of you!'

'But Nya,' Gudjo said, 'You know the teachings! There's no other explanation for a young, healthy woman being unable to give birth! I tell you——'

'Nonsense,' Nyasanu said. 'Dirty, sluttish nonsense, like all things you women believe. You heard me, Mother! Get out of here!'

'No!' Gudjo said. 'I won't. Not until she confesses, tells who it was she made her dirt with! For——'

She stopped short. What was in his eyes then reached out and choked off her voice like a strangler's hand.

'Nochi,' he said, 'go. My father is waiting for you. At least he *was*. And, little mother——'

'Yes,' Gudjo whispered. 'Yes, my son——'

'Promise me you won't slap him too. Or is dying only a sin when women do it?'

'Nya!' Gudjo said.

'Yes,' Nyasanu said, 'my father is—dying. Ku has breathed upon his wounds and rots him into death. He stinks worse than a corpse at the second burial. For what sin, Mother? Loving you? Getting you with me? Or for the two great evils we're all guilty of: the sin of being born, the crime of drawing breath?'

'Nya,' Dangbevi whispered, 'I'm sorry. Your father——'

'Was a great man. I know. But then, so was your husband, Dangbevi——'

'*Was?*' Dangbevi said. '*Was?*'

'Three feet of Auyo steel through a man's belly aren't likely to improve his health, woman. Oh, Yalode, protectress of female evil. Get out of here, all of you!'

He stopped short, staring at Dangbevi. She had bent all the way over, and pressed her forehead against the earthen floor. Her two tiny fists went pounding against the hard-packed ground, like *asitan zeli*, the funeral drums.

Gently, Nyasanu bent and raised her up; stood there holding her in his arms, while she put her face against his chest, and scalded it with her tears. Out of the corner of his eye, he saw his mother's still graceful skip and scamper, as she plunged head down and sobbing, through the door.

'Dangbevi,' he groaned; but whatever he was going to say to her, he never finished, or even afterwards remembered, for it was then that Nyaunu wi said it, her voice tired, ragged, slow.

'Couldn't you—couldn't you both—have waited—at least until I'm dead?'

'Nyaunu!' Dangbevi said. 'You mustn't think, believe——'

'Think—Dangbevi?' Nyaunu wi shaped the words like an unskilled carver, hacking them out of solid gusts of breath. 'Believe? The word is—*know*. Don't—worry. I shan't make you wait. Not—too long, anyhow. Tonight—tomorrow—you can lie with him—naked—atop my grave——'

'Nyaunu,' Nyasanu said. 'I swear——'

'Don't swear,' she said, 'oaths—you cannot keep. Nor trouble—your heads—about me. My ears—will be too choked —with earth—to hear—your kisses—or your bellies slap together—or all the *aga glee* words you'll say. The—the worms——'

'Nyaunu!' he said.

'Will have eaten—away—these lips—you kissed—and even *this*—you used to fill me—with giants, devils—gods, too big— too big—to burst forth into life——'

'Nyaunu,' he said, crying now, openly, terribly, like a child.

Nyaunu wi lay there staring up at him, her eyes holding all the life she had left in her. They glowed like coals in the greyish-blackness of her face.

Then, very slowly, she smiled.

'Nya,' she murmured. 'Older person mine——'

'Yes, little black one?' he wept, seeing how it was with her now, seeing clearly how her ghost went dancing through the doorway, upside down, head on the ground, feet in the air. 'Yes, my little love?'

'Kiss me,' Nyaunu wi said.

He kissed her. Her mouth was hot and dry. Her breath stank of fever—and of death. He drew back, kneeling then beside her, looking at her.

'I thank you, husband,' she whispered; then her voice suddenly ringing desperately strong: 'Dangbevi! Come here!'

'Me?' Dangbevi faltered. 'You want me to——'

'Come—kneel here. Beside—Nya. Take—his hand——'

'She's—she's raving!' Dangbevi wept. 'Legba's eaten her brains! She's suffered too much, and——'

'Yes,' Nyaunu wi sighed. 'Too much. Must die now. So— *chiosi*! The first time—in all of memory—a woman—makes *chiosi*. I—bequeath to you, Dangbevi—my husband—thus taking——'

'Nyaunu!' Nyasanu said. 'Little woman, I——'

'My vengeance on—the—arrogance of men! Enough. Don't make me—talk. No breath—no——'

She closed her mouth. The silence in the little beehive-shaped, mud and wattles house was absolute. None of the three of them breathed. Nyasanu leaned close. Her breath rustled against his face, smoothly. She seemed to be sleeping. He leaned back against the wall of the house, watching her. Dangbevi crouched there beside him, her eyes sweeping from Nyaunu wi's face to his. In the darkness they glowed like a leopard's in the night. Adje eased her thin, taut body down upon a low stool. She sat there, staring at her daughter, and crying without sound.

Two hours later, Nyaunu wi woke up and began to scream. She screamed for hours. Dangbevi and her mother had to hold her down upon the sleeping mat by force. Nyasanu knelt there, gone beyond tears, watching that. Each time Nyaunu wi opened her mouth and shredded the night with the high, piercing shrillness of her voice, the sound became an Auyo spear-point, embedding itself in his guts. The pain of it was so great that he was sure that if she launched one more hard-flung javelin of a scream upon the night, it would split his heart, burst his lungs, free his three souls to moan and gibber and dance upside down just beyond the village gate——

201

He saw her head arch back, back, her mouth tear open like a tortured beast's; but before she could get that one last great death cry out, Gudjo came through the door. She stood there looking at her son, and her eyes were wild.

'Your father,' she said. 'Dying. Asking for you. Come!'

'No!' Nyasanu said. 'I can't! I won't! Mother, can't you see that she——'

'Is dying, too?' Gudjo said harshly. 'Yes. But she is only your wife. And you'll have many wives. While, my poor husband is the *only* father you'll ever have. So, you heard me, Nya! Come!'

Nyasanu looked towards the moaning, twisting, monstrously swollen figure of his bride; she was still, suddenly. Her voice was the rustle of a little wind moving through the savanna's grass.

'Go. Nya,' she murmured. 'Honour your father, for that's your duty. I'll wait—I'll wait——'

'Until I come back?' he said. 'Will you, little black one? Can you?'

She nodded dumbly. He bent and kissed her. Then he plunged out into the night.

But when he came back, an hour later, after having received Gbenu's dying blessing and public acknowledgement of him as heir, she had left him forever, gone to her ancestors, beyond the dark river of time.

And, as the custom was, they took the *hohovi*, the sacred twins, from her belly, ripping her open like a slaughtered goat, and gave them high and holy burial beyond the compound gate. But, since nothing could shake the stubborn Dahomean belief that death in childbirth is the god's punishment for unconfessed adultery, they bundled Nyaunu wi's body in a winding sheet, bore it into the brush, unwound the sheet, and left her sprawled out, naked and unburied upon the ground.

One hour later, in open defiance of his people's customs and their laws, Nyasanu came to that place bearing with him his hoe, a spade, a dagger, and all poor Nyaunu wi's wedding clothes. And seeing at once what was needed, he went away again and came back with a clay jar of water, some native soap, and many flasks of perfume.

Tenderly he bathed the butchered body of her who had been his bride, combed her matted hair, anointed her with perfume.

Then he covered her knife-torn nakedness with her finest robe of silk, and after that, rolled her gently upon the winding sheet, kissed her death mouth at the last before he wrapped her face and body in the big white cotton cloth to protect them from the earth, at least for a time.

That done, he fell to work, digging her a decent grave in the iron-hard ground. It was hard labour, and dusk was at hand before he had it deep enough. But finally, he picked her up, murmured a prayer to the Sky *Vudun* of whose cult she was, and laid her in her last resting place.

To cover her with earth was a far easier task than digging her grave had been; in less than half an hour he had it done, pounding the loose clay into place with a sawn-off tree trunk so that no prowling hyena or jackal might be able to dig her up again.

Afterwards, he took off the sweat- and earth-stained toga that he had worn, and bathed his body with the rest of the water he had brought, rubbing what remained of the perfumes into his skin. Then he dressed himself again, putting on the rich, green silk toga he had worn on his wedding day. Last of all, he buckled the ornamented belt with the jewel dagger that had belonged to S'ubetzy, the Auyo prince, hanging from it in its brass and silver sheath. All that done, he went to the edge of Nyaunu wi's grave and knelt there, sorrowing.

Then, after having said a prayer to every god he could think of, he put his right hand down diagonally across his body and grasped the jewelled hilt of the dagger. But, when he did that, Dangbevi came out of the bush and knelt beside him, putting one slim arm around his neck.

He stared at her in wonder; but she smiled at him so the tears that were flooding her black cheeks clung to the upturned corners of her thin-lipped Arabic mouth and quivered there. With her free hand she pointed to the fresh grave.

'*She* gave you to me,' she said, 'so you're mine. Don't cheat me, Nya. Or her either, since she wanted it that way. Among my people, the wishes of the dying are sacred, so even if I didn't love you—I'd marry you anyhow, out of respect for her. Even so, she only took away part of my sin——'

'Your sin?' Nyasanu said. His voice was heavy, uncomprehending, slow.

'Loving you while I was still Kpad's wife. Long before I'd become his widow. From the first hour that I saw you, if you

203

must know. And him your first friend eldest, at that, which makes it more shameful still. He was a good man, Nya. But I don't need to tell you that, do I? Though how good, how fine, how gentle, you can't even imagine, not being a woman.'

Nyasanu bowed his head. Looked up again, his eyes awash and glittering.

'Can't I?' he said. 'When he took three feet of Auyo steel through his guts to save my worthless life?'

She stared at him, and now her smile wavered, went away. He could see the grief, guilt, pain she was trying to hold back jerking her throat.

'Only,' he went on, his voice dust dry and rasping from the hurt that shredded his insides with vulture's claws, 'he made me promise him before the battle that if anything happened to him, I'd marry you. So that makes *two* sacred wishes we're supposed to respect, doesn't it? Doesn't it, Dangbevi?'

She nodded, dumbly. Then she pointed at the dagger at his waist.

'That,' she said. 'Give it to me, Nya.'

He looked at her, but she held him with her eyes. Slowly he drew the dagger out and handed it to her, hilt first. She took it and threw it into the brush as far away as she could. Then she put her hand down inside the waistband of her skirt and took out another dagger. It was the type the priests used to sacrifice animals with, and one glance at its edge told him he could have shaved with it. He hung there watching her and his brain formed the question; but couldn't force it into words until she had hurled the second dagger into the undergrowth after the first one; then he did get it out:

'That one—what was it for, Dangbevi?'

She smiled at him then, slowly, peacefully.

'For me—if I didn't get here in time or couldn't stop you after I got here,' she said. 'Now come on, we've got to go make the arrangements for your father's funeral. You heard me, Nya! Come on!'

But he went on kneeling there until she put out her hand to him. And even after that, instead of getting up, he took her proffered hand and jerked her down beside him, drawing her into his arms, holding her to him, and crying.

'No,' she said, 'don't kiss me, Nya. Not unless you want what *she* said to come true. . . .'

'What she said?' he got out woodenly.

204

'That I'd profane her grave by lying with you atop it. She was right. I would. So turn me loose. Life has another day. But the dead can't wait. Please, Nya. Come——'

He turned her loose then. And the two of them got up from there and walked down the winding path under the cottonsilk trees towards the compound, hearing, as they approached it, the terrible *avidochio* howling shriek of the women mourning for Gbenu, and the slow, steady, never ceasing thump and thunder of the *zeli* drums.

But they were both young. And though sorrow had begun to pile its slow accumulation of crushing weight upon their backs, they were not yet bent. So it was another rhythm that they marched to, heard, swift pounding in their hearts. Not Ku's drums, but life's. And knowing that, sensing it, they averted their eyes from one another and were ashamed.

PART TWO

FIFTEEN

Nyasanu, *toxausu*, or chief, of Alladah, lay is his great hammock, attended by all four of his wives. The first of them, his *hwesidaxo*, Dangbevi, the honoured housewife eldest, and hence something of a commanding officer over the others, wiped his brow with a perfumed cloth. Alihosi, one of the two *chiosi* wives, that is, widows of his father whom he had inherited, fanned him with a huge woven palmetto fan. Sosixwe, the other *chiosi*—though to tell the truth about it, he hadn't inherited her, but had bought her from his elder brother Gbochi, to whom Gbenu had left her—held the ornamental chief's umbrella over him to shade him from the sun. And Huno, the youngest of them all, since she wouldn't reach her fourteenth birthday until the next month, and who had been a slave girl before he'd also bought her, freed her, then married her, crouched at his feet holding the big brass spittoon for him to spit into, if he so desired, and looked up at him with so much adoration in her eyes that he couldn't bear the sight of it, and turned away his face.

He was, on that morning—some three months and eight days after Gbenu's and Nyaunu wi's death—a sight to see. His *chokoto chaka*, the short breeches that every male Dahomean wore, were woven of the fibres of the cottonsilk tree, and their whiteness was snowy; his *awo*, or sleeveless shirt, was of pure European silk, dyed a vivid red; and his *bone*, the chief's cap that marked his new rank, and his toga were of the green, embroidered silk traditional in his father's house, as were his sandals. He was smoking his father's clay *koko*, the chief's pipe, though he hadn't really mastered the art of smoking tobacco, and it still made him dizzy. But he persisted, for ceremonial smoking was one of the things expected of a great chief.

'Look, older person mine!' Dangbevi said, and pointed.

Nyasanu raised himself up a little and saw the procession going through the gate. At its head was his great Granduncle Hwegbe, that malicious old scoundrel of a woodcarver, who—

though only Legba himself knew how he'd found out about it—had come back to Alladah for Gbenu's funeral. But just behind him went Gbochi and Yu, followed by Gbochi's wives, three of the four *chiosi* women Gbenu had left him in a sure-to-be-futile attempt to cure—from across the river of death itself, Nyasanu thought wryly—his effeminacy; and these were followed by Yu's servants and slaves, who were many, for Yu, due to her shrewdness in business and the continued favour of her patroness, the Princess Fedime, was a wealthy woman in her own right.

'I was expecting that,' Nyasanu said a little sadly.

'So was I, my lord,' Sosixwe said. 'But I don't understand why you sound so sad over it. I'm glad to be rid of them, and so's everybody else in this district, except Yu's lovers, maybe. And the only reason they aren't is she paid them to lie with her. Old and ugly as she is, she had to——'

'Sosixwe,' Nyasanu said, warningly.

'It's true, my lord!' Sosixwe said. 'Don't you see how she held back to keep from touching your father's body, the way all his wixes were supposed to, during the *maudaugbugdo* rite? And if that's not the same thing as admitting to adultery out loud, I don't know what it is! Besides, as far as that perverted little swine you saved me from is concerned—ugh!' she stopped short without finishing her thought and shuddered visibly.

'Where are they going?' little Huno said, in her soft, sweet voice.

'Look who's asking questions!' Alihosi said. 'Who gave you leave to speak, slave girl?'

The excessive bitterness in her voice when she said that caused Nyasanu to turn and stare at her. Alihosi was thirty-two years old and anything but pretty, while all his other three wives were. One of them, Dangbevi, except for her thin-lipped mouth, which robbed her face of a certain necessary sensuality, could legitimately have been called beautiful. And they were all years younger than Alihosi, as well. Huno, in fact, could easily have been her daughter. Then suddenly, Nyasanu remembered another thing about the widow of his father he'd inherited: never, in all the years she had been married to his demonstrably virile sire, had she been able to present the now departed Gbenu with a child. So she had reasons to be bitter. But it was damnably unfair of her to take her frustrations out upon poor Huno, whose lowly status in Dahomean society left her

208

almost without defence. Or would have so left her, if Nyasanu had not been what he was.

'Alihosi,' he said quietly, 'Huno is free now. I freed her. And she is my wife—through my own choice.'

Alihosi bent her head. The rebuke was a stinging one. A man *had* to take a *chiosi* wife. To refuse her was to insult his father's cult as a *tauvudu*, or ancestor-god. But for him to buy a slave girl, free her, and then marry her was something else again.

He felt Dangbevi's eyes on him, and the pain in them was naked. He realised suddenly that she, too, believed that he loved and desired Huno. Instead of merely pitying her, he thought, which was what drove me. Pity—and disgust. Minona, Goddess of Women, witness *that* was an ugly thing. . . . Anger tore him, and since he couldn't reveal the source of it, Alihosi suffered, became the butt of all his ill humour.

'Answer Huno's question, Alihosi!' he said.

'Yes, my lord!' Alihosi whispered. Then to Huno, 'They're going to another quarter of the city, to buy land and build a new compound, as far from this one as they can get. They haven't any other choice. Since Kausu, my late husband's first friend eldest, confirmed at the *ka tu tu*, the "will reciting ceremony", what everybody already knew anyhow, that my—oh, all right, Sosixwe—*our* departed lord wasn't going to have a pervert, a *gaglo* like Gbochi, succeeding him as *toxausu*, and brought forth that chief's ring our new lord and husband now wears in proof of his words, they feel disgraced. They're right. They *are* disgraced. So they have to go. All the other members of the family would treat them like dirt if they stayed. And, as Sosixwe has said, we're far better off without them——'

'I—I thank you, my lady,' Huno said humbly, 'and I beg you not to be angry with me.'

'Huno!' Nyasunu said sharply. 'You're no longer a slave. You're a lady now, and a chief's wife. Take care you act like one!'

'Yes, my lord,' Huno said, so low he almost couldn't hear her.

Again he felt Dangbevi's gaze upon him. Looking at her, he could see the tears misting her lovely, yellow-brown eyes.

'Danh and Dangbe both, aid me!' he thought. 'This business of managing women is going to be a trouble. Of course, after tonight, she'll feel better. At least I hope so——'

As his number one wife, it was Dangbevi's indisputable right to be the first of them all to share his sleeping mat. For the strange truth was that all four of his brides were, so far, wives in name only. The reasons for this curious state of affairs were both simple and complicated.

In the first place, the mourning period for a chief was a full three months. And to lie with a woman during that time was an act showing so terrible a disrespect for the dead man that the *tauvudum*, the ancestor gods, would punish it at once by striking both the lecherous son and his paramour dead. For that reason, he had refrained from knowing Dangbevi; though, by the expressed will of his late and achingly mourned first friend, Kpadunu, as told to Mauchau, the sorcerer, just before the two friends had marched away to war, she was already Nyasanu's legal wife. And, though he had bought Huno during the funeral rites, thus making her his slave, with the right to use her as a concubine, the same prohibition applied, since the *su dudu*, the tabu, employed the word *'Nyaunu'*, woman, instead of *'asisi'*, wife, thus making the sin all-inclusive.

But the other two, Alihosi and Sosixwe, had only become his wives eight days before, at the *ka tu tu* ceremony, when, as was customary, the *xauntau daxo*, the first friend eldest, of the dead man—in this case one Kausu—had recited the deceased's last will and testament as told him by the departed.

By then, of course, the mourning period was over. So theoretically, Nyasanu could have consummated his weddings to either Alihosi or Sosixwe, or both, at once.

'If I'd wanted to,' he thought bitterly, 'if I had the slightest desire now for any woman born. Even Dangbevi, whom I've always been fond of—no, to tell the truth about it, more than fond. Of course it would have been an insult to her—as housewife eldest. And even to Huno as my number two wife. Yet, it was within my powers to set them aside, for Sosixwe's sake at least, just as father set Gbochi aside for me. But Ku sits upon my heart, reminding me of too many deaths: Kpad's. Alogba's. Poor Badji's. My father's. Nyaunu wi's. Surely I'd have failed any woman then—even one so—so female as Sosixwe is. Danh be praised I had the *xwetade* ceremony as an excuse!*

* The son who has been named heir is obliged to build a little house over his father's grave and to give a feast lasting from at least two to more than ten days. This rite is called *xwetade*, 'roof building over'.

210

I've stretched it out as long as I could—all of eight days, now. But I can't any more. I'm belly-sick of both feasting and prayer! Neither serves for anything; food turns to excreta in your gut and your body to carrion in spite of all the gods we invent to pray to. . . .

'Besides, Dangbevi's hurt. She thinks I prefer one of the others. Huno, likely. Oh, Legba take women, anyhow! I——'

'They're gone,' Alihosi said then, in her rather harsh and strident voice, 'and besides, it's getting dark. So, since the Serpent's Child is too polite, too subtle, likely, to kick us out of here, I think we'd better go back to our houses, sister-wives, and leave Dangbevi to her bliss. That is, if our young and lusty lord hasn't any objections. . . .'

'Alihosi,' Nyasanu said, 'the world and your own *fa* have treated you badly, haven't they?'

'Alihosi bent her head. Looked up again.

'Yes, my lord,' she said. 'They have——'

'But now, you're starting a new life,' Nyasanu said. 'The past is gone. It went across the river with my father. I want you to be happy. I mean to see that you are. In proof of which, I ask Huno to give you her week as my housewife. Next week as is her right as my number two wife. Will you, Huno?'

'Yes, my lord,' Huno said, almost too quickly—so quickly that Sosixwe laughed. Huno was virgin. They all knew that, absolutely. And so, naturally enough, she had all a virgin's fears.

Alihosi was staring at him with wonder in her eyes. He saw her incline her body as if to prostrate herself before him. Being an intelligent and sensitive man, he couldn't bear worship. He found the total mindlessness of the concept demeaning to worshipper and worshipped alike. He wondered suddenly how the *vudun* could bear the quantity of it they got. But then maybe the gods were different. That is, if there were such things as gods. . . .

'Don't bow!' he said sharply. 'Or throw dirt on your head. There's only one thing you can do for me, Alihosi——'

'And that is, my lord?' Alihosi whispered.

'Stop biting and scratching everything that comes near you,' he said. 'You aren't an alului, the wildcat of the woods, but a woman. And practise singing——'

'Singing, my lord?'

'Yes. It will make your speaking voice sweeter. A musical

211

voice is an excellent thing in a wife, Alihosi. But I think that
once I've cured you of your bitterness, that grate and scrape
tone in your voice that hurts my poor ears so will go away.
Now, good night all. Sleep well.'

'And Serpent's Child,' Sosixwe said in her mischievous way,
'will she also sleep well, my lord?'

'You may ask her tomorrow how well she slept,' Nyasanu
said. 'Now leave us, will you? Go!'

After they had gone, Dangbevi busied herself with preparing
his supper. Kpadunu had boasted upon more than one occasion about her abilities as a cook.

'I only hope I can do her cooking justice,' Nyasanu thought,
'for Sagbata witness my appetite is gone. . . .'

He watched her moving about his house. She was as slim
and graceful as a loko sapling, her movements as sinuous as a
serpent's. His mind—which always worked in odd ways, so
that he quite often looked at things in a manner inconceivable
to most Dahomeans, a trait he'd inherited from his father—
occupied itself with the question of whether she was more or
less beautiful than Nyaunu wi had been. He found that question impossible to answer. He simply hadn't had the necessary
experience to answer it, because, to do so, he'd have had to
have seen enough Arab, or even darker Mediterranean types of
European women to have got used to them. For, apart from
her soft, velvety, nightshade colour, that was what Dangbevi
looked like. She had almost no Negroid characteristics at all, a
fact that caused a remark his dead first friend had once made
to come jarring back into his mind. 'She looks,' Kpadunu had
said, 'almost like one of the Furtoo women dyed black. . . .'

'If she does,' Nyasanu thought, 'then the Furtoo women
can't be as ugly as people say they are—for Minona witness
she's a lovely thing. . . .'

He realised that she had seen him looking at her and was
trembling like a wild woods thing under the curious, searching
insistence in his gaze.

'What's the matter, Dangbevi?' he asked her. 'Are you
afraid?'

'Yes, my husband,' she said.

'Not of *me* surely?'

'No, older person; not—of you . . .'

'Then of what?' Nyasanu said.

'Of not pleasing you,' she said. 'Before—I wasn't. But now,

212

you have other wives. And little Huno is so pretty and so sweet. And Sosixwe—she—she looks——'

He grinned at her, said:

'She looks like she could set the savanna afire even in a rainy season by merely walking through the grass. Is that what you meant Dangbevi?'

'Yes. Oh yes! Exactly that. And that's important, isn't it? At least to men. Isn't it, older person mine?'

'Very,' he said, solemnly.

She bent her head; when she looked up again, he could see the tears in her strange, light-coloured eyes.

'Then you must let me divorce you,' she said. 'For *that*, I am worthless.'

He stared at her. It was not the way she put the matter that surprised him. In Dahomey, women always divorced men, and not the other way around, because for a man to put a wife by was held to be a refusal of his duty to provide future worshippers for the *tau-vudun* and Sagbata's pantheon, the *vudun* of the earth, and, therefore, an insult to his own ancestors and to the gods of fertility, causing them to punish him by making him totally and permanently impotent—to the Dahomean male, the one fate worse than death. Even the word for divorce in Ffon, *asugbigbe*, meant 'to refuse one's husband'. What was surprising was that she said it at all; for, up to that moment, she'd given him a great many shy and delicate indications that she loved him.

'How would you know *that*, Dangbevi?' he said.

'Kpad,' she whispered. 'He always said so. Not only when he was angry with me, but even when he wasn't—which makes it more grave, doesn't it? Besides, he was right. I—I don't even like what men and women do together. If it weren't the only way to make a child, I'd *never* do it.'

He studied her face before he spoke. Her mouth. Her eyes.

'You want a child, Dangbevi?' he said.

'Not *a* child,' she whispered, '*your* child, my husband.'

'Why mine, housewife eldest?' he said.

She faced him squarely.

'Because I love you,' she said.

'Minona who is their goddess, tell me,' he cried out in mock astonishment, 'is there any way of understanding women?'

Dangbevi smiled at him then, gently.

'No, Medaxochi; no, older person mine; how can you men

understand us, when we don't even understand ourselves?' she said.

The supper was good. In fact, it was delicious. As was customary, Dangbevi stood beside the table and served him. She wasn't supposed to eat until he had finished. But he doubted that she would or could, even then. He was finding it very nearly impossible to get the flesh of the agbanli antelope, cooked with yams and millet grains, down. It was wonderfully prepared, but his throat tightened up on him, and would not let it pass.

'You're not eating!' Dangbevi wailed.

'I can't,' he said. 'It's very good; but I can't. The tears I've swallowed in the last two months have ruined my belly. Scalded it to rags. And my throat is raw from so much wailing. So, let's go to bed. To *sleep*. Hard as it is for a woman to believe, there're times when a man doesn't feel like making love, either——'

He smiled at her perplexed expression, at the warfare between relief and disappointment visible in her eyes. Then he added with grave mockery:

'You'll forgive me, won't you, Hwesidaxochi, housewife eldest mine, for cheating you of one of your four nights?'

'As you wish it, husband,' she faltered, a little uncertainly, then whispered. 'Will you let me ask you a question, older person mine?'

'Of course,' Nyasanu said.

'Would you have said—*that*—if this had been Huno's turn? Or Sosixwe's?'

'Yes,' he said, 'but not if it had been Alihosi.'

'Oh!' Dangbevi said.

'Because I pity her so much,' he said gently, 'and she wouldn't have understood.'

'I—I'm not sure *I* do,' Dangbevi said.

'I love you,' he said, 'and I don't any of the others. I'm probably trusting too much in your good sense, to tell you that. I only hope you won't throw it in their faces the first time they provoke you into a quarrel, as they will. Women are strange little beasts! Though it doesn't matter, really. What I meant was that you and I have time. All the rest of our lives, maybe. And, apart from the fact that it seems almost a sin with both our dead scarcely underground, I'd rather wait with you. No, for you.'

214

'*For* me?' Dangbevi said.

'To come to me. Wanting *me*. All three of my souls, of course. But my body too—and not just the child we'd make by doing a thing you don't even like. So now, come on. Let's get some sleep, shall we? Gu help me, but I'm tired!'

But, to her own surprise, Dangbevi found she couldn't sleep. She lay there warm and soft and trembling in the crook of his arm and stared at the thatched roof. She was aware that he wasn't asleep either; so out of sheer nervousness, perhaps, she began to make talk, asking him things that she knew already, or that she wasn't even too interested in, or really wanted to know.

'Husband,' she said, 'did you *know* your father was going to pass over Gbochi?'

'Yes,' he said. 'Didn't you?'

'I thought he would. How little man is Gbochi! He disgraced himself when he fainted outright at the first *chiosuso*, didn't he?'

'I don't blame him for that,' Nyasanu said. 'I almost fainted myself. And at the second it was even worse. . . .'

She stared at him in the darkness.

'The second, I understand. It must be awful to have to dance all over the city, bearing a dead man who has been dug up after lying in the earth twelve days, in your arms. The smell—was dreadful. I was far away, and even with six perfumed cloths over my mouth and nostrils I could scarcely support it. But at the first *chiosuso*, the first "dancing with the dead", your father had been dead only two days so——'

'It was hot,' Nyasanu said. 'And he died of gunshot wounds that had festered. Even while he was still alive, the smell of him was unbearable. Poor father! I hope he's content with the funeral we gave him. . . .'

'He should be!' Dangbevi said. 'Twenty-two full days of funeral rites! And at night, all the little funeral lamps, what does one call them, husband?'

'*Fau meaun tagbive,*' Nyasanu whispered.

'All the *fau meaun tagbive* twinkling in the trees like stars,' she stopped short, stared at him. 'Why do you shudder, my husband?'

'Two of them went out,' Nyasanu said, 'and that means two more—persons whom I love, will die——'

215

'Oh!' Dangbevi whispered. She was silent for a while after that. But woman-like, she had to go on chattering with seeming aimlessness about the things that didn't interest her, in order to get to the ones that did.

'People say,' she began, 'that the Lady Yu also disgraced herself. At—at—what do you call that ceremony, older person?'

'The *maudaugbugbo*. You know. Dangbevi, you speak Ffon so well that I forget you're a foreigner. Your people don't have such ceremonies, do they?'

'No,' Dangbevi said. 'They have—different ones, I think. I— I don't remember my people, husband; Kpad always said that I'm a Fanti, so I suppose I am. And the language I always spoke is very like yours anyhow, so it wasn't hard to learn to speak Fau well. But tell me, *how* did she disgrace herself? I was there. I was standing right behind your sister Axisi—how beautiful she is! Tall as a goddess—and so stately——'

'Axisi is anything but stately,' Nyasanu said.

'Well, she was then. She's the tallest girl I've ever seen. Only five fingers shorter than you are, Medaxochi. And when she made her gifts the—the—what, my husband?'

'*Adjoko tau madje kwi*, which means "the river crossing go towards death cloths". She *was* impressive, then, wasn't she?'

'Very. But to get back to the Lady Yu. I didn't see her do anything disgraceful, so how——?'

'That's just the point: it's what she *didn't* do that disgraced her. At the *maudaugbugbo* ceremony, apart from the many, many gifts that are made the departed in order that he may lift up his head and speak with pride in the land of the dead— that's what the word means: "allow him to speak dead land" —the sons hold up their father's body, and every wife must touch his face, as she makes her gift. But any wife who has been unfaithful to him while he lived will fall down dead the moment she touches him. So—Yu didn't care. She hung back and made her gift from a rod away, thus admitting to all the world she was an adulteress. She wasn't smart——'

'Smart?' Dangbevi said.

'Yes. Precisely that. There were at least three others who didn't touch him either. And one of them, to make it even worse, was among the *"Ma yalau ni che o"* women, those with child, which is why they say that "Do not call my name, O!'

216

because if their names are called out as the others' are when
the gifts are made, they'll lose their babies. But the other three
were clever enough to pretend to touch poor father, putting
their hands so close to his face it was hard to see whether they
did or not. But I was watching, and I saw. That's one of the
reasons I don't mean to marry too many women. There are
limits to a man's strength. And if a man doesn't keep all his
wives contented on the sleeping mat, they'll find somebody else
who will.'

'Husband,' Dangbevi said.

'Yes, Dangbevi?'

'I—I don't believe you! It's only three months since your
father died and already you've got *four*!'

'Four. One of whom my father left to me, and therefore I
had no choice——'

'Another whom, when you saw the *dokpwega* was going
to—to do *that*—to her, you got so jealous that you offered him
two thousand cowries for her, and——'

'Dangbevi!' he said, anger and hurt shaking his voice. 'You
don't understand!'

'Don't I?' she said. 'Don't I? When he took all her clothes
off her, you saw—how—how beautiful Huno is! And then
when he laid her down on your father's grave and tried to—to
push that huge and ugly—part of himself up into her, and
couldn't because she was too little, you——'

'Not because she was too little,' Nyasanu said sadly, 'but because she was chaste. I—I wasn't prepared for that. I'd never
seen a chief's funeral before. I never want to again—except my
own—and that I won't be able to see, I'm sure.'

Dangbevi stared at him, her leopard's eyes luminous in the
darkness.

'Listen, Dangbevi! he said. 'You don't know me. All my life
I've had this weakness: I can't stand seeing people humiliated,
hurt, shamed. I wept for the men I killed during the war. If—I
can avoid it, I'll never kill any man again. I—I'd thought my
father's funeral was all over—twenty-two days of rites; over
two hundred separate and distinct ceremonies, two dances with
my father's body, men fighting for the chance to hold up his
putrid, stinking corpse and dance all over Alladah with it!
Two burials, the first for eight days, then they dug him up
again to pollute the air so that not all the *gbedjeleku, sosal-*

217

ekwi, tike, nuhweku, and *ywaywado** or any other perfumes you can name could drown that stench. All his sons-in-law with their societies and their *dokpwe* drumming, chanting funeral songs, dancing funeral dances, until the beat of *zeli* drums was about to burst my poor head. And women wailing, wailing, wailing! Night and day for twenty-two days, the *avdochio,* the "tears give the dead", never ceasing. People beggaring themselves to make imposing gifts which will only rot with the stinking lump of human carrion my father has become, deep in the earth. Whole societies ruining themselves "pushing" one of my brothers-in-law or another, so that he might outshine all the others with his funerary gifts———'

'Huno,' Dangbevi said stubbornly, 'get to that. Why you bought her. I want to know.'

'And then, finally, I *thought,* it was over: the *dokpwega* in charge, the *legede,* his first assistant, the *asuka,* his second, and the *asafaga,* his public crier, have been given gifts enough to make them wealthy for life, drinks enough to make even their great grandchildren drunkards from the liquor inherited in their ancestors' blood! The *yaukutau,* the gravedigger, has been paid a young fortune and ceremoniously chased beyond the gate. Even the *dogbwlehw djito,* the "death spoiled house sing men" and the *dogbwlehwe dudu,* the "death spoiled house dancers", have been paid and sent away. The *bokono* kills my father's *fa,* and his *legba*—pouring peppers, mustard, and goat's blood over them and smashing their images with his club. *Amasi,* a medicine made of leaves, is brought to disinfect my father's house, where he lay so long, with an old woman there night and day to attend him and to cook food he couldn't eat, until the only way I'll ever get the stink of death out of it will be to burn it down———'

'Husband,' Dangbevi said.

'Shut up! Nyasanu howled. 'Hold your tongue, silly, jealous, female fool, and listen! I'd have you understand me, by Fa! And now, I think, it's over. Now I can rest, can allow my heart to brood, quiet and slow, over a pain so great it has no need for ceremonies, gifts, or show. Now, I can weep in the darkness of my house, slow-dripping, quiet tears, that cool my grief, instead of having to howl aloud in public like a demented

* These names of native aromatic plants have no English or French equivalents, probably because the plants themselves are unknown outside of central Africa.

beast to demonstrate my sorrow——

'But no! There's this one more ceremony! The *djauno tutau*, "come sleep", the wake. And instead of decent solemnity, what do I see? Licentious riot! We're supposed to amuse poor Father now! So we dance, and play *adji** and *akau*,† and drink rivers of rum, and tell all the dirty stories that we know. Then we go back to his grave and do the *kodido kodji,* "sand raise on the dead", ceremony to make the earth lie less heavily upon him, sing the forty-one *yotaya*, the "grave head" songs, and do the *zehwi xwe*, putting the small pot on the grave. After that we sing the sad and beautiful old woman's song, and the song of the avenger, and the song of the hidden singer. I'm beginning to feel better, now. And then, then!'

'Then?' Dangbevi whispered.

'The *dokpwega* begins to sing: "Give water for him to drink, a drinker of water is dead!"'

'And they brought a calabash full of water, and he drank it,' Dangbevi said. 'Then he sang about the rum, didn't he?'

' "Give drink for him to drink, for a drinker who drinks is dead!"' Nyasanu chanted. 'So the *dokpwega* drinks the rum they bring him. Then he sings for my father's *koko* and tobacco, and they bring the pipe and he smokes it; and then——'

' "Give a woman!"' Dangbevi sang, her voice vibrant with a mockery doubly shocking in this delicate creature he had often held up to his headstrong Nyaunu wi as a paragon of gentleness. ' "That someone may lie with her! For a lover of women is dead!"'

She stopped short, looked at him and said:

'And that was when you, older person mine, disgraced yourself and broke my poor heart at the same time!'

'Dangbevi,' Nyasanu said, his voice a grate, a scrape, rasping against the silence, 'when they pushed poor little Huno forward, didn't you see her face? It looked like a trapped she-monkey's does, when you put your hand into the cage to draw her out. And when she got a good look at that grizzled old blubberlips of a *dokpwega*, I thought she was going to lose her dinner, that is, if she'd had any, which, considering the fact that she was Yu's slave, I doubt. How can you be so stupid? You thought I *wanted* her? Minona, Goddess of Women! Have you never

* Dahomean checkers or chess.
† Dahomean craps with cowries used for dice.

219

heard of pity? But even forgetting that side of it, when I saw that rusty black scoundrel gleefully preparing to turn my father's grave into a roofless whorehouse, my guts revolted in my belly! Custom or not, I couldn't let him do that. If they thought to honour my father's manhood thus, they're fools, for they insult it! My father was such a man who could be considerate and thoughtful with all his women and never publicly shame them. He'd never have dreamed that his virility needed proof, much less of giving a free demonstration of it by rutting like a billygoat in the street! That's why we build houses in the first place: in order to eat and sleep and urinate and move our bowels in private. But most of all to be alone and unwatched when we make love. Because Dangbevi mine, a man's nakedness and a woman's are together a high and holy thing. For thus souls are made, wife of my heart. And love, and even lust, are not meant to be watched by spectators as though they were some kind of wrestling match, say. So I couldn't let my father's tomb be dishonoured like that, nor allow little Huno to be so shamed. I bought her. And freed her because I believe slavery is the greatest curse that men inflict upon one another, and married her, because since she is a Maxi, an orphan and alone, she would have surely starved, otherwise. So now——'

'Now?' Dangbevi whispered.

'Stop insulting me by believing me an animal, or a slave to my seed sacks and my dangling gut! I'm a man, Dangbevi; and if you don't know what a man is, what a creature with souls in him, how compounded of dreams, compassion, tenderness, intelligence, pain—and joy—oh yes, and sometimes, rarely, joy! If you don't know that a shaft of moonlight can transfix him, the otutu's singing stop his breath, if you don't know he can bury half his heart in one woman's grave, and that the other half's alive only because his love for another, *one* other, stopped his pushing a dagger through his ravaged guts—why then, I'll allow you to divorce me, for I have no other choice!'

He could hear her crying. She sounded as though she were strangling to death.

'One thing more,' she wept. 'I'll go cut you twenty green rods and peel them myself—allow you to beat me to death for asking it; but I've got to know. And Sosixwe, Nya! Sosixwe—what about *her*?

He sighed, long and deeply. Then he said:

'All right. I'll have no peace with you until I've stilled your doubts. My father spent years trying to cure my brother, Gbochi, of his homosexuality. Even on his deathbed, he tried again. So before he died, he called his first friend Eldest Kausu to him, and indicating his four youngest, prettiest, and most sensual wives—for there *are* a few rare women, as lecherous as she-monkeys, Dangbevi, as Yu herself has abundantly proved —the same four over-heated females, who'd made his last days a darkness with their incessant demands, and told Kausu they were to go to Gbochi. The *chiosi* he made was useless, for Gbochi is perverted to the bitter bone. But anyhow my father tried. So, when, at the *ka tu tu,* Kausu recited my father's will and Sosixwe found out she'd been left to Gbochi, she threw herself at my feet, embraced my ankles, and swore she'd disembowel herself before she'd let him touch her, or kiss her with a mouth that had drunk male seed from its very source, so——'

'You bought her from him,' Dangbevi whispered.

'Yes. Do you know how much he asked for her?'

'No,' Dangbevi said.

'One cowry—to show his contempt for women and all their works, and now——'

'Now?' Dangbevi said.

'You make me wonder if he wasn't right; if any of you is worth even a cowry. Now go to sleep, will you? Haven't you tormented me enough for one night?'

'No,' Dangbevi said. 'For I'm going to torment you a little more, though in a different way. I've changed my mind; so now, you'll just have to change yours, that's all! Make love to me, husband! It's my right, you know. I insist upon it!

Nyasanu turned and stared at her.

'Minona, Goddess of Women! he swore, 'you said——'

'That I didn't like it. I don't. But I want a baby, your first son eldest, which is a great honour. Do you know any other way of making one?'

'No,' Nyasanu said, and looked at her sadly, where she lay waiting, her body tense, rigid, trembling, her mouth twisted into the same expression of anticipated disgust and terror usually seen upon the face of a child who has been commanded to take a bitter medicine. 'But tell me something; have you ever seen the figures that my first friend—by reason of poor Kpad's death—Amosu, the brassworker, makes?'

'Yes,' Dangbevi whispered, 'they're—beautiful. But I don't see——'

'What that has to do with this? An example, merely—or a lesson. Amosu takes a long time to make his figures. He works with skill and care. And he *enjoys* his work, housewife eldest. Pours all of his heart into it. So they're beautiful, because they're joyfully made. But how can a woman who hates love itself make a beautiful child? Tell me that? Or her husband either, if he's labouring upon a wooden statue? As rigid as wood—as unfeeling?'

'Nya,' she whispered. 'I—I'll try—I'll——'

'No,' he said. 'I'll show you what a master sculptor can do with even wood, how an *azaundato* can chase away the little evil spirits who arm female flesh against the strong invader, bringing cringing, tightening, disgust, pain, instead of welcome, opening, a flood of balm to ease his passage, mutual joy——'

'How?' she got out in a strangled voice.

'Like this,' he said, and bending found her mouth.

When the others came up to the house in the morning to attend their lord and master during the daylight hours as the custom was, they could hear Dangbevi singing even before they reached it. Her voice erected arabesques of liquid silver upon the dawn, sweeter than the otutu's cry, made flute runs and trills that weren't silver, but golden, sunbursts of happiness, little, laughing staccato bursts of joy.

And hearing her, little Huno stared at her two companions in wonder, while Sosixwe let out a little mocking snort of laughter. But Alihosi, poor, forlorn Alihosi, hearing it, feeling it in her heart like the death of hope, bent her head and wept.

SIXTEEN

'My lord Toxausu,' Gudjo said, 'a word with you, if you will be so kind!'

Nyasanu looked at his mother. She had prostrated herself before him as a commoner was supposed to when addressing a chief. He sighed. It was the nature of women to be troublesome, he supposed, and his mother was as much woman as

222

any he had ever known. No, more. Except his lost Agbale/ Nyaunu wi, maybe.

'Nochi,' he said, 'get up from there. You're the widow of one chief and the mother of another—or at least you will be when the *dada* confirms me in the office at the next Customs. That is, if he doesn't change his mind by then. You don't have to kneel before anybody, except the king. So stop acting like a Maxi slave-woman, will you? You heard me, Mother! Get up from there!'

Slowly Gudjo got to her feet.

'As my lord wills,' she said.

'Sagbata, God of the Pest!' Nyasanu exploded. 'Must such empty things as rank and titles come between us, Mother?'

Gudjo looked at him.

'Yes,' she said, 'for they already have. My house is empty. I have no tall and handsome son to eat my cooking and ask counsel of me. In his place there is—a chief. Distant, haughty, occupied with the affairs of Alladah, and with husbanding his wives. Natural enough, I suppose. . . .'

Nyasanu stared at her. Then he drew himself up very stiffly on his ornamented chief's stool.

'Then, as chief of Alladah,' he said, 'I give my subject the Widow Gudjo, a command!'

Gudjo took a backward step. Bowed her head.

'Which is, my lord?' she said.

'That she kiss me,' Nyasanu said. 'That she remembers I am her son. . . .'

'Oh, Nya!' Gudjo wailed, and came to him.

He kissed her. Stood there holding her in his arms and letting her cry. Women needed to cry at times. He already knew that much.

'Nochi,' he said. 'Little Mother, tell me: there's something wrong, isn't there? Something else besides father's death, I mean?'

'Yes!' Gudjo sobbed. 'It's Axisi, Nya! She—she's with child! And she won't even tell me who the father is! When I asked her if it was her promised, Asogbakitikli, she told me in words that would have disgraced a drunken woodcarver that before she'd let that fat little slug touch her, she'd cut her throat!'

'I see,' Nyasanu said. 'Can't say I blame her too much. That's the trouble with betrothing a couple when they're still

223

babies, Nochi; you can never tell what either of them will turn out to be. . . .'

'Asogbakitikli is a nice boy,' Gudjo said, 'and . . .'

'Mother,' Nyasanu said, 'was father a nice boy?'

She stared at him; then suddenly she smiled, through her tears.

'No!' she chuckled. 'He had more mischief in him than Legba, himself. And a temper like the Thunder God's! Why once he . . .'

Nyasanu stopped her with a lifted hand. Once embarked upon her memories, his mother would talk until nightfall.

'Nochi,' he said, 'has any woman since the beginning of memory ever loved a nice boy?'

Gudjo looked at her son long and thoughtfully.

'You're a chief, all right, my son,' she said, 'for though your years are few, your wisdom is a man's. You're right. There's nothing duller than a nice boy, is there? If a man has no *afiti* nor *ataki* in his blood, no pinch of Legba in him, naught of thunder, sea, nor storm, what use is he to a woman?'

'None,' Nyasanu said. 'Don't worry about this. No. Go home now, and tell Axisi to come to me the first hour after there is light, tomorrow morning.'

'She won't come,' Gudjo said. 'I tried to bring her with me and she said . . .'

'Go tell that long, tall, black giraffe of a brother of mine that he may be chief of Alladah to everybody else, but he's still only my snot-nose brother to me!' Nyasanu quoted solemnly.

'Her exact words,' Gudjo sighed. 'How did you know?'

'I know Axisi,' Nyasanu said. 'Time she was taught a lesson, it seems to me.' He clapped his hands suddenly. Two huge men, blacksmiths from the looks of them, from the knotted coils of muscle with which their upper trunks were covered, came running towards them from the direction of the chief's stables.

When they were close enough, Nyasanu said to them:

'If by the third hour of tomorrow morning, my sister Axisi has not appeared before me, you will go to the house of my mother, the Lady Gudjo, and bring my stubborn little beast of a sister before me. By force, if need be.' Then turning to his mother he said:

'And, Nochi, tomorrow you must bring with you the *tayino*, and my father's *akauvi*. Aunt Chadisi, too—and a council of

224

women. I'll sit in judgment but you women must carry out the sentence. . . .'

Gudjo stood there. She opened and closed her mouth two or three times before she could force enough breath out to shape it into words.

'Nya,' she said, 'you aren't going to order her . . .'

'Beaten?' Nyasanu said sternly. 'Yes, mother of an unchaste and wayward daughter! And with many rods at that!'

'Nya,' Gudjo began, 'please, you . . .'

'If you want to remember that I am *toxausu* of Alladah, now is the time to do it, woman! Go home. Tell Axisi that if she thinks she can disgrace you, me, and my father's memory, and get away with it, she's wrong. Advise her to come before me on her own two legs, or by Legba, Lord of Lust, Soye and Alihonu here, will drag her to my house, feet first! You heard me, Mother, go!'

After she had gone, Nyasanu sat there thinking. Then a smile stole over his lean black face. He was well aware that all three of his wives had heard his loudly voiced threat to have Axisi beaten half to death. And, true Dahomean that he was, it occurred to him at once to take some small profit from the fact, for among the many problems confronting him, not the least important was the establishment of peace in his own household.

For only this morning he had come upon his three younger wives, Sosixwe, Huno, and what had shocked him to his heart's core, Dangbevi, dancing in a ring around poor tired Alihosi and singing the cruel song Dahomean wives taunt one another with:

Woman, thy soul is misshapen
In haste was it made, in haste
Too fleshless a face speaks, tell me
Thy soul was formed without care
The ancestral clay for the making
Was moulded in haste, in haste
A thing of no beauty art thou,
Thy face unsuited for a face,
*Thy feet unsuited for feet!**

* Translation from the Fau by Mrs Francis S. Herskovits.

They'd all fallen silent at noting his presence, and even scampered away with a largely false show of fear, leaving poor Alihosi weeping there. Whereupon, he had taken his eldest, *chiosi* wife in his arms, kissed and comforted her.

But he thought now grimly, 'It's high time they all learned a lesson!' So shaking his head he roared out lion-mouthed:

'Dangbevi! Sosixwe! Huno! Come here!'

They came out of the house at once, and stood before him with downcast eyes.

'Women,' he said, 'you will each take a knife and cut me ten slim branches of the anya tree. After that, you will cut away the twigs, and peel off the bark. Then you will bring the bundles of peeled rods to me.'

Sosixwe stared at him in utter astonishment. Huno started at once to cry, like the child she was. But Dangbevi stood there looking at him, and her eyes widened in her soft black face and her mouth began to tremble.

'My Lord ...' she said quietly, 'the anya tree is sacred to your god, Gu, isn't it?'

'It is, woman,' Nyasanu said.

'And it is called ironwood for that, but also because it is the hardest wood there is, is this not so as well, older person?'

'It is,' Nyasanu said. 'What's more, it is one of the most flexible of woods, when green. One can strike more than a hundred blows with one anya rod, and still it will not break....'

Dangbevi bowed her head, looked up again.

'A hundred blows will—kill a woman, my lord,' she whispered.

'I know that, too, woman,' Nyasanu said.

'And—and still you order us—to bring them, my lord?'

'I do,' Nyasanu said.

Dangbevi stood there, looking at him. Sosixwe and Huno were howling and blubbering and begging for mercy, but Dangbevi stood there proudly, like a queen.

'So be it, my lord!' she said at last; then to the others, 'Oh, stop your screeching, you she-jackals! Save your breath. You'll have need of it, I think!'

Then, turning on her heel, she went back into the house. She was, at that moment, the most regal creature Nyasanu had ever seen.

There was a grove of anya trees just behind his house. His great grandfather had planted them there as a sign of respect to their god Gu, the *Vudun* of Iron. So it was the work of no more than a quarter of an hour for the three women to cut and peel the rods. Then they came back and laid the bundles down before him. Sosixwe and Huno were trembling like loko saplings in a high wind, their faces flooded with tears. But Dangbevi stood there facing him and did not cry.

'Kneel!' he shouted. 'Press your faces to the earth!'

The three women knelt before him. Huno and Sosixwe shivered and shook; but Dangbevi curved her body into something his Granduncle Hwegbe, at his miraculous best, might have carved out of ebony wood. As still as that, as unbreathing.

'Alihosi!' Nyasanu called out.

Alihosi came out of the house and stood there. She stared at her three sister wives. At the bundle of peeled rods beside each of them. Then very slowly out of the purest, most exquisite satisfaction possible to a Dahomean wife, she smiled. But, then abruptly, her smile went away. The gaze shifted to her young husband's face. Became unsettled. Confusion invaded it.

Nyasanu was almost able to watch what was going on inside her mind, for he saw the warfare that broke out among her three souls show visibly upon her plain, tired face. It was this he had been gambling upon. Alihosi was less hurt now, less bitter. His never failing patience, his especial consideration for her, the very real tenderness with which he restrained all the excesses of passion while making love to her, had had their effect. So he dared now, because he knew he could—and, having in any event, the power to reduce or annul any too great severity on her part—to put the matter of discipline into her hands.

'Tell me, beloved wife,' he said sternly, 'how many stripes do you consider the insult these three she-cats offered you this morning to be worth?

Alihosi looked at the younger wives. Fifty or a hundred blows, she knew, would ruin her rivals utterly, leaving them scarred, or even crippled, for the rest of their lives. A hundred blows from a peeled rod had been known to kill a man. In either case, she'd be left in undisputed possession of her young lion of a lord, whose heart was as tender as a woman's. But it was precisely this aspect of his temperament that made her stop and think. He'd punish them as she directed, she knew that. All three of his souls were as straight as the loko tree, down which, the ancients hold, the gods had climbed to earth.

227

But—afterwards? Would that tender heart of his forgive her her cruelty? Besides, as a barren wife, all too frequently she'd known her late Lord Gbenu's displeasure; she, herself had been beaten bloody half a dozen times, though, she was honest enough to admit, her own soured temper had nearly always been the cause of her receiving a punishment largely fair, for Gbenu's souls had been as straight as his son's were. So she knew how a peeled rod felt. The memory of its searing bite moved her to pity.

And there was one thing more—she hugged the secret to her heart with fearful joy—her menstrual period was more than three weeks overdue. If she could be the first to give her princely young lord a son, nothing the others could say or do would prevail against her. She glanced at his face, set in lines of unaccustomed stress. How good he is! she thought, how tender! What would please him most? That I ask for a light punishment or——

She stopped short, all three of her souls flooded with light. What she had arrived at was almost incomprehensible to the African mind. The black man's legal genius was praised throughout the ancient world, but while it fully understood and meted out pure justice, mercy was not, and is not, an African word.

'My lord,' she said gently, 'I consider the pranks and babblings of three silly girls powerless to injure a true woman. Therefore, if my husband would favour me, I beg him to forgive them fully, as I already have. . . .'

'Forgive them?' Nyasanu said. 'No. Remember that when they made sport of you, Alihosi, they insulted not only you, personally, but the institution of *chiosi*. To taunt a widow of my father is to offend his memory and his sacred cult. But since you're disposed to pardon them, I'll make their punishment light.'

He turned to where the three young women knelt.

'You will come forward one by one, crawling on your knees —which is the position proper to she-cats, and kiss Alihosi's feet. Then you will tell her you are sorry for what you have done. What's more, for one full moon, she and only she, will occupy my house. Your turns to be my housewife are cancelled until next month. And I'm warning you, they can be cancelled again if you don't behave yourselves!'

At that Sosixwe came to her knees, her hands clasped in the

228

attitude of prayer.

'Beat me!' she howled, 'fifty stripes! A hundred! Take all the skin off my bones! Anything but that, my lord!'

Nyasanu stared at her. His father had been right to select her as one of the four he had left as *chiosi* wives to Gbochi. Sosixwe was as lecherous as a she-monkey. It was a singularly unpleasant trait in a woman. He wondered why this was so. Normally, a man would think that the possession of a woman always ready for the great act to, and of, which all men are born—even, he admitted ruefully, when *he* wasn't—should be a glory. But it wasn't. For one thing, it ruled out courtship, all the delicate art of persuasion, so that the whole thing became mechanical somehow, and thereby robbed of tenderness. 'By being a she-monkey,' he thought bitterly, 'she makes of me an ape. We don't make love. We fornicate. While with Dangbevi, now, and little Huno, and—even Alihosi—it's always pleasant and occasionally very fine. Though Huno and Alihosi spoil it by being—too submissive, too—grateful. Only Dangbevi knows what it is to be a wife. To be lover, mistress, companion, friend . . .'

'My lord, please!' Sosixwe wept.

'Do as I command you, Sosixwe,' he said coldly. 'And if you don't shut up, I'll take still another week away from you.'

He saw, with a curious sense of satisfaction, as the three of them got up, after kissing Alihosi's splayed, rusty, and none too well washed feet, that Dangbevi was crying too, now. Not sobbing aloud like the other two, but weeping great crystalline tears that streaked her black cheeks with light and holding her mouth hard shut, so that the sobs she wouldn't let out, was too proud to voice, quivered her lips, made her chin shake.

But he didn't say anything to her then. It was better to let her suffer awhile. For when a man lost control over his household in a country where polygamy was the rule, he was in bad trouble indeed.

That night—after having done his husbandly duty by Alihosi, and there was guile in this, too, for, by leaving her thoroughly worn out and sleeping the sweet sleep of satiation, he was able to avoid a good many questions that Alihosi's growing confidence in herself, in her hold upon his affections, would have nerved her to ask him—he slipped out of the night and moved as silently as a ghost towards his mother's house.

And except for a loincloth of dark grey cloth—white would have been too visible—he went as naked as the day he was born. He bore only an Ashanti *assegai*, and the jewelled dagger he'd taken from Prince S'ubetzy, heir to the Auyo's saddle-throne. For Dangbevi had gone back into the woods on the first night of his father's funeral and found the beautiful weapon for him, though she hadn't given it to him until some weeks later, when she was sure he'd overcome his mood of despair.

He had no intention of killing or even wounding anyone, unless forced to do so in self defence; he bore the weapons only as a precaution. For who, in the name of Legba, the *Vudun* of Salacious Mischief, could tell what a reluctant lover, forced into a marriage he didn't want, might not do or attempt in defence of his freedom?

'If it is freedom,' Nyasanu thought bleakly, 'Fa grant that he doesn't have a dozen wives already, whoever he is.... Axisi's not bad looking. In fact she's quite pretty—if you can apply that word to a girl who towers by half a head over every living soul in Alladah except me! Strange, the way men react to that.... I'm married to little Huno, who even standing on my chief's stool can barely reach high enough to kiss my chin, and it doesn't bother me. But a man walking down the road with a woman who can eat off his head looks and feels a fool....

'So I hope he's single. And even too poor to afford a little bought and paid for sleeping mat play from time to time. Because if he's too well satisfied in that department, I'm going to have my work cut out for me....'

He went on swiftly, through the night. But what was puzzling his poor head now was another thing. How in the name of Yalode, Goddess of Women, had Axisi managed to get herself pregnant in the first place? Normally, postpubescent girls lived not with their mothers but with their *tauchinoe*, their paternal grandmothers, the Dahomean belief being that a *tauchino* would be far more vigilant of her son's interests—and what was a daughter if not marketable wealth in terms of an advantageous marriage?—than a mere mother would be in watching over her daughter's virtue.

But, he reasoned now, the belief left out the factor of age. His father's mother was very old. It surely had been laughably easy for Axisi to evade her grandmother's vigilance upon many an occasion. And the fact that Gudjo had insisted that

Axisi return to her house some weeks ago probably meant nothing; by then the harm had already been done.

But now he stopped short, brought up hard against a thought that was truly a formidable obstacle to what he had planned to do. For if Axisi slept once more in their mother's house, the possibility of her slipping out to meet her lover and thus enabling him to follow her and discover who the culprit was, simply didn't exist. He knew his mother only too well.

'Even though the yams have already been stolen,' he thought bitterly, 'she'll take great care to lock the storehouse door!' Then he went on. But he moved with his head bent, his footsteps dragging; for he was sure now that on the morrow, he was going to have to order the secret beaten out of his sister's remarkably stubborn hide. And he knew Axisi. If she'd made up her mind not to talk, she wouldn't. That was very bad. For in Dahomey, corporal punishment was administered on the basis of the number of rods broken over the criminals back; the individual blows were not even counted. So, even as big and strong as his sister was, the danger that she would die of that terrible beating was very real.

Still, once he had come to his mother's door, he lingered in the shadow of a nearby baobab tree, waiting. There was nothing else he could do. Having come this far, he'd have to trust to luck. His mother was a sound sleeper, that he knew. Many were the times, during his earliest boyhood, when he had still been too small to live away from home in the communal hut of the older boys, that he had used that knowledge to slip out at night upon some mischief of his own. Even armed and irritated by her suspicions as she was, the weight of her years upon her would surely cause Gudjo to fall asleep at last. The only question was: would his mother succumb to weariness in time to leave enough hours of darkness for Axisi to be able to reach her meeting place? And the sole answer to that question was to wait and see.

So Nyasanu, chief of Alladah, crouched on his heels in the darkness like a waiting thief. And was rewarded. Not half an hour later, he saw his sister's tall figure come through the doorway.

Following her, for a hunter of his practised skill, was child's play. He moved like a ghost, black upon blackness, lost in the jungle night, fitting his footsteps to the exact rhythm of Axisi's so that when they moved, the two of them made but a single

231

sound. Actually, as well he knew, his precautions were largely unnecessary. With all the despair, anger, grief that went trooping through her heart, her mind, Axisi wouldn't even have heard a rogue elephant trumpeting his battle charge.

It took her a long time to reach the place where she was going. More than an hour, Nyasanu judged. But finally, in a moonlit clearing, she stopped, stood trembling, her long, good body sculpturing tension, expectation, hope, against the silvery night. A long time. A very long time. Until he could see her tense form slacken, loosen, give as hope died; assume the head bent down drooping posture of defeat.

A coward, this lover of yours, sister, Nyasanu thought. A thing of little manhood. Having cooled his weapon between your long thighs, he flees responsibility. So be it. I'll have his name off you tomorrow, even if I have to flay the last inch of hide from your foolish back, Legba take you! Why . . .

Then, far off and faint, he heard a little sound. So small a noise that only ears as trained as his were could have heard it. It broke through all the other sounds, for an African rain forest is not a silent place, whispering through monkey screech and chatter; the big-beaked ibis, raucous voiced in a shallow pool; leopard cough, and from the jungle's edges, where the great trees abruptly halt and the grassy savanna lands begin, the whoop of hyena, the bark of jackal, and the felt reverberations of the lions' drum-deep voices, dark spoken, their muzzles placed close to the ground to make their menace carry. The reason he could hear it was that it was alien. No scampering brushcat, no tiny dik dik, made a sound like that. No. Quietly, carefully coming on, was the padding footfalls of that cruellest of all the beasts: man.

And now Axisi went flying towards the far edge of the clearing. The man stepped out of the brush, out of midnight into moonlight; and Nyasanu saw who he was; Kapo, son of Hwesbeyu, a poor tenant farmer upon one of his late father's estates. Kapo, a ne'er-do-well, known for his success at gaming, at wenching, at all else except work. But a handsome young man. Better looking, in all probability, than even Nyasanu himself was. And, perhaps best of all, tall enough to look Axisi straight in the eye.

'Gbo,' Kapo said loudly, so that his voice carried over to where Nyasanu was, using the word in its sense of 'charm'. 'Enchantress, who has enslaved my heart . . .'

232

'Shut up!' Axisi howled at him. 'This is not time for pretty words! So keep your lying speeches, Kapo, before I knock you back on your rusty black tail again! What I want to know is what you're going to do about us! My mother knows. By now she's told my brother. And you know how straight his souls are. He'll probably order me beaten to death if I don't tell the name of the man who made me find my belly. *Your* name, lover! So ...'

'Look, Axisi,' Kapo said, 'I've told you a hundred times. We've got to run away. It has to be an *xadudo* mating. I haven't a cowry. So how can I pay back Asogbakitikli for all the work he's done for your late father, and for your mother, for the gifts he's made? And his *dokpwe* and his *gbe,* for their work and help on top of that? Why it must amount to thousands of cowries by now! And your brother—how can I pay him for your bridal price? Look, sorceress mine, I love you; but there is no way under Mawu-Lisa's heaven I can make you an *akwenusi* bride. ...'

'You'd better find a way!' Axisi said, 'for by Sagbata, I ...'

'Axisi! Axisi!' Kapo groaned. 'Why have you changed so much? You used to say that *xadudo* was the only honourable way for a free woman to wed! To come to her man out of love, alone. Demanding nothing, defying her family, conventions, the world. ...'

'Dung!' Axisi shrilled. 'Goat dung! I hadn't found my belly then, Kapo! So I only had *me* to think of. Besides I was a fool. Everybody knows what you men do with *xadudo* wives! The minute our breasts start to sag, the first grey hair that sprouts on our heads, the first wrinkle on our faces, and out we go into the streets to starve! There's no law to make you feed this bastard you've given me. I go to my brother for help, and straight souled as he is, he kicks me out of his door. And rightly! For since I've been fool enough to disgrace him and our family, why should he help me, when the shiftless brushcat I opened my legs to out of an excess of folly won't? Oh, Yalode, Goddess of Women, help me! For I ...'

'I'll never desert you, Axisi,' Kapo said. 'You know that.'

'I *don't* know it! You've deserted at least twenty loose-kneed idiots before now! And the only reason you're still here now is that I'm not far enough along to be unable to beat the daylights out of you. But the minute I'm too swollen to move, you'll take off for Maxi land, or hide out among the Yorubas

233

or the Fulani, or ...'

'Axisi,' Kapo whispered, and took her in his arms.

Nyasanu went away from there, then. Axisi was his sister; she shared his heritage. And he was only too aware of the tendency that any child of Gbenu and Gudjo had towards compounding romantic folly. That she would let Kapo make love to her again, he was bitterly sure. What he wasn't sure of was his own right to prevent or stop this one more sin, since it could neither add to nor subtract from the consequences of previous indulgences in common carnality. 'Let them enjoy each other,' he thought sadly. 'What difference does it make now?'

What he could do—and did do—was to wait for Kapo on the edge of the trail that led to the plantation—now his, Nyasanu's own—on which that reckless sinner lived with his father Hwesbeyu. Again his wait was long: Kapo was an athlete of a lover. But at last, just as dawn was pearling the edge of the sky, he saw that ne'er-do-well stumbling towards him, his face grey and drawn with weariness. Axisi was a big, lusty girl; husbanding her properly was nobody's easy task.

Then very quietly, Nyasanu rose up from his place of concealment and with one smooth motion put the point of his *assegai* against his throat.

'Come with me, Kapo,' he said.

Kapo stared at him. His breath made a dusty, dry rattle in his throat.

'While a man lives, all things can be arranged,' Nyasanu said. 'But crossing the river ahead of time ends all possibilities, don't you think? You heard me, Kapo, come!'

But even after he'd left his prospective brother-in-law bound hand and foot in the stables where he kept the miserable, scrawny nags he'd inherited from his father, there to be fly-tormented along with them, he still had another thing to do: selecting five of the stoutest anya rods his wives had prepared the afternoon before, he carefully ringed each rod with a deep cut near its thicker end. The way he had weakened them, the rods would break upon the impact of a single blow. But then he stopped, and stared at his handiwork. All too clearly the fresh cuts showed. He stood there, frowning. Then his eyes cleared. Taking up a handful of reddish earth, he mixed it with water, and packed the wet clay into the cuts. The clay was a darker red than the anya wood. If you looked closely you

234

could still see that something was wrong with these rods. But he had to gamble on the probability that whatever woman was chosen to administer the whipping wouldn't think to examine the rods. At least he hoped she wouldn't.

For he had no intention of killing his she-devil of a sister; or even hurting her too much. Truth to tell, he loved Axisi dearly; and it was her very devilry, compounded, as it was, of gaiety, mischief, impudence, and mockery of all authority, that most appealed to him.

After that, finally, he went to bed, and slept the blissful sleep of the straight souled, the just.

What wakened him at the third daylight hour, was the sound of women's voices. He heard his sister's fluting above them all. Axisi was cursing like a woodcarver, using a language that blue smoked and made sulphurous the very air.

He listened, judging how far away they still were by the way their bleat and titter and cackle came over to him. Then he relaxed; he still had time. He got up from the sleeping mat, urinated in the clay pot kept for that purpose, washed himself in the warm water that Alihosi quickly brought him, cleaned his teeth with the pounded and shredded twigs of a fragrant herb, perfumed his neck, armpits and crotch, and last of all attired himself in his green silk toga and chief's cap.

By the time he'd finished his toilet, the women came trooping into the square before his house. They were led not by his mother but by the *tayino,* the eldest woman member of his father's clan, in whose person was vested almost as much magical and spiritual authority as was granted to the *xenuga,* or clan head, himself. She was followed by the *akauvi,* the woman who had cooked his father's last meal, and who presided over the washing of his body, the clipping of his fingers and toenails, the shaving of all hair from his head, face, armpits, chest, legs, pubic regions and the like as a precaution against such personal relics falling into the hands of an evil sorcerer, who, by making *gbos* of them, could easily have brought all the dead man's children under his absolute control. Therefore the *akauvi,* in a way, was the living representative of Gbenu's ghost, and, as such, had great authority in all matters touching the lives and future of the family.

After her came Gudjo, and Nyasanu's Aunt Chadisi, both of them weeping bitter tears. The rest of the council was made up of respectable married women, as well as several free

235

women, by which term Dahomeans meant only that they were not responsible to any man, the word being no reflection upon their personal morals. Two or three of the free women present were heads of their own compounds and 'father' of many children. This was a pure convention. All Dahomeans understood that by one of the twelve forms of marriage, *gbausu dono gbausi,* 'giving the she-goat to the buck', these very wealthy women, widows or women who had never wed, but who through their own efforts as traders or by inheritance possessed independent fortunes, and even occasionally wives of noble or royal birth, who were past the age of childbearing, would themselves 'marry' a number of younger women. By no means did this imply that such women were lesbians, as dirty old men like Nyasanu's granduncle Hwegbe loudly claimed. What such rich women did, actually, was to call in younger male relatives and friends of theirs to mate with their 'wives'. But the children born of these strictly supervised matings belonged to the female founder of the compound, took her name, and called her 'father', just as her 'wives' called her 'husband'. Dahomean life was rich in variety, which was why, maybe, it produced the proud, intelligent, forceful people whom nobody ever successfully enslaved.

The only men present, beside Nyasanu himself, were his men-servants Soye and Alihonu, who half carried, half dragged the kicking, screaming, cursing Axisi between them. Nyasanu sighed. He had hoped that his sister would have come of her own free will, thus making the proceedings a trifle less unpleasant. But he should have known better. Axisi was Axisi —a rebel to the core of her proud and tender heart.

'Tie her hands and feet,' he ordered the two menservants. 'Then wait nearby in case I should need you....'

Soye and Alihonu tried to obey his command. But Axisi was her father's daughter. For one thing she was six feet one inch tall, and had all the lean, lithe, graceful strength of a black panther. In the end, he had to help them, at the cost of some little blood, drawn from his arms and face by her nails, and a considerable injury to his chiefly dignity. When they had it done at last, he heard a titter of mocking laughter, and glaring in the direction from which it had come, saw that the woman who loosed it was Yu, his father's number one widow, and mother of his half-brother Gbochi.

He wondered who, in the name of Legba, Lord of Lust and

Mischief, had invited Yu to join the council. Then it came to him that no one had. She had simply heard about it—next to boasting, gossip was the most prevalent of Dahomean vices—and had come of her own accord. The worst of it was that no one could stop her; as his father's widow, she was fully entitled to take part in the deliberations.

Nyasanu lifted up his voice:

'Dangbevi!' he called: 'Sosixwe!'

The two young wives came flying out of the house and stood before him, trembling.

'Bring stools for the venerable *tayino*, and for my father's *akauvi*, to whom great respect is owed. Tell Huno and Alihosi to bring my parasol and two others. Alihosi will hold my parasol over my head, while you and Sosixwe will shade the heads of my two oldest living ancestresses. Huno will fan both of them. Is all this clear?'

'Yes, older person mine,' Dangbevi whispered. He could see the great hurt in her eyes. Even in so small a matter as providing him with shade, he was favouring Alihosi, and she knew it.

'Lay down the palm fronds,' he said to his men servants. Soye and Alihonu laid the fronds, or rather the bare stalks of palm frond, on the ground before Nyasanu's house in such a way that they formed a square. Inside that square his wives placed the three stools, his own, the richly carved tall chief's stool he had inherited from his father, and the two lower, plainer stools upon which the female clan head and the sacred she-guardian of his father's relics and memory were to sit. No other woman could enter that marked-off square until she was called upon to testify.

The *tayino* and the *akauvi* took their seats. Dangbevi and Sosixwe opened the gaudy parasols over their white heads. Alihosi opened the chief's parasol, decorated all over with appliqué cloth designs that depicted many of Gbenu's feats of valour, and stood here waiting. In time, Nyasanu would order a great chief's parasol of his own and the appliqué pictures on it would show his own heroic acts. Young as he was, he could already picture a scene that outdid any of his father's; for how many men could boast of having won a war singlehanded, captured an enemy prince, and saved the life of a king?

With great dignity, he sat down.

'I, your *toxausu*, have enstooled myself,' he said. 'This constitutes a court. Before us stands the prisoner, Axisi, accused of unchastity and of betraying the trust of the man to whom she is formally promised. And as your chief, I should like to make clear one thing: though Axisi is my *novichi nyqnu*, mother's child female, my full sister, not half, that fact will have no influence upon my decision except, perhaps, to make my judgments more severe. For it is my father's honour that she sullies, if the charges be true, and my own. Now let the prisoner come forward.'

'How can I,' Axisi said, 'when you've tied my feet together like a sacrificial goat's?'

'If you had kept them—and your knees—together as a maiden should,' the *akauvi* said sternly, 'you wouldn't be here now. One of you women cut the cords that bind her ankles!'

It was quickly done. Axisi came forward and stood before the two old women and her brother.

'Are you with child, woman?' Nyasanu said.

'Yes, Brother,' Axisi said mockingly.

'I am not your brother, woman!' Nyasanu roared, lion-mouthed, 'but your judge! Now tell me: is Asogbakitikli the father of your child?'

Axisi smiled.

'Can a potter shape a clay image with the drooping stem of the lotus flower?' she said.

All the women present gasped at that. Nyasanu could hear the words 'Shame! Shame!' float above them upon the riptide of their breaths. He stood up then, and picked up a peeled anya rod from one of the bundles of those he had not notched to make them break. He walked quietly behind his sister. When he swung that rod, the whistle it made was like a storm god's wind screech howling over the unmarked tombs of the sinful dead. The flexible anya wood wrapped itself three quarters of the way around Axisi's body. It opened up her flesh like a blunt knife. The force of the blow was so great that she measured her full length out upon the ground.

She lay there crying very quietly. Then for the first time she saw the three bundles of anya rods. She stared at them. By Dahomean custom, the blows wouldn't be counted, only the number of rods broken over her bare back. And one anya rod would last through a hundred blows, two hundred even. Three bundles of ten rods each meant an absolute minimum of

238

three thousand lashes. By the time they'd done with her, skin, flesh, muscle would all be gone, and the bare bones of her back would be showing through.

'My lord Toxausu,' she said quietly, 'since you mean to kill me for having so dishonoured our *gbwe*, our house, I ask only that you use a knife.'

'Silence, woman!' Nyasanu said. 'I have made no judgment yet. What that judgment will be, depends upon you. I warn you to keep a respectful tongue in your head, and tell me who fathered the child you have in your womb. What is his name?'

Axisi grinned up at him.

'Names,' she said. 'There were three of them.'

Again all the women gasped aloud. Surely never had there been a more shameful confession made in all the memory of the spoken chronicles.

Nyasanu looked at his sister. Then at his mother. She and his Aunt Chadisi had buried their faces against each other's necks and were sobbing loudly.

'And you have no idea which of the three with whom you've dishonoured yourself and your house is the actual father?' he said tiredly.

'Yes, my lord,' Axisi said. 'All three of them are. You see they are ghosts—and ghosts have great powers. Their names are Mase, Agadeyaunsu, and Siligbo. And maybe Hwesiyo too. But I was so tired by then, I couldn't be sure about him. . . .'

What burst from the throats of about one third of the women present was a howl of rage. The women who cried out, Nyasanu knew without even looking at them, were all members of his father's clan. For unlike most clans, the Ayatovi Gaminu had not one *tauhwiyo,* or founder, but four. And that mistress or mischief and mockery, his sister Axisi had named them all—or at least their ghosts—as the fathers of her child.

He stood there looking at her, with a sort of reluctant admiration in his eyes. As an example of pure Dahomean guile, her answer was masterly. He was quite sure that no woman, at least, ever believed another when she claimed that her child had been fathered by the ghost of the founder of her clan; not even when the *bokono*, the diviner, substantiated her claims. Everyone knew that the diviner could be bribed. And it was at least highly suspicious that the women who made such claims were nearly always unmarried or wives whose husbands had been so long absent on one of the *dada's* military campaigns that they *had* to claim that or the even more dubious proposition that they were victims of a prolonged pregnancy. Yet both beliefs were part of Dahomean religion. Many a bastard child had gone through life honoured by all because some *bokono* had declared him the son of the ghost of *tauhwiyo*. And some women had given birth to a legitimate child, after their husbands had been held prisoner by the Auyo a full three years, because a friendly *bokono* declared that an *azaundato*, an evil sorcerer, had put a spell on them which had kept them from giving birth to a child sired by their own husbands during all that time.

These things, Nyasanu knew, were escape doors wisely provided to supply a needed human relief from the rigidity of Dahomean religion and morality. He didn't believe they could really happen; he was sure his sister was lying, but then, who could tell? All things were possible to the *vudun* of Africa.

'Son-chief,' the *tayino* said, her lips muffling the words, because she was eighty years old, and had long since lost the last tooth she had, 'we'd better call Zezu, the diviner.'

'Not yet, Nochi,' Nyasanu said, calling her Nochi, my mother, as a sign of respect. 'First we shall see if she persists in her claims.' He turned and looked at the crowd.

'My Lady Yu!' he cried out.

Yu came forward, a look of astonishment on her face. It was matched by the expression upon Gudjo's, upon Chadisi's, even upon Axisi's. But Nyasanu was exercising all his native guile. He knew that so terrible a humiliation as having Yu serve as executioner would break his sister's resistance faster than any number of lashes would.

'You will take these five rods,' Nyasanu said, 'and break them over this woman's back. After every five blows you will pause that I may ask her if she persists in her claim that her child was fathered by the mighty dead.'

'Nya—my lord,' Axisi said. 'Choose somebody else. Beat me yourself. But don't shame me like this! Don't have me whipped by this whore who opened her legs to even the monkeys in the forest!'

Nyasanu said:

'Silence, woman! You insult my father's memory when you insult his widow!'

'And she insulted his honour while yet he lived!' Axisi shot back at him, 'for Mawu-Lisa witness that not one of her chil-

240

dren have his face!'

'The Lady Yu is not on trial here,' Nyasanu said quietly. 'You are, woman. And believe me, my father's ghost weeps at the sight of you, from beyond the river. . . .'

Clearly, it was a thought that had never occurred to Axisi. She looked up at her brother, and her eyes were appalled.

'My lord,' she whimpered, 'kill me. Decree my death. I—I am not fit to live!'

'No,' Nyasanu said tiredly. 'You have but to speak the truth and . . .'

Stubbornly Axisi shook her head. Nya knew why, and even admired her for it. Since Kapo was too poor to marry her properly—for except for *xadudo*, *chiosi*, and *axovivi*, which is to say, common-law, inherited wives, and the wedding of a princess, all Dahomean marriages involved substantial exchanges of money and goods—what point was there in getting her lover in trouble over a sin that had been mutual and that he was powerless to remedy?

Quietly Nyasanu turned to Soye and Alihonu, his menservants.

'Go to the stables,' he commanded, 'and bring the male prisoner before me!'

The two big men loped away at a fast trot. Came back again dragging Kapo between them. Ignoring his sister's startled gasp, and the astonished cries of the women, Nyasanu stared at Kapo, solemnly.

'Kapo, son of Hwesbeyu,' he said, 'I have ordered this woman beaten with five rods for the sin of unchastity. That is, if she doesn't name the man who fathered her child. What have you to say to this?'

'Free her, my lord,' Kapo said at once. 'I am the father.'

Nyasanu turned to his sister. Except as a lever to pry the truth out of her, Kapo's confession was meaningless. If accused, no male Dahomean ever denied siring a child. Even if he'd been away in Benin or Kumassi when the actual conception took place, he'd still take upon himself the guilt. For if he didn't, his dead ancestors and the gods of fertility would punish him with impotency on the score that to reject a child was to diminish by one the number of their worshippers.

'Is he?' the young chief said.

'Him?' Axisi hooted. 'He's another drooping flower, my lord!'

241

'Beat her!' Nyasanu said to Yu.

Yu sought Gudjo's face. Smiled at her, a smile of pure undiluted malice. Stood there holding the anya rod, her eyes alight with mockery, with triumph. Then she swung it with all her force. But the instant it touched Axisi's naked back, it broke off short in the Pig Woman's hand.

Yu stood there, staring at what was left of the rod. Then she took another from that carefully selected bundle Nyasanu had given her. Swung it fiercely. The result was identical. But now, as she stared at the second broken rod, a wavering glint of fear showed in Yu's eyes. Yu was, after all, a Dahomean, and every Dahomean knew that the *vudun*, the gods, intervened on behalf of their favourites. As she took up the third rod, Yu's hand shook visibly.

'Get on with it!' Nyasanu said.

The other three rods broke easily and at once, so that Yu, for all that she was as strong as a buffalo cow, was unable to raise a single welt on Axisi's glossy black hide.

And it was only then that Nyasanu saw to what degree he had outsmarted himself by his trickery. The women were staring at Axisi in awe.

'The *vudun*,' they whispered, 'protect her! The ghosts of the founders break the rods in mid-air before they touch her back! She's telling the truth? It was the *tauhwiyo* who ...'

Nyasanu lifted his hand.

'I order Kapo, son of Hwesbeyu, beaten with ten rods,' he said, 'for the self-confessed sin of stealing a girl promised to another!'

Axisi stopped grinning.

'My lord,' she said, 'please ...'

'Unless you tell the truth, woman!' Nyasanu roared, lion-mouthed. 'If you name the father of your bastard, I'll stop the beating at once.'

Axisi was no fool. If she confessed the truth, Kapo stood convicted by her very words of bride-stealing, an offence punishable by a least one hundred lashes. So she bargained. Like all Dahomean women, she was good at it.

'I'll confess,' she said slowly, 'if you, my lord Toxausu, will promise upon your honour as a judge to spare Kapo all punishment, no matter *what* name I say.'

Nyasanu was hard put to suppress a grin.

'Done!' he said. 'Upon my honour as a judge!'

'It was him,' Axisi said slowly, 'Kapo, I mean. I—I love him, my lord; I know he's nothing much, but . . .'

'Silence!' Nyasanu thundered. 'Trial's over. The council is dismissed!'

'But—but,' Yu protested. 'Nothing's been decided! No sentence . . .'

'Has been handed down,' Nyasanu said. 'Nor can one be, now. The matter is beyond the jurisdiction of a woman's council. It now lies between my clan. Asogbakitikli's, and Kapo's. Asogbakitikli has just claim for damages against me, as head of my father's household after his death, for not making sure this slut kept her knees together. . . .'

'Nya!' Kapo said. 'By Fa and Legba both, I'll . . .'

'And against this champion whore-hopper for sneaking into other people's houses,' Nyasanu went on imperturbably. 'Tell me, Kapo, how many women have you caused to find their bellies by now?'

Axisi got wearily to her feet. She smelt of sweat. The one terrible stripe that Nyasanu had given her was stiffening up on her; but she was smiling. No, grinning at her brother.

'One,' she said, 'me. He knows better, Brother! I've already proved to him I can whip his rusty tail for him without even half trying. And don't tell me what a no-good he is. I know that, too. But you're looking at the straightest-souled man in Dahomey from here on in. Right, Kapo? Or do I have to knock you right back on your skinny seat again in front of all these people to prove it?'

'No,' Kapo said ruefully. 'You know I've been faithful to you, Axisi. . . .'

'Only because you knew I'd have broken your worthless neck if you hadn't,' Axisi said. 'Nya . . .'

'Yes, Sister?' Nyasanu said.

'Will you—forgive me? Will you—please?'

'I'll have to think about it,' Nyasanu said gruffly. 'Dangbevi! Huno! Take her into the house! Wash her. Dress her stripes. I've got things to do. *We* have things to do, Kapo and I. Now get to it, all of you!'

Two hours later, Nyasanu sat before the *xenuga* of his father's clan. With him was Kapo, crouching there with downcast eyes. Around them were all the elders of the Ironworkers' Clan.

'What is your verdict, venerable elders?' Nyasanu said.

Adjasmi, Nyasanu's paternal grandfather and also the *xen-uga* of the clan, spoke calmly.

'Vivu,' he said, 'Grandson—if this lecherous young billygoat can pay back the girl's legitimate suitor the money and work already expended on her behalf—and make the proper gifts due in a normal *akwenusi* wedding, we'll accept him as my granddaughter's husband. If not, no...'

'But, my lords and venerable elders!' Kapo protested loudly. 'I am poor! I haven't the money to...'

Nyasanu leaned forward, his proud nostrils flaring with suspicion. For, even as he voiced his groaning protests, Kapo's right hand had flown upwards to half cup itself around a bulge under his toga.

'Kapo,' the young chief said quietly, 'how much money do you have in that pouch you've got tied around your neck under your shirt? All of it, I happen to know, cheated out of the poor devils foolish enough to play *adjo* and *akau* with you. Don't lie to me, now! How much have you got there?'

'Two thousand cowries,' Kapo whispered. 'But Ny—my lord —that won't even start to pay back....'

'Give them to me,' Nyasanu said. 'You heard me, Kapo! Give them to me!'

Wonderingly, Kapo pulled the leather drawstring purse out from under his shirt and poured the cowries out into Nyasanu's two hands.

'Great Xenuga and venerable elders,' Nyasanu said, 'I accept the money as a downpayment on the estate where the scoundrel lives with his father, a hard-working and an honourable man. Every growing season, Kapo must pay me two-thirds of his harvests for ten years, at the end of which time the estate becomes free and clean and his property. I call upon all of you, venerable elders, to bear witness to this contract.'

'But—but...' Kapo stuttered, 'Asogbakitikli? How can I pay him?'

'I'll lend you the money to pay all his claims and to bear the expenses of a proper wedding to my sister—all of which I'll sweat out of your mangy hide with a couple of years more hard work,' Nyasanu said. 'Only one thing do I require of you, Kapo, from this day forth....'

'And that is—Brother?' Kapo said, happily.

'That you break your *adji* board, and throw your *akau* dice into the fire. Now, today, in the presence of these witnesses.

Go and fetch them. We will wait. And I don't think I need point out to you what will happen to your rusty tail if you fail to show up for work in the fields you've just bought—or rather started to buy—for even one day. Even if you're dying, you'd better crawl to work on your belly, Kapo! You have heard what I said?'

'Yes, Brother—I mean my lord!' Kapo said.

Some hours later, when Axisi heard of it, she came flying to her brother's house, prostrated herself before him, kissed his feet, threw dirt on her own head, and howled and blubbered like a demented thing.

'Oh, get up from there, Axisi,' Nyasanu said, but then he stopped short, staring.

The three Half Heads, the royal messengers, were bowing low before him.

'Great Chief,' they said. 'The Customs begin next week. Our lord, the Leopard, commands us to bring you before him that he may reward you for your mighty deeds. We pray you, great Gbonuga, prepare yourself for the journey!'

When Axisi and Nyasanu's wives heard that, they all let out a squeal of joy. For although *gbonuga* and *toxausu* both mean chief, a *toxausu* is chief of but a single town or city, while a *gbonuga* is ruler over a province.

But hearing it, knowing that his dizzy climb to power had already begun, Nyasanu felt a sudden stab of fear. How many men had the Leopard kings lifted to the skies, only to dash them down again, for some slight, trifling fault? It was not wise, he knew, to attract too much attention in Da's Belly. Only men in some lost village, far away from Abomey—men 'without names'—were really safe.

The reflection came too late. He had a name already—*gbonuga*, ruler of a province. A most weighty name. He sat there savouring it. Then, deeply, sadly, he sighed.

'I hear and obey, most noble lords,' he said.

SEVENTEEN

Nyasanu soon discovered that the preparations for a journey to Abomey, where the Leopard kings held their court, was enough to try the nerves of one of the brass figures that his friend Amosu made. For a man simply couldn't go up to the capital with the same slight effort it took to go to any other Dahomean city, a matter, merely, of buying provisions for the trip, leaving foodstuffs and money in the hands of his wives to support his family during his absence, calling together his bearers and hammockmen, and setting out. No. He had to carefully decide upon the number of his people to take with him, how richly he dared dress them and himself, choose suitable gifts for the king and the more important officials of the court, select the means of transportation; in short, arrange every detail of the journey in a manner calculated to please the *dada* once the omnipresent royal spies had reported these matters to the Leopard, as they were sure to do. And what plunged the young *toxausu* into a really painful state of indecision was his certain knowledge that any slight error in protocol on his part could cost him not only the king's hard-won favour, but even the permanent separation of his head from his neck.

Worst of all, there was no one he could consult. For, while it was true that there were several old men in Alladah—among them his paternal grandfather—who had attended the royal Customs, their visits had outdated the present *dada* reign. And what had pleased one Aladaonu king was like as not to infuriate his successor. All the world knew that.

So thinking, Nyasanu walked down to his father's stables and stood there, looking at the horses he had inherited. There were five of them. Four of the five were miserable racks of bones, as were nearly all horses in the land of Da's Belly. But the fifth, a snowy Arabian stallion, was very fine indeed. And for this state of affairs, Nyasanu was himself responsible. Some years before, Gbenu had brought home not this stallion, but its sire, a fine mount he had captured from an Auyo horseman in one of King Gezo's earlier raids, and Nya had clapped his hands and cried out at the sight of the animal's great beauty. Whereupon his father had said, sadly:

'Yes—he is beautiful, isn't he? More's the pity. For inside

246

three months he will be dead.'

'Why, Da?' the boy had asked.

'Don't know. Auyo horses always die down here. I think it's the flies. They don't have them in Auyo country—or at least not the same kind. Too hot and dry up there, I guess. So the only thing we can do with this beauty is to serve one of the mares with him and hope the colt, having half the blood of a dam accustomed to the tsetse flies, will live——'

So it had been done. And when the mare had foaled, the colt she dropped proved to be even more beautiful than his sire—already dead by then of the sleeping sickness just as Gbenu had predicted. For that reason Gbenu called the spindly-legged little fellow N'yoh, a Fau phrase meaning 'It is good'. And it was then that Nyasanu had ventured the suggestion which had made all the difference.

'Da,' he'd said, 'why don't we put him—and his dam—in a special stable hung with netting to keep out the tsetse flies? That way he could grow up to be big and strong without them draining all the life out of him.'

Gbenu had stared at his son. Then he smiled.

'Good,' he'd said. 'You have much head, Vi. It might work at that.'

And it had worked, though for a reason beyond their concepts. The netting had sharply limited the number of tsetse that could get to the white colt. Therefore, instead of being swarmed from head to hoof with the maddening, stinging, biting insects, the way Dahomean colts and fillies always were—with the result that the rare exceptions who had lived to grow up at all developed into the world's most miserable examples of horseflesh—N'yoh was bitten only occasionally, so that his blood developed a *gbo* against the tsetse similar to the one that Furtoo, the skinless people, had invented against Sagbata's scourge, the smallpox. N'yoh was by long odds the finest horse in all Dahomey.

Looking at him now, Nyasanu put out his hand and caressed the white stallion's forehead. The horse stretched out his neck and whinnied with pleasure.

'Shall I ride him?' Nyasanu thought. 'That would make a fine impression. Me dressed in green silk mounted on N'yoh and——'

Then he stopped. The memory of the *dada*, King Gezo himself riding into battle against the Maxis came jarring back into his head. The king's mount had been as worthless a nag as anyone he could imagine. Of course, part of that had been strategy; but even so, the mounts of the *munga*, the *meu*, the *gao*, the *kposu*—his own father—had been very little better. He was suddenly quite sure that not even the *dada* had in the royal stables a horse anywhere approaching N'yoh in strength and beauty——

Therefore, he reasoned, I cannot ride him. To outdo the *dada* is one of the quickest forms of suicide known to mortal man. . . .

He leaned against the doorframe thinking:

'A hammock, then? As a chief, and certainly as a *gbonuga*, that is my right. The finest hammock of all hung with embroidered green silks and shaded with my father's biggest, richest parasol would——'

He stopped again, a light of slow and sly mockery beginning to glow in his black eyes.

'That is what they'll expect,' he mused, 'all the envious ones who from this day on will be plotting my downfall, scheming ways to deprive me of the *dada*'s favour: that I'll come in finery, making a great show. And then they'll say: "Look at him, this provincial bullfrog, puffed up with pride, pretending to lord it over us as though he were an *axo* of royal blood!" Then they'll whisper and whisper: "Have a care, O mighty Dada! Such a one as this, lacking in all humility, will surely scheme to seize the throne from you, as you seized it from your elder brother, Adanzau!"*

'So now to fool them by doing precisely what they don't expect. I'll go as a pilgrim, dressed in white cottonsilk cloth. I'll take only ten bearers with me, of which six will carry gifts for the *dada,* and the other four our provisions for the journey. Then when the *dada* sees me, he'll think: How modest a young man! How humble! And to think that such a one as this saved my conquest for me—and my life!'

He stood there, smiling at his own thought. That it was the wisest choice of all was unquestionable. So, having decided, he

---

* Historical note: Gezo was able to overthrow Adanzau, because this king, an older half-brother of Gezo, was the most hated ruler in Dahomean history, due to his sadism, and the people flocked to support the younger brother. Among Adanzau's proven crimes was to sell Gezo's own mother and all her women attendants into slavery in Brazil.

dismissed it from his consciousness and turned his mind to other matters.

Clapping his hands, he waited until Soye and Alihonu, his menservants, came running from the direction of his forge. When they were close enough for him not to have to shout, he said to them:

'Go to the compound of my half-brother Gbochi and bring my granduncle Hwegbe to me. Don't ask him to come, because the old scoundrel has spent his life defying all authority. Bring him. And his woodcarving tools as well. When you've got him here, lock him up in that empty storehouse at the back part of this compound. Then I'll deal with him.'

'We hear and obey, great Gbonuga!' his menservants said.

Nyasanu stared at them. Then he sighed. That they addressed him as *gbonuga,* governor or excellency, was proof enough that some or all of his wives were talking too much. Sooner or later he was going to have to carry out his often voiced threats—which he was wryly sure they laughed at behind his back, knowing he had no belly for cruelty—and give the lot of them a good beating.

'I am not a *gbonuga*', he said quietly, 'but only a *toxausu.* Perhaps when I come back I will hold a higher rank than chief of a village. And perhaps not. That's for the *dada* to say. But I'd thought both of you were too smart to listen to the cackling of silly hens who don't even know how to lay an egg!'

The menservants looked at him and cast down their gaze, much ashamed.

'Oh, forget it!' Nyasanu said. 'Go get me that wicked old fool. I need him—but for Legba's sake, don't tell him that!'

Watching them loping away, he was again seized with a disquieting premonition of impending trouble. But then he shrugged it off. The things you did about a future trouble you were afraid of cost too much time and money. He had the money, but he hadn't the time to spend up to five days in Zezu's *fafume,* forest of hate, listening to gibberish designed to ward off evil. He was beginning to suspect that everything the *bokonoe* and *azaundatoe* did was pure nonsense, that even when it worked, it was coincidence that achieved the miracle.

So, consigning diviners and sorcerers both to the nether regions, he set out in the direction of the storehouse next to his forge. In it he had a number of *ase,* the decorated iron altars used to worship the *tauvudun,* the ancestors-become-gods. He

249

had made these *ase* himself and they were very beautiful. Now all he had to do was to select the finest one of all as an offering to the royal ancestors. Surely a gift of such great piety could not fail to please the king....

But before he had gone four steps he became aware of Alihosi. She was kneeling before him with her forehead pressed to the ground and was busily engaged in throwing dust on her head with both hands as a sign of humility.

'Now what?' he almost groaned. 'Have those three she-cats been taunting you again?'

'No, great and noble Gbonuga, whose very shadow honours his servant and his slave,' Alihosi got out, and now he could hear the pure triumph vibrating her rather shrill and harsh voice, 'it is only that I—I——'

'That you what?' he said impatiently.

'That I heard what my noblest and most exalted of all the great lords who dwell in the Belly of Da said to Soye and Alihonu. Therefore if my *axo*, my prince, his excellency will permit——'

'Oh, for Legba's sake, call me husband, woman!' Nyasanu said. 'Haven't you got sense enough not to put store by any reward or title that the Leopard has not given yet? Don't you know from my father's time that the only unchangeable thing about leopards are their spots? Certainly not their tempers or their favours. So if you've got something to say, say it! But make sure that it's important, for I have no time!'

'I—I think it's important, Medaxochi, older person mine,' Alihosi whispered, 'though whether my lord will agree I cannot say. Put it this way: here you have one hen at least who has all the right to cackle in this world!'

Nyasanu stood there. The feeling that invaded him was hard to put a name to. He was going to have a son—which was, or should be, a source of joy. But by the plain, faded relic of his father's instead of by Dangbevi, as he'd hoped with all three of his souls. What kind of a manchild could poor, tired Alihosi give him, conceived in pity as it had been, shaped in the until now barren womb of a woman close to the end of her childbearing years? A weakling? A coward? A *gaglo* like his brother Gbochi?

He was aware, finally, that she was studying his face; and from the expression on her own, it was clear that she had read his disappointment all too well. So he willed himself to smile at

250

her most tenderly and voicing in his heart the silent prayer 'O *Vudun* of Earth, Sky, Sea and Thunder, let it be a girl!' he raised her up, drew her into his arms, kissed her, and whispered:

'Praised be to the *vudun* for you, Alihosi, who are truly a woman!'

She stared at him, her eyes small, suspicious; then they cleared. She could forgive him his disappointment, because now, considered coolly, it didn't matter. She had won. No matter how powerful the weapons her rivals had—beauty, youth, sensuality, charm—she had already outdone them. For when he saw the son she was sure she was going to be able to give him—tall as a loko sapling, made of the night's own beauty, eyed with stars—he would be bound to her forever. Of that she was very sure.

'Have you told the others?' he said.

'No, husband,' Alihosi said. 'I—I thought it best that it should be you——'

'Who tells them? All right. But later—when they've given me some other occasion to rebuke them, which, as sure as Legba is Lord of Lust and Mischief, they will. Now, go back into the house. Lie down. You mustn't do any heavy work. I'll send three Maxi slave girls to do all your chores and——'

But Alihosi shook her head. At that moment, standing there enwrapped in her dignity, her pride, she was almost handsome.

'I am a true woman,' she said, 'just as my lord was kind enough to call me. I shall cook his food, and tend his house, and love him with my body until the belly I have found grows too big. To give my lord a son is so great a joy that it will sustain me. So, please do not send me three silly, chattering wenches to be always underfoot, breaking and spoiling things and burning the food. I can do a wife's work by myself.'

'As you will, wife,' Nyasanu said, and kissed her again. 'We'll talk about it tonight. Now I must go.'

'Where, older person mine?' Alihosi said.

Nyasanu stared at her. For her to question his goings and comings was a kind of boldness she had never displayed before. But she was with child, would probably be the mother of his at least nominal heir, so she was, he judged, well within her rights.

'To consult the Half Heads,' he said, 'for they, if they will, can tell me how I must prepare for this journey....'

251

'That they counsel you well, my husband!' Alihosi said, and turning, went back into the house.

When Nyasanu came up to the guest house he had had his *dokpwe* build for the royal messengers—a feat that had taken them less than one afternoon so zealously had they worked— only one of the Half Heads was in sight. He, the eldest of the three, sat before the door of the guest house and slowly turned his head from side to side so that alternatingly the half of it that had been shaved and the half of it that was thickly thatched with his own non-grey kinky wool came into sight. What the Half Head was doing, Nyasanu saw, was watching every approach to the compound. And his beady little black eyes were cold sober. What was more, the Maxi slave girl Nyasanu had given him for his pleasure sat two rods away from him, with her back propped up against the house, and dozed peacefully in the afternoon sun.

But from the sounds that came out of the guest house, the other two Half Heads were making full use of his gifts to them of wine and lithe young slave girls. He turned his face away from the door, closed his mind to the sounds of panting, moaning, thumping that came from within. This, too, was a part of life; an important part, its cause, and its beginning; but by Mawu-Lisa, witnessing it as a spectator or listening to it was—ugly. Nothing that people do, he mused, demands more privacy than this. . . .

But the eldest Half Head had climbed to his feet and was bowing deeply before him.

'What is your pleasure, my lord Gbonuga?' the Half Head said.

'Some small sharing of the wisdom of which your store is great,' Nyasanu said. 'I have never before visited Abomey. And, it seems to me, that he who treads beneath the trees wherein the Leopard dwells would do well to walk softly and to have eyes in the back of his head. . . .'

'Well spoken!' the Half Head laughed. 'What is it that my already wise young *gbonuga* would like to know?'

'Many things. First of all: I have decided to go very simply dressed much less well than I can afford; and that my people should be very few, and likewise simply dressed. Am I right?'

'Fa hath endowed you with your father's brains,' the Half Head said.

252

'Further, we shall walk——'

'That, too, is wise,' the Half Head said, 'but if one of your wives is with child, say, a hammock and bearers for her would be—well—permitted you. . . .'

'Then I'm to take my wives with me?' Nyasanu said.

'Yes. You see, young lord, there're going to be certain cere- monies in which their presence will be useful—even necessary,' the Half Head said.

'I see,' Nyasanu said, calmly enough; but his heart shrank within his breast. For, almost surely what the Half Head meant was that he was to be given a princess as his bride. That was the only rite he could think of—aside from his own fu- neral, of course—where the presence of his wives would be obli- gatory. And the idea didn't make him happy. Far from it. For a man to be given a princess of the blood, one of the king's own daughters in fact, as his wife, as a reward for his valour, was a very great honour to be sure; but it was an even greater trouble. Because when a man married a woman over whom he hadn't, and never could have, the slightest control he was purely begging for disaster. Even when the girl in question wasn't even of the royal family, but merely a lady in waiting to some princess, as his father's wife Yu had been, and given to him by her royal patroness, her immunity to punishment for anything she might choose to do—even flagrant adultery—was complete. Brave as Gbenu had been, a great chief and a gallant gentleman, he'd had to close his eyes, accept dishonour as far as Yu had been concerned. The alternative in such cases was simple : you swallowed your pride of manhood or you died.

Which wasn't a matter to be discussed with a Half Head, so Nyasanu fell back upon a simpler problem.

'Hammocks, then?' he said, absently.

'*One* hammock,' the Half Head said, 'a simple one, not too ornamented. And that only, as I said before, if one of your wives is with child. You're a *gbonuga*, now; but you asked my advice, so I give it, frankly. Do not arouse too much jealousy before you're firmly established. Later on, the position you're going to have will demand of you a great deal of show. Now, as you seem to have already gathered, your first concern must be to give no offence. After all, even the *kpausi,* the Leopard wives, walk when they go to bear the food to the officials with names——'

Nyasanu knew what he meant, for Gbenu had told him of

this strange custom: all the higher officials of Abomey, no matter how many wives they, themselves, possessed, had their meals cooked for them by the royal spouses, and what was more, delivered to their residences by the self-same *kpausi*.

'A terrible nuisance,' Gbenu had said. 'Apart from the fact that the cooking of the majority of the *dada*'s women is abominable, there's the additional trouble that when they're abroad on this stupid errand, all traffic in the capital comes to a dead halt. Since no man can look upon the Leopard's wives, they're preceded by little slave girls who ring bells—at the sound of which every mother's son in that street, even if he's a stone-blind beggar, has to stop where he is, and turn his back on the procession or else off comes his head!'

'Only one of my wives is with child, my lord Half Head,' Nyasanu said. 'If it will not give offence, I'll leave her here. . . .'

'Do it,' the Half Head said. 'Is there anything my wise young lordling would like to know?'

'Gifts,' Nyasanu said, 'of what nature should they be?'

'Well,' the Half Head said cautiously, 'that's a more difficult matter. They needn't be too costly—because, since you're just beginning to rise in life, that, too, might awake too much envy on the part of people in a position to do you harm. Besides, the *dada* won't be impressed by their value; for, in sober truth, everything and everybody in Da's Belly belong to him already, anyhow. What they should be, son of Gbenu, about to add much weight to your name, is rare. Curious. Unlike most things ever seen before. For instance—like that!'

Nyasanu followed his pointing finger, and saw Soye and Alihonu coming up the trail. Between them trotted, as agile as a boy of twenty despite his seventy-odd years, the woodcarver Hwegbe. And on his head was the most beautiful chief's or king's—or king's!—Nyasanu's mind exulted—stool ever seen in Dahomey.

Hwegbe was grinning like an ancient monkey, his sly old face alight with mockery and with mischief.

'So,' Nyasanu said sternly, 'they didn't have to drag you before me, Granduncle.'

'No, Grandnephew—oh, I beg your pardon!—Your Excellency Gbonuga of this province!—I came of my own free will, as you can see,' Hwegbe cackled.

'And now I suppose you're going to tell me that you carved this stool as a gift for the *dada*, in the three days that the royal

Half Heads have been here?'

'No, Nephew,' Hwegbe said. 'I am not going to tell you that. The mere facts that you are Gbenu's son and *my* grandnephew are enough to safeguard you from being a fool.'

'Then when did you carve it?' Nyasanu said.

'I began it the day you brought your poor father home,' Hwegbe said quietly. 'And at first it was only my intention to make a chief's stool for you—as a peace offering between us, Nephew. I am too old to move along again, and it is unwise to have the enmity of a chief.'

'You have *never* had mine, Taugbochinovi,' Nyasanu said.

'I know that, now. Your friend M'bula told me finally that it was Kpadunu and his gang of apprentice sorcerers who beat me almost to death before your wedding to Agbale, and that you neither knew of nor had anything to do with these plans. So, as I said, I started to make this for you, whipped to my task by my disgust at seeing the activities of your half-brother Gbochi, and his mother Yu—too close at hand. That Gbochi takes his pleasure from men at both ends, I knew; but that Yu provides him with lovers—bought lovers—and that servicing *her* is also part of the bargain struck, I didn't.'

'I see,' Nyasanu sighed. 'But, from the looks of this stool, which is far too fine for a mere chief, you afterwards changed your mind?'

'Yes, or had it changed for me. For I hadn't even finished blocking it out upon my finest, biggest piece of anya wood, when I began to hear the tales of your valour: how you won the war singlehanded by capturing the Axo S'ubetzy, heir to the Auyo's saddle-throne. So since this grizzled old pate I have atop my scrawny neck *works,* Nephew, I realised at once that you had already added enormous weight to your name—and that from now on were sure to stand high in the favour of the king. So——'

'So?' Nyasanu echoed.

'Even reflected favour can be useful to a tired old man, Nephew. You would be called up to Abomey, I realised—and the presence of these distinguished visitors confirms my guess —and hence must, out of courtesy, bear offerings to the *dad.* How better to ensure having a roof over my head and food in my belly throughout the few years remaining to me than gaining the king's favour through one who already has it—namely *you* Nyasanu?'

'One way, Taugbochinovi,' Nyasanu said, 'a way that has never been closed to you: returning to *my* compound and throwing yourself upon my mercy. Did it never occur to you that I'd have provided for you gladly—that I've always loved you, despite your many sins?'

'Not *despite*, Nephew!' Hwegbe said. '*Because of*! Like all solemn, pompous young idiots—you got that trait from your father, no doubt!—you envied me my savouring of life. But no matter. Tell me, how do you like my masterpiece?'

Nyasanu studied that regal stool. It was, he realised, exactly what his *taugbochinovi* said it was: a masterpiece. Hwegbe had carved the serpent Danh—with his head resting upon the base of the stool, which in turn rested upon the ground—in the act of swallowing a goat. The goat's head protruded from the serpent's mouth, and one could see the terror in the animal's eyes. But, from just behind the neck, Danh's sinuous body looped upwards in three enormous coils, placed side by side, with every scale lovingly carved in low relief, until his tail arched up beyond the last coil, and flattened itself into a plane parallel to the head, which is to say, it extended itself horizontally above the base and the ground. Upon the tail itself rested the seat, most cunningly shaped to contain the king's anatomy. And no part of the stool had been fitted or joined to another. The whole thing had been carved out of a single huge block of ironwood.

To call it a masterpiece was but to do it justice.

'It is very fine,' Nyasanu said. 'In fact, it is your best work, Granduncle. What will you take for it?'

'Nothing,' Hwegbe laughed, 'except your favour, Nephew—and the king's!'

On the morrow, Alihosi was left weeping bitter tears because her princely young husband would not allow her to undertake the risks and the fatigue of the journey. Both Hwegbe's magnificent stool and Nyasanu's own almost equally magnificent *ase*, or iron altar for the house of the royal ancestors, had been carefully covered with thick cotton cloth. The oldest Half Head, who had taken an immense, fatherly liking to the young chief, as valiant old men always did, had suggested that.

'Wouldn't do,' he said, 'for some informer to tell the *dada* ahead of time what your gifts are, and thus spoil the effect of surprise. By the way, you've brought the heads you took in the campaign with you, haven't you, young lord?'

Nyasanu looked at the long rows of baskets, each of them containing an Auyo's or a Maxi's head, carefully smoked and dried to preserve it, and shuddered.

'Yes,' he said. 'I was told it was necessary.'

'You were told rightly,' the eldest Half Head said. 'It is a custom that the *dada* pay in money and goods for each head taken for his sake. And you've fixed in your memories all the details of the behaviour expected of a man at the *dada*'s court that I've told you?'

'Yes, my lord Half Head,' Nyasanu said; 'and I thank you for it.'

'Good! Then let us not talk any more; for we shall need our breath for walking!'

They marched briskly up the trail towards the high plateau on which Abomey sits. Soye and Alihonu took turns holding the chief's parasol over Nyasanu's head, while other men-servants performed the same service for the three Half Heads. Each of Nyasanu's wives had their heads protected from the murderous African sun by a simple undecorated white parasol held over their heads by a Maxi slave girl.

Their route led them, at first, through the farming country near Alladah, where the Gletanu, the great cultivators, had their estates. And of the Gletanu, Nyasanu's departed father Gbenu had been one of the greatest, since no less than five huge plantations devoted to such crops as palm oil, dates, manioc, millet, maize, yams, beans, and cane had belonged to him. All five of those plantations had been left to Nyasanu, since Dahomeans held it unwise to break up land into too small units, which is what dividing it among a man's all too numerous sons would do. But implicit in this custom of primogeniture—honoured as much in the breach, if not more so, than in the observance—was the obligation of the heir to assume responsibility for all his brothers and sisters, whether full or half.

Upon his return from the capital, Nyasanu realised he was going to have his hands full: first, with finding suitable occupations for his brothers, many of them only a few weeks or even days younger than he, and providing them with money and goods with which to buy wives; second, it was his duty to find suitable husbands for his numerous sisters of marriageable age, though this wouldn't be much of a burden financially, rather, the work and gifts their suitors would have to render him as head of the household would actually make him richer than he was already.

But even so, he wondered if he had been more than a little foolish to have practically given away one fifth of his holdings to that ne'er-do-well Kapo in order to protect his sister Axisi's future. What brought that recurring worry to mind was the fact that the safari was passing at that moment through the very plantation he had ceded to his *novichesu*, his brother-in-law, Kapo, for a price that, while fair enough, he had reasons to doubt he'd ever be able to collect.

And, as if to confirm his worries, at that very moment he saw his brother-in-law. Kapo lay sprawled out in the shade of a baobab tree—fast asleep. A long line of Maxi slaves crawled down the rows in the sun, taking an occasional languid chop at the quick-sprouting weeds and savanna grass with their short-handled hoes.

A vein stood up in Nyasanu's temple and beat with his blood. Grimly he started towards the sleeper, thinking: 'Oh why did Axisi have to be such a fool? With a good-for-nothing like this for a husband she is lost!'

But before he got there, he saw his sister. Axisi came very quietly out from behind the baobab tree and stood there looking at her husband with great sorrow in her eyes. Then she lifted the slim anya wood rod she had with her—brought, Nyasanu was sure, out of her absolute certainty of what she was going to find upon her arrival—and swung it with all her force. It whistled like a wicked man's ghost bemoaning all his sins. Kapo let out a howl that split the day apart, leaped three full yards into the air, and came down already running. Behind him Axisi went—for she was not yet great with child—swinging the anya rod with every stride.

Nyasanu stopped. That this scene was repeated almost daily he was dismally certain. Then very slowly, he smiled. He needn't worry about Axisi's future. That his sister could take care of herself stood abundantly proved.

He turned then and came back to where the Half Heads, his wives, bearers, and slaves waited. Just as he got there he heard the half-smothered gasps of Sosixwe's and Huno's laughter. But Dangbevi looked upon him with grave and troubled eyes.

'My lord Half Head,' he said loudly, 'there is a slave market in Abomey is there not?'

'Yes, Gbonuga,' the eldest Half Head said, 'but why do you ask me that? Surely you don't mean to dispose of such excellent people as yours seem to be?'

'Of my people, no,' Nyasanu said, 'but of two whooping hyena bitches, I could easily be persuaded!'

At once Sosixwe and Huno were kneeling there before him, pressing their foreheads to the earth, and throwing dust all over themselves, while they howled and moaned and blubbered in an extravagant counterfeit of fear and contrition.

'Oh, get up from there!' Nyasanu said tiredly. 'I won't sell you, as you know only too well. But tonight, when we make camp, I'll see if I can't teach you both better manners!'

And he kept his word, though it sickened him to do it, knowing it necessary. In the presence of the whole company he gave both his young wives a beating, which consisted of about ten or fifteen stripes each administered with bamboo rods so light that they broke before even raising any appreciable welts upon Sosixwe's and Huno's glossy black skin.

The beating hurt them scarcely at all; but the humiliation of it almost broke their hearts. They crawled away to their hammocks with their faces averted, and, instead of sobbing aloud as they usually did, making a great show of purely faked grief, they wept silently, their young and lovely faces awash with anguished tears.

And to drive the lesson home, Nyasanu took Dangbevi by the hand and led her into the hut made of woven brush mats carried along for that purpose, so that it could be set up and taken down in a scant half hour. But she lay beside him propped up on one elbow and stared into his face.

'My lord,' she said, 'may I ask you a thing?'

'If your question is: will I beat *you* if you deserve it, the answer is yes, Dangbevi!' he said.

She bowed her head, looked up again, said:

'So be it. And will you also give me—honourable burial, my lord?'

He turned over, looked at the dim and shadowy image of her face.

'I did not say I should beat you to death, Dangbevi,' he said harshly, 'any more than I did those two laughing hyenas. There is a difference between justice and cruelty, housewife eldest!'

'I know there is,' she said, 'but if I should ever so far lose

259

your love, older person mine, that you need to strike me even one blow, you will have condemned me. For the glow of the setting sun of the first day that you reduce me into—a thing—that can be beaten, will be the last light I'll ever see.'

He lay there without moving; but all the night was loud with the halt, release, sudden rasping of his breath.

'You threaten me thus, Dangbevi?' he said.

'No, Nya—no, my lord, my love—I don't threaten. I promise. It's not a threat to say the sun will rise tomorrow. It's a certainty. And as sure as that is the fact that I should die—by mine own hands—before enduring so great a hurt.'

He stared at the roof of the hut. It was badly thatched. In one place the light of a single star shone through. He lay there a long time without speaking. Then he sighed.

'Very well,' he said quietly, 'you have my promise: I shall never strike you, no matter what you choose to do.'

He heard a single sob pulsate against the night. Then he felt her arms as they stroked softly about his neck.

'And what I choose to do,' Dangbevi whispered, 'is to love my lord, with all my heart, with my three souls, with my body—and to give him twenty sons!'

He lay there, frozen, despite the heat of the night. Agbale/ Nyaunu wi had said that too, and where was she now? There was, he thought bitterly, a kind of fatality about those words. It was a mistake to taunt Fa thus, by voicing such big promises. . . .

He closed his eyes, seeing again the *fau meaun tagbive*, the funeral lamps they'd lighted at his father's final rites, twinkling amid the trees like little stars. And even as he watched them in his mind's eye, two of them flickered, and winked out. A shudder rippled through his long, lean form. Dangbevi felt it.

'Why do you shudder, my husband?' she said.

'For nothing. No reason,' he said; and bending to her, found her mouth.

EIGHTEEN

When they came up to the earthen walls of Abomey, the empty eye sockets of human skulls glared down at them from the roofs of every sentry box and from above the gates. Glancing back, Nyasanu could see his three wives looking up at them; but although little Huno, too, cringed under that blind and eternal gaze, it was Dangbevi who was most visibly affected by the sight. Her face went greyish, her lips quivered, a trembling got into her slim form. For a moment, Nyasanu feared that all three of her souls were going to take leave, temporarily at least, of her; but then she recovered and strode proudly forward, head up like a queen. Yet, for all that, Nyasanu saw, she kept her eyes averted from those monstrous proofs of Dahomean valour.

'You are different from the others, aren't you?' Nyasanu thought. 'Better surely. Finer, gentler. More tender. Huno—little Huno—looks at these hundreds of bleached skulls and is afraid. I can see the fear in her eyes. She wonders what harm their ghosts might do her. Sosixwe—true to form as usual!—imagines what great sport it would be to reward each valiant taker of each head in her own peculiar fashion. For surely the warriors who took these poor crow- and kite- and ant-cleaned globes must be strong enough to make her scream with delight —ride her till she faints from ecstasy.

'But you and I—and I! my Dangbevi—remember that these hollow horrors once cradled—dreams. From those grinning, macabre jaws hung lips that kissed beloved women, favoured children. Within them were tongues that savoured wine and flesh, that shaped wisdom, or babbled folly. Ended now—forever ended. And by us. For what? To prove we're crueller than leopards, fiercer than lions, ravenous as jackals, madder than whooping hyenas—that we are beasts, not men.'

He stared back at the baskets his bearers bore. 'And I am come,' he thought, 'to add to their numbers. To prove that I'm a man-killer too. Great honour! To be greatly rewarded! I'd rather make one of Amosu's bronze figures, weave one of poor Badji's cloth designs, carve one of Granduncle Hwegbe's *bauchie,* dance one fine dance, sing one true song than to kill the greatest warrior in the Auyo hosts. . . . Which means I'm out

261

of step with life, as life has always been lived here in Dahomey, ever since our first King Taconda ripped the guts out of Da, ruler of this city, then built a palace over his disembowelled victim's grave. And thereby changed our name. Before that we were Faus. Afterwards everybody started calling us Dahomeans, "the people of Da's Belly" in memory of that murder, for even our origins are drenched in blood——'

But it was no good thinking such things and he knew it. Such thoughts weakened a man, chilled the fire of life in him, bemused his wits, all of which could be fatal in a city where just staying alive took all a serpent's guile. So he bent his head and followed the Half Heads through the gates. And after him came his wives, his bearers, his servants, and his slaves.

Inside the gates, the first buildings they passed were the royal sheds. These were long, low, thatch-roofed, unwalled buildings designed to protect from the sun the people waiting for an audience with the *dada*. Here the notables of the city squatted on their haunches, for no man at the Leopard's court —except in time of war and then only to confuse the enemy— was allowed to publicly sit upon a stool, that privilege belonging to the king alone.

Seeing the notables of Abomey squatting there in the dirt, clad in their fine robes, smoking their long pipes, and fanning away the flies, Nyasanu's face tightened in disgust. Here were governors, chiefs, privy counsellors, heads of societies, great land-owners, immensely rich merchants; and they all sat in the dirt and scratched themselves like dogs. Days might go by before the *dada* finally condescended to call any one of them into his royal presence; but they dared not leave until they had been dismissed by the *minga* or the *meu* on the king's behalf, for if a notable summoned to the court were called and was not there to answer, at the very least he could expect to have five or ten rods broken over his bare back for his wilful neglect of the courtesy due to the king.

'Things of the Leopard!' Nyasanu thought. 'But then, aren't we all? How many days and nights did poor father have to squat like this in the dirt, waiting for the *minga* or the *meu* to shout his name aloud? And I have earned myself a place among these "notables", risen so high in life that I, too, can spend most of the future crouched upon my hams, awaiting the king's pleasure and fanning flies!'

He moved on, following the Half Heads. A little farther away he saw another row of long, thatch-roofed open sheds. Under them more people sat; but they wore no finery; in fact, except for loincloths, they were quite naked; and—he felt a sick, hurtful rush of pity engulf him at the sight—their arms and legs were manacled, chained together at wrists and ankles, with the added precaution of their having been forced to sit with their limbs straddling the poles that held up the roofs of the sheds, before the handcuffs and the leg irons had been applied.

Most of these were, Nyasanu knew, prisoners of war. As a general rule they would be sold to either the Dahomean Galentu, the great farmers, or to the Furtoo, the people without skins who called themselves white men, as slaves. But some few of them would die, sacrificed before the altars of the royal dead. For what crime? 'For not having fought long enough, or run fast enough,' he thought bitterly. 'For being less brave than lions, less swift than jackals. In short for being—men instead of ravenous beasts. . . .'

He stopped dead. For the prisoners beneath the next row of roofs were neither Maxis nor Auyo, but Dahomeans. And though they were equally naked, he had as little trouble distinguishing them from their former foes as a European would have had in telling a Portuguese from a Dane, say. To his eyes, the only thing the three races had in common was the blackness of their skins. In all else, bone structure, features, height, build, carriage, the differences between Maxis, Auyos, and Dahomeans were marked.

And now, looking at them, the feeling of sadness deepened in him. These men were doomed. Surely, they had played the coward, thrown down their muskets and fled the battle. Or had been caught stealing from some Galentu's storehouse. Or——

But across from them, now, he saw the probable reasons for their arrest: women. Chained with their legs and arms round the posts as were the men. Stark naked, with even their loincloths taken away to cause them greater shame. Most of them were weeping very quietly—and by now, close to four months since the end of the—thanks to Nyasanu's own valour —victorious campaign, the crime for which they had been imprisoned and were awaiting trial, was visible upon them. They had all 'found their bellies' in the classic Ffon phrase. And, since they were all *ahosi*, female soldiers, and, by that very token, at least nominally wives of the king, the fifty-two women sitting there naked in the dust were—along with, of course, their male partners in the crime—going to die for adultery, in spite of the fact that almost surely not one of these so-called royal spouses had ever shared the *dada*'s sleeping mat, their married state being but a fiction, a device for preventing the whole *Ahosi* Corps from rendering themselves useless for war through love, as these had already done.

'So now you must die, poor stupid bitches,' Nyasanu thought, 'for being human beings, having human weaknesses, human desires. May all the *vudun* have mercy upon you, upon this our land!'

Then shaking his head to clear it, he followed the Half Heads towards the lodgings that had been provided under the *dada*'s own command, for him and his people by the *meu*.

At the head of his people, Nyasanu passed a large and imposing bungalow, richly, newly thatched and whitewashed to a degree that the sun's glare reflected from its walls stabbed into his eyes with a real, physical pain. So it was that to him, and to his people, the windows of that house appeared as black holes in the general whiteness. It was impossible for him to see within.

But the two people inside its cool and dim interior could see him very clearly.

The Princess Taunyinatin, a name meaning 'my father's name shall live', stood to one side of a window and looked out at the procession passing through the street. She held herself well back in order to avoid being seen from the street, for two excellent reasons: she hadn't a stitch on, and her brother, the Prince Atedeku, crouched on his knees beside her and was busily engaged in running his right hand up between her long, lovely thighs and fingering that part of her anatomy that, considering the degree of consanguinity between them, he should not have touched at all.

'Stop it, Ate,' said the Princess.

'Why?' Atedeku said. 'You're going to tell me you don't like it, Taunyi?'

'Shut up!' Taunyinatin hissed. 'I want to see these people— I'm almost sure——'

The Prince Atedeku raised up until he could see above the window sill; he gave a low, throaty chuckle.

'You're right,' he said. 'It's him all right. The conquering hero. The man father's going to marry you to. Look at him! A black giraffe! The tallest man in the kingdom. An oaf—a country oaf from Alladah——'

'*We* come from Alladah originally,' the princess pointed out, 'that's why we're called the Aladaxonu, isn't it?'

'Yes,' Atedeku said, 'and the only smart thing our ancestors did was to leave that miserable place! I've been there and—well, Sister, how d'you like your husband-to-be?'

'Well,' Taunyinatin said, letting a small purr of mockery breathe through her voice, 'he doesn't seem *too* bad. Awful lot of him, isn't there?'

'Meaning,' her brother said, 'that you think he might do for a couple of months until you can think up some excuse to make father grant you a divorce, and bring you home again?'

'Well,' the Princess drew the word out, savouring with almost feline delight this opportunity to torment her brother-lover, 'he is good looking. Very. Even you have to admit that, Ate. . . .'

'You can tell him from a monkey, if you look hard,' Atedeku said, 'likely because his mother horned his great baboon of a father with a giraffe. Tell me, Taunyi, d'you s'pose his arse is blue? Most baboons——'

'Oh, come off it, Ate!' Taunyinatin laughed. 'I might even decide to stay married. Provided——'

'Provided what?' Atedeku said.

'That I can teach him to dress decently, for one thing. His clothes are dreadful—like a peasant's. And I'll bet he never washes, doesn't even know what perfumes are, stinks like a goat, and talks Fau with that thick back-country accent nobody can understand. Still . . .'

Atedeku grinned up at his half-sister.

'Still, peasants are—strong, eh, Taunyi?' he mocked. 'And if his—weapon is as long as the rest of him, you just might be in for a *very* happy honeymoon—that's what you're thinking, aren't you?'

Taunyinatin whirled then, and slapped her half-brother with considerable force. He came up from the floor and grappled with her; they wrestled skilfully until Atedeku finally managed to put one of his legs behind his sister's, pinned her to the floor. Then very slowly began to kiss her mouth, her throat, her breasts.

After that, they both forgot the little band of country people passing through the street.

'I'll *never* leave you!' Taunyinatin wept. 'I'll die first! Cut my throat! Get a poison from the *azaundato* and——'

Full of the blissful calm of sexual satiation, Atedeku yawned.

'Oh, don't be a fool, Taunyi,' he said. 'Go on, marry your long oaf. I'll get you free of him soon enough. . . .'

Taunyinatin came up on one elbow and stared at her half-brother.

'How?' she said.

'Remember the time that father exiled me to a farm near Alladah for killing my manservant Gbokauhwe?'

'Yes,' Taunyinatin said.

'The farm was next to *his* father's. The Kposu Gbenu, I mean. So I got to know the *kposu.* Proudest man I ever did meet. Treated me like dirt—always maintaining the most perfect outward show of respect and courtesy at the same time. Don't know even yet how he managed it, but he could, he could *look* at me and shut me up. My souls would shrivel, and the words wouldn't even come——'

'Ha!' Taunyinatin said.

'I don't know this long oaf; but I've heard of him. People say he's his father's image in all ways——'

'So?' Taunyinatin said.

So his pride will be his vulnerable point. When you marry him, Taunyi, wear white! Put on the tall cap——'

'That only virgins are allowed to wear? It'll fall off. They say that the Sky Vudun always expose a bride who pretends to be a virgin when she isn't, by knocking her cap——'

'Nonsense!' Atedeku said. 'Wear it! So when on your wedding night, he finds out he could ride a buffalo up it, he'll——'

Taunyinatin slapped her brother-lover again. Hard.

'Well, maybe not a buffalo,' Atedeku grinned, 'but a zebra anyhow. Stop it, Taunyi! This is serious. Hold still and listen, will you?'

'All right,' she said sullenly.

266

'He'll say—or do something you can consider an insult. Maybe he'll even hit you, forgetting that to strike a princess could cost him his head. . . .'

'But,' Taunyinatin said, 'why should he get angry? What difference does it make that I've lain with other men?'

'In his world it does. Since a commoner must work hard to pay for a bride, he takes it as an insult to find he's bought second-hand goods. Third or fourth hand in *your* case, isn't it, Taunyi, dear?'

'That's none of your business,' Taunyinatin said, 'go on, lover. . . .'

'In fact, those country oafs show the sleeping mat to the bride's father the morning after the wedding night. And if there's no blood on it, back she goes, whereupon the old fool has to pay back the husband for all his gifts, work, and the work of his *dokpwe* as well—or give him another certified virgin to replace the girl who'd opened her legs out of season. . . .'

'How strange!' Taunyinatin said.

'No, it isn't,' Atedeku said a little sadly. 'It's what *we* do that's strange, Sister. In a way, we don't count at all, we younger sons, nor any female children of the *dada*. Do you know why? It's because neither we nor our children can inherit the royal stool. Our ancestors were nobody's fools, Taunyi. So they laid down the law—the iron-clad law of patrilineal primogeniture, though they, themselves, sometimes break it by passing over the oldest for a better endowed younger son. But I can imagine what would happen if *any* member of the royal family could inherit. Chaos. Civil war. Every one of you screeching she-cats with your claws out, biting and scratching to put *your* brat on the stool! But we can't, and you can't. So we're nothing. Less than nothing. Parasites. Which is *why*, Taunyi, we're allowed to eat and drink and rut our lives away like pampered pariah dogs! We're permitted to lie with anybody, even one another, an act any self-respecting commoner would call incest, and put us to death for practising——'

'He *would*?' Taunyinatin said. 'Why, Ate?'

'Because children born of too close a degree of consanguinity are accursed, Taunyi. Legba eats their brains before they're born, sending them into this world as witless idiots. That's why I've always made you drink the lime juice mixed with the foaming stone. But here, in the royal compound, we're *all* brothers and sisters, or first cousins, at the very least, since only our aunts' and uncles' children, aside from us, the *dada*'s direct descendants, are allowed to live here. So, for us, it's incest or chastity. Fine choice, what?'

'No choice,' Taunyinatin laughed, 'no choice at all!'

'I—I envy the commoners,' Atedeku went on soberly. 'They live *good* lives. While we're useless and drunkards and lechers. Fa take me! I'm in a mood, I suppose. Funny. A man's always sad after making love——'

'Women aren't,' Taunyinatin said. 'We're *happy*. Very happy, at least when our lovers are good at it. And you are, Ate. But suppose he doesn't do or say anything that——'

'Then I'll visit you. By daylight, at that. Let him catch us at it. I know those hot-tempered Alladah people. Even though you're a princess and all things are permitted you, he won't be able to control himself when he sees us lying naked in each other's arms——'

Taunyinatin thought about that. Then very slowly she smiled.

'All right. Now you stop controlling yourself, too,' she said.

That next day, for Nyasanu and his wives, was one of total horror. For Gezo, who was not a cruel man, crowded all the punishments to be meted out at the royal Customs into that one day, in order to get them over with before his own stomach revolted. And, as all the crimes committed in the nation during the whole year were by old tradition bound over for the time of the celebration of 'the Customs to the royal Ancestors', the culprits were many.

First came the turn of the soldiers who had displayed cowardice in the last war. Towards them, the *minga* announced, the Leopard had decided to be merciful: he would not exercise his right to take their heads. Since they had been facing Auyo horsemen afoot, their panic was in part understandable; for that reason the good, the wise, the patient *dada*, father of the people, had commuted the sentences to ten rods apiece to be broken over their bare backs.

So Nyasanu and his people had to stand in the square and watch that. He had seen it before, which didn't help matters at all. First the culprits were forced to kneel in the dirt, with their hands tied together above their knees. After that, a rod was thrust through the bend of the knees and the crooks of their elbows at the same time, thus arching the victims' backs like a bow, stretching their skins tight to await the blows. Then two muscular fellows were placed on either side of each victim and the whippings began. The only redeeming feature, Nyasanu saw, was that the peeled rods weren't made of anya wood, but of another, rather brittle sort he'd never seen before, so that they broke after only a few blows. Even so, the culprits' backs looked like so much chopped meat before it was over; and he had to support Dangbevi on one arm and Huno on the other to keep them from fainting outright as the sick, wet smashing sounds of the rods, and the screams that rose and rose and rose, going woman-shrill, tearing the day apart, came over to them. On the other hand, Sosixwe bore it well. In fact she seemed to be enjoying the spectacle.

Then it was over. The executioner flipped the victims over, and, catching them by the heels, dragged them around the square so that their bloody, lacerated backs scraped across the sand. The way the beaten men screamed then wasn't to be borne. Nyasanu felt Dangbevi go heavy, her knees loosening, so he snarled at her:

'You want me to be next, Dangbevi? That's what'll happen if you disgrace me by showing weakness now!'

He felt the shudders mount her slender form in waves the way a sea surf mounts the beach at Whydah. Yet, with terrible effort, she recovered at this command, gathered all three of her souls into her belly, and stood there, head up, nostrils aquiver. But all her face was awash with tears.

What followed next was even worse. The fifty-two *ahosi* and the seventy-six soldiers—for some of the female soldiers had been a trifle generous with their favours—accused of the high and treasonable crime of adultery were dragged forth to face the king.

Mounting the *attoh*, the high broad platform constructed for these ceremonies, Gezo addressed the people. Nyasanu worked his way forward followed by his wives and his servants, not because he couldn't hear Gezo perfectly well from where he was, but because he wanted to study the *dada*'s face. It was whispered everywhere that the king hated killing and would, were matters left entirely in his hands, have ended human sacrifices altogether.* Most people were scandalised by such

* See Herskovits, vol. I, p. 21.

269

shocking irreverence towards the royal dead; for, if their tombs were not well watered with blood every year what would become of the nation? But a few sensitive souls, such as Nyasanu himself, agreed with all their hearts.

The king's speech was short; and his big, good speaking voice was shot through with sadness. Even his imposing figure seemed bowed under its weight. In short, shorn of all the flowery turns of phrase that a formal discourse in Ffon, or Fau, imposed upon an orator, what Gezo said amounted to this:

'I, your father, am sad because certain ones among you, my children, have betrayed me. In spite of all the care I have lavished upon your welfare, leading you victoriously in war, making the yearly *so-sin* customs to insure that the royal ancestors, the great *tauvudun*, the fathers-become-gods, intercede for you before all the great gods, certain of my soldiers have laid lecherous hands upon my *ahosi*, who, though soldiers themselves, are also my wives, and sacred to me. And, to be fair, certain of my *ahosi* have only too willingly lent their persons to such lewdness and carnal play. . . .

'Therefore I, Gezo, *dada* of Dahomey, decree the punishment of death by decapitation upon all such who have thus betrayed me——'

At this, a fiendish yell from all the crowd cut off the king's voice. Gezo raised his hands and the cry ended, cut off as though it had never been.

'Still,' the king said softly, sadly, 'the guilty are many, one hundred and twenty-eight men and women; and I would not send so huge a number to tremble before the *nesuxwe*, the souls of the princely dead. Therefore I commute all the sentences except eight, four men and four *ahosi*, to service, in the case of my she-soldiers in the *achi*, the bayoneteers, and in the case of the men, in the Gate Opening Company. . . .'

Dangbevi looked at her young husband, formed with her lips with the shape of the word 'Why?'

'The two most dangerous companies,' Nyasanu whispered, 'they always lead the attacks. So it's fitting. By bravery and luck they can still save their lives. And if they must die, it will be with honour. . . .'

But the *dada* was speaking again.

'Therefore I ask the royal *bokono* to pass among the prisoners and choose those to be sacrified by lot . . .' he said.

It was quickly done. Three minutes later four trembling wretches were kicked forward before the *attoh*.

'Don't look!' Nyasanu warned his wives; but almost before the words were out of his mouth, the king's club wielders had knocked the four soldiers upon the head. Then a crowd of *assegai*-bearing soldiers, all former comrades of theirs, were upon them, their blades flashing in the sun. Five seconds later the ghastly trophies were held high as all the world roared their approval. All the world that is, except Nyasanu, his women, and the king.

Nyasanu saw the *dada*'s face go grey, saw how he struggled to control the jerking of his mouth.

'You are good, aren't you, my King?' the young chief thought. 'Tender and good. It will not be hard to serve you. . . .'

The four *ahosi* who had also been selected to die were led away into an inner court. For unlike his European contemporaries, who made public spectacles of the execution of female criminals, the only concession to modesty being the act of tying a cord around their skirts below the knees to keep their legs together as the hangman hoisted them aloft, Gezo held it unseemly to kill women, at least, before spectators.

Half an hour later, the *gundeme* and the *yewe,* the female generals of the right and left wings of the *ahosi* army, came back to announce the sentence had been carried out. . . .

The rest of the day was enough to try the nerves of the *vudu* Gu himself. From the victim shed atop the *attoh*, twelve prisoners of war, clad in the long nightshirts of condemned victims, with the tall conical cap—exactly like a European dunce cap—upon their heads were brought forth in the little boat-shaped baskets, each basket borne aloft upon the hands of a single huge, muscular man, and paraded around the *attoh*. Then one by one they were placed on the parapet, where they teetered in their basket until the king himself upset their balance with his foot, hurling them head down into the pit, where the ugly, blood-smeared monster of a royal executioner cut off their heads slowly with a butcher's knife.

By then, Nyasanu's people had been forced to make a protective ring about Dangbevi, to shield her terrible retching from the other spectators; but even so, a tall and burly chieftain, clad in the silken toga of a *gbonuga*, his voice filled with hoarse mockery, said to Nyasanu:

'What ails your woman, young fellow? Is she with child?'

Nyasanu eyed him up and down. Decided with a sigh, that discretion was, here and now, under those circumstances, the better part of valour.

'No, your Excellency,' he said. 'It is only that she is not of our nation. She is Fulani. Among her people they don't make the *so-sin*, so she is not accustomed to so much—blood.'

'You'd better train her better then, young fellow,' the *gbonuga* said, 'or else she'll get you in an awful lot of trouble. There are those who might interpret her attitude as—an insult to our customs, say. . . .'

Nyasanu faced him then, squarely.

'Then let those who so interpret it,' he said, 'deal with me. But let them be also warned that that will be no easy matter.'

The *gbonuga* roared then, lion-mouthed:

'Just who in Legba's name do you think you are, peasant! By Xevioso, I'll have my servants thrash the hide off you!'

'Is his Excellency, then, tired of life?' Nyasanu said very quietly.

'You'd threaten me!' the *gbonuga* howled. 'By Sagbata, I'll——'

Nyasanu put out his hand and caught the *gbonuga* by the arm, as the big man turned to call his servants to his side.

'Wait,' the young *toxausu* said. 'You're making a mistake. Don't judge me by my dress. I wear these simple clothes because of a vow I took. But in spite of them, I am a person with a name. And that name, your Excellency, carries its share of weight. So, before you start something you may not be able to finish, hear it: I am Nyasanu, son of Gbenu, lately *kposu* to the king.'

The *gbonuga* took a backward step. The way his eyes bulged suddenly in the blackness of his face would have been funny, if it hadn't been so sad. A moment later, he had prostrated himself before Nyasanu and was clawing up dirt with both hands and pouring it on his own head; his big voice came out earth-muffled and shaken.

'Young lord, forgive me! I didn't recognise you! How could I, seeing the way you dress and your lack of years? Who'd have thought that the great hero who saved the *dada* from the Auyo hosts would be but a boy? Besides you can be merciful, I think, for on the morrow the Princess Taunyinatin, the love-liest of the king's daughters, will be betrothed to you, and you'll be showered with all high titles, powers, and wealth! So pardon me, I beg you! Believe me had I known you were he, who——'

'I know,' Nyasanu said, 'courtesy is a virtue we practise only in the presence of the strong. No matter, get up from there, will you please? You're making a spectacle that shames us both....'

Slowly the *gbonuga* got to his feet.

'Then you accept my apologies?' he mumbled.

'They're unnecessary,' Nyasanu said. 'I bear you no ill will, and here's my hand upon it....'

the *gbonuga* took the young chief's hand, stood there gripping it, and staring at the youth. When he spoke, a crafty look had got into his eyes.

'These are all the wives you have, my lord?' he said.

'No,' Nyasanu said. 'There's one more at home. She has found her belly so I couldn't bring her.... Why do you ask?'

'I have many daughters,' the *gbonuga* said slowly. 'Those as yet unmarried are all virgins, and good to look upon. To link my house with a house of so great fame as yours, son of the *kposu*, would honour me. And to make amends for my rudeness it seems to me that——'

Nyasanu stood there, his face impassive; but inside him his heart was cold and sick. He didn't want another wife. The four he had now were enough trouble for any man to handle. Yet age-old custom forbade his refusing such an offer. The *tauvudun*, the ancestors-become-gods, did not look with favour upon a descendant of theirs who wouldn't take a woman, thus denying them a pious increase in the number of their worshippers. They usually spoiled his luck for him for that.

That was one thing, another was that this *gbonuga* was quite obviously a notable; a man with a name—and probably a strong name at that. To refuse a daughter of his would be to make a lifelong and deadly enemy, all the more so because from now on, he would proceed with caution and with cunning. As high as Nyasanu had risen now, so low could he fall, if he made too many powerful enemies in Abomey. So quietly, thoughtfully, he said:

'You honour me too much your Excellency. But it seems to me that now is not the time to discuss so weighty and delicate a matter. Let us postpone it until my next visit to your city, shall we! In fact, I think we'd better....'

The *gbonuga*'s heavy face grew heavier still.

'Why do you think that, young lord?' he said.

'Two reasons, both of them having their share of strength,' Nyasanu said. 'First, by then, both you and I will have had time to consult our diviners, insure ourselves that such a match will bring good fortune to both our houses. And, second, by letting a few moons go by, we lessen the risk of offending the Leopard....'

'Offending the *dada*?' the *gbonuga* said. 'I don't understand——'

'Tomorrow, according to *you*, I'm to be given a princess. So great an honour should be allowed to stand alone, don't you think? Or do you actually believe that the king, having bestowed his daughter upon me, will be pleased at the spectacle of my betrothing myself to a child of one of his governors almost at the same time? Won't it appear to the Leopard that I bring the princess too low, or raise *your* daughter too high, to marry them both within the same season? Who treads beneath the trees wherein the Leopard dwells, should walk softly, it seems to me——'

The *gbonuga* peered upward into the young face towering half a hand above him.

'You have your father's wisdom, son of Gbenu!' he said, 'and more guile than the Serpent Gods, Danh, Dangbe, and Aido Hwedo put together! You'll go far in life; of that I'm certain. You're right. The matter *must* wait, or we'll both run grave risk of offending the *dada*; but on your next visit, I shall expect you to stay in the guest house of my compound so that you may choose for your wife the daughter of mine who most pleases you. My name is Gbade, *gbonuga* of Savalu....'

'But, your Excellency,' Nyasanu said, 'Savalu is in that territory we took from the Maxis! So how——'

'Can I be governor of it, and still have my compound in Abomey? Easily enough. I have seven great chiefs under my control. They do their work well, thus insuring themselves that they'll stay as long as possible on *this* side of the river. Which is why I can live here in Abomey and visit that wild northern marshland only occasionally. I'd advise you to make some such arrangement once you're raised in rank. Life in the provinces in intolerable! Will you at least dine with me before you go?'

'Of course,' Nyasanu said, and bowed politely. He'd been

274

wise, he realised, not to offend such a man. Gbade, governor of Savalu, was a very great chief indeed.

That night, as he lay in the guest house to which he and his wives had been assigned—for so crowded was Abomey at the season of the royal Customs that no vacant compound, with three or four women's houses set apart from the master's house as elementary decency demanded, could be found—Nyasanu became aware that all three of his wives were crying! Sosixwe and Huno blubbering aloud, but Dangbevi almost silently, as usual.

'In Legba's name!' he roared. 'What's the matter with the lot of you?'

'A—princess!' Sosixwe sobbed. 'And—very beautiful! All the women here say she's the *most* beautiful of all the *dada*'s daughters! They've been taunting us all afternoon about it!'

'So she's beautiful,' Nyasanu said. 'Now tell me, you lecherous little she-monkey, what's that got to do with *you*?'

'Everything!' Sosixwe howled. 'She's *very* beautiful, so you won't love us any more! She's a princess, so she'll have all your favour! And she'll queen it over us, and call us names and pull our hair and spit on us and kick and beat us if she so sees fit; and there's nothing anybody can do about it, not even *you*, older person!'

That, Nyasanu reflected sadly, was the bald and ugly truth. A princess, brought into a commoner's compound, all too often made the lives of his other wives absolutely intolerable. And the bitter fact that her husband, being far below her in rank, had not the slightest control over her, made matters even worse.

'I won't stand for it!' he thought. 'Princess or not, she'll obey and respect me or else——

'Or else what?' the sober, realistic part of his mind demanded. 'Are you prepared to die to defend your manhood, and your mastery over your household?'

He sat there like one turned to stone, oblivious to the whimpering of his wives. Then slowly, stubbornly, remembering the lifelong disaster of his father's marriage to the Lady Yu, the iron answer formed itself in his mind.

'Yes,' he thought. 'I am so prepared, if it comes to that. For to live as a thing, I cannot, will not, do.'

Then very quietly, he got up and went out into the night. As he closed the door behind him, he could hear all three of his wives shrieking his name. But he moved on, walking slowly, softly, as Kpo the leopard does.

Or as goes Ku, who is death.

NINETEEN

The sound of the shots blasted them up off the sleeping mats that next morning. The three women clung nakedly to one another and screamed. In two wild thrusts, Nyasanu got into his short *chokoto chaka* pants. Then, picking up his *assegai*, dashed out into the street.

People were streaming past the guest house towards the gates of the city. The women among them stared at the young giant, naked except for the tight-fitting short pants, standing there holding a bare blade in his hands, and loosed a flute run of giggles.

'What's happening?' Nyasanu said to an old man. 'An attack? The Auyo, maybe? The Fanti? The Hausa? Or—or the Ashanti?'

'None of these, my son,' the old man said calmly. ''Tis only the ceremony of the "Firing Down to Whydah". Go and get dressed, for it is well worth seeing. Don't worry, you'll have time. It'll last all the morning!'

Sheepishly, Nyasanu turned and went back into the house. Long ago, Gbenu had described to him the rite, invented by Gezo himself, of the 'Firing Down to Whydah'. Actually what the whole thing amounted to was the climax of the Dahomean vice of showing off. For, to demonstrate his wealth and power, Gezo had stationed men, soldiers and civilians alike, so close to one another in a double row that their outstretched hands could touch each other's shoulders, all the way from Abomey to the great seaport of Whydah, the second largest city in the kingdom, a distance of some ninety-odd miles.

When they were all in place, at the Gao's command, the first soldier fired off his musket; then another, at the limit of the range that the sound of the first shot would carry, shot his; and still another just within hearing distance of the second jerked the trigger of his blunderbuss and another and another so that

276

the crack of muskets and the belly-deep booming of blunder-busses ran like a train of fire all the way down to Whydah.

Once the signal had reached the port, the European-made cloths, liquors, perfumes, jewellery to be used in the Customs would be picked up in bundles, and literally handed from man to man all the way from Whydah up to Abomey, covering the full ninety-odd miles in a little over two hours, a speed of trans-port that none of the white men's mechanical devices had yet equalled and in sober truth, never would.

Nyasanu, his wives, and his retainers, spent the morning watching the steady flow of bales and bundles bobbing up the human trail from as far away as they could see.

'Truly he is a great king, the *dada*!' little Huno said.

'He is, indeed, child-wife,' Nyasanu agreed; but he thought: 'Is the possession of power the measure of greatness? Is it not rather the manner in which that power is used?'

Later in the morning, Glele, the crown prince, and heir to the throne, made a little *attoh*. His platform was far smaller than his father's and lacked entirely the victim shed. From it the prince, a handsome young man indeed, flung great hand-fuls of cowries to the people, and followed that by throwing down a cock, two ducks, a sheep, a goat, and a monkey. These animals were immediately placed in the canoe-shaped baskets exactly as the human victims of the day before had been, and paraded around the square. After that, they were beheaded and then blood was sprinkled on the ground before the *ase*, the iron altars of the *nesuxwe*, the princely dead.

Following as it did, the *dada*'s mighty *attoh* of the day before, with its terrible spectacle of men being beheaded to please the *nesuxwe tauvudun*, the royal ancestors-become-gods, Prince Glele's little *attoh* seemed an anticlimax to Nyasanu, a rite having little excuse. Then it came to him that its anticlimactic nature was deliberate; that Gezo wanted to show the people how absolute the royal power was. Only the *dada* could sacri-fice the most costly of animals: man. Not even the crown prince was permitted so great a luxury. 'And a good thing it is,' Nyasanu thought, 'or there'd be nobody left alive in Dahomey.'

By the time the prince's *attoh* was finished, it was near the hour for the noonday meal. Sosixwe, Huno, and Dangbevi vied with one another in preparing the highly spiced, savoury Dahomean dishes for their lord and master, rushing about and

277

jostling each other, until, their tempers wearing thin, they began to call each other names. Whereupon, Nyasanu picked up a long slim anya rod.

'Who wants to be first?' he said.

That silenced the screeching cat fight at once. Now they knew he *was* capable of administering a husbandly beating when necessary, and that knowledge had a most salutary effect upon their manners and their behaviour, both.

But, before he could sit down to eat, he had a visitor. There was a great ringing of bells before the guest house, with the result that the street immediately emptied itself of people, as if by magic. Everyone knew that the sound of the little brass bells indicated that one or more of the *kposi*, the Leopard's wives, were going to pass that way. Therefore the townsfolk fled, because, for a man to look upon one of the wives of the king, in the absence of his majesty himself, was to make sure that there'd be a severing of all relations between his head and neck.

Nyasanu sat there, his food untouched, hearing the footsteps of many people come to a stop outside his door. From the way some of the feet had shuffled, he judged them to be hammock bearers, for the immense weight of a ceremonial hammock with its noble or royal burden, swinging beneath huge poles that rested upon cushions placed upon the bearers' heads, caused these human pack animals to bend their knees and take a curious shuffling step. He had heard that step many times before, because, as a chief, among his privileges was that of being hammock-borne. He really didn't like it; it shamed him to see his servants bending under his considerable weight; but, apart from walking, being carried in a hammock was the only really feasible means of transportation in a country in which the flies sooner or later killed all the horses.

Slowly, not knowing what else to do, he got up, walked past his terrified, trembling wives, and went out into the street. He saw at once that the slaves were helping a woman get down from a most costly hammock. Her dress of silks, her clanging clatter of gold, silver, and bronze jewellery, proclaimed her to be an *axovi*, a princess; but her snow-white hair, her seamed, lined, and wrinkled face, the bent and quaking way she moved, told him that she was not one of Gezo's wives; but very probably a widow of the late Dada Agongolu, the present king's father.

278

In any event, courtesy was due her, so immediately the young chief prostrated himself, and scooping up a handful of dust poured it on his own head.

'Oh, get up from there, son!' the old crone cackled. 'I've come to break bread with you, eat your salt. You see, I am your mother.'

Nyasanu stared at her. He thought: 'Hath Legba eaten this old witch's brains?' But then it came to him: Every high official at the *dada*'s court had a 'royal mother' appointed by the king, from among his own wives past the childbearing age or from the widows of his father. These official 'mothers' had the important function of being present at every interview between the *dada* and the official in question and memorising what was said. The fact that nobody had ever invented an alphabet or even hieroglyphics for Fau, made such devices necessary. Since the Dahomeans didn't know what a convenience writing is, they took memorising everything as a matter of course, and thereby developed the most prodigious memories in all the world.

'You honour me, Nochi,' Nyasanu said gravely. Then he called out, '*Asisichi!* Wives! Prepare another place at the table! A princess glories our house with her presence!'

But, when he escorted the old woman into the guest house, he saw that although Huno and Sosixwe were scurrying about, preparing the plates, the clothes, the stool, Dangbevi hadn't moved. She stood there in the middle of the room, as still as though an *azaundato* had turned her into an ebony statue. And what was in her eyes was very death. Then, suddenly, she saw the old princess's white hair, her bent figure, her shambling gait. Her eyes went very wide and soft, and she prostrated herself before the old woman. Then, remembering their manners, Sosixwe and Huno did the same.

'Your wives?' the old princess said. 'Comely enough wenches! You've taste, my son....'

'I thank you, Nochi,' Nyasanu said. 'Will you be so kind as to take this seat?'

The old princess sat down. At once Sosixwe began to heap her plate with the steaming, savoury-smelling, highly spiced food. The ancient *axovi* tasted it.

'Hmmm, good!' she cackled. 'Let us eat, my son!'

Not until she had eaten a great deal of everything did she say another word.

279

'Apart from making your acquaintance, son,' she said affably enough, 'I have come to guide you a little, so that you don't make any mistake. You're a provincial, though nobody could tell it from your speech. You talk beautifully, and your manners are good, too. But now, since the *dada* has put you in my charge, I mean to take care of you. ...'

'I thank you, my mother,' Nyasanu said.

'Today,' the old woman said, 'you will be rewarded for your valour. The king's going to make a *gbonuga* of you. You know that, don't you?'

'I—I'd heard it,' Nyasanu said; 'but I didn't *know* it, mother. 'Tis scarcely wise to give too much ear to idle talk.'

'Good! Good! Good!' the old crone cackled. 'You'll do! I like you, son! Come here and give me a kiss!'

Gravely, Nyasanu bent and kissed her withered cheek.

'Well now, you *know* it,' the princess said. 'So I must instruct you in the rules of courtesy. First, you must lead all your people, including your wives, about two hundred rods outside the city gates.'

'I hear and obey, Nochi,' Nyasanu said.

'There, guards will bring the Axo S'ubetzy to you.'

'The Prince S'ubetzy!' Nyasanu said.

'Yes, son. You see, all men of valour, at the close of a campaign, must deliver publicly the heads and the captives they've taken there to the *dada* so that he may buy them, thus relieving himself of moral responsibility....'

'I knew that,' Nyasanu said, 'but——'

'Don't interrupt your mother, son,' the old princess said calmly. 'Aside from the fact that *all* the captives taken were, at bottom, taken by you, the only one you took physically was the *axo*. But since the king let you go home to try to save your father's life, you *couldn't* take part in the victory celebration. So now you have to do what you should have done then....'

'I understand,' Nyasanu said.

'Another thing you neglected to do was to come up to Abomey to be confirmed as *toxausu* of Alladah, the post your late father, the Kposu Gbenu, left you. I know! I know! You were meaning to, but you had many things to attend to first—a good many of them by night——' The old princess shot a mocking, merry, and malicious gaze at the three wives. 'It won't be held against you, the more so because you have to pass that office on to one of your brothers, since you can't be

280

governor of a province and mayor of a city at the same time. . . .'

'As my Lady Mother wills,' Nyasanu said.

'As the *dada* wills, son! You will wait there with your people until you hear your name called. The sound of it will be lifted in the royal courtyards, then people will shout it to one another until it reaches your ears from where you're waiting outside the city gates. D'you know what to do then, Vi?'

'No, Mother. I suppose I shout *"wae!"* and come at once?'

'Neither. For to do so would be to display an unbecoming eagerness. You sit there where you are and let them shout their silly heads off. Only when a group of notables led by a pair of Half Heads come close enough to you that you can no longer deny having seen and heard them do you answer "Present!" and follow them. Is this clear?'

'Very, Nochi,' Nyasanu said.

'Good, Vi. When you come into the *dada*'s presence, you will have with you those trophies you took in the war, borne by your menservants. You, personally, will lead the Axo S'ubetzy by a cord attached to his manacles. Treat him with courtesy. He is, after all, a person with name——'

'I realise that, Mother,' Nyasanu said.

'Besides, his father, Ibrahim T'wala, ruler of the Auyo, will be present to ransom him from the *dada*. The Auyo are a powerful people. Wouldn't do to offend *them*——'

'If I haven't already,' Nyasanu said.

'No. T'wala has been informed that you spared S'ubetzy's life when you might easily have killed him, and that you risked your own by so doing. I'm told he wishes to thank you, personally.'

'Good, Nochi,' Nyasanu murmured. 'Am I on this occasion permitted to make my gifts to the king?'

'Gifts?' the old princess said, 'Hmmmm, I'm not sure that would be wise. It might be interpreted as an offensive display of wealth. Depends upon the nature of the gifts, I should think. Shouldn't be too showy. Have you got them here?'

'Yes, Nochi,' Nyasanu said; then to Dangbevi: 'Go tell Soye and Alihonu to bring the gifts in here. . . .'

'Lovely child that,' the old princess said, watching Dangbevi as she scampered away. 'Seems northern. What is she anyhow? Auyo? Yoruba? Hausa?'

'Fanti—I think. I really don't know, Mother,' Nyasanu said. 'Her native tongue is Ewe. But all the tribes to the north and east speak Ewe——'

'When they don't speak bastard Arabic—which is what she really looks like. Only she's too black to be an Arab. Tell me, son, why don't you *know* what she is?'

'Well,' Nyasanu hesitated.

'Tell me!' the ancient *axovi* said imperiously.

'All right, Nochi,' Nyasanu said, 'but first, let me admit that I can't vouch for the truth or certitude of a single word I'm going to say....'

'Why not?' the old princess said.

'Because they were told me by my first friend eldest, who wasn't sure of them, himself; and I've no way to test the matter because, unfortunately and to my great sorrow, he is dead....'

'Tell me, anyhow,' the *axovi* said.

When Nyasanu had finished with the tale of how Kpadunu had met and married Dangbevi, his 'royal mother' laughed until the tears ran down her withered cheeks.

'What nonsense!' she cackled, 'what delicious nonsense! But you, of course, Vi, have a more rational explanation for your wife's origins?'

'Yes,' Nyasanu began. 'I think ...'

But the old princess stopped him with a lifted hand.

'*Don't* tell me. I like the nonsense better. So little romance and magic is left in the world nowadays, son. How about those gifts——'

Nyasanu clapped his hands. At once Soye and Alihonu came through the door with the iron *ase* and the beautiful stool wrapped in cloths. They had been politely waiting outside for Nyasanu to finish his magic tale.

'Hmmmm,' the old princess said. 'Not bad. Not bad at all! You're *very* intelligent, aren't you, my son? Nobody can say that an iron *ase* is a costly gift, nor a royal stool either, for that matter. At the same time, no man can deny that those are by far the most beautiful objects of their respective kind ever seen in Da's Belly! Where'd you get 'em, Vi?'

'The altar I made. I am of the Ironworkers' Clan and it seemed to me that so pious a gift couldn't possibly offend——'

'You were right, and the stool?'

'Was made for me by my granduncle Hwegbe who is the

282

prince of all woodcarvers and of all scoundrels at once and the same time!'

'They'll do,' the princess said. 'Have your people bring them along. One more thing. You must have in mind a strong name to name yourself when you are made *gbonuga* of Alladah, for such a high office requires that you change your name thus cutting off as far as is possible, all your associations with the past....'

Nyasanu thought about that. Decided at once that he would invent no new name for himself, but would honour his mother by selecting one of the five secret strong names she had given him at birth. But which one? His names were Dosu Agausu Hwesu Gbokau Kesu, called Nyasanu, son of Gbenu. Thinking about it he decided to call himself Hwesu, which meant 'He whose eyes behold the sun'. It was sufficiently ambiguous not to cause trouble. In fact the spectators—and the *dada*—might well assume the flattering interpretation that by 'the sun' Nyasanu meant the *dada*, himself. Even if they did guess its true meaning: 'He whose eyes look upon glory', it couldn't be considered too boastful, because to look upon glory and to attain it were two different things altogether.

So he was to be governor of Alladah! That was a great and fearsome thing. For though, having watched his father do it for many years, managing the city of Alladah hadn't proved too difficult, governing the whole province of which the city was the capital, was quite another matter. For the province of Alladah was made up not only of the city bearing the same name, but of five immense districts called Ugbiya, Aladagbe, Nwacheme, Agbogbove, and Hwedjisi. It meant that he'd *never* be at home. He'd have to travel constantly from place to place to check on the activities of the great district chiefs, the *togans,* who now would become his subordinates and, being men of middle age, of wealth and influence, they were sure to resent his authority furiously. He'd have to watch over the *gevi* as well, the men placed in every town to see that no man killed his slaves; and the *toxausu,* the chiefs of the villages, towns, and cities, from whose ranks he himself had so recently risen. It was a grave thing, and very troublesome.

So clearly did his feeling of disquietude show on his face that his 'royal mother' reached out and patted him reassuringly on the arm.

'You'll manage,' she said. 'You're a smart boy, son. Besides,

you'll have me to help you. Now one more thing: lean close
that I may whisper in your ear the strong words you're to say
to the king after you've been appointed *gbonuga*.'

Nyasanu did so. Straightened up, moving his lips and frowning, as he repeated the strong words over and over again until
he had them in mind.

'Got them?' the old princess said.

'Yes, Nochi,' Nyasanu told her.

'Very well. After that ceremony, you will be dismissed. Start
back towards Alladah. But don't travel too fast, nor too far;
for tomorrow morning you will be called back to Abomey....'

'Why, No?' Nyasanu said.

'The *dada* is going to engage his daughter Taunyinatin to
you. You realise that this is a very great honour.'

'Yes, Mother,' Nyasanu whispered, 'I realise that....'

'You don't seem pleased,' the old princess said.

'Say—I am afraid,' Nyasanu said frankly. 'Marrying a princess can be a very great trouble, as well.'

'Ha!' the *axovi* laughed. 'You have brains, Vi! You're right.
Princesses are spoiled, headstrong, ungovernable, slothful, and
lecherous as she-monkeys. I know. *I* am a princess.'

'Forgive me, Nochi!' Nyasanu gasped, 'I quite forgot——'

'Doesn't matter. Taunyinatin is the most beautiful of my
stepson's daughters. It's said she is the most beautiful girl in
Dahomey. And she *is* a very great trouble. I know her well.
But I remember that in my youth I was far worse than she. But
my father engaged me to a man. A real man. You think that
because you can neither scold, hit, beat, or otherwise punish a
princess that you'll have no control over her? Well neither
could *my* husband; but before six months were out, he had me
crawling on my belly to kiss his feet, and he was a commoner,
a real commoner, not the son of a great chief and a *kposu*, the
way you are——'

'How'd he do that, Nochi?'

'By making me love him. Which is the simplest of all *gbos*
and the most complicated, at one and the same time. I won't
tell you his methods. They wouldn't work for you. You'll have
to invent your own. And my guess is it won't be hard for you
to do so, since these three wenches plainly adore you. One hint
though: *don't* treat her like a princess. Don't seek her favour.
Treat her as though she were a Maxi slavewoman—by which I
mean kindly enough—but with indifference. If there's any one

thing that can drain the pride out of a high-born heart, 'tis that.'

'I thank you, Nochi,' Nyasanu said.

'Don't mention it. And now, I must go. Help me up, will you, son?'

Nyasanu took her arm and led her to the doorway. Outside in the street her people scurried about preparing the hammock, the sunshades, the cushions. The old princess stared up at her new 'son'.

'You're a giant, Vi,' she said mischievously. 'Lift me into the hammock. I want to see how strong you are.'

Nyasanu bent and swept her up. She weighed nothing. All that there was left of her was skin and bones. But as he laid her gently down in the great hammock, she tightened both her withered arms about his neck and kissed his forehead with great and maternal tenderness.

'Thou'rt fine, my son,' she said. 'Ayi, but thou'rt very fine!'

From where he sat, on the edge of the clearing, Nyasanu could hear the voices calling his name.

'Ahgo!' they roared. 'Ahgo, son of Gbenu! Ahgo Nyasanu!'

He didn't answer them. He sat very still, looking at Dangbevi. Her eyes were swollen and completely shut from crying. And nothing he could do or say would comfort her.

'A princess,' she sobbed, 'the most beautiful of the king's daughters! The most beautiful girl in all Dahomey! That old woman said that! I heard her! And she didn't lie!'

'Oh, for Legba's sake!' Nyasanu said. 'What's all that got to do with you, Dangbevi?'

'I'm your housewife eldest,' Dangbevi whispered, 'and once you—you said you loved me. That—that you didn't love any of the others. Yet you—you've made Alihosi find her belly—and now you're going to marry a princess——'

'I'm not going to,' Nyasanu said. 'I'm obliged to. I'm forced to. There's a difference.'

'Is there? Maybe! But hear me, older person mine; listen to me well! The day I see the slightest sign that you *love* her. That you prefer her to me—that day I die!'

'All right,' Nyasanu said coldly, 'I'll bury you with all due rites and ceremonies, housewife.'

'Ohhhhh!' Dangbevi wailed. 'You won't even care! Oh, I'm

285

not going to wait! I'll do it now!'

'Go ahead,' Nyasanu said. 'But first, know this, Dangbevi: only one woman on earth can rob you of my love. And she's *not* the Princess Taunyinatin.'

'Then, who?' Dangbevi whispered.

'You. You yourself. And you're making a first-class number one start at it right now.'

Dangbevi opened her mouth to say something but whatever it was, she never got it out, because the cries of '*Ahgo*, son of the *kposu*!' were like thunder, and then the Half Heads broke into the clearing leading the Prince S'ubetzy by the ropes attached to his hands.

The ceremony was very long and tiresome. First Nyasanu's servants brought the twelve smoked and dried heads and built a little pyramid of them before the king. For each head, the king caused the *minga*, the prime minister,* to ladle up a headful of cowries, using a polished skull for the purpose. Therefore Nyasanu received a great deal of the shell money for his grizzly trophies. It cost him anguish to keep his face impassive at the sight.

Then the *vuduno* of Gu, God of War, sang:

'*E bo-hun e diegi!*' which meant 'The sound of the war-drum is good!' and that part of the ceremony was over.

'You will now,' the *gao*, or commander-in-chief of the army, said, 'bring forth your prisoner with a name!'

Nyasanu led S'ubetzy forward. The Auyo prince made no resistance. In fact, he seemed to regret being freed. He might very well have; for, Nyasanu later discovered, during his captivity he'd been lodged in one of the apartments of the palace, given every delicacy imaginable to eat and drink, supplied with twenty-five concubines to ease his rest at night, and it was said, visited secretly by all the younger, prettier princesses, including the beautiful Taunyinatin, herself, who found his dress, bearing, and manners irresistible.

At that point, Gezo, *dada* of Dahomey, got up and made

* The *minga* and the *meu*, the two most important civilian officials of the kingdom, had duties which make it impossible to decide which of them more closely corresponded to a European prime minister, and which to the chief justice of a supreme court. But the *meu*'s disciplinary power seems, to the writer, to qualify him more nearly as chief justice.

one of his famous speeches. In it, he praised the late Gbenu as one of the greatest of his warriors, shed not entirely theatrical tears at speaking of his death, and concluded with the remark that the *vudun* had been kind to him personally and to the kingdom, for they had sent a worthy replacement in Gbenu's son, here present before them.

Thereafter, Gezo made a brief description of Nyasanu's heroic feat, which, it could truly be said, had saved not only the kingdom, but his, the *dada*'s own sacred life. Therefore, no ordinary rewards were sufficient for the hero.

At which point all the people cried out; the drums thumped and thundered, flageolets and cymbals sounded softly.

'But,' Gezo said, 'let us complete the business of buying from the young lion his prisoners. My lord Gao, award this *kposu*'s son fifty heads of cowries, and twenty rods of cloth for his prisoner!'

All the people shouted at that, the more so when the bolt of pure European manufactured silk was unwound to its full length. In Dahomey, the value of such a cloth was very nearly incalculable.

At this point, a tall stately old man, black as the night itself, clad in robes of dazzling richness, his lean aquiline features made all the more striking by the snowy turban that he wore, stepped forward.

'Have I the Leopard's permission,' he said in Ewe, 'to say a word to this young man?'

'Of course, great caliph!' Gezo said.

Ibrahim T'wala, king of the Auyo, stepped up to Nyasanu.

'My son,' he said, 'I am told you held my son and heir's life in the hollow of your hand and generously spared him, at great price. Is this so?'

'At very great price, my lord,' Nyasanu said clearly, 'for my first friend eldest, my third friend, and one of my sisters who served in the Woman's Corps, all died in that fight.'

'Yet, you spared him,' Ibrahim T'wala said, 'for which Allah the Compassionate shower eternal blessing upon thee! And from my poor hand, I beg you to accept—this.'

It was a jewelled dagger, hung upon a chain of gold. Its sheath was of brass and silver, garnished with rubies.

Nyasanu took the beautiful weapon.

'I thank you, my lord,' he said.

'Know all men present,' Ibrahim T'wala said, 'that Nyasanu

son of Gbenu is from henceforth safe forever from Auyo steel! For the sacred dagger I have given him is his passport; he may come and go in the Saddle Kingdom as he pleases, and I shall expect him at Alakpawe within the coming years, whereupon I shall award him with much treasure and a princess of the blood as his wife!'

'Oh no!' Nyasanu groaned inside his mind. 'I have all too many wives now, though none of them as yet is a princess! And *two* princesses in the same compound will be any man's definition of disaster!'

But he kept a tight grip on his nerves and bowed deeply.

'My lord honours me too much,' he said.

In the brief pause while the king of the Auyo was taking his seat, Nyasanu waved Soye and Alihonu forward. Before anyone was aware what they were going to do, they had set their burdens down and had prostrated themselves before the *dada*.

'What is this?' Gezo said, a little angrily.

'Some poor and humble gifts, my lord,' Nyasanu said. 'Since you, my king, have deigned to honour me for my poor efforts on your behalf, I would like, my lord permitting it, to present to him and to his great ancestors these small tokens of my gratitude, my loyalty, my esteem....'

'Uncover them!' Gezo said.

When the *ase*, the iron altar, was uncovered, the exclamations of surprise and approval ran like a crackling fire around the square. But when the stool was unveiled, all the people fell silent. In the shifting afternoon light, it seemed to be alive; the serpent coils to move.

Gezo picked it up, examined it from every angle. Then, turning to the *minga*, he thundered:

'Remove my stool! From this day on, this gift of the late *kposi*'s son will be the royal stool! For truly its beauty is unmatched!' Then after a pause, he added, 'And let this glorious *ase* be placed in the house of the royal ancestors; for truly it, too, is worthy of such honour!'

A babble of whispered comment broke out at this unprecedented act on the part of the king.

'How greatly doth the *dada* honour him!'

''Twould be wise to court this upstart stripling's favour, it seems to me....'

'Don't worry—a country clod like that will come a cropper

soon enough! The higher you rise, the harder you fall!'

'I don't know.' [A woman's voice.] 'So handsome a lad as this is sure...'

'To crawl into your house if I don't watch you!' [Her husband's.]

After that the *minga* rose.

'Young man, come forward,' he said.

Nyasanu did so, prostrating himself three times on the way.

'Stand up!' the *minga* said.

Nyasanu got to his feet. At once, one of the *minga*'s servants threw a heavy and costly cloth over the young chief's shoulders. With his own hand, the *minga*—or prime minister—hung a string of red beads around Nyasanu's neck. A stool was pushed forward. It was very like a chief's stool, except that it was much more intricately carved, and was far finer.

'Sit!' the *minga* said.

Nyasanu sat. The *minga* then placed an anya wand in the crook of Nyasanu's arm. Then, causing Nyasanu to cup his two hands, the prime minister poured a handful of sand into them, as a symbol of the territory which he was to govern.

Then the *minga* made ready to deliver the set speech of eleven clauses, which has been made at the inauguration of a man's term of office in Dahomey since the beginning of memory.

He began by asking:

'What is your name?'

'My name is Nyasanu,' the young chief said.

'From this day, you will no longer be called Nyasanu but Gbonuga, his Excellency, or governor of the province of Alladah! You will be in command of that province; all *togan*, *toxausus*, and other lesser officials will be at your command. But before allowing you to take your departure, let me call to your mind the ancient prescription of the king.'

Whereupon the *minga* launched into the eleven clauses. Nyasanu didn't listen to them, he knew them all by rote anyhow, and he was rehearsing in his mind the reply he'd have to make.

So when the *minga* reached the last and noblest of the clauses:

'In closing, the king orders you to allow even the poorest man to come to him, and the strangers who have no protectors in the capital, so that he may help them. And here is the rule of Dahomey: put dust on your head, and rise to vow to the king your devotion, and give us your surname. . . .' Nyasanu knew what to do and say.

Again prostrating himself, he threw the double handful of sand on his head. Then rising, he made a princely speech, assuring the *dada* of how faithfully he'd do the royal bidding. He swore this by the royal totems, Kpo, the leopard, and Agbali, the spotted antelope. He called upon the *nesuxwe*, the ghosts of the princely dead, to aid him; he called upon the royal *tauxausu*, the ghosts of those princes abnormally born, those having six fingers on each hand, or huge heads, or a tail like a monkey's, and other such deformity, for in Dahomey such people are held to possess more powerful spirits than normal folk; he called upon Gezo himself to aid and comfort him in his endless labours. And he finished it with age-old formulae, calling upon Agasu Tauhwiyo, or founder of the Gbekpovi Aladaxonu, the royal clan.

'With the help of Agasu!' he cried out.

'He will aid you!' the people shouted.

'With the help of the ancient kings!'

'They will aid you!' the people cried.

'With the help of Zumadunu!' There was a little pause at that, because all the people's throats tightened with fear. For Zumadunu was the legendary chief of the abnormally born, and no ancestral spirit was so greatly dreaded as he. But managed at last, with many a quaver, the response.

'He will aid you!'

'With the help of the *dada*, who is present!'

But now, instead of shouting, all the officials and the people dropped to their knees, wringing their hands in supplication and crying: 'Kuse, Kuse, Kuse! Please! Please! Please!'

The *dada* Gezo did not answer; for the *minga* was serving as his linguist, or spokesman. From now on, Nyasanu would have to find himself a smooth talker to serve him as linguist, for great officials in Dahomey usually spoke through the mouth of a spokesman, it being held beneath their dignity to address their subordinates directly, except on rare occasions.

Now the *minga* placed a *gbo* in Nyasanu's hand. It was of the kind called *holauhaulaugho*, designed to give its owner strength and confidence in dealing with people. Actually, it was a kind of bracelet made of woven raffia cloth called keleku, the cloth sacred to the Sky Gods, to which bristles from the neck of Agbo, the ram, had been attached. Swiftly, Nyasanu slipped it onto his left arm, murmuring at the same time the magic formula:

'*Akaunda agbo kuno xo xu gbo hauku ndyedo tanmeho*— *Akaunda*, when the ram goes to fight, he does not die in his place!'

'With this magic charm,' the *minga* said solemnly, 'you will never fail, for the *dada* is your living benefactor.'

Then Nyasanu turned to his wives and his people and said: 'With the aid of the ghost of my father!'

All his people murmured: 'The ghost of Gbenu will help you.'

'With the help of all the governors who ever lived!'

Now the king joined in the chorus: 'They will aid you!'

And now the young, newly made *gbonuga* turned towards the throne, and said:

'Today is my naming day!'

Whereupon the people cried out: 'Yes! Yes! Yes!'

'I shall work!' Nyasanu said. 'At night I shall not sleep, during the day I shall not rest, because rest is not a thing of the day and sleep not a thing of the night. The commands the *minga* has given me, I shall not forget, but shall keep them for my pillow. When *dada* commands anything of me, I shall leap to obey, for when *dada* raises only so much as his index finger, there is no man in Dahomey but instantly responds. When the king goes hunting, he kills much game; when he makes war, he takes many captives. *Mpahwe!* I praise the king!'

He stopped then, ran his gaze around the square, let it linger a moment on Dangbevi's face. Then loudly he cried out:

'My friends, from this day forth I shall call myself the Gbo-nuga Hwesu!'

The *dada* stood up then, clapped his hands, and led the people in the cheering:

'Hail to the new *gbonuga* of Alladah! Hail to Hwesu! He whose eyes hath seen the sun!'

Bowing, the new Hwesu, for never again would anyone call him Nyasanu—any more than they had called poor Agbale by that name after Nyasanu as her husband had changed it to Nyaunu wi—led his people through the great Kannah Gate. Three times they marched around the Dange-la-Corde Palace, with the newly made, newly named *gbonuga* shouting:

'*Chu-o-o! Kohwe-kohwe! Cho!*'

For these were the strong words that his 'royal mother' had whispered in his ear at the noonday meal. And though their meaning is not precise, what they signified was: 'All praise and thanks to the king!'

And, as he marched, followed by his beaming wives, his laughing, prancing, dancing servants, all the people gazed down at him, tall as a giant, proud as the Thunder God, as he passed crying his great cry. They marked his face, his bearing, his gait, with great attention, knowing that never before had a commoner risen so swiftly in the king's esteem. And among the people who watched him were the Princess Taunyinatin and her half-brother, the Axo Atedeku. Taunyinatin studied her husband-to-be with care, the ghost of a smile playing about her full and lovely lips. Seeing it, her half-brother frowned. He stopped looking down at Hwesu, *gbonuga* of Alladah, striding so proudly down below. Instead, the *axo* studied the faces of the other spectators. Within half a minute he'd found what he sought:

Among the people with names, the notables, three-quarters were all but strangling on the green tides of their own envy, seeing their paths to power blocked by this provincial upstart. From now on, Atedeku knew, every move the newly named Hwesu made would be watched, and at his slightest wavering, his first mistake, the pack would be upon him. For that, Prince Atedeku reasoned, is the greatest weakness—or the greatest strength—of the kingdom of Da's Belly: That the king's power is absolute. And around a lion, only jackals gather.

But, the *axo* thought, as he raised the hand of his half-sister-mistress to his lips, even jackals have their uses. So now to devise a means to deal this upstart so grave a wound that even such cowardly carrion eaters as these won't hesitate to attack!

He didn't know how that could be accomplished yet. But standing there so close to Taunyinatin that the dark, musky odour of her oiled and perfumed body rose like a cloud about his head, he knew he'd find a way.

He had to.

TWENTY

They made camp a little over five miles from the walls of Abomey and rested there, though it was not yet night. The servants and the slaves laughed and gesticulated and even danced, bursting with pride to suddenly find themselves being pointed out as the people of a personage with so great a name, as their young master had become.

But his Excellency Hwesu, governor of the province of Alladah, lay in his hammock and was silent and the thoughts that moved through his head were long, long thoughts.

'I'll have to build a compound in Abomey,' he mused, 'or near it. And at least a house in the largest towns of each of the five districts of the province. If not, I'll be forced to accept the hospitality of the *togans*, and that's not a good idea at all. In the first place, they're all men of my poor father's age, or older, and being commanded by a stripling is sure to offend them. The only question is: how will they react to my ordering them around?'

He lifted his head and gave a little snorting laugh. His three wives—who were standing by the hammock, fanning him, and wiping his forehead with perfumed cloths, and bringing him cooling drinks—stared at him. But he paid them no attention at all.

'They'll react in two ways, the district chiefs,' the newly named Hwesu thought. 'Or three. Though, come to think of it, the first two ways are just about the same. They'll try poisoning me: or get their sorcerers to make *gbos* designed to induce Legba to eat my breath or my brains. And if the first two methods fail, they'll move on to number three: trying to influence me by giving me their daughters as wives.'

He lay there, thinking about that. His own experience of it had convinced him that plural marriage was far from the best way to arrange one's life. He was quite sure that had Nyaunu wi lived, and if he'd been able to run away with her to some other country—the Bight of Benin say, or Ashanti—he'd have been far happier with her alone than he was with four wives. Even with Dangbevi, he could be at least contented, if it weren't for the others. But four bickering women made happiness impossible; and when the children came, inspiring each wife to fight all the others like a lioness to insure that it was *her* son who inherited his father's rank and titles, a man's compound became a battlefield, causing him to have to strain his nerves to the breaking-point exercising tact, diplomacy, and brutal force by turns, merely to keep some semblance of peace.

'That being so,' Hwesu reasoned painfully, 'why did a man as intelligent as my father was, acquire so many wives?'

He sat upright in the hammock, throwing up one hand in the same gesture that a trapped beast does, clawing against the netting. 'Trapped,' he thought morosely: 'That's it. That's the word. As my father was before me, by a system so close woven there's no escaping it. In Dahomey a man *has* to marry. The ancestors and the earth *vudun* demand children of him to increase the ranks of their worshippers. Even if he's dirt poor, hasn't a cowry, he has to. The meanest beggar can't escape it. Even for him there's *adomevaudida*, "empty belly marriage", the form of wedding where your first friend, backed by his *dokpwe* and his society, lends you everything you need for the ceremonies in return for your first daughter by your new wife as his future bride, some thirteen or fourteen years hence. But if you stay poor and unknown you can at least hold the number of your wives down to two or three. Only who *wants* to stay poor and unknown? So you make some money, do something that gains you a name, and men who'd have kicked your skinny tail out of their compounds before push their daughters into your arms. How many can you refuse? If your *bokono* is willing to read the *du* the way you want him to, three or four, say. More than that, and the whispers start: you're *gaglo*, or impotent, or Legba's given you a disease; and you're ruined. Just let them start whispering *gaglo*, homosexuality, even though there's not the slightest truth in the rumours, and all doors are closed to you. So to prevent the evil of becoming an outcast, you accept the many evils of belonging to your world. Which means one day you wake up and you've twenty wives, thirty, forty—and among them a princess—to make your life utterly miserable. Rutting with any man who takes her fancy like a jackal bitch in eternal heat; and you powerless to——'

He stopped. Again that strong thought came to him:

'No man is powerless who's prepared to suffer the ultimate consequence for his actions.' He lifted his head. His broad nostrils flared. 'My life, yes,' he thought. 'But bow me, never!'

294

Then he smiled and put out his hand to Dangbevi.

'Come, let us go to bed, housewife eldest,' he said.

It was midmorning when the Half Heads came to summon him back to Abomey for the *nayanunu*, or royal betrothal ceremony, a word meaning 'princess drinks drinks' because of the glass of palm wine that was one feature of the rite.

Just outside the gates, the old princess who had been appointed Hwesu's 'royal mother' met them. She took the young *gbonuga* aside and explained to him how he must behave at the ceremony; as usual, the actions required of him were demeaning to the ultimate extreme; but since they were no more so than those demanded of the *minga*, the *meu*, the *gao*, the *kposu*, and all other highest officials of the realm, he could not take them as a personal affront, the more so since the honour of becoming husband to one of the *dada*'s own daughters more than compensated for them.

'But one thing more, my son,' the old *axovi* said. 'The *dada* has ordered one of the other *gbonuga* to lend you his compound near the palace. Alladah is too far away: and for the next three months you'll be too occupied with the business of your wedding to travel back and forth....'

'Only three months?' Hwesu said. 'But I thought——'

'That the marriage of a princess was a matter of two or three years. It is, usually. But the *dada* means to honour you still more, by speeding this match. Besides——'

The old princess stopped, a little flustered, and did not say her thought. The result was that Hwesu substituted for it one worse than she'd intended.

'Besides,' he thought bitterly, 'she's probably found her belly already, with the assistance of one of her first cousins, or even one of her half-brothers. That's what you mean, isn't it, Nochi? So the thing must be done before she begins to bulge too visibly....'

'You'll remember everything I've told you, Vi?' the old princess asked him.

'You may be sure of that, my mother,' Hwesu said.

His wives and his people came up to the barrier, which consisted of nothing more than long rows of palm branches denuded of their fronts and laid end to end to form a hollow square. But he, Hwesu, hung back, standing some rods away as modesty demanded. Inside that square, a royal shed had been erected, and beneath it upon the stool that Hwesu in his former existence as Nyasanu had given the *dada*, Gezo the Leopard sat. He was, of course, devotedly attended by several of his younger, prettier wives. But what was obvious to those versed in court etiquette was the presence of the Princess Taunyinatin, dressed in a golden-coloured, flowered silk robe, her arms so weighted with bracelets she could scarcely lift them; rings on all her fingers, including her thumbs; silver anklets around her ankles—for, unlike Ashanti, Dahomey was not rich in gold—and dozens of necklaces, ranging from such traders' junk as coloured stones bored through and strung as beads, with bits of broken glass interspersed here and there to catch the light, to master-works of bronze and silver, swung from her neck.

From where he was Hwesu could not see her clearly; and he dared not crane his neck, or come forward for a better view, for either action would break the polite fiction that he was totally unaware that he was to be betrothed to a princess on this day. He had the vague impression that she was pretty; but that was hardly surprising since the Leopard Kings has an absolutely unlimited choice of wives and concubines. Whenever the *dada* happened to see a woman beautiful enough to awake desire in him, he immediately had her carried off to his palace even though she were a priestess of the sky cult or wedded to the highest official in the land. Therefore the fact that the princesses were generally lovely was no accident, considering what beauties their mothers always were. 'Of course,' Hwesu thought ironically, 'some of them take after their fathers, which accounts for the ugly ones.'

But even here, he admitted, he was being unjust, for except for a cast in one eye, Gezo was a superbly handsome man.

He looked around the crowd. Close to the stool, just outside the bamboos, the *meu* stood. That was to be expected, for among his other duties, the chief justice was supposed to supervise the princes and princesses, a task no man envied him, because one slight mistake in the direction of over-strictness on the one hand or of over-laxity on the other, depending upon the Leopard's mood at the moment, might well cost him his head. A considerable distance away from the *meu*, closer, in fact, to where Hwesu's own wives and people waited, stood that official's 'mother' the *meuno*, which is to say the old princess appointed to memorise all the sayings and doings of the chief justice, being no more his real mother than the *axovi* who had visited Hwesu that morning was *his*.

Nor was the *meuno*'s presence surprising. Just as the *meu* himself was required to discipline the princes, being empowered to give their royal hides a good whipping, or to rusticate them by exiling them for a time to one of the *dada*'s country estates if they did something absolutely outrageous such as killing a slave in a fit of rage or getting one of their full sisters with child, so, too, could his 'mother' take a peeled rod to the princesses' bottoms or shut them up in their own apartments on maize cake and water, if they overstepped the rather loose bounds of convention—apart from commoners and slaves the only lovers forbidden them were their full brothers—in which they were held.

But Hwesu could see Dangbevi from where he stood, or at least her left profile. And the front half of it was outlined by light, caught and reflected by her tears. He felt his own breath stop at that sight. Pity tore him. An unmanning stab of tenderness. And fear. Then, most of all, fear. For Dangbevi to thus openly show her jealousy, her grief, was a kind of silent rebuke to the prerogatives of royalty—and the Aladaxonus' power to punish any hint of rebuke was limitless. The trouble was that he couldn't even move up close enough to her to warn or comfort her, so he prayed to Minona and Yalode, the special goddesses of women, to keep him safe. But then he stiffened, for the ceremony had begun.

Gezo lifted his head.

'Taunyinatin, my daughter,' he said, 'come to me.'

Slowly, laden with so much jewellery that she clanked as she walked, the princess came to where her father the king sat. And though her slow, stately gait lent her much dignity, the cause of it was anything but dignified: she had been making love with her half-brother the Prince Atedeku all night long and she was so stiff and sore she could hardly move. What was more, that parting passage at arms had left her seething with rebellion; her father might give her to this peasant oaf, but by Legba, Fa, and Danh, she'd make the sweaty, unwashed lout regret the day his dam had foaled him!

With great ceremony Gezo lifted an ornate flask, and poured liquor from it into a silver cup. As Taunyinatin leaned forward to take it, the king whispered something into her ear.

The princess turned, then, and walked towards the bamboos, moving slowly, quietly, her face turned earthward, her eyes half closed. When she had reached the spot where the chief justice's 'mother', the *meuno*, stood, she bent swiftly and whispered one word into the old princess's ear.

At once the old woman cried out:

'*Ahgo!* Hwesu! I call the Gbonuga Hwesu, governor of the province of Alladah! Let him come forward! Let my lord the Gbonuga come!'

At that all the people—with the exception of Dangbevi, of course—took up the cry: 'Hwesu! His Excellency Hwesu! Let him come forward! Let him come!'

With perfect timing—to rush forward would have been to show unseemly eagerness, to delay too long unseemly pride—Hwesu came up to the barriers and knelt before the princess who was to become his bride.

And it was then that the first two nearly fatal details struck him: Taunyinatin was so beautiful that to him, at least, she was breathtaking. That beauty is subjective, that it lies in the eyes of the beholder, that there were men present who wouldn't have agreed with him, holding this one or that of her sisters lovelier still, is beside the point. And that point was that Nyasanu/Hwesu inhabited his own skin, possessed his own three souls, was living his own breath-gone, stunned, absolute moment, as he looked into that smoothly oval nightshade face, peered into those slanted almond-shaped eyes, their pupils the darkness on the deep before a *vudun*'s footstep troubled the waters; but with a whole galaxy of fallen stars glowing within, their whites blue smoky pearl, their lashes long and sweeping.

But he was raving and knew it, so he dropped his gaze, which thereupon fastened itself upon her mouth. Her mouth. Adjectives failed him: description was impossible. He tasted its wide, hot, wet fullness from a rod away. And then he saw it twist into what was clearly bitter disdain, and taking her hand away from the rim of the cup which she had been covering with her fingers, the Princess Taunyinatin deliberately spat into the wine. Then very coolly, with a smile of infinite mockery upon those glorious lips, she held it out to him.

Hwesu hung there. There were fishhooks in his belly, broken pottery, knives. The rage that tore him was absolutely pure. And the strong thought he had vowed—that no man willing to suffer the ultimate consequences of his acts is ever morally

298

helpless—came roaring back into his mind. So then he put out a hand, held it a moment so that all the spectators could see how it trembled—for not even in his act of defiance could he escape his native tendency towards subtlety, towards guile, and clumsily, jerking, reached for that cup, with such showily overplayed awkwardness that he knocked it from the Axoni Taunyinatin's hand and spilled its contents upon the ground.

At once all the spectators set up a howl of amazement, anger, and fear combined. But the *meuno,* who had seen Taunyinatin spit into that cup, and who, moreover, knew the princess only too well, said quietly:

'Go and ask your father for another cup, girl. And if he asks you tell him *you* spilled it out of nervousness. Or do you want me to tell him what insult you offered the man who saved his life?'

Taunyinatin got up and went back to her father. What explanation she gave him, Hwesu could not know. But it must have been the one the *meuno* suggested, for Gezo, with very little grumbling, gave her another cup of wine.

This time when she came back and knelt before Hwesu, she handed him the cup without a word. And without a word he took it, his hand as steady as a rock, drank it down, and said so low that only she could hear him:

'I drink to the humility and obedience of true wives!'

Taunyinatin's eyes opened wide at that; but very simply she got up and went back to her father.

Then all the people cried: '*N'yoh!* It is good!'

And Hwesu answered: '*Maphwe!* I praise the king!'

Then he and all his people and his wives prostrated themselves and threw dirt on their heads in sign of submission to the Leopard's awful power. After that Hwesu poured two great pots of water on the ground and humbled himself still further by rolling in the mud.

Finally the king stood up and led his wives and daughter back into the palace. At its gateway he turned and cried out:

'From this day forth let my daughter be known as Hwesusi!'

'*N'yoh!*' the people cried. 'It is good!'

Hwesusi meant very simply: wife of Hwesu.

But watching Taunyinatin as she disappeared into the *hwe-pa,* or woman's entrance, Hwesu wondered bleakly in his heart:

'Is she? Will she ever be?'

299

Then rising from the stinking mud, he walked away, leading his people towards the borrowed compound on the edge of the town.

TWENTY-ONE

'Today,' Hwesu said to Dangbevi, 'we move to my new compound. Go tell Sosixwe and Huno to start packing their things. . . .'

But Dangbevi didn't answer him, or even turn away to obey his command. She stood there, looking at him, a long, slow time. A shade too long, perhaps, so that a tiny stirring of anger awoke in him, but then he saw once more how thin, how taut and drawn she was, and what was in her eyes—again, and his anger died.

'I have favoured her too much,' he thought, 'and, by so doing, brought her more grief than happiness. By Mawu, why can't she accept the world as it is?' But before he had half formed that rhetorical question, the critical, doubting part of his own mind, a trait he'd inherited from Gbenu, shot back at him: 'Why can't *you*?'

He sighed, reached out, took her hand, said:

'What is it, Dangbevi?'

'Many things,' Dangbevi said. 'Will you forgive me, older person mine, if I ask you a few things I shouldn't? That I haven't any right to ask, I mean?'

'Haven't I always answered everything you've asked me?' he said wryly. 'And truthfully at that. Though maybe I wasn't smart. For it seems to me that instead of doing you good, I've harmed you.'

'Oh no!' Dangbevi said. '*You* haven't, my lord. Say—life has. And Fa. And Legba. Especially Legba with his dirty tricks!'

Hwesu looked at her with amused pity.

'What dirty tricks, housewife?' he said.

'To make the man I love grow so great that I can't keep him for my own, I suppose,' she said slowly. 'That isn't *your* fault, husband. The *vudun* willed it so. And Fa, who is Fate. And it surely isn't your fault that I can't give you a son——'

'At least not so far,' Hwesu said.

'And perhaps never,' she said sadly. 'Maybe that time I fell down and lost my baby—while I was still poor Kpad's wife, I mean—hurt me—too much. Crippled me—as a woman. Left me—barren. Oh, Hwesu! Wouldn't it be awful if I never——'

'I don't think you'll fail me,' Hwesu said. 'I think you worry about it too often, getting yourself into such a state that——'

Sosixwe and Huno have both found their bellies since we've been here, my lord,' Dangbevi said, 'while *I* haven't. I've prayed to Yalode and Minona and Taunsu, all the special *vudun* of women. To the Earth Gods, too; and to your *tau-vudun*, your ancestors. I've made sacrifices. But—they don't answer me!'

Hwesu thought, 'Do the gods ever answer anybody?' Remembering how Alogba, and Kpadunu, and Taugbadji and his father and Nyaunu wi had died, though he'd lifted prayers enough to shake the foundations of the sky. 'Are there gods at all? Don't we—well—sort of invent them, because this world's a jungle filled with savage two-legged beasts, and most of the time we're too lonely and too scared?'

'They will, little Serpent's Child,' he said. 'Give them time——'

'Husband, older person mine. I'm going to ask you—things. Forbidden things, maybe; I don't know. May I?'

'Of course,' Hwesu said.

'Are we going to stay here in Abomey always? You've built a new compound here and——'

'No,' Hwesu said. 'We're going back to Alladah, Dangbevi. This compound is only for the many months we'll have to live in Abomey out of each year, from now on, due to my new position. I'm also going to build smaller ones, or at least houses, in each of the chief cities of the five districts of the province, because I'll have to travel constantly to attend my duties. So maybe *you're* the lucky one among my wives, because the others will have to stay home and nurse their babies, while I can take you with me.'

He saw joy sparkle in her eyes at that; but just as swiftly, they dimmed.

'My lord,' she said, 'tell me: how was it that you were able to build a new compound in so little time? And one so great that people are saying you risk angering the *dada* with its size and splendour at that?'

He stood there, looking at her, and considering how to answer so thorny a question. He thought it might be kinder to lie to her, but then he decided it wouldn't be. The answer wasn't one of those things that could be kept hidden. By the natural course of events she'd find out the truth later on, anyhow; better to tell her now and get it over with.

'Because Gbade, governor of Savalu, loaned me the services of his *dokpwe* and his *gbe* to speed the work,' he said.

'That old, ugly man you almost got into a fight with,' Dangbevi whispered, 'when he insulted me because I got sick at the sight of men being butchered like goats—loaned you his work group and his mutual aid society to build your compound?'

'Yes,' Hwesu said.

'Might I ask—why, husband?' Dangbevi said.

'Because I have made a pact with him. Later on, after this business of my wedding to the princess is over with, I am going to marry one of his daughters.'

Dangbevi stood there. She did not even bend her head. She simply let her great, yellow-brown eyes fill, brim, spill, tracing star tracks down her nightblack cheeks.

'You don't understand!' Hwesu said, a little rasp of exasperation getting into his voice. 'Look, Dangbevi, you've seen Gbade. If he isn't *the* ugliest man in the world, I don't know who is. And his daughters all look like him. The one I've picked out is a little less ugly than the others—which is only to say she looks like an ordinary she-monkey, instead of a female baboon or a lady gorilla. So if you must cry over something, pick a better reason, for Fa's sake?'

'Then—why?' she whispered.

'You could call it—politics,' Hwesu answered. 'Or even neck saving, if you want to. For one thing, Gbade's no fool. On the occasions I've dined with him, he's made me see just how intense the plotting and intrigue that go on in Abomey day and night are. And how dangerous. The notables are always jockeying for positions closer to the royal stool. And precisely because of that, today, *hwesidaxo*, housewife eldest mine, your husband is one of the most bitterly hated men in Abomey....'

'But why, my love?' Dangbevi said; 'how could anyone hate *you*?'

'They do,' Hwesu said, sadly. 'They—all the personages with names hold that their names have lost strength precisely because mine has gained it. The king sits on a stool I gave him.

302

My *ase* holds the place of honour in the house of the royal dead. And while the *dada* has married some of his princess nieces to notables, so far his own daughters have been wed only to their cousins, sons of *his* cousins, and even his own brothers. Taunyinatin will be the *first* of his daughters to wed outside the Aladaxonu Clan. All of which scarcely pleases the envious, Dangbevi. So, therefore, I must protect myself against plotters. One of the ways to do it is by making alliances with powerful clans through marriage. And Gbade's clan is the Ohwegbo Geyaunu, which is a branch of Gbekpovi Aladaxonu, the royal clan, itself. So marriage to his ugly little she-monkey of a daughter, when it occurs, will be pure policy, that's all. . . .'

'And, by the same token, you'll marry the daughters of other powerful chiefs, won't you, husband?'

Hwesu sighed. 'Women!' he thought. But he said, mildly:

'I'm afraid I'll have to. Or would you prefer waking up one fine morning to find yourself my eldest *widow*, Dangbevi?'

'Oh no!' she breathed. 'Not even if you have to marry a thousand chieftains' daughters, Hwesu! You mean they'll try to—to kill you?'

'If I give them the slightest chance,' Hwesu said soberly, 'now go tell the others to——'

'Pack their things? No, husband; I'll do it for them. It is morning, so they're both sick as she-goats bitten by serpents. Poor little Huno can scarcely lift her head. She's vomited so much she's green. Besides, I'll have the Maxi slave girls to help me. So please talk to me a little longer. You so seldom do, these days. . . .'

'All right,' Hwesu said. 'What other impudent question are you going to ask me?'

'Don't know. Your lady mother and—and Alihosi. When will they arrive?'

'Today, I hope. Why?'

'Alihosi—isn't it dangerous to make the journey all that distance? She must be great with child by now. . . .'

'No. I'm having her and mother hammock-borne all the way from Alladah. So Alihosi, and my first son eldest to be, will be all right. Now what else, *hwesidaxo*?'

'*Hwesidaxo*,' Dangbevi whispered. 'Your housewife eldest— and therefore to be honoured above all other women. Do you know, Hwesu mine—I—I never dreamed that the day would come when I should *hate* being that——'

303

Hwesu stared at her.

'And now you do?' he said.

'And now I do. I'd rather be a—a slave girl, whom you took to your mat out of lust! Because then I wouldn't be tortured to death by inches the way I am now. . . .'

'Tortured?' Hwesu said.

'Yes, yes, my husband! Do you know what it was to stand before the bamboos and watch a—a princess, so beautiful that she stopped even my breath, and I'm a woman!—come forward to offer *my* husband the betrothal drink? And afterwards I had to prostrate myself and throw dirt on my head, not only that day but the next one, in the *kaudide* ceremony—that means "earth throw everywhere", doesn't it?

'Only I wasn't throwing it everywhere, Hwesu—I was piling it up on the grave—of every hope I ever had. Maybe even on my own tomb, I don't know. . . .'

'Dangbevi!' Hwesu said.

'No—I won't try to kill myself, if that's what you're thinking, older person mine. If—if you love her too much, I won't have to—I'll just die. My heart will burst from too much grief. . . .'

'Dangbevi,' Hwesu said. 'You're far more beautiful than she is and——'

'Liar!' Dangbevi snapped. 'I *saw* how you looked at her, husband! And it was then I started to hate being your house-wife eldest. For not only do I have to get my hair full of dirt to let royalty know how grateful I am to the king for breaking my heart—all your wives have to do that—but I alone had to receive the *meu*'s servant when he came to tell you that his master bade you build a house in your compound for your new bride—no longer Taunyinatin now, but Hwesusi, "bride of Hwesu". I had to give him food and drink and stand behind his chair and service him as though I were a slave girl!'

'That was only courtesy, Dangbevi,' Hwesu said, 'and——'

'I know! I know! As your *hwesidaxo*, I have to do all the important things—all the things that are killing me! I had to take your calabash filled with flasks of the finest liquors money can buy up to the palace. And if that wasn't bad enough, when the *meuno,* the *meu*'s mother—she really isn't, is she? I mean they just call her that, don't they? She can't be! She's no more than fifty or so, while he's almost that old himself——'

'It's a title—go on, Dangbevi——'

'She took a fancy to me, she said. Wanted to know of what race I was, what tribe, what nation. Said it was clear I wasn't Dahomean——'

'It is,' Hwesu said.

'Anyway, she invited me to stay for the ceremony. The *ayabadudu*. What does that long word mean, husband?'

'"Drink burden load",' Hwesu told her.

'Another load upon my heart,' Dangbevi whispered, 'for I had to stand there and watch while the *dada* poured all that fine liquor that cost you so much money out on the ground before the tombs of the royal ancestors and listen to him praying to them to prosper his daughter's marriage to *you*, my husband! And there's still one more ceremony that I—and only I—because I'm your housewife eldest—must do. I have to take your basket—how is it called, Hwesu?'

'*Kaublibi,* which means "earth roll over",' Hwesu said.

'Your *kaublibi* basket, filled with precious gifts, to *her*! To Taunyinatin! To Hwesusi! And on that day, surely I will die!'

'No, you won't,' Hwesu said calmly, employing all his Dahomean gift of guile. 'But she will, maybe. Burst her sides with laughter, likely. Or at least make herself sick from so much mirth, when she sees what a scrawny she-goat I have for my housewife eldest. A skeleton dancing around inside a shrunken skin. No flesh on her bones. Her beauty—if ever she had any, completely gone. Have you no pride at all, Dangbevi! Aren't you woman enough to want to make her sick with envy when she sees how lovely you are—I mean how lovely you *were*, and can be again, if you work at it? Or do you want to help her along by conceding defeat? Reducing yourself to such a thing as no woman could possibly feel jealous of? Or getting completely out of her way by starving yourself to death the way you're doing now?'

He saw from the appalled expression upon her face that he had taken the right tack. He thought with relief, 'From now on, she'll stuff herself like a sacrificial pig,' then he went on with the lesson he was trying to drive home.

'If Legba hadn't eaten half your brains by now, you'd know you've nothing to worry about,' he said. 'For one thing the marriages of princesses *never* last. When they get bored with a husband, they simply leave him, and there's nothing he or anyone else can do about it. And even if they remain on good terms with him—a thing that almost never happens because of

305

the way they're brought up—they still go back to the Royal Palace at the end of two years, whereupon the poor devil has the great privilege of visiting them there, like a thief in the night. Moreover, all their children take their mother's name, belong to the royal clan, and can never inherit either their father's rank and titles or even the kingship itself. All they can be is princes and princesses, which is but another word for parasites to my way of thinking. So——'

'So?' Dangbevi whispered.

'So forget Taunyinatin and remember this: I don't *have* to make Alihosi's child my heir even if he turns out to be a boy and my first son eldest, any more than my father made Gbochi his, child of the python. I should much prefer to name the first son I have by my favourite wife, my only truly beloved, as my heir, if she'd ever give me one, which she can't as long as she keeps on ruining her own health and my sleep with her groundless fears. . . .'

She stood there looking at him; and her eyes were wide and soft, suddenly.

'Hwesu,' she murmured. 'Older person mine—you are making me have wicked thoughts——'

'Such as?' he said.

'Such as—although it's Huno's turn now to be your housewife she's already found her belly. And she's so sick anyhow that I know she wouldn't mind if—if I asked her to—change with me—and——'

He smiled at her, a little mockingly.

'Then you prefer to continue as my housewife eldest?' he said. 'You have decided not to die?'

Her answering smile was alight with mischief. 'No,' she said. 'I haven't decided that. How can I? Maybe I—I'll get so tired from trying all night long for too many nights to make you a man-child that Legba will eat my breath. But that's a good way to die, isn't it? At least I think so. . . .'

She went to the door. Then she stopped, looking at him flirtatiously over one smooth shoulder. Clearly she was expecting him to invite her to stay. But he didn't say anything, out of a perverse desire to tease her. So, very quickly to cover her embarrassment, she said:

'Guess I'd better go to start those lazy wenches of yours packing——'

'No,' he said solemnly, 'don't. We have time I think to make

306

our son's foot, at least, or his nose, or his ears, anyhow.
So——'

'So I stay with you, my husband,' she whispered, laughter
bubbling through her voice, and came to his waiting arms.

On the next morning, the bearers came trooping into his new
compound with the hammocks in which his mother Gudjo and
his *chiosi* wife Alihosi reclined. Alihosi was great with child
now, and it became her. Round and plump, beaming with pride
and happiness, she was almost pretty. Even her voice had lost
its stridency. And when she learned of Hwesu's approaching
marriage to the princess, she took the news calmly enough; for
she had known of similar cases in the past, and was aware that
while a princess wife of a commoner could be a very great
trouble indeed to his other wives, that trouble was almost never
lasting. A year or two at the most, and the haughty creature
was gone. Besides, to Alihosi, the fact that the children of a
princess did not belong to her husband made up for all the
other difficulties; for such children could not inherit. Not even
the news of Sosixwe's and Huno's pregnancies could shake her
equanimity. Hwesu—as she now had to call her husband—
loved neither of them sufficiently to put aside a true first son
eldest for offspring of theirs. And the fact that Dangbevi was
not with child set her heart completely at ease. Dangbevi's son
was to be feared; the sons of the other two, no.

So she bubbled with good cheer as she joined with Gudjo in
telling Hwesu all the news from home: *gaglo* that he was,
Hwesu's half-brother Gbochi was rising in life. He now had
many wives and dozens of babies on their way to be born; and
his wealth, due to his mother's shrewdness in business, was
great. . . .'

'Considering the number of men he puts to work at making
them for him,' Gudjo said drily, 'in order to secure for himself
their manly favours as the price for the pleasure his wives
afford them, the babies are hardly surprising—nor is the
wealth, I suppose. . . .'

Old Hwegbe had disappeared, wandering away from the
compound, unable, despite his years, to endure a fixed existence. And Yu was still—Yu. 'The biggest whore in the uni-
verse!' Alihosi spat.

'And my sister Axisi, how fares she?' Hwesu asked.

'Well. Very well indeed,' Gudjo laughed. 'She's as big as the

Royal Palace by now, of course. But the *bokono* says she'll give birth easily and that the child will be both male and have a great future before him.'

'And that worthless scoundrel she insisted on marrying?'

'Kapo? That's the surprising thing, my son. He's really trying to reform now; I'm sure of it.

'You're to blame for that, husband,' Alihosi said.

'I doubt it. As long as I was there, maybe. But now I'm too far away to reach his rusty buttocks with an *anya* rod, he'll——'

'No,' Alihosi said seriously, 'he's changed. Life does that, you know. The last time he visited your mother and me, he talked—sense. Said that since he was getting rich by honourable means, trickery and gaming no longer appealed to him. And that it felt awfully good to be looked up to and respected for a change. People seek his counsel now—and on serious matters, not merely upon how to manipulate the dice. . . .'

'You needn't worry about Axisi, son,' Gudjo added. 'Kapo's being very, very careful to her. News travels fast, you know. And as the greatness and strength of your name grows, your brother-in-law becomes increasingly proud of the relationship. In fact, I happen to know he brags about being *your* sister's husband now. He's nobody's fool; he can see the wisdom of maintaining so important a connection. . . .'

'I see,' Hwesu said; then, remembering how glib of tongue Kapo was, a thought struck him: 'I'll make him my linguist! That way he'll have to travel with me everywhere and be my spokesman when I address the *togans* and the lesser chiefs. Have the beggar where I can watch him then, and puff up his already over-swollen pride, neither of which will do any harm. . . .'

Two weeks after his mother's and Alihosi's arrival, the bells sounded outside the gates of Hwesu's new compound. The gates were opened, and all Hwesu's people prostrated themselves as his 'royal mother', now called everywhere the *gbonugano* Alladahonu, 'the mother of the governor of Alladah', was borne into the courtyard.

Hwesu, his wives, and his mother presented themselves and prostrated themselves in their turn before the ancient *axovi*.

'Oh get up from there,' the merry old witch cackled. 'I'm sick of people grovelling on their bellies and throwing dirt on

308

themselves. Get up, all of you. . . .'

And, as they did so, she at once noticed Alihosi and Gudjo.

'The wife you told me about, eh, son?' she said. 'Fine belly you've hung on her for a fact! And this lady?'

'My mother,' Hwesu said. 'The Lady Gudjo, widow of the late *kposu* to the king. . . .'

'I knew your husband, Lady Gudjo,' the old princess said, 'and a fine figure of a man he was—pity he's gone. But he's left you a worthy souvenir, hasn't he? You'll have to share him with me, though, for the *dada*'s appointed me his court mother.'

'I knew that,' Gudjo said with great dignity. 'I trust you will counsel him well, your Highness.'

'I'll do my best,' the old princess said. 'Now let's all go and have a bite to eat and some palm wine and talk. As friends talk. For that's what we're going to be. . . .'

Half an hour later, they had her news: the *meu* had sent her to inform her official 'son' that if he cared to send word to the *dada* through, of course, the *meu* and the *meuno*, that he was now ready to take possession of his new bride, the news would be received with favour.

At first Hwesu sat there, speechless with astonishment, because, generally speaking, a commoner engaged to a princess had to wait for a minimum of six months to a maximum of two years before he could send his *kaublibi* basket to his bride-to-be, thus informing by that act, the *meu*, the *meuno*, and the king, that he was ready for the actual wedding to take place. That Gezo had speeded matters up in this fashion was a very great honour indeed.

He looked quickly at Dangbevi. She had regained some of the weight she'd lost in the two weeks since his mother's arrival. And the sheer amount of love, physical and otherwise, that Hwesu had lavished upon her in those two weeks had left her literally glowing. She smiled at him now with real confidence in herself, and in her charms, her powers.

'Thy basket is already prepared, my husband,' she said.

Hwesu turned to the old princess.

'Tomorrow I will send my *kaublibi* up to the palace,' he said.

That next morning, Dangbevi dressed with unusual care. After bathing all over and literally soaking herself in perfume she put on her best silk robe. What was more, she wore all her best jewellery and fluffed out her hair into the ball-shaped coiffure much affected by those ladies of the court who had enough hair to accomplish it, which be it said were very few. Then she slung the basket, containing thirty-five small cloths, various large figured cloths, flasks of perfume, beads, earring, mirrors, and various other kinds of jewellery, beneath one arm, since she had no intention of spoiling her coiffure by bearing it on her head as she ordinarily would have, and set out for the palace.

And well did she know the value of her burden, for the flasks of perfume were made of hammered silver, and all the jewellery, whatever its nature, was either of silver, or gold, a material Hwesu had procured from a wily Ashanti trader. He had taken a terrible beating on the question of price, for he simply hadn't the cunning to outsmart an Ashanti trader. But he didn't care very much, since gold was a metal all but impossible to procure in Dahomey, so he was absolutely sure that Taunyinatin was going to be the first princess in recent history to have jewellery made of it.

What was more important, perhaps, was the fact that the workmanship was absolutely superb, for Hwesu had found his old friend Amosu, whom long ago the *dada* had summoned up to Abomey to work as royal silversmith, and had asked him to make the very finest pieces he was capable of. Inspired by the opportunity, Amosu had outdone himself. The earrings, brooches, bracelets were masterpieces of the silversmith's art.

So Dangbevi set out for the Dange-la-Corde Palace with a mind as divided as it was possible for a woman's mind to be. On the one hand, she was proud of the richness and beauty of her husband's gifts to the princess; she was fully aware of how great an honour the king had paid Hwesu by betrothing one of his own daughters to him; but, on the other hand, being entirely cut off from her own background by whatever it was that had blotted all memory of her childhood from mind so completely that she didn't even know whether she was a Fanti, or a Fulani, or even from some other tribe of the Ewe-speaking Yorubian people to the north, she regarded Hwesu's approaching marriage to Taunyinatin with all the pristine fury of a jealous woman. In this, she was unique, for unless she were actually miraculously transformed from a pythoness into a woman, as all her contemporaries—even, occasionally, Hwesu himself,

310

who could not entirely escape the superstition of his people—
believed, her childhood would have prepared her to accept
polygamy with a certain grace.

Though only with a *certain* grace; for the strict truth of the
matter was that most West African women, in their heart of
hearts, hated it. Even Dahomean custom, rigid enough on
most questions of morals, provided two outlets for female rebellion against becoming the ninth, the twentieth, or the for-
tieth wife of some grizzled old chief their fathers had engaged
them to out of policy: *asidjosi*, in which the girl in question
ran off with the younger, handsomer, simpler man with fewer
wives or none whom she preferred, whereupon the lover made
the relationship legal by paying back the rejected official
suitor's gifts, and work; and *xadudo*, which was exactly the
same thing except that nothing was paid back, and the marriage
rites never performed so that the couple went on living in sin,
as it were.

So on the way up to the palace, Dangbevi reached such a
state of desperation that she toyed with the idea of killing the
princess once she had been admitted to her rooms.

'Only,' she thought miserably, 'what good would that do
me? She wouldn't have him; but then, neither would I. For the
only thing a man can do with a woman whose head has been
hacked off is to bury her....'

She was passing through the Kannah Gate as she thought
that, and the palace lay immediately before her. 'The only
way,' she reasoned now, slowly, 'is to convince the Axovi
Taunyinatin that she *shouldn't* marry Hwesu. That it isn't a
good idea at all. That—that she'll be unhappy. I—I'll tell her he
drinks much rum, and has a terrible temper and beats all his
wives bloody with peeled rods! And——'

She stopped, bowed her head and watered the very earth
with her tears. Because she realised suddenly that her proposed
strategy was useless: no man beat a princess wife, ever. Even
to slap her face was enough to cost him his head.

'I—I'll think of something!' she thought. 'I—I've got to! O
Danh, Dangbe, and all the Serpent Gods, masters of all cun-
ning and all guile, help me! Show me the way to be rid of her!
For beautiful as she is, my Hwesu will love her too much. And
I—and I——'

But nothing came to her. So head down and sorrowing, she
moved on towards the *hwepali,* the gate of women.

She was shown at once into the apartments of the *meuno*, the 'mother' of the *meu*, or chief justice of the realm. That shrewd, middle-aged princess studied her, for the second time, with some care. What the princess saw pleased her: 'Time,' she thought, 'that that vicious little she-cat of a Taunyinatin is brought down a peg or two. And if anyone can accomplish *that*, this proud and lovely creature can!'

So, smiling most graciously, she said: 'Sit down, my child, while I send for the *meu*. . . .'

Then with an imperious gesture, the *meuno* called a slave girl to her side: but instead of speaking to her aloud, she whispered something into her ear. The girl scampered away at once; and within minutes, the beaten-earth corridors of the palace resounded to a heavy tread. The *meuno* got up and opened the door to her apartment herself, the moment that the knock sounded; and the *meu* strode into the room. Like most important Dahomean officials, he was a big, heavy man, with a stern, even menacing, kind of face. His robes, Dangbevi saw, were gorgeous. But by then she'd recovered enough from the terror the chief justice inspired in her to remember her manners, so she prostrated herself before him.

'Get up, child,' he growled in a drum-deep bass; and, as she did so, stared at her long and thoughtfully. 'And who might this pretty little thing be, Nochi?' he said to the *meuno*.

'*His* wife,' the *meuno* said drily; 'Hwesu's. His housewife eldest come to bring the *kaublibi* basket, in token that he's ready to have the *dada* set the date. . . .'

'He already has,' the *meu* said heavily. 'Two weeks from today. But I must say the boy has taste! What are you, child? Fulani? Fanti? Auyo? That you're a northerner is evident!'

'I—I don't know, my lord,' Dangbevi whispered.

'You don't *know*?' the *meu* said. 'Don't make mock of me, girl! What are your origins?'

'I—I'm called Serpent's Child,' Dangbevi got out. 'People say I—that I'm the daughter of the Sacred Python——'

'Now I've heard everything!' the *meu* said. 'You'd better explain this, daughter!'

Whereupon, with much stammering, and many hesitations and pauses, Dangbevi did. When she had finished, the *meu*, who was a shrewd judge of human nature, was convinced she wasn't lying. But being a most intelligent man, his belief in the *vudun* and in miracles was something less than keen. So since

312

Dangbevi's utter sincerity was apparent, he decided she was mad. Only the *meuno*, his 'mother', who was even more intelligent than he was, and had, as a result, the brilliant woman's natural hatred of male arrogance, wasn't disposed to allow him such easy comfort.

'Get up child,' she said to Dangbevi in a kindly tone. 'Now walk to and fro ... that's it—that's it! Tell me, Vi, my son, have you ever seen a more lovely way of walking?'

But the *meu*'s face had gone grey with fear. For the sinuous, serpentine gait that Dangbevi possessed rivalled the grace of the great constrictors, and to even a fairly enlightened mind was enough to inspire doubt that rational explanations existed for it.

'Danh and Dangbe save me!' the *meu* whispered; then: 'Has Taunyinatin seen her?'

'Not yet,' the *meuno* said drily; 'but if my ears serve me she will in about a moment, for I hear her coming now....'

Taunyinatin came into the room with a sullen look upon her face. Ostentatiously, she stifled a yawn. Then her gaze rested upon Dangbevi, and her almond-shaped eyes opened wide.

'Tell me, Nochi,' she said to the *meuno*, 'who or *what* is that!'

'The daughter of the Dangbe, the Sacred Python,' the *meuno* said calmly, 'transformed into a woman in order to become Hwesu's housewife eldest. Hwesusi, I'd advise you to treat her well. The *vudun* don't look kindly upon people who abuse their children—even when such people are of royal blood. She has brought you the *kaublibi*——'

'Good,' Taunyinatin said. 'Have the slaves take it to my rooms.' She stopped then, and stared at Dangbevi, a long, slow thoughtful time. Then:

'And you come with me, child of Dangbe; I want to talk to you,' she said.

Dangbevi sat on a low stool and stared at the princess as she tried on all the rings and brooches from Hwesu's gift basket. When she saw how many of them were of beaten gold, Taunyinatin/Hwesusi turned to her visitor.

'He must be a wealthy man, my husband-to-be,' she said.

'He is your Highness,' Dangbevi whispered.

'*How* wealthy?' Hwesusi said.

'He owns five great farms, left him by his father the *kposu*,'

313

Dangbevi said, 'each of them run by a Galentu, and each of them bigger than the city of Alladah itself. One of them, at least, is as big as Abomey. No, bigger.'

'Humph!' the princess snorted. 'A great Galentu, then. A countryman. For all their wealth, nobody's ever been able to teach them civil manners. . . .'

'He is *not* a Galentu, your Highness,' Dangbevi protested. 'He is city born and bred. What's more, his father—his late father, the *kposu*, Gbenu—was not only one of your father's finest generals, but also *toxausu* of Alladah itself. So *my* husband has had every advantage of birth and breeding, both. He was a personage with name from the day he was born. He did not have to acquire one, though, to my sorrow, he has——'

Hwesusi/Taunyinatin looked at Dangbevi more keenly now.

'Why to your sorrow, child?' she said.

'Because—I—I love him very much. And he loves me. His other wives don't count. They're plain, or silly, or dull. But you, your Highness, are much too beautiful! And you're a princess, too! I'm afraid . . .'

Taunyinatin laughed merrily at that.

'Don't worry, child!' she said. 'I don't mean to rob you of your sweaty peasant oaf!'

And at once Dangbevi was on her feet, her yellow-brown eyes afire.

'Sweaty peasant oaf!' she whispered. 'He whose very breath is sweeter than the smell of the savanna's grass in spring! Who bathes and perfumes himself thrice daily! Whose voice is the sound that Xevioso, the Thunder God, makes when he really isn't angry, but is only murmuring to himself far away out on the edge of the sky. Like slow drums. Deep and—and tender, and sad. Whose touch—whose touch——'

'Ah!' Taunyinatin said, 'why do you stop there? What of his touch, Dangbevi?'

Slowly, stubbornly, Dangbevi shook her head.

'No,' she answered. 'It can't be said. Maybe when the *vudun* first climbed down the loko tree to earth, and shaped men and women out of clay, it felt like that. Like his touch I mean. Life—passing into one's body through the fingertips of a—a—god. Forgive me, your Highness! I should show more respect, I know; but when you talk about him so—so mockingly, to me it's the same as seeing someone smearing filthy *su dudus* over the image of a *vudu*. A *vudu* of those cult I'm high priestess, and chief devotee....'

'You mean you *worship* him?' Taunyinatin/Hwesusi said.

'On my knees,' Dangbevi said. 'And love him and adore him and have no being, no existence, nor any souls, apart from those he gives me. Please, your Highness, may I go now?'

'Of course,' the Princess said. Then curving her full lips into a slow smile, added, 'I have no further need of you, little she-snake, for you've told me all I need to know!'

TWENTY-TWO

'She's hateful!' Dangbevi stormed. 'Hateful and evil! And cruel! Maybe that's why the *dada*'s so anxious to be rid of her!'

'Then he's set the date?' Hwesu asked her.

'Yes, he has! And instead of six months or a year from now, the way people say he always does with princesses—he's giving you that witch in two weeks! Two weeks from today!'

It was no good trying to calm her now and Hwesu knew it. So very quietly he opened the door and went out into the yard. As he did so, his eye fell upon Soye sitting idly in the shade of a cottonsilk tree. In Alladah, Soye and Alihonu attended to his horses, in addition to their other duties; but here he had no horses, so they had very little to do.

Then, suddenly, Hwesu stiffened. He stood there, with his eyes half closed, thinking. Dangbevi's all too faithful repetition of the Princess Taunyinatin's mocking words had, although he'd have died before admitting it, stung his pride. 'Sweaty peasant oaf,' he thought. 'Why——'

Then his eyes cleared; what he'd thought of, what he proposed to do, was actually dangerous, for the Leopard kings were quick to strike down any man daring enough to make too brave a show. Yet that, now, was precisely what he had to do—and in eight short days, since Dahomean weeks have only four days each. 'For if I don't,' he thought; 'there'll be no living with this royal sorceress!'

'Soye!' he called out. 'Come here!'

A moment later Soye was kneeling before him.

'Soye,' he said, 'how fast could you get down to Alladah?'

'Well, my lord,' Soye hesitated, trying to think of a way to protect his vested interest in sweet idleness, 'it seems to me that since I'm smaller than Alihonu, and my legs are shorter, he could do it much faster than I could and——'

'No,' Hwesu said, 'he weighs too much. How long, Soye?'

'In three days, my lord,' Soye said, 'if the matter is urgent. . . .'

'Urgent enough to cost you ten rods broken across your rusty seat,' Hwesu said, 'if you fail me. Go tell the women to give you food and drink for the journey. Then come back to me for money. I want you to get down to Alladah in less than three days and then ride N'yoh back up here. If you reach Abomey during the daylight hours, wait outside the city until it is dark. I don't want anybody to see what a beautiful beast N'yoh is before my wedding day. Understand?'

'I hear and obey, great Gbonuga of the most mighty name!' Soye said, and, leaping to his feet, started off at a dead run towards the women's quarters.

And now at long, long last the evening of that day of days was at hand. On the morning of it, as was obligatory, Hwesu had sent a trunk so heavy that it had required four men to bear the poles of the little platform on which it rested up to the palace. In the trunk were silks, velvets, and printed clothes, all of the finest European manufacture, bought in Whydah and brought up by runners from the great seaport. What the whole thing had cost him, Hwesu refused to think about, because it offended his naturally frugal nature. But in addition, the trunk contained the finest of perfumes and jewellery, as well as—and this was of supreme ceremonial importance—two huge cloths, one a man's, the other a woman's.

But now, one hour after sundown, all was ready. Dressed in his finest green silk toga, with the jewelled dagger Ibrahim T'wala had given him slung around his slim waist on a highly ornamented belt, his chief's cap on his head, scrubbed until his black skin shone, drenched in perfumes, and preceded fore and aft by whirling, leaping, dancing torchbearers who could and did hurl their torches end over end into the night sky, catching them with marvellous dexterity as they fell, Hwesu set out for the palace, but not, like every other commoner about to wed a princess in all of previous history, afoot. No, he came riding like a prince, a king.

Better, in fact, than any king anyone had ever heard of, for no *dada* of that land where, if sober truth be told, the night warrior ants and the tsetse flies are the true and undisputed lords, ever possessed a horse of half the beauty and strength of N'yoh, the white Auyo stallion that the young *gbonuga* rode.

He was aware that he was going to lose the horse by this gesture, because the only way out of the dilemma his own pride had forced him into was to make a present of the white stallion to the king. But he took some comfort from the news Soye had brought them: no less than three of the mares had foaled since his departure from Alladah; and all the colts had been sired by N'yoh himself. Best of all, they were all being carefully screened from the flies by his stable-keepers who had been convinced by his success in making a horse out of the colt N'yoh had been, instead of the dull-eyed shambling, half-dead racks of bones that even great lords had to ride in Dahomey, because the flies didn't leave them anything else, that his methods were very great *gbos* indeed.

Behind Hwesu as he rode, trooped not only his wives and his people, but Gbade's people as well, loaned him for the occasion by the governor of Savalu, to swell the number of his retainers, and add, by their singing, drumming, dancing, laughter, noise, all the more splendour to the show.

Most of the drumers bore the gay-toned *boyuyayi* cala-bash drum, but, except, of course, for the *zeli*, funeral drum, every type of percussion instrument made in Dahomey thumped and thundered the intricate syncopated rhythms that descendants of West Africans have made the music of the whole world, while flutes, flageolets, cymbals, and various stringed instruments caused the night to vibrate with what was perhaps the finest art of one of the most artistically gifted peoples in the world.

Even poor Dangbevi was soon so caught up in the hypnotic current of the proceedings that she forgot her jealousy and her grief, and she danced and sang along with the rest.

Arriving before the palace. Hwesu and his followers put on what must have been very nearly the finest show that Gezo's royal eyes had ever seen: for not only did the drummers and musicians of all kinds make even the palm trees sway to their rhythms, but the dancers, acrobats, and jugglers performed without ceasing during the four long hours that royal dignity made them wait until it condescended to take notice of them.

Hwesu contributed his share to the performance by intricate feats of horsemanship, duplicating all an Auyo cavalryman's tricks—including the one of turning in the saddle and catching in mid-air a javelin hurled at his unprotected back. But then he withdrew, as protocol demanded that he should, and waited to be called to take his place beside his royal bride.

Precisely at midnight, the *meuno* came out of the palace through the *hwepali* entrance, leading the princess by the hand. When the people saw *how* Taunyinatin was dressed, the roar of 'N'yoh!'—'It is good'—shook the sky. For not only did the princess have on white, but she wore upon her lovely and arrogant head, the sacred white cloth arranged into a headdress, by which she proudly proclaimed herself a virgin. From where he sat on his white stallion, some distance away, Hwesu felt his heart both melting within him and swelling with pride at the sight of that headdress, which two completely contradictory and simultaneous actions only the hearts of fools and sentimentalists are capable of. And, at that moment, drunken and enthralled by the sight of so much loveliness, poor Hwesu was both a sentimentalist and a fool.

For, from concealed vantage points within the princes' apartments, an appalling number of young royal wastrels and rakes were laughing themselves sick at the sight of that headdress and making bets with one another as to whether it would droop or fall off as tradition held always happened to the virgin headdress worn by a princess who lied about her condition. And the worst of it was that they made their bets and loosed their laughter out of a very perfect individual and personal knowledge that as far as virginity was concerned, Taunyinatin should have been dressed in scarlet and should have crawled towards her future husband on her hands and knees.

But they reckoned without Taunyinatin's cleverness: that very morning she had sewn slivers of bamboo into the cloth of the headdress; and upon putting it on, she had pinned it to her thick, bushy hair with long ivory pins. Short of a hurricane, nothing could make it fall off, and less than a war club's blow, no force could make it droop. Unless, of course, the *vudun*, themselves, decided to intervene. But when, in what land of earth, have the gods ever bothered to save a fool from the consequences of his folly?

And now the *meuno* drew ahead. Lifting up her head, she

called out: 'Hwesu! Hwesu, *gbonuga* of Alladah! Let Hwesu come forward! Let him come!'

All the people echoed her cry, making the very heavens shake as they thundered out the young *gbonuga*'s name.

'Hwesu! We call Hwesu to his wedding! Let Hwesu the mighty warrior come forth! Let Hwesu, the king's saviour, come!'

Sitting there on N'yoh, Hwesu was trembling. But he restrained his impatience, and counted slowly up to a thousand before he urged N'yoh forward at a brisk canter, riding into the square, tall and proud in the flare of the torches.

At that sight the Princess Taunyinatin's almond-shaped eyes opened very wide. Then, she lowered her gaze from Hwesu's stern and handsome face, and a slow smile lifted the corners of her mouth. This wedding, which she'd fought against with every weapon at her command, was turning out to be somewhat less than bad. Going over a long row of faces —and, be it said, of bodies, for Taunyinatin, tropical daughter of a tropical race, would have been astonished, then appalled, then moved to wholehearted mirth at the belief of her European contemporaries (be it recalled that a girl named Victoria would within a very few years occupy the British throne) that a woman wasn't supposed to enjoy sex—Gezo's royal daughter was suddenly sure that none of the men she had known—in both the antique and modern senses of that word—could in any way compare with the proud and princely young lordling who had swung down from his mount and stood there before her.

'Lord Hwesu, governor of Alladah,' the *meuno* said, 'I ask you for a flask of rum and a calabash of water!'

Slowly, and with immense dignity, Hwesu turned and clapped his hands twice. At once Soye and Alihonu were kneeling before him with the rum and water. Hwesu made a courteous gesture towards the *meu*'s 'mother'.

'Give them to my lady,' he said.

The *meuno* took the flask and opened it. Slowly, in the midst of a silence so heavy it could be felt, she spilled out exactly sixteen drops of rum upon the ground. Then, taking the calabash, with the greatest of care, and moving even more slowly still, she spilled out sixteen drops of water with such precision that each drop fell exactly upon the damp spot left by each of the drops of rum.

319

Wordlessly, the older woman then took up the flask of rum and gave it to Taunyinatin.

The princess held the bottle out to Hwesu. As he stretched out his hands to take it, their fingers touched; and a current of feeling ran between them like unto the bad lightnings made by Gbade, Xevioso's youngest son; but Hwesu dominated his nerves, took the flask from her, and drank deeply from it. Then he gave it back to her.

Taunyinatin stood there holding the rum flask a long, slow dead-stopped time, until the bad lightnings of the thunder god's youngest and most evil child were crackling along poor Hwesu's nerves. Then with a little, mocking smile, the princess lifted the flask to her lips and drank as deeply as Hwesu had done. The same ceremony, repeated with the calabash of water, went better; for Taunyinatin, by drinking the rum, had acknowledged her consent to the marriage; so to play tease with the water made no sense, and she knew it.

The next half hour was spent in indulging the Dahomeans' dearest vice, that of ostentation. To the left of where the almost married couple stood, slaves now piled up a small mountain of gifts sent by the king. And one by one, the *meuno* showed each and every gift to the spectators who dutifully roared out as each precious object was held high, 'N'yoh!' When the long, long *mawaluhwe* necklace, and the shorter *kaxodenu* necklace of coral beads, were shown, the 'N'yohs!' were as thunder, for, by giving his daughter these two symbolic necklaces as wedding gifts, the *dada* publicly acknowledged that the marriage was by his consent and enjoyed his royal favour.

The display went on, to poor Hwesu at least, seemingly forever. The princess's throne-like stool was shown. Her cloths, which the *meuno* counted one by one. Hwesu's nose itched; he dared not scratch it. His left foot went to sleep; he shifted his weight slowly and with great caution; for any sign of impatience on his part would have been the rankest kind of discourtesy, and he knew it.

And now, the *meu* himself came forward, leading a row of twelve lovely young girls, ranging in age from thirteen to seventeen.

'These girls, daughter of the king,' the *meu* cried out, 'are given into your care, as your ladies in waiting. Over them you will have all power even to choose their husbands, and their children will be your children. I bid you, therefore, give them names!'

Nobody, least of all Hwesu, was surprised at this last command. At every important event in a Dahomean's life, his or her name was changed, so that as a man or woman advanced through life their friends and families had constantly to make the mental effort to remember the new name, and never to call them by the old—which was not really discarded, but rather stored in everyone's memory as one of the personage's strong or secret names, so that by the time a Dahomean of either sex died, if his or her career had been at all brilliant, he might well have forty names. . . .

The princess stood there, pretending to be lost in thought. Then, in her low, throaty voice she began, taking each highborn maiden by the hand in turn, and saying: 'I name you Dohwe; I name you Agausi; I name you Nwesi; I name you Kausi; I name you Kauhwi; I name you Wume;' then tiring of pronouncing the whole phrase, she called out: 'Gbokausi; Wuhwe; Kesi, Tosi; Alogbahwe and Taushwe!'

As she called out each name, Hwesu looked at the face of the girl being named at that moment. By the time she'd finished, Hwesu had the name of each of her attendants graven forever upon the tissues of his brain. He would never forget them or mix them up. As each of these girls acquired husbands and new names, he'd remember them, too. He had to; it was as simple as that.

And now it was his turn to indulge in the dear vice of showing off, for the coffer he had sent up to the palace that morning was now brought forward, opened, and its contents displayed. There were genuine gasps of astonishment at the sight of the gold and silver jewellery; no one present could recall ever having heard of a commoner's being rich enough, or even having nerve enough, to make such a display. And when Hwesu presented to the *meuno* and the *meu* his gifts of magnificent large cloths, the people split the sky with their 'N'yoh! N'yoh! N'yoh!' for the cloths were Portuguese and Spanish velvets embroidered with gold threads.

Seizing the opportunity, Hwesu demonstrated all his Dahomean guile: looking towards the crowd of notables who were examining his white stallion, the green of pure envy discolouring their black skins, the young governor called out, loudly:

'And further, Oh mighty *meu*, I consign to you my horse

N'yoh, as my humble gift to the father of my bride. For surely so noble a beast as this should be ridden only by the king!'

But Taunyinatin almost spoiled the gesture for him. Pouting visibly, she said:

'Ask Father to give the horse back to me, O *meu*—and if he won't do that, at least to lend me the beautiful creature, for I should like to ride on him behind my husband, to our new home!'

Everyone stared at her when she said that, for among the sternest *nowaidu*, or 'things that must be done', as opposed to the *su dudu*, 'the things that must *not* be done', was the obligation of a princess to ride to her new home on the bare back of a slave called the *mesau* or man-horse. But princesses are always capricious, so the people shrugged their shoulders and looked at the chief justice to see what he would do. Frowning, the *meu* whispered something to a servant. The man set off at a run towards the door of the palace.

The display went on. Coffers, boxes, trunks, baskets arrived from the palace; and the *meuno* counted and displayed everything. Last of all, the personal objects of the princess, her dishes, her kitchen utensils, her broom, her stools, her mats, and two mosquito nets, one for herself, one for Hwesu, were shown. All these humble objects were inlaid with brass and silver, and one or two with gold. But even so, the *meuno*'s voice lacked confidence when she said:

'Look you, here is what a princess brings! It is not you who enrich her family, but she who brings wealth to you!'

For it was very apparent that while the princess brought many more gifts to her new husband than he to her, Hwesu's gifts were far finer and more valuable. The sad fact was that if it hadn't been for his shrewd gesture in giving his beautiful stallion to the *dada*, he would have already been in grave trouble by then, because of his ostentation and his pride.

But now the *meu* took a huge sack and handed it to his 'mother'.

'In this sack,' the *meuno* cried out, 'are fifty thousand cowries—a gift to Lord Hwesu from the *dada*! With this money he is to defray the wedding expenses: so generous is the father of us all! Moreover, the princess will be provided with her own servants, labourers, slaves, and slave girls, so that the Gbonuga Hwesu need not so occupy himself with the demands of his royal wife, that he must allow his other wives to want.'

Then at long last, the *meuno* took Taunyinatin's hand, and cried out:

'My Lord Hwesu, approach!'

Hwesu had, of course, knowing the ceremony, moved five or six rods away during the display of gifts, thus allowing the *meuno* to perform the rites correctly. So now he came to Taunyinatin's side. The *meuno* then placed the princess's warm, soft, trembling hands between his big ones, hard as iron, but equally trembling from real emotion, and said:

'In the *dada*'s name, I give you this woman who is a daughter of the royal family. Do not abuse her honour. She is of a rank whose members may not be struck on the cheek. Do not insult her father, for if you do, you insult the king. Do not insult her mother, for if you do, you insult a queen. No demands were made of you when this girl was promised you, and no demands are made of you now that she is coming to live with you. You did not give the gifts that are customarily required of husbands. You did not perform the *xaungbo,* the giving of the money and the salt. You did not even ask that she be given you. All this the *dada* has kept for you as a surprise. . . .'

Hwesu stood there very quietly, waiting for the rest of it. And though he stiffened his spine, crowded all three of his souls deep into his belly, the *meuno*'s further words, expected as they were, seemed to him exceptionally brutal, came in fact, despite all his efforts to prepare himself for them, to accept them, as a distinct shock:

'Wherefore, know that you have no rights over this girl. She is your wife, and you are her husband, but the children born of your mating will be members of the royal family. Yours is not the right to ask of a *bokono*, a diviner, the name of the ancestral soul from which the souls of any of your children derive, for their souls will come from the souls of the royal ancestors.'

The 'mother of the *meu* paused then, and, with a singularly mocking smile, looked up at the tall young bridegroom. Then she went on:

'We shall supply you with the special magic for making women faithful so that if your wives betray you, it will be their death!'

She stopped again, and her smile became even more mocking. Then she said, spacing the words out, pausing between them to give them greater impact.

'Yours is not the right, however, to give this magic to the girl you are now marrying; for if you do this, it will be your own death. You must not take her to your *tauhwiyo*, the founder of your clan, to tell him you have made this marriage, for your clan founder has no right over this girl, who is a daughter of Agasu, the *tauhwiyo* of the royal clan. It is forbidden to any of the other women of your family to insult this girl. The princess on her part, is not to annoy her co-wives.'

Then only did the *meuno*, the *meu*'s 'mother', turn to Taunyinatin.

'My child,' she said, 'on behalf of your father, I give you today into the hands of this man, who has been chosen as a husband for you. Respect him more than do any of his other wives, for yours is the task, as a member of a great family, to set them a good example. Let this man see, from the work you do for him, that verily your great father commands. Taunsu, the *vudu* who watches over women, tells you not to eat the flesh of the panther or of the spotted deer. He tells you that when you are no longer satisfied with this man, you may leave him, but only for reasonable cause. Do not take advantage of your *su*, your clan laws, however, to break the house of this poor man.'

And now once again the *meuno* turned to Hwesu.

'Young lord,' she said, 'here is your wife, your true wife. She is not a beam to be transported by two men. She is a "load" you must prove able to carry yourself and not allow another to carry for you. If you fail in this, remember what we have told you, and do not say later we have been evil in our dealings with you....'

The *meu* stepped forward then and stared upwards at the immensely tall young bridegroom.

'Gbonuga Hwesu!' he roared out, lion-mouthed, 'the king has done you a great honour! Give your wife a name, to show your gratitude!'

At that, all the people present dropped to their knees. More than a thousand pairs of eyes turned towards that stern yet wonderfully handsome young black face, frowning now, intent, as if struggling to come to a decision, though everyone present knew that that decision had been made long ago. Upon the occasion of the naming of his bride, a Dahomean groom always pretended to be pondering weightily over various choices. But for once, the spectators were wrong: Hwesu was

struggling to come to a decision, for his mind was torn between two choices, whether to call his bride Chiwaiye, a lovely
flattering name which did indeed carry the implication of
gratitude towards the king, for it meant 'My future is assured',
or proudly, defiantly, the name which hurled his own manhood into the very teeth of all his foes, and had a sound like
the reverberations that the lion makes when he puts his muzzle
close to the ground and roars and roars and roars so that the
felt vibrations, heavy with menace, seem to come from everywhere:

'Yekpewa!—I have no conquerors!'

From the stunned expression upon the faces of the spectators, he realised suddenly that his decision had been made, that
without meaning to, or being really conscious of his choice, he
had spoken that great and terrible name aloud, so that from
this hour forth, every ambitious and envious lordling in Da's
Belly was going to regard it both as a direct insult and a challenge.

But there is something infinitely admirable about sheer
nerve, about the possession of both intestinal and testicular
fortitude, or to put it more politely, of valour and manhood
both. Despite themselves the spectators responded to them.

'Yekpewa!' they roared, 'the Princess Yekpewa! Yekpewa!
Well said! For truly the Gbonuga Hwesu hath no conquerors!'

'Arise!' the *meu* thundered.

'Arise!' his 'mother' echoed. 'Bear the Princess Yekpewa to
her new home!'

At once three ancient crones, all of them princesses themselves, came forward. One of them, Hwesu was pleased to see,
for he had taken a great liking to her, was his own official
mother. The three old princesses formed a guard of honour
around the newly named Yekpewa, and stood there waiting.
At once a huge, exceedingly muscular man, naked, except for
a loincloth, rushed forward and knelt before Yekpewa.

Hwesu was not surprised at this either, for one of the tasks
of his royal mother, the Gbonugano Alladanu, had been to
explain to him the *su*, the special laws, of the royal clan as
they would affect the princess in her marriage to him.

So he knew why the huge slave knelt before his bride: for
this was the first *nowaido* in an *axovivi* wedding, that the princess must ride to her new home on the bare back of a slave

called the *mesau* or man-horse; the second *nowaido* was that the bridal house to which she went must be entirely new, built especially for her occupancy; the third was that the husband must never have entered it; and the fourth was that three days must elapse, and certain ceremonies must take place before the newly weds could have sexual relations.

But what did surprise him, and every person present, was Taunyinatin/Yekpewa's reaction to the sight of the kneeling slave. Her lovely young face twisted in anger. Stamping one tiny, daintily sandalled foot, she screamed out:

'No! I want to ride to my bridal house behind my husband on his great white horse!'

'The king's great white horse, child,' the *meu* corrected her, 'for the *dada* has graciously consented to accept the Gbonuga Hwesu's gift. . . .'

'Then ask father to lend it to me for tonight only,' Yekpewa wheedled like a child. 'I'll send it back by the *mesau*. Surely being half a horse himself, he should be able to treat his brother gently!'

'It's not that, child,' the *meu* said, 'it is the *nowaido*. Your father, the king, will gladly lend you the horse; but how could you ride it without breaking sacred law?'

'Oh, Legba take sacred law!' Yekpewa said. 'I don't want to ride this greasy, stinking ape! I want to ride that beautiful white horse!'

'But child,' the *meu* began; but, at that moment, Hwesu touched his arm.

'If the great and exalted chief justice of the realm would condescend to listen to his humble servant,' he said smoothly, 'I might be able to suggest a way out of the difficulty. . . .'

The *meu* stared at him, thinking, 'This upstart brat of Gbenu's could be dangerous; for well does it seem that he's inherited too many of the wily old scoundrel's traits!' But aloud, the chief justice said gruffly:

'Suggest it, then, my Lord Gbonuga!'

'Let my lady wife, the Princess Yekpewa, mount the king's horse, but sitting sidewise, which not only is more becoming to her modesty, but will allow her to rest her feet upon the *mesau*'s shoulders. That way, she can both comply with the *nowaido* and have her heart's desire. . . .'

'Dangerous!' the *meu* thought. 'As subtle as a serpent!' He

326

said: 'A good plan, my Lord Gbonuga! And you—how will you go?'

Hwesu smiled. Clearly he saw the trap the *meu* had prepared to catch him. For him to mount the horse he had already given to the king—as, up to that moment, he had intended to—was to encroach upon royal prerogatives, to say the least, and, added to the arrogance of the name he had given his bride, might well lead him to the parapet above the headsman's pit, if not today, then tomorrow, which was what the *meu*, who had remained in power a very long time by the simple process of cutting down threats of danger before they grew too strong, was counting upon.

'I my Lord Chief Justice,' he said quietly, 'will walk ahead and lead N'yoh. He knows me, and therefore will go gently.'

Despite himself, the *meu* had to smile in reluctant admiration of Hwesu's skill in the subtle use of guile.

'Thou'rt a true son of Gbenu, young Hwesu!' he said.

So it was done. The Princess Yekpewa rode to Hwesu's compound mounted on N'yoh, but with her dainty feet resting on the shoulders of her slave. And humbly as though he were himself a slave, Hwesu walked and led the horse, a sight which brought tears of purest rage to Dangbevi's eyes.

At the new compound, the celebration was of such a magnitude that even the eldest guests could not recall ever having witnessed its equal. Tons of food, rivers of wine were consumed; everybody clapped and laughed and danced. Even Gbade, *gbonuga* of Savalu, forgot his dignity—and the menace implicit in his name, for Gbade means 'Thunderbird' and is the name of the lightning thrower, the youngest of the children of Xevioso, God of Thunder—and displayed, for a man of his size and weight, astonishing skill as a dancer.

The feasting went on all the rest of the night, all the next day, and all the following night. Yekpewa, of course, retired with her three guardian dragons, the ancient princesses, to her bridal house whenever sleepiness overcame her. And at last, his head reeling from wine, Hwesu found he could endure no more and stole away to his own house to sleep. But he had no sooner laid himself down than two arms wrapped themselves about his neck and the mouth that found his was warm and trembling and salt with tears.

He tore his mouth away from hers, got out:

327

'What in Fa's name——' But no more; for drunk as he was he had recognised her.

'Love me—or else I—I'll kill her—and myself!' Dangbevi said.

And afterwards, counting back, it was very clear that it was upon that very night that his housewife eldest finally conceived.

That next day, reeling with weariness, his head a hollow, echoing cavern through which huge black bats flitted, his stomach occupied by an army of zaxwa, night warrior ants, his knees atremble, Hwesu performed the *xwesaya* ceremony. The word meant 'Pig Palace', and, although his hands shook wildly, Hwesu performed it well. Which is to say, with the aid of Soye and Alihonu, he caught a pig, hung it up by its hind legs and cut its throat. Once the animal was drained of blood, the two menservants butchered it most skilfully. Whereupon Gudjo and Dangbevi prepared many different kinds of savoury dishes from the meat. These dishes Dangbevi, accompanied by three of the Princess Yekpewa's youthful ladies-in-waiting, took up to the palace. The *meuno* received them graciously, and led them to the *tauvuduno*, the high priest of the *nesuxwe* cult, that is the cult of the princely dead.

The *tauvuduno* took the pork dishes, and, entering the *dexoxo*, the tomb house, laid them solemnly before the *ase*, the iron altars to the royal ancestors. After that, he came out and told the four young women that Hwesu's *xwesaya* sacrifice had been received by the royal-ancestors-become-gods with favour, and that his marriage to the princess could now be consummated.

Dangbevi was sure that never in her short life had she been forced to be the bearer of news that caused her, personally, greater sorrow; left to her own devices, she probably would not have reported it to her husband at all, or she would have even lied to him, saying that the royal ancestors looked upon this match with great disfavour. But Yekpewa was far too shrewd to leave a woman so insanely in love with her husband—which was the exact phrase the princess used when speaking of Dangbevi, for to her, to whom love was a pleasant physical activity and nothing more, the kind of devotion that the serpent's Child demonstrated towards Hwesu was madness—to report so important a matter alone. Therefore, the princess had

328

deliberately sent the three ladies-in-waiting with Dangbevi, leaving Hwesu's poor, grief-stricken, jealousy-tormented house-wife eldest with no alternative but to tell the truth.

But the rest of the matter lay, finally, in Yekpewa's own dainty hands. For until the day that she herself went to market, bought food, and cooked it for her husband, inviting him to partake of the evening meal with her, he had no rise to cross the threshold of her door.

And Yekpewa let a full four days pass before, accompanied by all her ladies-in-waiting, a host of serving girls, and slaves of both sexes, she went to the market. She probably would have let even more time elapse except for two things: the more she saw of her tall and princely husband the better she liked him; and her little army of female spies, that is, her attendants, ladies-in-waiting, slave girls, and the like, dutifully following her instructions, provoked Alihosi, Sosixwe, and Huno into ardent and furiously sincere defences of Hwesu's abilities as a lover, by making sneering little remarks, calling into question his obvious maleness. Dangbevi, of course, the princess in-structed her spies to leave alone, holding that she had informa-tion enough from that particular source.

So it was, after enduring a day of waiting terrible enough to test the nerves of one of the little brass figures that his friend Amosu made, Hwesu found one of the ladies-in-waiting, the girl the princess had named Wuhwe, bowing low before him.

'My lord,' the girl whispered, 'my lady, the Princess Yek-pewa, asks that you do her the honour of dining with her tonight....'

'Thank you,' Hwesu said; and reaching his hand into his pouch, came out with a necklace of filigreed silver. 'This,' he said quietly, 'is for you, lovely Wuhwe, for bearing such wel-come news. Tell my lady wife, I shall arrive the second hour after the sun has set. I suppose that will be agreeable to her? If it isn't, she has only to send me word....'

Then, after Wuhwe had gone, he set about preparing himself for his ordeal. For, beyond the obvious things such as clean-ing his teeth with the frayed stalk of a fragrant shrub, bathing all over, and perfuming his body, and dressing with great care, he had also to prepare his nerves. For that he relied upon a trick his late first friend Kpadunu had taught him: he took up a substance that looks like yellowish stone but really isn't, called *akamu* and dropped it into a pot of palm wine brought

329

to a boil. Instantly the *akamu* began to foam and dissolve. When it had all dissolved, he took the pot off the fire, and set the doctored wine aside to cool. Just before setting out he would drink it, and its effect, as he knew well from the two occasions he had used it before—the night of his wedding to Agbale/Nyaunu wi and the night of his wedding to little Huno —was not to make him drunk but to ease tension in him completely, leaving him utterly calm.

That was important, because Taunyinatin, before she became by his choice Yekpewa, had worn the headdress of a virgin. And a man driven by lust and impatience could easily make of his mating with a virgin bride a species of butchery. That was to be avoided. That was to be avoided at all costs. With Nyaunu wi he had avoided it by prolonging the tender and worshipful little acts of love so long that ablaze with desire, she had thrust upward and forward, impaling herself upon him, achieving penetration by her own act and her own will, so that although her pain was terrible, she could not blame him for it, nor accuse him of brutality. And even so, by the use of soothing balms, he had been able to so ease her that before the morning of that self-same night, she had reached not only once but several times the climax that older women had warned her she would not know before many moons of marriage.

With little Huno, it had been more difficult, for she had been so terrified, and so disgusted by the *dokpwega*'s act of near rape upon her at Gbenu's funeral, that not even the then called Nyasanu's skilful caresses could ease her trembling, cold rigidity. So he'd had recourse to wine; and after getting her pleasantly drunk, had warmed her with kisses, played with her tender and relaxed young body until she achieved orgasm from his touch alone. After that, being a most inventive lover, he did a thing that most Dahomeans would have considered disgracefully unmanly; he lay on the mat and let her lie upon him so that she controlled the act absolutely, stopping each time the pain became too great, until at last, their male and female flesh was wholly united, engorged, penetrated, and there was no more pain but only joy. To do that, of course, had required a degree of self-mastery on his part that he would have been incapable of but for the help of Kpad's matchless *gbo*.

With his other three wives, Dangbevi, Sosixwe and Alihosi, no such elaborate precautions had been necessary, for all three of them had come to him as widows. Having suffered the ordeal of consummation with a girl of authentic chastity, he felt their experience a great relief.

'What they served for,' he thought with cheerful amusement now, 'was to demonstrate to me how great the difference is!'

Later that same night, he would remember that thought.

The supper that Yekpewa prepared for him was, he was surprised to find, one of the most exquisite he had eaten in all his life. It was so good that he suspected that his princess bride had cheated in this ritual—for by age-old tradition the wedding supper must be cooked by the bride herself, that too being one of the *nowaido*—just as she'd cheated upon the command that she ride to her new husband's compound upon the back of a slave.

But Yekpewa saw the doubting quality of his smile and stretched out the fingers of her right hand before his face. Three of them were blistered from the heat of the cooking fire.

'I'm sorry,' he said. 'I did doubt you cooked this. I admit it. It seems strange that a princess——'

'We're trained in all the domestic arts from childhood,' she said in her rather husky voice, 'and by the best teachers in the land. Those of us who aren't utter idiots learn. The truth is I rather liked cooking, so I learned.'

'And very well indeed,' Hwesu laughed. Then tasting another dish, he made a face. It was much too highly spiced for his taste. Then suddenly, astonishingly, it came to him why, and the first cold and slimy worm of doubt began to gnaw at the core of his heart.

'Did you think you needed to heat my blood, Yekpewa?' he said, a little mockingly. 'Even lovely as you are?'

She smiled at him then, a smile of pure luxurious sensuality.

'Yes,' she said, 'and I still think so. You're much too calm, older person mine! I've seen your wives. The oldest one, the one who's found her belly, is nothing much. But the others! Especially the one who claims she's the daughter of the Serpent God—with such ardent creatures as these to ease you, your blood must flow like the little rivulets of spring, slow and quiet and at peace....'

'It does,' he said then quietly. 'But surely to one who wore the tall peaked cap to her wedding, that shouldn't be a trouble

331

should it? Most girls—of your condition—would be scared to death by now.'

'But I am a princess,' she said, her voice vibrant with mockery, 'and we're trained to be afraid of nothing, certainly not so unimportant a thing as a mere man——'

'And especially not of a "sweaty peasant oaf",' he said then, bitterly.

She stopped—stared at him.

'So she told you that—your sad and stupid Serpent's Child?' she said. 'I was sure she would, Legba eat her breath and brains!' Then very swiftly she crossed to where he sat, and kissed him slowly, lingeringly, upon the mouth.

'What was *that* for, wife?' he said.

'To say I'm sorry I said that. I was wrong. I've been wrong about a good many other things as well; and now I'm afraid I'm going to be sorry about them, too. Sorrier than you can know or are going to believe....'

'Is this an apology in advance?' he said.

'Yes,' she whispered.

'Might I know for what?' he asked her.

'No. You'll find out soon enough,' she said, and turned away from him.

He was a Dahomean, which is to say he was a highly intelligent, very sensitive man, as complex as his exceedingly intricate and ritualised culture could make him.

So now, he sat there cold and sick and tried to decide how to deal with the situation facing him. Because already he knew that the tall white headdress had been a deliberate lie. Everything about her proclaimed it: her freedom of manner, her ease with him, her utter lack of timidity, of shyness. Her kiss —had either Nyaunu wi or Huno known how to kiss open-mouthed with tongue tip serpentine and busy about its play?

With a girl of his own class, it would have been his absolute right to send her back to her father and demand recompense for his gifts, his work; for no man suffered and struggled for secondhand, shop-soiled goods!

'But would I have done it?' he thought now, the cold, realistic part of his mind in full command. 'Probably not—especially not if she were as lovely as this royal whore is. Most men don't. They keep or burn the sleeping mat that hasn't any bloodstains on it and treat the lying little wenches a little rougher than they do their other wives. Beat them more often.

332

Watch them more carefully to see that they don't adorn their foreheads!'

So now, history repeats itself! My father and the Lady Yu all over again. No, worse. For father was forced to marry Yu without loving her, and I came to this match with tenderness, with joy. Yet this lovely witch of an *axovi* dared to publicly proclaim herself a virgin, knowing that a commoner is powerless to punish the daughter of the king for anything—unchastity, lies, flagrant adultery, what you will—unless he is prepared to die in defence of his manhood and his pride....

'As I am prepared. But is she worth it? Must I leave my sons fatherless, my women helpless and alone because this jackal bitch dared...?'

He saw she was staring at him then; saw how deeply troubled was her gaze, and a soft, slow stirring of pity moved on tiptoe through his heart. Sternly he repressed it, and stared back at her.

Then suddenly, blindingly, the idea came to him: a method of punishing her—not for unchastity, for he was more than sophisticated enough to realise how truly unimportant mere physical virginity is—but for lying about it, for holding him up to public ridicule when, on the morrow, as he must, he sent the three ancient princesses back to the palace, without his night's sleeping mat, so that all the world would know that she had made a fool of him by coming to him dressed as a virgin bride. Because, on those rare occasions when a notable risen from the ranks of the commoners found himself married to a princess who, somehow, miraculously, had escaped the attentions of her half-brothers and her cousins, he *always* sent the sleeping mat stained with chaste blood up to the apartments of the *meuno* and thereafter gave a feast that lasted a week or more.

So now, slowly, peacefully, Hwesu smiled at her.

'Two favours, dear wife,' he said.

'Which are?' she said, her voice a little harsh and strident with nerves.

'More wine—and another kiss,' he said.

And because Kpadunu's *gbo* had calmed him utterly, but even more so because his heart, his nerves, his breath all ambled to the rhythm of his cool, half-bored contempt, he made of his lovemaking a masterpiece of mockery, and achieved the beginnings of tragedy because she, out of her considerable store of amatory experience, recognised it for the masterpiece it was, without perceiving the mockery behind it.

Gaily, playfully, he crouched beside her where she lay on the sleeping mat and lifted the sole of her left foot to his lips, then, taking all the time in the world about it, he ascended her body kiss by kiss, making—to her acute disappointment—a small detour around the part of her that her lover-brother Atedeku would have lingered greedily over, teasing her flesh with his lips and tongue tip, awakening her breasts to a tumescence, her nipples to a quivering rigidity that, though it was a very small agony, was almost impossible to bear. But having reached her mouth at long, long last, he did not stay, but kissed her eyes closed, tormented the hollow of her throat, going on like that, slowly torturing her; breasts, flank, umbilicus, thigh, knee, calf, and foot again, until she was moaning and thrashing about and clawing at him with her hands, and he, still ice cold, deadly in his mockery, murmured silently inside his mind:

'Beg. Beg, you whorish royal bitch. Ask for it. Beg.'

'And then he heard her.

'Please. Don't you see I can't stand any more? What are you waiting for? You—you aren't human! You're a—sorcerer! Or—or one of the living dead!'

'Am I?' he said, and arching his body like a bow, thrust forwards brutally, forcing her thighs into bifurcation by sheer impact, opening her, ramming his male flesh home, close clasping her to him, his powerful fingers biting into her flesh, holding her like that, grinding, sweat glued together, the crisp crinkly mats of hair on both their bodies entangling, working into her without haste, but with a male force, a virility none of the soft and pampered princelings she had known before could ever dream of matching, until she was moaning into his ear, chanting the *aga gbe* language, sending up a breath-gone litany of linked and prayerful obscenities that mounted and mounted the tonal scale, becoming flute notes finally, the crash of cymbals, then nothing, no sound, the gasp and gulp of tearing lungs fighting for air, until with a strength reborn of very nearly intolerable anguish she threw her head from side to side thrashing against the pillow and screamed and screamed and screamed.

He brought his hand up and clamped it over her mouth. Then thinking to end it, he thrust into her with absolutely murderous intent, breaking through at last the protective, deadening sheath the foaming *akamu* had built around his nerves, his tactile sense, jetted his life into her loins in a kind of terminal agony, in a kind of small, but no less awful, death.

When he came back, was resurrected, born again, won the sobbing fight for breath, he saw she was propped up on one elbow looking at him, or trying to, because her lovely, almond-shaped eyes were scalded blind, and the great tears chased one another down her soft, velvety night-black cheeks.

'What is it?' he said harshly. 'Why do you cry?'

'Because—because you *hate* me!' she whispered. 'Hate me enough to—to——'

'Brutalise you that way?' he said. 'Sorry. I really didn't mean——'

But she shook her head wildly, so that the tears were flung out from her cheeks in an arc, making a semi-circular, iridescent spray.

'Wrong word!' she wept. 'Not—brutalise. You can't. No man can ever be too powerful for a woman who *is* a woman, really. No. The word is——'

'What?' he grated.

'Enslave!' she whispered, and reaching upwards, found his mouth.

This time he was very gentle with her, very tender. But she clung to him and cried and swore she'd never leave him, that she'd worship him on her knees lifelong, and that he'd never have cause to doubt her.

He looked at her, and his smile was very bleak. Outside the dawn was greying the sky, putting edges on things, recreating form out of primordial blackness, the mother of all that is.

'Get up!' he said to her.

'Get up?' she echoed. 'Oh, Hwesu, I couldn't! I don't think I could even move!'

'You must,' he said sternly, 'there's a thing I have to do——'

Groaning, she got to her knees. He put out his hand and helped her to her feet.

Then, from where it swung beside the door, he drew from its sheath the dagger Ibrahim T'wala had given him.

She backed away from him, her face going grey, her mouth trembling.

'You—mean to kill me!' she said.

'No,' he said, 'this is for another thing. . . .'

335

Then swiftly, he knelt beside the sleeping mat. With one smooth motion, he plunged the point of the dagger into the crook of his left arm. Then blood spurted, hot and thick and red. Smiling at her, he let it pour down his arm, and off his fingers until it made the same deep, dark, oval-shaped splotch that ruined virginity does, there on the sleeping mat, amid the semen stains.

Then taking up a cloth, he pressed it into the crook of his arm to stop the flow of blood.

'Get dressed,' he said. 'Go call thy women. Especially the old princesses that they may take this sleeping mat up to the palace and show it to the "mother" of the *meu*.'

She hung there, staring at him.

'Hwesu,' she moaned.

'You wore the high cap,' he said, 'and who am I to shame you? Go on, Yekpewa; get dressed!'

Bending, she began to grope for her clothing in the dim morning light. And, as she dressed herself, she wondered in her heart what manner of man was this whom she had wed.

For either his gesture was the tenderest proof of love ever dreamed of, or a mockery so terrible that if she had to live with it, Legba would eat her brain and breath, send her screaming beyond the river.

And which of these it was, she didn't know.

She simply didn't know.

TWENTY-THREE

Of all the things that a man learns as the years bend and burden him, the most important is that life is totally unpredictable despite all the diviners in this world; and the saddest is that there really aren't any solutions to anything. Most men, of course, waste half their lifetimes before they learn, and the other half, usually, before they resign themselves to these two iron laws of living; but Hwesu, the young governor of Alladah, had them pounded into his skull within two years after his elevation to power and his marriage to a princess.

On the score of unpredictability, he could add up an impressive list. Item: confronted with the fact that the Princess Yekpewa, convinced that she was truly in love for the first time in her life, had, early in their honeymoon, given way to that most absolutely idiotic of all romantic compulsions: a remorse-driven desire to purge herself of her former sins by confessing them; and listening to her detailed recounting of a previous promiscuity so appalling that he came to the conclusion it would have been simpler and far less time-consuming for her to have named the men she hadn't bedded with instead of the endless list of those with whom she had, how was Hwesu to believe it possible for a woman so conditioned and so trained—for all things were permitted a Dahomean princess—to transform herself into a tender, loving, dutiful, and submissive wife? Yet Yekpewa had done just that, and still lived in his compound, resisting both his somewhat half-hearted efforts to force her to divorce him and the time-honoured tradition that princesses always returned to the Royal Palace after six months or so in their husbands' compounds, there to be visited by their semi-deserted grooms if their relationship remained warm.

Item: who would have believed that Alihosi, pregnant for the first time in her late thirties, would have presented him not only with a fine and sturdy son, but that the child, whom he immediately named Gbenu, after his late father, would be so outstandingly beautiful that he knew in his heart of hearts that he would never pass over him for even Dangbevi's child. Fortunately, thus far, the problem had not arisen, for his housewife eldest's child turned out to be a tiny sprite of a girl, remarkably like her mother.

It did not, of course, fall under the category of life's unpredictability that Sosixwe should have given him another son, but it did that this son, a huge and lusty child, even in his infancy, promised to be a trouble, roaring like a lion cub at all hours to be fed, and throwing terrible temper tantrums, in which he literally lost his breath for rage, and had to be slapped on the back to start him breathing again. So wild was little Kausu, that the great bokono, Zezu, had had to be called to determine whether an evil spirit had invaded the baby's body. The diviner decided that such was not the case; that the child had been specially favoured by the *vudun* of his father's clan and was designed to become the mightiest of warriors—a logical enough explanation, when one recalled that Gu was the God of War as well as of iron and ironworkers.

But that his child-wife, Huno, had presented her young lord and master with *hohovi,* twins, the most prized of children among Dahomeans, no one would have been able to predict, because she was the youngest, smallest, and slightest of all his wives. Yet she had, giving birth to a boy and a girl after so prolonged and terrible a labour that he had despaired for her life. Thanks, perhaps, to his prayers and sacrifices to the Sky Gods, however, she had survived and now was doing well.

Still, to Hwesu's mind the most unpredictable fact of all was that Gbade's daughter Xokame, whom he had described with merciless accuracy to Dangbevi as being 'uglier than a she-monkey' and whom he had married mainly to force a truce in what he ruefully called the Dangbevi–Yekpewa War, should have made him happier than all the rest of his wives put together. She had accomplished this feat by being the merriest, most mischievous, fun-loving, gay, and eternally good-humoured little creature anyone could possibly imagine. Also, although she thoroughly enjoyed making love, and never, never refused him, she managed, month after month, to avoid 'finding her belly' in the classic Ffon phrase, by—though he didn't know it—making use of *gbos* and methods taught her by a wandering Fulani sorcerer, since such life-defying wickednesses were beyond Dahomeans. Her reasons for this were a tribute to her cleverness; for, since all his wives except the princess were now absent from his sleeping mat because of the stern Dahomean prohibition against a woman's indulging in sexual relations during the whole of the two or three years she was supposed to nurse her child, Xokame was simply making sure that she would not lose the hold on him that their retreat into sweet and sober maternity provided her.

But if life's unpredictability was at least endurable the situation he was now confronted with forced him reluctantly to the conclusion that his departed father's gloomy view of Dahomean life was almost entirely justified. Its greatest evil lay in the fact that the king's power was absolute, so that all the means for a man's personal advancement rested in the royal hands, the appointment to, or confirmation in, every office in the kingdom down to the chieftainship of a tiny miserable village being a privilege of the king.

This, of course, was a very great trouble, for it caused a brilliant and ambitious young man like Hwesu to find his life in actual and almost constant danger from a host of his glory-hunting fellows, who, only too well aware that there were only a limited number of offices to be apportioned in the kingdom, looked upon his appointment as governor of the province of Alladah as a slamming in their greedy faces of the door to that particular opportunity for almost unlimited looting, gratification of lechery, and grandiose ostentation.

And, since an official could only be removed from office in the unlikely event of his becoming so careless or so foolish as to offend the *dada*, day and night Hwesu had to occupy himself with thwarting plots—usually clumsy, but sometimes almost fiendishly clever—designed to trick him into doing or saying something that would cost him at least the lesser penalty of being sold into foreign slavery, if not the greater one of decapitation.

Being Gbenu's son, he managed that easily enough; but he was forced into spending small fortunes upon the types of *gbos* called *gboglo*, which are a preventative against all effects of magic sent by another; *afiyauhweji*, which not only prevent evil through sorcery from happening to him, but also cause black magic to recoil upon the sender; and *sukpikpa,* which have the same effect, but more specifically against the terrible *gbodudo*, those evil *gbos* designed to kill.

He didn't really believe in black magic, but since he was of his own time, race, and culture, he wasn't completely sure of the truth of his own scepticism either; being, in this, somewhat like a former Christian who has become an agnostic, yet who, out of simple prudence, occasionally goes to church. So he kept Mauchau, the sorcerer, busy supplying him with preventative charms and thereby made the old scoundrel rich into the bargain.

But what was intolerable to him was the absolute necessity of taking at least three or four Maxi slaves with him as tasters every time he visited the five *togans* under his command. Not that the *togans* were so stupid as to attempt to poison him in their own houses, or even in the capital towns of districts over which they ruled. In Bolizo, capital of Ugbiya, Mochi, capital of Aladagbe, Audi, chief town of Mwacheme, Sowakau, principal village of Agbogwe, in Idjesi, the trading centre of Hwedjisi, he was perfectly safe, and could eat anything that was brought to his official residence in any of the five capitals by the wives or daughters of the *togans* themselves. No, it was always in some remote village of one of the five districts that the village chief, acting under the secret orders of the *togan*, tried to kill him.

Each of the first three attempts had cost the Maxi slave who served Hwesu as taster his life; whereupon the *toxausu* in question was immediately beaten bloody by the officials of the same *togan* who'd ordered the poor devil to make the attempt in the first place and sent bound and gagged up to Abomey where, since the taking of human life was a privilege strictly reserved to the *dada*, the poor, failed-instrument of the *togan*'s envy, malice, and hatred was decapitated with all due legal form.

What was most maddening about this was that Hwesu was never able to obtain conclusive evidence against the true and original authors of the murderous attempts, and hence was forced to maintain a studied politeness in his dealings with the district chiefs. One thing he could and did do, however, was to liberate himself forever from any necessity of having to marry any of their daughters.

In his first audience with his royal father-in-law, Hwesu made a very cunning and flattering speech. After receiving the *dada*'s permission to rise from the ground and brush off at least some of the dust he had ceremoniously thrown all over himself, he said:

'My mission, Great Father of us all who dwell in the Belly of Da, is to control the *togans*, and to prevent, or report to you, all-wise and all-powerful father, the most flagrant of their abuses, is it not?'

'It is, Gbonuga,' Gezo said.

'Then I beg of the great father of us all his permission to refuse—or better still, his direct order forbidding me—to marry any of their daughters.'

Gezo stared at Hwesu, a carefully concealed glint of admiration in his dark eyes. Being a most intelligent man he had already caught the drift of the young governor's remarks. But he wanted to hear how the late *kposu*'s son was going to put it.

'Why, son of Gbenu?' he said.

'Because, as Your Majesty has already demonstrated to me, his humblest servant, there is no more potent *gbo* in all this world. By giving me the fairest, sweetest, chastest of your daughters, you, great father of us all, have bound me to you forever, personally, by ties even stronger than the natural

340

veneration and respect which a subject normally feels towards his king. I love your daughter, my wife Yekpewa, utterly, Your Majesty; her beauty, and the purity in which she came to me have enslaved me forever. . . .'

Gezo sat there, his little eyes narrowing with distrust. He had had many complaints from the *meuno* about Taunyinatin's outrageous behaviour; on more than one occasion he had consented to allowing the *meuno* to give her a good beating; and now this young fool—was he? could he be?—was raving about a point he should have kept decently silent about: Taunyinatin/Yekpewa's alleged chastity. If Hwesu wanted to refuse further wives out of love of his princess wife, his plea— though flattering enough to paternal sentiment—was the plea of a fool. And for fools and sentimentalists, Gezo, being a wise king, had no use whatsoever.

'About my daughter's chastity, I've had my doubts,' he said drily. 'Few restraints are placed upon princesses of the blood, you know, young Hwesu. But, as her husband, you doubtless know of what you speak. . . .'

'But I *do* know, Great Father!' Hwesu said. 'Did not the "mother" of his excellency, the chief justice, show the bridal sleeping mat I sent her, to you, my king?'

'Night warrior ants,' Gezo thought, 'packed alive into her vagina to make her bleed. Truly a heroic deception. But why, in Legba's lustful name, did she bother? What difference would it have made if this tall lout found her used goods or not? Or had she somehow seen him, been so impressed that. . . .'

Suddenly the king leaned forward staring at the young *gbonuga*'s left arm.

'How came you by that scar, my son? I'm sure that the last time I granted you audience, the only scar you had was that ugly mark of the arrow wound infected with Sagbata's scourge that I still see upon you and that you got before the Maxi's capital. . . .' He turned to Hwesu's royal 'mother' who, of course, witnessed the interview.

'Gbonugano,' he said, 'mother of the governor of Alladah, did young Hwesu have a scar in the crook of his left elbow before his wedding night?'

'No, Great Father of us all!' the merry old witch cackled, 'but on the morning after it, when he gave us a remarkably bloody sleeping mat to take up to the mother of the *meu*, he had

341

a bandage round his arm!'

'I see,' the *dada* said solemnly, 'and I withdraw the question. It is, after all, a private matter, isn't it? But apart from your great love for your chaste and pure and excellent princess wife, have you any sensible reasons for wanting to be able to refuse the daughters of the *togans*?'

'If Your Majesty will permit me the observation, that to me, is the most sensible reason of all; I think that a *gbonuga* of a province should be allowed to avoid any temptation, any influence which might even slightly alter the absolute quality of his loyalty to the great father. I think you, all-powerful Leopard, know that your interests and those of the *togans* don't exactly coincide. They want to keep as much of the wealth they sweat out of their subjects and their slaves as possible; you, my father and my king, want them to pay the taxes necessary to the maintenance of the state.'

He paused, looked Gezo straight in the face, then said boldly:

'I don't think that either of us, my father and my king, are deceived as to who were actually behind those three attempts upon my humble life. My absolute loyalty to your person is both feared and resented. Poison having failed, why should not they try to see what a few pairs of soft and amorous arms about my neck would do? And that way, I confess myself afraid of my own weakness. Nearly all of my wives are giving suck to children, and, upon your orders, Great Father, I am often away from home....'

'So, aside from the distress that my bringing a new wife into my compound would cause the princess....'

'A distress, according to my informants, you have *already* caused her, Hwesu,' the king said drily.

'Your Majesty,' Hwesu said, 'if he will forgive me the boldness of the suggestion, should change his informants, for surely they are all stone blind. Certainly there can be no other reason for their having failed to inform you, father of us all, that my new wife is daughter of Gbade, governor of Savalu, all of whose female offspring look as if they've just swung down from the trees. Xokame causes your daughter no distress at all, but only merriment, since it is all too obvious to anyone who's seen that dear little she-monkey that I married her only because I could not risk refusing the offer of so powerful an official as Gbade is....'

342

'Which risk, in the future, you wish to avoid—out of loyalty to me and love for my daughter?' Gezo said.

'And also, Great Father of us all,' Hwesu said solemnly, 'to insure that my head maintains at least diplomatic relations with my neck!'

Gezo threw back his head and roared with laughter.

'Thou'rt clever, son of Gbenu!' he gasped. 'Nay, more: intelligent even! Having sense enough to occasionally tell the truth. I greatly admire cleverness, and that you have in greater measure than even your late father had. That sleeping mat, now—that was a marvellous gesture! Most men would have kept silent, sent no mat at all, and . . .'

'But, father of us all!' Hwesu protested solemnly, 'I do not understand! It is always the custom to send the proofs of a chaste wife's virginity to her father to thank him for having guarded her so carefully, so naturally, I . . .'

'Oh, for Legba's sake, Hwesu!' the king said. 'Get out of here! Your request is granted. I hereby forbid you to wed the daughter of any official under your command! But don't push your cleverness too far, or you'll offend me by making me seem a fool. Audience is over; you're dismissed. Out of my sight, you son of a serpent, you!'

'I hear and obey, Great Father of us all!' Hwesu said.

But that measure was only partially successful, for having only two active wives now, and being away from home for weeks on end, Hwesu found his growing belief that there really aren't any solutions to anything being demonstrated out of mere belief into devastating proof.

Simple sexual hunger—he was, by then, entirely unaccustomed to a solitary sleeping mat—led him to accept the loan of one of the lovely slave girls that were one of the stock courtesies offered to visiting dignitaries by the village chiefs. Formerly, he'd always passed such favours on to his linguist, or spokesman, his brother-in-law Kapo, in the belief that the involuntary servitude in which his sister held that poor devil while at home deserved some such occasional measure of relief. And in the middle of the night, as she had been instructed to do by the *toxausu*, acting in his turn upon the orders of the *togan*, the girl tried to stab him to death.

The young *gbonuga* took the knife from the poor little creature with the greatest of ease, and then, having hurled the weapon out into the night, led the weeping and terrified girl

343

back to his sleeping mat and took a full and tender revenge upon her for the rest of the night.

But in the morning, professing himself smitten most mightily by her beauty, her carnal accomplishments, and her charms, he offered the quaking old *toxausu*—all the more sunk in abysmal terror because Hwesu made no mention at all of the attempted murder—a princely sum for her, out of his wry knowledge that poor Nwesi would not survive his departure from the village by one hour.

The village chief, of course, dared not refuse Hwesu's offer; what he did refuse—thereby making his own share of guilt in the conspiracy abundantly clear—was to take any money for Nwesi; loudly insisting that the great, the mighty, the all-wise, the most excellent governor of Alladah would honour his humble home, his miserable village, by accepting the slave girl as a gift.

Finally to end the long-winded argument, Hwesu did just that, taking the girl back to Alladah with him when he returned home, and thereby bringing on a renewal of the Dangbevi–Yekpewa war.

The war, as if to demonstrate the gods', and especially Legba's, capacity for complicated mischief, opened not upon a single but rather upon triple fronts: first of all, Yekpewa found poor little Xokame, whom she was genuinely fond of, having made a sort of personal court jester out of the rather simian little creature, weeping bitter tears. Now this was astonishing, for in all the time she'd been in Hwesu's compound, nobody had ever seen Gbade's daughter so much as frown, let alone cry. Usually she laughed and sang and danced all day long as though there were nothing in this world but joy.

'What ails you, child?' the princess said.

'It's Hwesu!' Xokame sobbed. 'Our older person, Your Highness! He—he's brought home a slave girl! And—oh, Legba eat her breath!—she's so beautiful!'

'I see,' Yekpewa said.

'And it is my turn to be his housewife, isn't it? At least I think so.... He goes away so much that I get all mixed up——'

'So do I,' the princess sighed. 'To tell the truth about it, I think it ought to be mine, since he's gone away to one of those miserable provincial towns twice now, when it *was* my turn, so——'

344

Xokame looked at her patroness thoughtfully. Yekpewa could almost see decision forming itself behind her little round and marvellously bright black eyes.

'That's Dangbevi's fault!' she burst out. 'She—she makes him go away then—so—so you'll get angry and leave him! She's a witch, you know. Her parents were serpents. I think she changes herself back into a snake at night so she can slither about and listen and hear everything and—and——'

'And what, child?' the princess said.

'And, oh, Your Highness, *you're* in trouble! She knows about that man—that beautiful, beautiful man—who's been to see you twice while our husband was away! She hasn't told Hwesu yet; but she will; I'm sure of that! She's just waiting for you to quarrel with her in front of people again, the way you used to do and then she'll shout out loud that you've been unfaithful to our lord and——'

'She can't,' the princess said, 'because I haven't and she knows it.'

'Oh!' Xokame said blankly.

'You seem surprised, child. Did *you* think that I—had?'

'Well,' Xokame said, 'he was awfully good-looking, that fellow. I love our husband too; but I'd hate for him to leave me alone with that one for more than half an hour, say. . . .'

Yekpewa laughed then, a little snorting laugh of quiet amusement.

'That fellow, dear little monkey, is my *brother*, the Prince Atedeku,' she said, 'and the reason that boneless little poison-fanged viper won't let out a single hiss from her fork-tongued mouth is that both times he visited me she was eavesdropping and heard me send him away lest his presence compromise me. So don't worry about Dangbevi. This slave girl now, tell me about her. What's she like?'

'Just beautiful,' Xokame sighed. 'Almost as beautiful as you are, Your Highness. Only—there's something odd about her. For one thing she doesn't love our husband. She—she's scared to death of him! Looks at him as though she expected him to kill her any minute. . . .'

'Then she's a fool. Hwesu is the kindest soul on earth. The fact that he hasn't beaten Dangbevi to death by now proves that. . . .'

'I think that Serpent's Child has put a *gbo* on him,' Xokame said seriously. 'All his other wives, Alihosi and Sosixwe and

Huno, say he's *never* beaten her, and Legba witness she can be provoking!'

'Or maybe he really believes she is the child of the Serpent God, and is afraid of offending the *vudun* Dangbe,' Yekpewa said.

'Well, *isn't* she?' Xokame said.

'Of course not, child! Snakes have snakes; and women, children. Nothing ever changes its form or its nature. That's all superstitious nonsense; and the people who believe in rubbish like that are idiots.'

'Then I'm an idiot. 'Cause when I look at Dangbevi, *I* believe it!'

'Of course you are—a dear, sweet little idiot, whom everybody loves, even I. Stay that way, little monkey-face; it becomes you. . . .'

At that the Princess Yekpewa got up and started towards the door.

'Where are you going, Your Highness?' Xokame wailed.

'To pay a call upon our lord and master,' Princess Yekpewa said.

When Yekpewa came striding unannounced into Hwesu's great house, the slave girl Nwesi was standing behind his chair and serving him his evening meal. Yekpewa studied her, looking her up and down from head to toe, with such a total lack of expression in her slanted, almond-shaped eyes that anyone would have thought the princess was examining some rare beast her *dega,* or captain of hunters, had brought in.

Poor Nwesi began to tremble under that steady gaze; and then only, at long, long last did Yekpewa speak.

'Get out,' she said coldly. 'I will attend my husband.'

'Yekpewa,' Hwesu said, 'you don't give the orders in my compound. I do——'

'I know,' Yekpewa said, 'and until now you cannot say, my husband, that you've ever had a more dutiful and submissive wife than I have been—out of love for you, and of my own free will. But when you bring home slave wenches you make me wonder if I haven't been wrong—not to insist upon my prerogatives say. . . .'

'In my house, my compound, and as my wife, your prerogatives are exactly the same as Huno's—who was born a slave,' Hwesu said quietly. 'Haven't you learned yet, Yekpewa, that

346

I'm no belly crawling peasant whom you honour?'

'I knew that from the first, my lord,' Yekpewa said quietly, 'from the hour you had the arrogance to come riding to our marriage like a prince, and the gall to name me "I have no conquerors"! I couldn't love you the way I do if you were a thing of no manhood and no pride. But now, I think, you wrong me. To have neglected me the way you have—at Serpent Child's request—or command!—for she, I think, does rule you——'

'No woman rules me!' Hwesu thundered. 'Why——'

'*She* does,' Yekpewa went on imperturbably, 'but let us not quarrel over matters of little consequence. She is your *hwesidaxo*, and as such I have always honoured her. But the shameful way you absent yourself from my bed, refusing to give me the child I long for, because *she* is trying to force you to provoke me into divorcing you——'

Hwesu glanced quickly in the direction where Nwesi had stood, but to his relief he saw the slave girl had gone, fled out into the night. He was glad of that, for these were not words he wanted her to overhear.

He stood up then, towering over Yekpewa.

'I don't stay away from you always, my lady wife,' he said with merciless cruelty. 'Isn't it rather that any vessel so worn from over-use cannot retain even the seeds of life?'

Yekpewa stared down at his feet, a long, long moment.

When she looked up again, he could see that she had tears in her eyes.

'I was a fool,' she said harshly, 'to tell you of my former life. It was no worse, Fa knows, than any high-born free woman's, or any princess's is. I offered you truth—ugly truth—as a kind of sacrifice upon the high *ase* of my love for you—as proof of that love—and—and to honour you, I guess. I was a fool. No matter; a woman in love always is. But now, hear this: I have come to stay with you, until we make a child. If you refuse me this, I'll make it with another. And every time you deliberately go away when it is my turn to be your housewife, I shall take a lover in your place. I can do that and you know it. I am a princess, and there is nothing you could do in such a case....'

Hwesu stood there. It was a long time before he spoke. When he did, his voice was quiet.

'Isn't there?' he said. 'Hear me, Yekpewa, listen to my words: if ever you betray me, I shall kill your lover first,

347

before your eyes—then *you*. For you forget one thing, my lady princess wife: a man can do anything—anything at all—if he doesn't count the cost. And I don't count it. I never have.'

She took a step forward, and now she was smiling at him through the wash and glint and glitter of her tears.

'Now you've made me happy, Hwesu,' she said. 'A man who cares enough for a woman to throw away his life for her sake has more than proved his love, I think. So let's not quarrel any more. Sit back down; I shall serve you. Tell me about this pretty wench. Where'd you get her? And why? You've no reason to be so hungry for a little love that you——'

Hwesu stood there, feeling a sickness in his belly. 'I should tell her,' he thought, 'that it wouldn't be my love for her I'd be defending in such a case, but rather—me—myself—what I am. What I have to be to go on living. And I won't put puffed-up words on it, like manhood and pride. Because—isn't it a kind of cowardice really? Am I not afraid that—that remembering I *took* that, accepted it, threw it all over myself as people dirty themselves before a king—Legba would eat my brains and leave me mad? Of—self contempt. Of hating the gelded thing I'd become, so much that——'

But he didn't say his thoughts. He couldn't because among the complicated bits and pieces that men fit together to make the shapeless, ugly *gbochi* idol they call the truth was the fact that he did love her. He was ashamed of that fact; he considered it a weakness; but there it was.

Slowly he sank down upon his stool.

And it was then, at that precisely awful moment, that Dang-bevi came through his doorway.

TWENTY-FOUR

She had on a red cotton skirt, with flowers printed on it, but, from the waist upwards, her body was naked. This, in itself, was astonishing, for Dangbevi had never bared her lovely breasts to the public view the way all Dahomean women did during the hot months of the dry season. Whether the custom of always covering herself to the armpits was a practice of her Ewe-speaking people, or simply an excess of personal modesty on her own part, not even she could tell, since she remembered nothing of her former life.

And, Hwesu saw now, her breasts were as beautiful as ever: proud and conical, up and outward pointing. So far, the bird-like appetite of doll-sized Hwesi—a name which was the feminine counterpart of his own and which Dangbevi had given their daughter to honour him, openly defying the Dahomean tradition that names must grow out of circumstances, as in this case that the child, like her father, had first seen the light of the noonday sun, which since Hwesi had been born just before midnight, wasn't true—hadn't been sufficient, nor the tug of her tiny lips enough to empty and drag them down into the flabbiness displayed by most nursing mothers.

And now, seeing him staring at them, she loosed a little trilling laugh of pure delight, and, lifting her hands, squeezed each of her nipples in turn.

'See!' she said, 'not a drop of milk! They dried up on me all of a sudden. So I've had to wean her. And now——'

She turned towards Yekpewa then, opening her eyes very wide as though she had only then become aware of the princess's presence.

'Your Highness,' she said in so humble and respectful a tone of voice that Hwesu, who had been repeatedly deafened by their screaming matches, as well as moved to genuine admiration by the inventiveness of the invective they applied to one another, felt his ears twitch with sudden suspicion the way a horse's do at the harsh buzzing of a fly. 'I—I don't know whether it's your turn to be our lord's housewife or not. But even if it is, I—I beg of you—it's been a whole year now—since——'

Hwesu frowned. Did his ears' delicate sense of nuance deceive him, or wasn't there the glint of menace underneath that courteous tone? He turned and looked at Yekpewa's face. The princess was trembling with suppressed rage, but her control of herself was absolute.

'Under the circumstances, I suppose I haven't any choice,' she said almost gently. 'But *one* week, Dangbevi, no more. And, my lord,' she whispered, turning to Hwesu now, 'if next week you ride off to one of those brush *krooms* you call district capitals, upon your head be the consequences!'

Then she turned and went towards the door. In it she paused long enough to take her small and deadly vengeance; a feline masterpiece of malice, sufficient, she was sure, to spoil at least this one night for them both.

'Don't worry about your lovely slave girl, my Lord Hwesu,' she said, 'although I didn't chase her away for Dangbevi's benefit, I'll see that she stays away. I'll keep her in my quarters this week to serve me—but only, of course, in lesser ways. Good night. The *tauvudun* and the Gods of Fertility make this night fruitful for you!'

And with that well-aimed parting flight of poisoned arrows, Yekpewa moved out into the night.

Dangbevi stood there. Hwesu was sure it was a full three minutes before she breathed. When she did let her breath out it made a long, long, tearing sob. Then, very quietly, and without a word, she started towards the door.

With one long stride Hwesu caught up with her, clamped his big hands down upon her shoulders, jerked her roughly around to face him.

'Where in Legba's name d'you think you're going, Dangbevi?' he said.

'To find my baby,' she said, 'to take her to the river. To—to throw her in, so that the crocodiles will spare her from ever having to learn—what utter beasts—are men!'

Hwesu brought his right hand up then, and slapped her hard, across the mouth. She didn't cry. She stood there, facing him, until a little trickle of blood came out of one corner of her mouth where his blow had broken the inner flesh of her lips against her teeth. And her eyes were the eyes of a leopardess, flaming through all the jungles of the night.

'Shall I cut and peel my lord twenty anya rods,' she said, 'that he may beat me to death for having insulted him? That is his right. But a woman has no rights, has she? Not even to refuse male flesh befouled and stinking from rutting with a filthy slave!'

Hwesu stood there, staring at her. Then, very slowly, he smiled.

'You came looking for me, Dangbevi,' he said, 'not the other way around. All right. Go, if you want to. But on your way stop off and tell the princess you've changed your mind.... You heard me Dangbevi—go!'

She hung there, then all her good body curved and crumped into the lineaments of abject defeat.

'Oh, Hwesu! How *could* you?' she wailed and hurled her-

350

self into his arms.

'Easily enough,' Hwesu said solemnly. 'She's a pretty little thing, that Nwesi: I might even decide to marry her——'

'Ohhhh, Hwesu!' Dangbevi screamed at him. 'You *are* mean! You're a beast! A lecher! A——'

'Husband,' Hwesu said gently, 'who has sorely missed his favourite wife——'

She peered up at him.

'Hwesu—older person mine—tell me——'

'What?' he said. 'Lies?'

'Yes, yes—if they will ease me! Tell me she's uglier than Xokame! Tell me that you bought her because you had to—tell me——'

'Now *that*,' Hwesu said, 'wouldn't be a lie. I did have to. If I hadn't, she wouldn't be alive by now. But first I'll strike a bargain with you: you tell me what *gbo* you used against Yekpewa that made her go away so quietly——'

'Oh!' Dangbevi breathed. 'Husband, older person mine—I—I'd rather not. Please don't ask me that.'

'All right,' Hwesu said, 'then I won't tell you why I bought Nwesi.'

'Hwesu,' Dangbevi said. 'I—I found out something about Yekpewa—something she's actually innocent of. I'm the only person in the whole compound who knows she's not guilty of—of doing anything wrong; the only one who could save her by telling the truth. Only she had to give in—because she thought I wouldn't tell the truth, that, like any woman in my place, I'd lie—and ruin her. . . .'

'Only she didn't know you,' Hwesu said.

'Only she *did* know me. I would have lied. Then. But now I can't. Because if I don't tell the truth, how can I ask you to?'

'What happened?' Hwesu said.

'A man came to see her—a young man. *Very* handsome. I hid behind her place and listened. Not only didn't they do—anything wicked, but they quarrelled—violently. Of course, I couldn't understand everything they said because they talked Fau so fast and with that aristocratic Abomey accent, but I did get most of it. He wanted her to come back to the palace. But she wouldn't. Said she was too much in love with you to *ever* leave you. That made him madder than ever. Up until then I was still thinking he was an—old lover of hers; but then she

351

called him "brother"——'

'*Novichi sunu?*' Hwesu said, remembering darkly all he'd heard of the Leopard Clan's peculiarities of behaviour, recalling Yekpewa's own confession which though it had not stated outright so terrible a violation of Dahomey's most absolute *su dudu*, had at least implied that her lovers had all been princes: and princes had to be at least her cousins if not—he dared not finish the thought. 'Or *tovichi sunu*?' he said.

'Child of the same mother?' Dangbevi put the idea laboriously back into Ewe: 'Or child of the same father?' Oh I see! Since a man has many wives, children of the same mother *are* brothers and sisters, truly, since both their parents are the same —or ought to be, if the woman's honest. While children of the same father but of different mothers aren't so close. I don't know which she said, Hwesu. I was translating inside my mind, putting it back into my own language to make sure I understood what they were saying, truly. And it came out "brother". That's all I know. What difference does it make?'

'A lot,' Hwesu said, 'but don't ask me to explain it. I'd rather not.'

'Please?' Dangbevi said.

'All right. You'll only find it out from some of the other women who'll make it seem even worse than it is. The Gbekpovi Aladaxonu, the royal clan, marry among themselves. That is, children of brothers, whom you'd call cousins in Ewe, are allowed to marry. We, the rest of us, don't permit that. And, among all the other clans of Dahomey, a brother and sister who lie with each other could be put to death. We call that act incest, and it's the most powerful *su dudu* among us. . . .'

'I should think it would be!' Dangbevi said.

'The Gbekpovi Aladaxonu take it less seriously, I'm afraid. Of course, they punish it severely, by whipping and banishment —if the guilty pair are of the same mother and the same father. If they aren't, if they're only half-brother and sister, they aren't allowed to marry; but they can be lovers and *nothing* is done about it, unless the girl finds her belly. Then the king finds her a commoner as a husband in a hurry, and ships her to——'

'Alladah, say,' Dangbevi whispered, 'as he shipped *her*.'

'Wife,' Hwesu said mildly enough, 'my royal wedding was three or four *months* in the making. And Yekpewa hasn't found her belly even yet. . . .'

'But if that young man is her half-brother, only, he could have been her lover, couldn't he?'

'Yes,' Hwesu said.

'Well, he isn't now. I have no reason to defend her; but out of simple fairness I say that because I'm sure of it. Now you be fair too. Tell me about your slave girl. Why did you *have* to buy her?'

'Because the *toxausu* of a brush *kroom*—a miserable little edge of the jungle village—sent her to my hut armed with a knife and with orders to kill me. So I took the knife away from her and——'

'Stabbed her in your turn, but with a blunter weapon,' Dangbevi said acidly, 'one that doesn't hurt at all, at least after the sheath has been stretched enough to accommodate it—as *hers* probably has been long ago. And, finding that sort of combat most delightful to lose, she begged you to——'

'Go on,' Hwesu grinned at her, 'tell me all about it.'

'Hwesu—older person mine—you aren't going to stand there and tell me——'

'That I tied her up and went peacefully back to sleep? No, but only because, being a woman, you won't believe me, and whether I did or not doesn't matter anyhow. The point is I knew that wily old scoundrel would cut her throat the minute I was fifty rods beyond the gates, both for having failed to kill me and for fear of her talking too much, as women always do. So, to save her life, I bought her from him. No, that's not true. I *tried* to buy her from him; but he wouldn't hear of it. He *gave* her to me, thinking thus to appease my anger. I brought her here. What else could I do? Tomorrow, if you like, ask her what happened. She'll tell you. Poor thing, she's still terrified of me. She thinks I mean to kill her. . . .'

'How?' Dangbevi said. 'By loving her to death?'

'Now *that's* a fine and princely method of execution if ever there were one! Come to think of it, now that we're talking about executions, it seems to me I remember somebody calling me a beast, a lecher, cruel, and even threatening to throw my prettiest daughter to the crocodiles. That threat alone merits the death penalty. So maybe I'd better both pass and carry out the sentence right now!'

Dangbevi made a mocking and merry face at him.

'Ha!' she said. 'I've had a *year's* rest, husband! Want to bet who it is that kills whom?'

He was too happy, and the feeling frightened him. So it was that when on Adjoxi, the final day of the Dahomean four-day week,* he lay in his hammock listening to Dangbevi's schemes to either poison Yekpewa or bewitch her into letting their second honeymoon go on forever and he looked up and saw his brother-in-law and linguist, Kapo, riding towards him on a bony, fly-infested brown nag, he knew his premonitions had come true, because for Kapo to ride up to his compound to seek him, lazy as his sister's husband was, meant that something was seriously wrong.

There was.

'It's the *tonukwe* and the *humekpaunto*,' Kapo explained; 'they've cooked up a scheme to cheat on the pepper tax. . . .'

Hwesu bounded out of the hammock at that. *All* the pepper for commercial sale in Dahomey was grown in the province of Alladah, specifically in the fields belonging to only seven villages permitted to grow *ataki* by the *dada* in order to make easy the royal control, maintained, as always, as a near monopoly over products deemed essential, as were, of course, the condiments: pepper and salt and honey. Even more than the others, pepper, in Da's Belly, was worth almost its weight in gold, because in Africa's tropical climate it kept leftover food from spoiling too fast, and disguised to a large extent the foul taste of that which had already gone bad, thus making it a real necessity even in the houses of the poor. The king, realising this, naturally enriched himself by holding an even stricter monopoly over its production than he did over salt and honey.

And since Hwesu was governor of Alladah, what went on in its villages was finally and fatally his responsibility. Therefore, if a *tonukwe*, a chief's assistant in agricultural matters, and the *humekpaunto*, the king's controller of death duties and inheritances—by his very office likely to get his hands on an occasional harvest whose owner had died—were out to put aside a few hundred sacks of black or red pepper with a view to selling them secretly to their own private profit, he, Hwesu,

---

* The other three were Miauxi, Adokwi, and Zogodu. But even in Gezo's reign, the Dahomeans were beginning simultaneously to employ the European seven-day week for non-religious and commercial purposes. The day names of the seven-day week are mere translations, Monday, being Teni; Tuesday, Tata; Wednesday, Azázâ; Thursday; Lamisi; Friday Ahosúzán; Saturday, Sibî; and Sunday, Vodu.

was in very bad trouble indeed. Because he knew well, the *dada* would be aware that such a thing could only be done through his ignorance or his contrivance, either crime, of omission or commission, equally likely to cost him his head.

'Does the *taukpau* know?' he asked.

'Of course not,' Kapo said. 'The old fool's honest enough, which is why the *dada* made him minister of agriculture in the first place. Besides, the king gives *him* a cut of all the fines collected for violations, as you know, Brother—I mean your Excellency—so being honest is profitable for *him*. But remember the last time we were in Bolizo? The *toxausu*'s so old he can't even fan flies off himself. You didn't get much of a look at his assistant, the *tonukwe*; but *I* did. Wouldn't sit down to a game of *adji* with *him*. Win the *chokoto chaka* drawers off you and leave you bare-assed on the second throw....'

'I see,' Hwesu said. 'Get down off that rack of bones; Dangbevi will give you something to eat and drink. I've got to get ready. This is serious.'

'You bet it is,' Kapo said gloomily. 'You'll be the original headless *gbonuga* of Alladah if you don't catch those two thieving rascals fast!'

They were halfway to Bolizo before it came to Hwesu that he hadn't even so much as said goodbye to Yekpewa, not to mention having explained to her his absolutely necessary and justifiable reason for cheating her out of, or at least postponing, her turn at being his housewife again. With a shiver of acute misery, he remembered her threat. But there was nothing he could do about it now, except to hope she wouldn't carry it out. For if she did, the consequences were going to be very bad. He had used strong words. Would he have to eat them like a coward or... ?

He kicked his nag in the ribs and rode on through the dusty day.

Three weeks later, he came riding back from Abomey itself, his wealth exactly doubled, which made him the third or fourth richest man in the kingdom. For, when he'd kicked the two bound and gagged scoundrels, whom he'd caught in their hidden warehouse busily counting their purloined sacks of pepper and sneezing happily over the fortune they were going to make, down on their bellies before the king, and showed the father of all who dwell in Da's Belly how much pepper they'd stolen over the years, the *dada* had awarded him half their estates, keeping the other half himself, along with their severed heads which he affixed to the Kannah Gate Tower to remind people how exceedingly unwise it was to try to cheat the Leopard.

But a mile outside of Alladah itself, Dangbevi met Hwesu. She clung to the stirrups of his horse and cried:

'Please! Don't come home now! Stay here—outside the city, tonight! I'll stay with you! I'll cook your supper! Bring you wine! Ease you——'

He sat there on his white stallion, son of the first N'yoh and looked at her sadly.

'So,' he said, 'she carried out her threat.' Then turning to his brother-in-law he said:

'Take Dangbevi up behind you. I can't. I have to ride fast—and this poor beast is already blown.'

TWENTY-FIVE

They weren't in Yekpewa's small but luxuriously furnished house. They were in his own big, almost palatial *gbonuga*'s bungalow, finding it more comfortable, perhaps, or wishing to make the insult of the humiliation more deadly. And they had neither locked nor barred the door. They were prince and princess, cubs of the Leopard; and nothing they did was punishable by a mortal lesser than the king.

He stood there looking at them—for they hadn't even heard him coming into his sleeping room, being much too occupied to hear anything less loud than Xevioso's thunderstones rolling across a leaden sky—and whatever evil spirit, what aspect or manifestation of Legba at his dreadful, mocking worst, that invaded him then was very bad. It poured a vileness into his belly as green and stinking as the marshes below Abomey; it rammed an ice-cold hand down through his groin, wrapped slimy fingers around his testicles and squeezed until the tears of a womanish effeminate gelding stood and scalded in his eyes; but did not, would not grant him the accidental mercy of robbing him of sight, so that he saw, discerned, even perceived the glossy sheen of those lean, black muscular buttocks, humping slowly between those matchless thighs that she held so high lifted that the calves of her long, beautiful legs crossed above the small of her lover's back, pressing him down upon her with considerable force, holding him to her like that, with an obvious and ardent reluctance to allow him even the necessary, partial, and momentary separation of their linked and united flesh.

The smell of mingled perfumes, sweat, and the pungent odours of sex came over to Hwesu and took him full in the nostrils, making him so giddy, sick, so that in another moment he would have vomited if Yekpewa had not at that precise instant loosed a low, throaty purr of laughter. Her voice, speaking, was infinitely mocking as she said:

'Y'know, Ate, you aren't *half* as good as he is!'

And released Hwesu from the grip of whatever evil spirit, or god, it was who held him.

He bent and locked his two hands into the sweaty flesh of Atedeku's shoulders, and straightened his own back in one long, smooth, irresistibly powerful jerk, tearing the young prince from the multiple embrace of arms, legs, vagina, stood him on his feet like a man-sized doll, whirled him about until they were face to face, then slapped him backhanded across the mouth so hard that his thick lips literally exploded in a rush of blood, and the whole of him crashed backwards into a wall. The prince hung there, shaking his head until it cleared; then he said, snarling the words with that unmatched arrogance that the cubs of the Leopard were born to:

'You fool! I'm a prince! And even if I weren't, she has every right——'

Then what was in Hwesu's eyes stopped his voice, choked off his breath.

'You,' Hwesu said, almost gently, 'are carrion. Kite bait. Vulture's meat. Dinner for ants and worms.'

Atedeku stared at him; then, clawing deep inside himself for whatever shreds of dignity he had left, he said:

'You mean you'll kill me—knowing *how* you'd die for it— because this royal whore——'

Hwesu shook his head. 'No. Not for that,' he said.

'Then for what?' the prince whispered.

'I can't say it,' Hwesu said, his voice sand dry, utterly bleak. 'Maybe it can't even be said.'

'Try,' Atedeku said, the wonder in him greater that moment

357

than his fear.

'Say,' Hwesu said quietly, 'that there are prostrations a man can't get up from, dirt that isn't ceremonial and won't wash off. Death—is nothing, however it comes. Pain, for all the headman's skill at prolonging it, ends sometime. It has to; what goes on too long is—remembering. What a man took, accepted, bowed to, I mean. It's not that I don't count the cost of killing a swine—an incestuous swine from the looks of you —and,' he jerked his head sidewise towards where Yekpewa lay, 'a jackal bitch who can't even whelp. It's just that there are other costs I haven't the wherewithal to cover, cannot pay. That the money that could pay them hasn't even been coined yet, and never will be, maybe. I wouldn't know....'

'What you're talking about, I suppose,' Atedeku said slowly, 'is—honour. A word much beloved of fools. That being so, what would you say if I proposed you upon mine—swore before the *nesuxwe*, the princely dead, to go away from here and say nothing to my father, the *dada*, of this? Leave you in peace with this—sister of mine, who actually is nothing to me: a hole to push my penis into when nothing better—less stretched and slackened, say—is available?'

'Kill him, Hwesu!' Yekpewa screamed. 'Kill him now, I beg you!'

'I didn't say honour,' Hwesu said. 'Don't like the word. It, too, has been used too often, stretched and slackened—I thank you for that phrase!—into a blown-up pig's bladder, full of nothing. But since you invoke it, I'll give you a chance at your life—if what you miserable royal parasites do can be called living....'

He turned, strode swiftly to the door, took down from above it the princely dagger Ibrahim T'wala, king of the Auyo, had given him. Then from his own belt he drew its twin, the weapon he had taken from the Prince S'ubetzy, old Ibrahim's son.

'See,' he said, 'they are exactly the same. Take which one of them you like.'

But Atedeku backed away from him, shaking his head.

'No,' he said. 'You give me no choice at all, Hwesu! With your height and reach and length of your arm you could kill me half a rod beyond the distance I could scratch your little finger!'

Hwesu stood there, staring at the prince, Atedeku was perfectly right in what he'd said, he had to admit, whatever the cowardice that drove him to say it. Then, very slowly, he smiled, for his gaze had fallen upon the pair of ancient shields, made of rhinoceros' hide—which proved how old they were, since that great beast had vanished from Dahomey hundreds of years before—and the long-bladed, beautifully formed throwing spears that an ancestor of his so remote that he was believed to have been the son of the iron god Gu, himself, had used to hunt lions, when man, lacking the skinless peoples' evil *gbos* of powder and ball, had had to be men indeed.

'Very well, your Highness,' he said, and going to the further wall, took them down. 'But these, at least, are fair. My height only makes me an easier target, and I have no greater skill than you in using them, for since the white men brought us their guns, neither you nor I in our lifetimes have had to learn how to throw a spear....'

'Ha!' Yekpewa said. 'Let's see you wriggle out of this one, Ate!'

'You seem to want him to kill me!' Prince Ateduku snarled at her.

'I do,' Yekpewa said. 'That will take away part of my shame, brother. And the rest he'll relieve me of shortly after. He always keeps his word, bless him!'

'And—and,' Atedeku got out, 'you—*want* to die?'

'I want to die. He called me—meaning it—a jackal bitch who can't even whelp. And he's right. So what have I to live for, now?'

Hwesu stared at her, less hearing the quality of her voice than feeling it in his guts, like a weight, a darkness. 'The weight of sincerity,' he thought, 'the darkness—of truth. The one absolutely insupportable thing there is in this world....'

He looked at the prince. Then jerking his head towards the door he said:

'Outside. We'll settle this there....'

They had taken their positions on the opposite sides of the square when Hwesu heard someone screaming his name. Lifting his head he saw Dangbevi racing towards him. Behind her came Kapo trying to catch her. Just before she got to the square he succeeded.

'Hold her, Kapo,' Hwesu said. 'Tie her up if need be——'

'Oh Hwesu, Hwesu, Hwesu!' Dangbevi screamed. 'Don't! Don't kill him! Don't because——'

'Put your hand over her mouth,' Hwesu said to his brother-in-law. 'Her screeching might spoil my aim....'

Then he heard Yekpewa's warm, throaty voice:

'Shall I count for you, my husband?'

Hwesu stared at her. Then he said:

'Yes. A three count. But slowly.'

'All right,' the princess said, and smiled at him.

'Spill his guts for him, Hwesu. He's lived too long, now....'

'And yours?' Hwesu said, harshly.

'Equally. Shall I begin?'

Hwesu nodded, dumbly.

'One!' the princess said.

The two powerful black arms went back, the spears slanted upwards at a diagonal to give them range. The sheen of their points was bluish. Time, it seemed to Dangbevi, no longer struggling against Kapo's grasp, had stopped. The world was ending. Her world.

'Two!' Yekpewa cried out.

The light had a new quality to it: the quality of stillness. The breeze stirred the savanna grass. From the baobabs, the cottonsilk trees, the palms, no bird cried. No lion coughed and grumbled at the waterholes. The antelopes themselves were motionless. Nothing moved. Nothing at all. Not even time.

'Three,' Yekpewa began: but before she could get the word out, the two spears arced across the clearing, blurring sight, whistling as they went and came. Hwesu stood there like a rock until the point of Atedeku's was almost upon him, then, slowly, gently, as the leopard moves, he stepped one foot to the left, and curved his immensely tall body a little further still. The spear bit the earth three rods behind him.

But now they were all staring at Prince Atedeku. The long shaft of Hwesu's spear protruded from the upper part of the rhinoceros hide shield. Yekpewa went racing towards him. He could not lower that shield. It was pinned to his right shoulder by the spear.

'Pull it out, Taunyi,' he wept. 'It hurts! *Vudun* of Earth how it hurts!'

Hwesu stood there, looking at the two of them. Then he put out his arm, caught the spear by its shaft, and jerked it free. A great foaming rush of blood followed it.

'Go into the house,' he said to Yekpewa. 'Bring cloths. Cotton lint, too. Bind him up.'

'Why?' the princess said. 'Why not just let him bleed to death? It won't take long. Or if you're feeling merciful, cut his miserable throat for him, and get it over with.'

'No,' Hwesu said. 'Do as I tell you woman!'

Yekpewa bowed her head. Then she went into the house, and came out with the cloths. But it was evident she had no skill at all at binding up wounds, Hwesu lifted up his head towards where Kapo stood holding Dangbevi.

'Turn her loose,' he said.

Kapo released Dangbevi. She came towards her husband, stood there looking at him.

'You do it,' he said, 'even for this she's useless.'

Dangbevi bent over the fallen, half-conscious prince. Her slim fingers flew, making the bandages. Her hands had magic in them. Atedeku's eyes flew open. He looked up at her. His broken, swollen lips made something like a smile.

'I tried to relieve you of the wrong woman, Hwesu,' he said mockingly. 'Next time I won't plough dirt where there's honey available. This one's a treasure.'

'Get up from there,' Hwesu said.

Slowly, awkwardly, Atedeku got to his feet. Swayed there.

'Does all your rigmarole about what you can't afford, what your peasant's honour won't let you accept, not include the cold-blooded murder of a helpless man?' he said.

Hwesu went on looking at him. A long time. A very long time. Until nothing could penetrate the walls of silence he'd built around the world. Not even the way Atedeku's guts were screaming.

Then the young *gbonuga* sighed. It was a slow sound, and very soft.

'Go to your house, Dangbevi—and bring him such food as will keep, a skin of water. Put some little wine in the water too, to dull his pain.... You Kapo, give him your *adradekwe*.'

Yekpewa stared at her husband as Kapo unstrapped the long hunting knife and passed it over to the prince.

'You're going to let him go?' she said.

Hwesu smiled at her then. But his smile was Ku's, enticing a man to cross the final river.

'I am going to put the question of evil back into the hands of the gods who brought it to earth with them when they climbed down the loko tree,' he said. 'You're a princess of Dahomey so you know our traditions. You know what ordeal means, really: that the *vudun* favour the honest, the just, the brave. So let him go back to Dahomey and report to the *dada* that I tried to kill him. But let him go afoot. He has only to cross the savanna——'

'Where the jackals are, and the hyenas who'll come howling to the attack the minute they smell his blood!' Dangbevi said. 'Oh Hwesu, no!'

'The *vudun* will protect him,' Hwesu said. 'The same gods who allowed him to cross savanna and marsh and jungle to lie with my wife. For the high and holy purposes of adultery and incest combined. The gods always favour their own, don't they? Besides, jackals and hyenas are cowardly beasts. He's only to wave Kapo's hunting knife at them and they'll slink away. Providing he doesn't stumble, doesn't fall. Providing it isn't a cheetah, the long-legged leopard of the plains, who scents his blood. Or a lioness. But the *vudun* love evil, don't they? Or else why'd they put so much of it in our world?'

'My horse,' Atedeku croaked. 'Let me mount him, ride....'

'You'd fall off him within a mile,' Hwesu said. 'Walking is safer. Pace yourself. Don't go too fast. Sit down and rest in the shade of a tree when you feel too weak, too tired. Looking first to see that there's no leopard above you in the branches. Nor any python, either....'

'Hwesu!' Dangbevi wept, 'you can't! You simply can't do this to him!'

'Why not?' Hwesu said, 'Are you in love with him, too?'

'No. I'm in love with a man I thought I knew: my husband and my baby's father. I'm asking that man—if he still exists—no *begging* him—to let me stay in love with him, with the kind, gentle, noble man I knew. I'm pleading with him not to change himself into—a stranger....'

Hwesu looked at her. His eyes were very bleak.

'You ask too much,' he said. Then, 'Go, get him the food and water woman! I'm giving him a chance at life. See that you further it!'

They stood there, watching Atedeku as he moved off at a shambling gait. It took him over an hour to disappear over the rim of the savanna. Then, at long last, Yekpewa said:

'And me, my lord? What manner of disposing of me have you chosen?'

'Kapo,' Hwesu said, 'go tell Alihonu to cut me twenty green

anya rods. Peel them. Bring them here.'

'*Twenty*, Brother? Anya wood doesn't break, y'know. Five will ruin her for life. Ten will kill her. But *twenty*——'

'Will leave the bones of my back bare to the sun,' Yekpewa said, 'so that the kites, the vultures can pull my guts through without having to trouble themselves to beak my flesh. So be it. But you named me ill, Hwesu, when you called me "I have no conquerors". For it seems to me that I have beaten you—even in this. . . .'

'Go tell them to bring the rods, Kapo!' Hwesu said.

'You thought you'd force me to leave you—and this snake-child witchdaughter wanted you to. But now you'll never be rid of me. Till the day you die, you'll remember the sounds the rod made, biting my flesh. And I wonder that even when the grave dirt plugs your ears at last it will be able to shut out the memory of how my voice tore the sky with its screaming. . . .'

'The rods, Kapo!' Hwesu said.

When Soye and Alihonu brought the rods, their faces were ashen and grey with fear. They prostrated themselves before him, threw dirt on their heads.

'What in Legba's lustful name ails you?' he said.

'She—is the *dada*'s daughter, O my master!' Soye wept, 'and we—but slaves. Don't make us do this! The headsman will have our life by inches with hot tongs and whips and knives and——'

'I release you from it,' Hwesu said. 'Go summon all my wives so they may witness it.'

Kapo licked his thick lips. They had turned blue.

'You—you're going to do it—yourself? Kill her like that, I mean? Beat her—to death?'

'What is the punishment for adultery, Kapo?' Hwesu said. 'What for incest?'

'That. But for Mawu-Lisa's sake, man! Don't be a fool! Don't leave your wives widows, your children orphans, just because this royal slut spread her legs one time too many! Whatever she did is not worth——'

'Kapo,' Hwesu said with a faint smile, 'I'll leave my women to you as *chiosi*. And my fortune, such as it is. As for the rest, I'm already a dead man. I have been since I struck that royal swine. So let me set my own valuation upon my dying. Upon my honour, too. If there's such a word. And if it means any-thing now. Or ever did, for that matter. . . .'

By then Alihosi, Sosixwe, Xokame, and Huno were there, their eyes wild as a doe thing's at the sound of a lion's roaring. And his mother, Gudjo. And, of course, as always, as though she could smell with that pig's snout of hers, the very presence of evil, the Lady Yu.

'Take off your clothes, woman,' Hwesu said.

'In public?' Yekpewa said; then she shrugged. 'It doesn't matter. One always dies naked and alone, doesn't one?'

'Kneel!' Hwesu said. 'Press your forehead to the ground. Your mouth, too; the better to sup your dirt, whore!'

He swung the rod. The sound it made was that of a bamboo striking a porous wine skin. A wet sound, curiously soft. It took him all of ten blows—each of which opened her black flesh into a pair of long, puckering lips that turned blue, then grey pink, then gaped, oozing thick red—to make her start to scream.

But at the eleventh blow she didn't scream, nor the twelfth, nor the thirteenth. And the sound the anya rod made biting flesh was different somehow. A tauter sound—less soft. The red haze cleared from his eyes; the world came jarring back from rage-distorted chaos into form.

And looking down, he saw Dangbevi lying across Yekpewa, taking the whipping for her, shielding the princess's lovely body with her own.

It took him a full ten heartbeats to force that 'Why?' into sound. Just that one word and nothing more, not any of the rhetorical qualifications: 'You hated her. You tried to force her to divorce me. You——'

'Because,' Dangbevi said, 'it's my fault, anyhow. If I'd have had to do without you as much as she has—because I twisted the messages you got to make you leave when it was her turn, delayed some, made up others—who knows what I'd have done. Another man? I don't think so. I'd have cut my throat, likely. So maybe—through my fault—you pushed her too far. She's—a princess after all—and they——'

'Get up from there, Dangbevi!' Hwesu said.

'No. It's my right. Ten rods anyhow. Kill both of us. Don't leave me alive remembering that—that my love turned crueller than the leopards are. That he hadn't in him what it takes to remember his slave girls—and free women in the towns—and Legba alone knows how many others—and was little-hearted enough, with souls as dwarfed and misshapen as *bochi* to beat

364

a woman to death for a sin that he, himself, has done a hundred times at least. Maybe more.'

Hwesu hung there, staring at her.

'I know! I know! A man's different. He can't conceive nor
bring his woman home an infant not her own. But he can
come to her reeking with another's sweat, with her bitch stink
all over him, his body hair caked and crusted white with her
female muck! With a tiredness in him, and the slow, pleased
smile of remembering——

'Oh, Hwesu, Hwesu! Every time I've come to you after
another wife had had her turn, however much you'd bathed
and perfumed yourself, I would smell her on you still. I've
died ten thousand deaths these last two years. So if you've
become such a thing as can kill her because of this, I beg you to
kill me, too! Because either way I'm finished, done for. I
couldn't live without the you I loved. Nor *with* the you if it *is*
you—you have changed into!'

He didn't move. Nor breathe. Nor think. He stood there.
Then he threw the rod down upon the earth, stooped and
gathered Dangbevi into his arms.

Wildly she shook her head.

'No,' she said, 'it's her turn now. Or it should be. So——'

'That's enough,' Hwesu said. 'Notability's one thing. Folly's
another. Or are they? Can a man ever tell them apart?'

'No,' Yekpewa said, 'nor a woman either.' Then she got to
her feet. She stood there looking at him. At Dangbevi.

'Hwesu,' she said, her voice harsh, strained. 'You want me
to go away? To—to divorce you?'

He stood there looking at her. Summoned all three of his
souls back from where they'd been. From deep in the earth,
maybe. From the dark caverns where Sagbata's fiends torture
the wicked dead.

'No,' he said. 'I want you to forgive me. You too, Dangbevi.
Both of you.'

Then he put his left arm around Dangbevi's shoulders, and
his right about Yekpewa's, and walked with them like that,
holding them close to him, towards the house that had become
a home again. His home.

No. Theirs.

TWENTY-SIX

'How would *you* like to be governor of Alladah, my son?' the Lady Yu said.

Gbochi didn't answer her. He was too busy following with his gaze one of his favourites, a plump and pretty boy who was walking languidly across the courtyard of the compound towards the sacred *aiza* above the gates.

'Gbochi!' Yu shrilled. 'I said ...'

'How would I like being *gbonuga* of Alladah,' Gbochi yawned. 'I heard you the first time, Mother. How could I help it, not being deaf? The answer is, I wouldn't. Too much trouble. I've got better ways to spend my time than wasting it riding out to some brush *kroom* to stop its chief from stealing everything that isn't nailed down and then having to watch him every minute to keep him from trying to poison me. Or, worse still, trying to push his stinking, sluttish daughters into my bed. Let Nyasanu—oh, I forget; he's Hwesu now, isn't he?—do it. He likes that sort of thing. I don't.'

'Fa and Legba both!' Yu moaned. 'What did I ever do that I should be cursed with such a son? My only son and heir. And he's——'

'*Gaglo*,' Gbochi said calmly, 'a man-lover. I am. I don't like women. They smell liked spoiled fish.'

The Lady Yu held onto her temper. Her quick wit immediately supplied her with crushing rebuttals: the coprolithic aroma of the sodomy Gbochi delighted in; the obvious fallacy of such fastidiousness on the part of a practitioner of fellatio; the ... But she refrained from expressing them. Her object was not to defeat such a thing as Gbochi was, nor her motivations any lingering maternal love for her only son. She was about as maternal as a viper or a crocodile; and her contempt for Gbochi was absolute. That even if she achieved the miracle of pushing him upwards onto the high stool of power, he'd fall off it into ignominious ruin within a month, she knew, being nothing if not clear-sighted. But being a Dahomean she did not need to love or romanticise the instrument used to break or the weapon used to kill; *fetiche,* after all is a European, not an African word. And a weapon was all Gbochi was to his mother now, its metal poor and base; but the only blade she had.

'But for this, he'll serve!' she exulted in her mind. 'In spite of all the miserable things he is, and all the worthy things he isn't, he'll serve to pull that arrogant black giraffe of Gudjo's down! I'll see that witch grovel on her belly, crawl, throw dirt and goat dung on herself begging for the life of—of this princeling she gave birth to! As if it weren't enough to steal poor Gbenu from me, rob me of the only man I ever really loved—*loved*, belly bumping aside!—she had to produce her young male *vudun*, her all but godling, while I—dropped this slug, this born gelding, who mouths men below the navel! A pity to have to cut down her loko sapling in his youth; but after all Hwesu did cause my poor bitch thing's death; for sure as Legba is Lord of Lust, Alogba threw her life away in battle because of him. . . .'

Raising her eyes to her son's face, Yu said then, mildly:

'All right; but you would like to get even with that long black baboon of a Hwesu, wouldn't you? Right now, this very minute, you've the perfect chance to do that.'

Gbochi peered at his mother, suspicion in his little pig's eyes. It was true enough that he hated his half-brother for the many, many times that Hwesu had—usually without conscious intent—humiliated him; but his fear of Hwesu's valour, manhood, and powerful fists was far stronger than his hatred.

'Now look, Nochi,' he said, 'the last time you thought up a scheme to get rid of Hwesu and sent me out to kill his fate-watcher tree, what happened? He almost killed *me*, and the *vudun* sent him a new fedi palm in the old one's place. . . .'

'But this is different.' Yu said. 'Listen to me, Gbochi! This morning Hwesu almost killed a *prince*—wounded him seriously over that royal slut he's married to. But at the last minute he lost his nerve or relented—how would I know why? —and sent the prince out into the savanna on foot, armed only with a hunting knife. . . .'

'Then the prince is dead. If he's gone out into the savanna armed with nothing but an *adradekwe* and wounded, the hyenas are crunching his bones by now. Mother, you know perfectly well that although jackals and hyenas won't attack a sound man, let them smell blood and . . .'

'Hwesu made Dangbevi bandage the prince's wound first! So there still is a chance! He's a son of the *dada*, Gbochi! If you save him there's no telling what the king. . . .'

But Gbochi was looking at her with a new thought glowing

367

in his perverse and swinish little eyes.

'The prince,' he said with elaborate casualness, 'what's he like? Is he—good-looking, I mean?'

Yu bowed her head. There it was—again. But for this particular sickness of the mind, the soul, there was, she was sadly aware, no cure. Then, very slowly, she smiled. If she had to use even this to gain her ends, then she would. When she spoke, her voice came out purring, warm. For all that she was postmenopausal now, she had not lost one iota of her genuine enthusiasm for lusty young men. Rather, it had increased, since the danger of the consequences was past.

'He,' she chuckled throatily, 'is absolutely the most beautiful male animal that these tired old eyes ever feasted upon!'

Gbochi looked at his mother long and thoughtfully—then he, too, permitted himself a gross-lipped and ugly smile.

'Then I shall share him with you, Mother—if he lives,' he said.

Prince Atedeku lay there amid the long, yellowish savanna grass and watched the hyenas. 'There is,' he thought, 'nothing uglier than you, you slope-hipped monsters! A jackal at least looks like a dog; but you—what do you look like—fiend beast? A living abortion. Speckled, naked hide, front legs half a rod longer than the hind ones. Teeth——'

He stopped there. He couldn't permit himself to think about the teeth. No beast on earth, not even the lion, has anything that could match them. Even though the hyena is essentially a scavenger, a carrion eater, he has the most powerful incisors and molars among the carnivores. A hyena could crunch half-way through the thighbone of a dead or sick helpless elephant with one bite. Other carrion eaters, the jackals, the kites, the vultures, scattered their victims' bones; the hyena, voicing his hideous laughter, left nothing, not even bones, crushing them to splinters to get at their succulent marrow.

Looking up, Atedeku could see the vultures circling above him. And the kites.

'What a way to die,' he thought bitterly. 'Because a fool valued a woman's hairy slit—or whatever relation her hot and squirming female parts bear to the mystic quality he's pleased to call his honour—enough to kill a man over them—over his exclusive possession of common country comforts! Over the easing of—a little groin itch, crotch tingle, ball ache, the swelling of his male flesh. Legba, Lord of Lust take him! Why...'

He could see the jackals now, slinking in, behind the hyenas. So far, neither of the really great predatory beasts, the lion or the leopard, had spotted him. That was the reason he was alive now; for all the animals facing him don't kill for meat, contenting themselves upon rotting carrion—unless their victim were so weak, so helpless that they dared forget their instinctive cowardice and kill on their own.

He lay there gathering his strength. The pain in his torn shoulder was very bad. The blood had soaked through the bandages that that lovely creature had wound around the wound—where in Fa's name did Hwesu find such women! —and the flies were swarming around him now, trying to get at it. That was the worst of his tortures: the flies—the true lords and sovereign masters of Africa. But even the gesture of brushing them off cost more strength than he could presently afford. He had to rest; but unless he got up soon, the hyenas would come whooping in. He had to anticipate them, calculate to the last second the time he could afford to lie there before they'd think him done, weak enough to start their noisy rush.

He lay so still that a flight of kites, emboldened by his motionlessness, swooped down upon him. He slashed savagely with Kapo's hunting knife and cut one of them in half through the thickest part of its body.

'Miserable birds!' he shrieked at them. 'Can't you wait till I'm dead at least?'

But it was the circling carrion birds who saved his life. For half a mile away, Gbochi's bearers and slaves saw them wheeling above that spot, and started on the run towards where Prince Atedeku lay.

'But, your Highness,' Gbochi said, 'it seems to me that we need only to send a runner up to Abomey, inform the *dada* of the criminal attack upon your sacred person and...'

Atedeku looked at him.

'Fat slug,' he thought. 'I'll have to accommodate you one way or the other, shan't I? Ram it up you or let you pull on it as though it were your mother's teat. Oh well, I've done the same things with the palace eunuchs as a boy, until my oldest sister, Yayui, taught me what it was really for....'

'You don't know my father, friend Gbochi,' the prince

369

sighed, noting Gbochi's wide grin of pleasure at being addressed as Nyni, my friend, by a son of the Leopard. 'He is very stern—but very just. Setting aside the fact that Hwesu caught me abed with his wife——' Atedeku paused, seeing Gbochi wince, his thick lips pursing in distaste at the very idea of this beautiful young man's wallowing in female filth—'my father will find it difficult to forgive the other, worse fact that the Princess Yekpewa is my half-sister. On top of all this, we have the additional circumstance that Hwesu actually saved my father's last campaign—and his life—for him. So even if he gives no credit to the witnesses your brother can produce to prove that it was a fair fight between the two of us and *not* a criminal attack, the worst sentence he'll make out to Hwesu will be a fine and a whipping. Which will solve nothing and leave us with a dangerous enemy burning to revenge himself upon us. . . .'

'Then . . .' Gbochi said, his voice a dying fall, abysmal with defeat. 'What *should* we do, your Highness?'

'Send your runner down to Whydah. There's a man I know there who . . .' Atedeku, stopped suddenly, glancing over his heavily bandaged shoulder. It was much better now, for it had been all of a week since they had brought him secretly, in the dead of night, into Gbochi's compound.

'Yes, your Highness?' Gbochi said.

'Lean close!' the prince hissed. 'I shouldn't like to be over-heard!'

Gbochi leaned his round bullet-shaped head close to those presumably royal lips. Listened a long time, and very carefully. When he straightened at last, he was smiling.

'Just perfect! I'll do it!' he said.

'Hwesu,' Yekpewa said, 'd'you know what?'

'No, what?' Hwesu said.

'I'm the happiest woman on the face of the earth. The most blessed of the *vudun*. The most fortunate . . .'

Hwesu looked at her. Lying there naked on his sleeping mat, she was very nice to look at indeed. He took a long pull on his chief's pipe, let the blue and fragrant smoke trail through his broad nostrils.

'Now that,' he said solemnly, 'is what I call a phrase of true and becoming modesty.'

'It may not be modest,' Yekpewa said, 'but it is true. For the

370

first time in my life a man has loved me. *Me*, not *this*!' To
make her meaning clear, she touched her mons veneris with a
wry, disdainful hand.

'I don't exactly dislike that, either,' Hwesu drawled, 'but as
much as I hate to admit it, I'm afraid you're right. I do love
you. I have from the first minute I saw you. Stupid of me, but
there it is. . . .'

She came up from where she lay on the sleeping mat and
caught his long, lean image of a *vudun* carved in ebony of a
face between her two hands.

'No. Not stupid, Hwesu. Intelligent, rather. Smart. Of all
your other women, who else is there who can appreciate
what it is to be loved? I—I'm a princess. Which means I've
lived a life of total licence. No, no! Don't wince! Such an
experience has its value too! D'you know the first time in my
life I've been truly happy? What it was, I mean?'

'No,' Hwesu said.

'When you were beating me. When I realised that—that I
meant so much to you that you'd kill me before letting me be
another's easy woman. That you cared. That I wasn't just
something you pushed it into—to ease yourself. I looked up,
and there you were, tall as a god, with the tears streaming
down your face. . . .'

'I didn't cry,' Hwesu said, 'I . . .'

'Oh yes you did! And I knew then, however much it hurt,
however cruel, however dreadfully, unspeakably cruel being
beaten to death is, I'd die happy. Because you loved me. Me,
Taunyinatin! No, Yekpewa—enough to go crazy mad with
rage because I let that worthless princely swine of a half-
brother of mine do what he's been doing to me—no, that's
not right, either! *with* me, for years, now. Oh, Hwesu,
Hwesu! Can't you understand? You've put value upon what
had no value! You've made me see that a quaint, back-country
peasant's word like violation could have some meaning, after
all. Because although a randy jackal bitch who crawled into
her own brother's bed before she was thirteen years old, herself
the aggressor, not the other way around, *can't* have anything
done to *her* that would matter in the least—if you smash a
clay chamber pot what do you spill beyond urine and offal?—
that there was something that could be violated, in the truest,
most antique meaning of that antique word! What was between us could be. What in your princely fashion you'd given

371

me could be and was. That warm and wonderful embroidered and bejewelled garment of great price, your love. That *could* be torn, dirtied, spoiled, couldn't it?

'While my love for you—*gbo*, miracle, rebirth though it was —had only a relative worth, being something of value only to me. What difference did it, could it make to you that a slut— king's daughter though she was—loved you?'

'It did make a difference, though,' Hwesu said slowly. 'It played Legba's own mischief with my accounting. With my sense of the fitness of things, say. You wore the high cap and came to me on the basis of a lie. And though I was surrounded by good women, true women, one of whom, at least, I loved. . . .'

'You love. Not past tense! Don't lie to me, Hwesu. It's not necessary. It—it kills me; but she deserves it.'

'All right. Whom I love. And who merits my love and more than my love and anything I can give her up to and including my life. Although, I started to say, I was surrounded by good women, and true, there came a day when I knelt before the bamboos and looked into a pair of slanted, almond-shaped eyes and was lost. And I knew then that for all the ways that a man adds and subtracts and keeps accountings of his life, his numbers are meaningless. That all the big and solemn words, honour, fidelity, chastity, wifely obedience, truth—even justice— are the wind's words, shaped of moving air, gone with the breath that utters them. That what any woman—however respected, however tenderly, truly beloved—deserves, has no strength, and little meaning before what another has and is. . . .'

'And what have I, Hwesu?' Yekpewa whispered. 'What *am* I? I want to know.'

'No, I can't say it. It comes out wrong. All the words I'd use—magic, enchantment, *gbos* enough to lure a dead man back from his grave—the true words, as far as they go, could be used of a dozen women, a hundred, I don't know. While the ones I *need*, would apply only to you. To whatever it is in you—that curiously inviolable quality you have—that not even you yourself could ruin or destroy, though Legba witnessed that you tried! To the thing—*gbo*, special magic, reborn soul of some ancient *tauhwiyo* who was surely a witch?—which makes you, *you*, and therefore very dear. Oh yes, I tried to put you by, force you to divorce me, because there was no peace in my house; and loving you—knowing the circumstances under which you'd come to me—seemed to me a humiliation all the greater because I couldn't free myself of it, or even will myself to really want to. So I—pushed you back into *his* arms, by cruelty, by neglect. . . .'

'And with the devoted assistance of my natural depravity,' she said bitterly.

'You are not depraved,' he said. 'None of my women has been a better wife. Strange—only Dangbevi and you have what it takes to be—persons. Persons with names—by Fa!—instead of merely women. Therefore, you're both damned troublesome!'

'Playing with dolls is a thing of children, Hwesu,' Yekpewa said. 'A man needs his equal for his mate. A lioness to run the kill towards where he lies waiting, or even make it for him should that be necessary. . . .'

'You'd equal me in cruelty then? Condemn me one day to death—as I condemned you?'

'No,' she whispered, 'for you are not cruel. You try to be; but you simply can't be. And it is—your tenderness, Hwesu, that makes you truly a man. You're brave and strong, but so is any of the great beasts. But you're wise and sober and have a kind of quietude in you. A peace. And great tenderness. Enough I hope—even to forgive—such a thing as I am. Oh, Hwesu, Hwesu—will you? Can you?'

'If you can forgive all my sins against you,' he said, 'my distrust, my neglect, my . . .'

'Oh, will you stop talking utter rot!' she said; and flung herself into his arms.

And it was then they heard the crash of the guns, coming from everywhere.

Hwesu leaped up, seized the only weapons that he had, the dagger Ibrahim T'wala had given him and an Ashanti *assegai*, and dashed out into the night. For all his guns were in an armoury storehouse next to the stables. In peaceful Alladah, the second or third largest city in the nation, except to go hunting occasionally, what need had a man for guns? Dahomey's borders were secure; the Leopard kings had made peace with the only nation powerful enough to threaten them, the Ashanti; the terrible Auyo, to whom for two hundred years the Aladaxonu *dadas* had had to pay tribute, were, since their defeat by Gezo, rushing pell mell downhill to self-destruction, engaging in ferocious civil wars, so that the majority of the slaves now being sent down to the factories, the barracoons, at Whydah were more often Auyos than Maxi; Benin, that ancient cradle of the arts, was peaceful.

'So who?' Hwesu raged in his mind. 'What nation, what tribe has had the nerve, the guts to attack us?'

Only it hadn't taken any excess of valour. For Dahomey wasn't being assaulted, nor even the city of Alladah. Just one fair-sized compound was under fire: his own. And unwittingly, he had made matters all too easy for his assailants; out of a desire for privacy, for peace, he'd moved out of his father's old extended compound where all his half-brothers and half-sisters, their wives, husbands, and children lived. He'd built the new one on the very edge of the savanna, hoping there to escape the petitioners, who, since he'd become *gbonuga*, harried him all day long, sure that their kinship to him entitled them to some small share of the spoils to say the least. So his new compound was ideally situated from his unknown enemies' point of view. He hadn't many people, being a frugal man, not needing nor wanting them underfoot; and the invaders, whoever they were, had not to contend with the hordes of his half-brothers who surely would have come to his defence, had he remained in the old *gbenusi* quarter. But he wasn't even thinking about his tactical errors; none of the considerations even came to his mind. He believed the whole country had fallen prey to a surprise attack, and all his astonished mind could shape was the single word! Who? Who? Who?

He heard a sound behind him, and whirled. Momentarily the glare of the torches blinded him. Then his dilated pupils readjusted themselves to the flickering light and he saw first the whole swathe of bandages around Prince Atedeku's shoulder, and then the rest of him, smiling with infinite mockery as he lifted the long, ancient, but at that range quite effective flint-lock pistol, pointing it at Hwesu's heart.

'Put down your blades, peasant,' Atedeku drawled. 'These are modern times—or didn't you know?'

Hwesu heard a high-pitched, entirely female giggle. Recognised it. Lifting his head, he saw his half-brother Gbochi at the prince's left, but some ten rods behind him, a location admirably chosen to afford such a jackal as Gbochi with both the

374

time and space for flight.

The rage that tore Hwesu then, exploding outwards along the network of his nerves, was very nearly mortal. But he mastered it and stood there, his mind ice cold and clear-thinking.

'Slattees. Slavers. But whoever heard of them attacking a city? Or even a village, as long as it's within our borders? They don't have to. They go out to some miserable brush *kroom*, get the chief drunk, and persuade him, playing on the ignorant swine's greed, to dream up crimes for which he can sell his own people : infidelity of wives, petty thieving; a cutting scrape—cheaper than buying foreign slaves, less dangerous than taking them in war. But this, now—the beautiful, beautiful audacity of it! No wonder it worked. It had to.'

'Stop where you are, Hwesu,' Atedeku said. 'I should regret having to kill you. To tell the truth about it, I don't want you dead. It would cheat me of something very fine : the pleasure of reflecting while I'm lying with that lovely, sinuous creature of yours—what's her name, Gbochi!'

'Dangbevi,' Gbochi said.

'That you're hoeing some Furtoo's field in Ame'ika under the lash. So be sensible and put down those knives, won't you? I can blow a hole clear through your guts at this distance. . . .'

'Only,' Hwesu thought slowly, coldly, quietly, 'You've gone too far. Miscalculated. When you said her name, you'd already lost. But I'll die to stop that. Taking you with me, cub leopard. . . .'

He bent very slowly then as though to lay his weapons on the ground. But at the perigee of the smooth, incredibly graceful arc his bending body made, he soared upwards again in one long, slight blurring rush, hurling himself straight at the white blooming flower of smoke, at its flame-stabbed heart, not even hearing the ragged coughing bark the flintlock pistol made with its tiny interval between the ignition of the flash powder in the priming pan and the explosion of the main charge; feeling, of course, the raking of fire along his side as the bullet grazed his rib, but coming on, despite that, until he was upon Prince Atedeku, his *assegai* swinging upwards, its point biting flesh; and he, stopping it there, saying :

'Call off your dogs, Atedeku—if you want to live.'

But the prince was smiling at him with utter calm.

'You still lose, Hwesu,' he said. 'Look behind you.'

Hwesu did not so much as turn his head.

'That,' he said, 'is the oldest trick in the world. Even if you do have a pair of musketeers aiming at my back, they can't save you. Even if they shoot me, I'll still kill you. Even dying, I'll do it. They can't finish me fast enough to stop my arm....'

'You underestimate me,' the prince sighed. 'Krumen! If he so much as moves his hand, cut her throat.'

Then Hwesu did turn and saw the two big *krumen*, of that seacoast race who were the original inhabitants of Whydah, holding Dangbevi between them. One of them had his fish knife, the scythe-sharp blade they used to scale and gut the fish that were their only food, pressed across her slender throat. And what invaded Hwesu then, at that sight, could not be put into words, and has no name. Because words, names, are only approximations, and this was an absolute. As death is an absolute. Except that death is kinder.

He drew the blade away from Atedeku's throat, hearing as he did so, her voice, choked off, taut, coming over to him out of that absolute, that horror—except that 'horror' too diminished that reality; as any descriptive term had to, then; what was happening, the way he felt existing on levels so far beyond ordinary experience that any attempt to think out ways to put them, even in a language as rich, as intricate as Fau, became the sort of meaningless and redundant absurdity that the phrase 'perfect perfection' is. She was saying:

'No. You can't. You can't. Let them kill me. Don't make me go on living. Not with this—remembering it.'

But he let the fingers of his two hands open and both the blades clattered to the ground.

'Tie him up,' Atedeku said, 'then bring out his women.'

An absolute. The ropes bit into the flesh of his wrists, where they'd crossed them behind his back. A loop of hemp dug into his throat, the longer end of it swung out, then looped again around Alihonu's neck, around Soye's. The only way any of them could even start to run was to drag all of the others behind him, strangling them. Even on the open savanna, they wouldn't get very far.

The *krumen* came out of the women's quarters, pushing the women before them. Their leader, one Koika, pointed a Gudjo.

'This one no good,' he said in his broken Fau. 'Too old. Nobody buy. I kill her, yes?'

'Yes,' Atedeku said.

The *krumen* wiped his crescent-shaped blade almost gently across the throat—of maternal tenderness, the long, long memories of Nyasanu's/Hwesu's youth, half his origin, his roots in love, in time. Gudjo didn't scream. She couldn't. The air from her severed windpipe made a whistling sound. Then she took a half step towards her tall son and went down upon the earth.

Hwesu didn't say anything. He did not moan, or scream, or cry. Absolutes. And the normal responses of human emotion are suspended before absolutes. Just as words are. And thought.

'Them babies,' the *krumen* said. 'No good. Die in coffle. Die on ship. In the way, prince.'

Now even Atedeku was caught and held by the thing men call horror, for want of a newer, better word, since the long tide of man's history have robbed the old one, and the thing itself, of all meaning, reducing them to routine, to casualness.

'For Fa's sake, Koika!' he said, 'I don't know . . .'

'You don't know. *I* know. Women young. Make more babies later on.' He pointed at Alihosi, said, ' 'Cept this one, maybe. Maybe I kill her, too, yes?'

'No!' Atedeku said. 'Take her along! And the babies. To-morrow we'll think of a way.'

But Koika shook his head. It was clear that the prince did not, and could not, control him.

'No way. Now.' He took Gbenu, Hwesu's first son eldest, from Alihosi's arms. The way she screamed was an absolute, too. Hwesu couldn't even hear the sound the baby's head made, smashing against the wall, as Koika swung him by his tiny, beautiful feet. All he could do was to stare and stare and stare at that red splotch on the grey-brown wall, dripping blood and brains in the light of the torches.

Sosixwe fought like a lioness. They had to club her unconscious to get little Kausu away from her. Huno fainted outright as the twins were torn from her grasp. Xokame screamed and vomited at the same time, on Huno's behalf, perhaps, having no children of her own. Or perhaps on Dangbevi's, who, when they brought tiny, exquisite Hwesi out of her house, stood there like a statue, then said slowly, carefully, quietly, in a voice that was the most absolute of all absolutes:

'Please. With the hands. Don't smash her head.'

Koika looked at her.

'You something, woman!' he said. 'All right. I choke her a

little only. Won't hurt. You make new one—tomorrow night; with the prince. With me.'

It was then that Hwesu broke or exploded or both. He surged forward, dragging Soye and Alihonu behind him as though they were tiny *bochi*, wooden dolls, big and heavy as they were. Koika growled something in his guttural tongue, and his warriors clubbed Hwesu to the earth with their gun butts, leaving him then in a sitting position, bleeding from the half dozen places their blows had opened on his scalp, his eyes without expression, blank and dazed.

One of the sentries they'd left to guard the gates came running towards them.

'People,' he said. 'Much people. *Toxausu*, too. Want 'em know what happen. Why much shooting. Told 'em what him prince said. Rested this one treason king. No believe. Want 'em *see* prince, hear why. Some of them belong longside him....' He pointed at where the bleeding, dazed Hwesu sat. 'Him brothers them, maybe.'

'I'll go,' Atedeku said. He walked over to where Koika's porters had left their baggage. Out of a basket he took a slender sheath of antelope's hide, dyed red. Drew from it a rod, beautifully, intricately carved of ivory. It was one of the royal sceptres that the king entrusted to a messenger, sent on royal business. Before it, the people had to grovel and throw dust on themselves, for it represented the symbolic presence of the king. Atedeku had stolen it, for his own purposes, long ago. And since there were many such messenger sceptres, it hadn't been missed.

As he walked towards the gate, they could hear the angry hubbub of many voices. But, when he came back again, a scant five minutes later, there was only silence.

'They're gone,' Atedeku said. 'Tell your jackal curs to bring the princess out now. It's safe enough....'

When they brought Yekpewa out of the house, Hwesu saw that her hands were bound, her mouth gagged. Great tears stole from her slanted, almond-shaped eyes, and crept down her nightshade cheeks. In the light of the torches they looked like amber beads.

'If you'd only have been reasonable, sister mine,' Atedeku got out in a choking voice, 'I'd have...' Then his gaze went helplessly past her, drawn inexorably to that heap of tiny, slaughtered bodies. He bent his head and retched, noisily, terribly, vomiting up his own disgust, his shame.

For once the absolutes have been reached, and passed, there are limits to everything, even human evil. At least until men get used to the things they do.

Which seldom takes them long.

Outside the city, they chained Soye, Alihonu, and Hwesu in the coffle of some fifty Maxi and Auyo slaves they'd already bought, separating them from one another, of course. Then the coffle started its long march towards the barracoons of Whydah, towards the sea.

On the first night of the march, when they camped at rest, Atedeku, Kioka, and Gbochi—for the prince had insisted that Hwesu's half-brother accompany them to share both the profits and the responsibility too, he said—got drunk as lords. Koika, because he liked getting drunk; Atedeku and Gbochi, because they had to. Liquor has always provided an escape of sorts when a man approaches a too clear perception of what he is.

'Women!' Koika boomed. 'Want me one! That little pretty one. Mine, yes?'

'No!' Atedeku snarled at him. Then in a more conciliatory tone; 'Tell you what, Koika, take the princess. Did you ever lie with a princess, you stinking black swine? They're good. Hot as fire. Agreed? The little serpent's child is mine. Appeals to me. She's got something. Don't know what it is, but . . .'

'All right. Princess pretty, too. Maybe more pretty. But less fine. Later on we swap, yes?'

'What about me?' Gbochi giggled. 'There are a couple of Maxi boys about twelve years old in the coffle. And it does seem to me that . . .'

'All right,' the prince said, 'let's all amuse ourselves in our own peculiar fashions! Koika, tell some of your cutthroats to bring Hwesu over here. Tie him to that tree. Want the beggar to watch me giving it to his woman. His favourite woman. The best.'

'All right. Princess his woman too, no? Watch that 'un too. We have a race, you, me, Prince. Man what keeps it up most long time win. Price one first-class slave. Whatcha say?'

'Done!' Prince Atedeku laughed.

Hwesu leaned back against the trunk of the cottonsilk tree they'd bound him to. He tried to keep his eyes closed, but he couldn't. He could see Koika coming towards him, dragging

Yekpewa by her thick, bushy hair. She wasn't struggling at all. Koika had already solved that problem by hitting her over the head with the barrel of his pistol. The big *krumen* stretched her out a scant two rods from where Hwesu was, ripped the clothes off her, and began to make use of her. Unconscious as she was, the phrase was unusually apt.

But Dangbevi was fighting the prince like a lioness. Already half his face was ripped and bloodied by her nails. Atedeku drew back his left hand and slapped her to the ground, threw himself upon her, clawing at her, clawing at her skirt. Then, suddenly, he was still. He rolled away from her, stood there, staring down at her, said, his voice a ghost's voice, husk-whispering:

'Yalode, Goddess of Women. Minona. Taunsu who guards them. Oh, Mawu-Lisa, I . . .'

Hwesu stared down at her, too. It was very dark; but enough light came from the camp fire for him to see what both her hands were clasped about. And what was flooding up around them, now.

'Don't know how she got it out of my belt,' Atedeku muttered. 'Just don't know. Couldn't raise it high enough to—to find her heart. So in the belly. Slow. Going to take her a long time to die.'

He whirled then, faced the long shadow bound to that tree.

'What manner of man are you, anyhow,' he screamed, 'that she'd die before she'd let . . .?'

'Hwesu,' Dangbevi's voice was very faint. 'Going. Crossing the river. But—staying too. In a true way. With you always. Inside. Forget me never. You can't. My ghost. Dancing forever. In your heart. Your mind.'

'Sorcerer!' Atedeku howled. '*Azaundat!* Magician! Tell me how—give me your *gbo*, and by Danh, I'll free you! What d'you do to them that they . . .'

'Die. For him.' Dangbevi's voice was a current moving beneath all sound. 'Nothing. Does—nothing. *Is.*'

Then she turned her face to one side and vomited blood. After that, she died.

It was then, perhaps, that the silence fell upon Hwesu. Surrounded him, invaded him. Nearly a hundred years later the Furtoo witchdoctors would invent a word to describe it: disassociation. But it didn't describe it. Nothing does. Hwesu fell silent. He didn't say anything all the way down to Whydah. He submitted to being manhandled by the hideous creatures with bearded faces, ghost's eyes, voices like the barking of jackals, and an absolutely insupportable smell, as they examined his limbs, his genitals, his teeth. He was silent when the Furtoo slavers branded him with a hot iron on his chest. He said nothing when the *krumen* rowed him and many, many others out to the blackbirder, *Mary Jane*. He was silent when the Furtoo sailors, hairy as the great apes, resembling them in other aspects, too, their hair being as silken straight as monkey hair, their lips as thin as monkey lips, their skins being as fair as gibbons' skins are, their mouths and cheeks the bluish pink of baboons, pushed him below decks, fitting him spoon fashion into the lap of another captive, and another into the lap of that one until they had crowded three hundred and fifty men, women, and children into a little schooner not big enough to hold one hundred in any comfort. He lay in that steam scald of urine and human excreta for the thirty-six days it took the *Mary Jane* to get to a nameless island hidden in the Florida reefs. He said nothing as he was brought ashore.

He was silent during the six months that the breaking-in period lasted, that time of acclimatisation when the wild African savages were taught 'nigger English', the rudiments of it, anyhow, and some notions of farm work, because, since the white slavers never ventured inland from their barracoons, forts, and factories on the coasts, depending upon bought and villainous black swine like Koika to do their dirty work for them, they honestly believed that Africans ate only bananas and lived in trees.

That the things they taught him to do were the scratching of children in the dirt, compared with his own highly developed agricultural and mechanical skills, he didn't bother to tell them. He was silent, never opening his mouth except to say 'Yes, Cap'n. No sir. All right,' though all unconsciously his brain, freed of all preoccupations, all desire, was soaking up not only 'nigger English' but real English—at least as much real English as the slave breakers and trainers who were in charge of him spoke, which wasn't very much at that. When years later, he again found it needful to talk, men found to their astonishment he spoke it very well indeed.

But on the day that Monroe and Matthew Parks bore him away from the slave auction in that hidden inlet of Chesapeake Bay, Virginia, where the swift coasting schooner of the slave smugglers had brought him once his training was done, he sat in their wagon and said nothing at all.

But his keen Dahomean brain was busy, sorting out the why of things very quietly in his thoughts. The only definite conclusion he came to was that the black men who sold other black men to white slavers didn't know what white men were, and couldn't even imagine how slavery in America differed from the rather gentle and indulgent variety of it practised at home. But beyond that, he found no answers. He'd seen his mother and his children murdered; his wives raped, branded, sold. There was no conception, no idea that meant anything any more. He had no certain knowledge that anyone he'd known and loved was left alive. He had been a man, almost a prince. Now he was a thing. A slave.

Riding in that creaking wagon, he approached the conviction that all men come to, soon, or late: that why is an unanswerable word: that there are no solutions to anything in life. And having almost reached that immense, empty, horizon-stretching, utterly barren plateau of always unacceptable truth, he was silent, making of his no answer perhaps the answer.

For silence at least has dignity.

THOSE ABOUT TO DIE   30p
Daniel P. Mannix

"He started forward toward the melee, blood
from his wounded side filling up the
footprints made by his right foot as he
staggered on. The armed *venator* and the
spearman exchanged looks. The crowd was
shouting, 'No Carpophorus, no!' But
Carpophorus paid no attention to them. He
was going to get another tiger or die trying."

This infamous but completely factual book
tells the story of the Roman Games, where
two armies of 5,000 men fought to the death
in a show lit at night by human torches. It
was the costliest, cruellest spectacle of all
time. And hundreds of thousands still crave
to satisfy their curiosity about the sport
every year – *Those About to Die* is a constantly
reprinting bestseller. No other title gives the
full facts and paints such a realistic scene:
this is an all-the-way book about man's
greatest aberration.

Write to **Mayflower Cash Sales Dept., PO Box 11, Falmouth,
Cornwall.**
Please send cheque or postal order value of the cover price
plus 7p. for postage and packing.

Name ....

Address ....

....

THE LITTLE BOOK OF

SPURS

SECOND EDITION

Edited by

LOUIS MASSARELLA

CARLTON
BOOKS

First published by Carlton Books in 2004
Reprinted with updates in 2008, 2009
Second edition 2010

This book is not an officially licensed product of
Tottenham Hotspur Football Club

A CIP catalogue record of this book is available from
the British Library.

ISBN 978-1-84732-686-7

Printed in China

INTRODUCTION

The greatest underachievers of the original Big Five, no English club has quite been able to inspire and frustrate in equal measure the way Tottenham Hotspur have. Since the Glory, Glory days of the early 1960s, successes have been few and far between, yet big crowds and high expectations remain at White Hart Lane, in the hope that one day not only will Spurs win major trophies once again, but – such is the club's tradition – they'll also do it with style.

When it comes to Spurs, people are never short of an opinion or two either. From chairmen to managers, players to fans, pundits to celebrities, this book of quotes is often hilarious, sometimes damning, but always intriguing.
A bit like Spurs themselves…

> The great fallacy is that the game is first and last about winning. It's nothing of the kind. The game is about glory. It's about doing things in style, with a flourish, about going out and beating the other lot, not waiting for them to die of boredom.

DANNY BLANCHFLOWER, 1972

" I love Spurs more than I love football. Unless a match has any real interest concerning Spurs – like Arsenal, who I would always want to lose, every time without question – then there is no link for me. I am first and foremost a Spurs fan, and then a football fan. **"**

DANIEL STERN, Spurs season ticket holder and shareholder, 1996

❝ It is a matter of record that at White Hart Lane in 1930, the Spurs winger centred the old type of leather ball with such velocity on a wet Saturday afternoon, it struck the centre-forward, bounced off him and hit another player, resulting in both of them being carried off with concussion. **❞**

VIN STANLEY, *Football Shorts*

" Tottenham is a disgrace. The commentary position is set low to the right of the players' tunnel. The camber of the playing surface means you can't tell if a foul is committed inside or outside the penalty area. You can't see at least one, and usually two, of the corner flags. **"**

BBC commentator **ALAN GREEN**, 2000

" Even now, when I go over to my mother's house and dig out some of the old tracksuit tops I wore, it makes the hair stand up on the back of my neck. I like to think I am part of a special family. I am no longer connected with the club on a daily basis, but I'm delighted with every win and sad about every defeat. **"**

STEVE PERRYMAN, former captain, 2001

66 The people who support other teams don't like me or the way I play, but that pleases me because if the Tottenham fans are happy then I have done well. If the papers say other fans don't like me, then good, I have done my job. 99

STEFFEN FREUND, 2000

> **"** At the moment, Spurs are not talked about as a big club, and they are a big club. They demand success and, if you don't give that to a club like Tottenham, the fans complain. **"**

LES FERDINAND, 1997

66 I have no doubt whatsoever that Spurs are one of the biggest clubs in the land. 99

SAM HAMMAM, November 2000

" Spurs aren't as big a club as they used to be. It's as simple as that. We have to get our heads around that, but that doesn't mean we can't be big again. If you live in the past, you're never going to move forward. **"**

STEPHEN CARR, 2001

> **"** I want to win things with Spurs. The League will take a little bit of time, but we're working towards it. How short are Spurs of a Championship-winning squad? Oh God, I don't know. **"**

STEPHEN CARR, 2001

66 We'll win the Double for you this year – the League and the Cup. **99**

DANNY BLANCHFLOWER, Double-winning captain, to Spurs chairman Fred Bearman on the eve of the 1960–61 season

"When I went to Spurs they were in the bottom four or five but started getting some decent players. Including myself."

DAVE MACKAY recalls modestly the turning point in the club's fortunes

> **"** He exemplified everything I want in a footballer – a majestic barrel of a man who tackled like a shark and ran like a wounded stag. A powerhouse with lungs like a marathon champion. Dave Mackay was the focal point of the '60s Spurs side that won the Double. **"**

STUART HALL, 2003

17

66 As far as the media were concerned, that Tottenham side were the bee's knees. They positively drooled over the men from White Hart Lane who could not put a boot wrong… Tottenham played with a style and a swagger that was to define their character over the years to come. 99

ALEX FYNN and **OLIVIA BLAIR**, *The Great Divide*, 2000

> **❝** I always felt there was
> a special role for Spurs; they were
> glam. They were great
> at attacking but they couldn't really
> defend. But you really didn't care,
> and you could feel special about
> them. **❞**

HARRY LANSDOWN, Arsenal fan, 1996

66 I did not enjoy dancing around, waving trophies in the air. I'm sure he didn't like it either. His comments regarding success were always cold… I was embarrassed by the boasting around us but I escaped it with humour. He gruffed his way out of it. Our satisfaction was in doing the job. 99

DANNY BLANCHFLOWER on Bill Nicholson, 1972

" Bill Nick always wanted us to win with style and entertain the fans. If we won a game and we'd played badly, he was disappointed. **"**

CLIFF JONES, 2001

66 Than the famous Spurs there is probably no more famous club in the whole of England. Did they not recover the Association Cup for the South? Did they not play pretty and effective football? Are they not scrupulously fair? Are they not perfectly managed? **99**

WILLIAM PICKFORD and **ALFRED GIBSON,** authors, *Association Football and the Men Who Made It*, 1906

" When I went to Tottenham
I was really in love with
the game. After six months,
I was ready for a transfer. **"**

ALAN MULLERY on the troubled start to
his Spurs career, 1972

" When we had been there as players, two bad games and the fans were on your back; three bad games and they were rocking your car, trying to turn it over. "

ALAN MULLERY, 1972

" The biggest regret of my whole football career was leaving White Hart Lane in 1970... My interest in football weakened after that. I was heartbroken. **"**

JIMMY GREAVES

" We couldn't believe Bill had done it. We were gobsmacked. Jimmy was still a great player. **"**

ALAN MULLERY on the departure of Spurs' greatest striker, 1972

❝ Intelligence doesn't make you a good footballer. Oxford and Cambridge would have the best sides if that were true. It's a football brain that matters and that doesn't usually go with an academic brain. I prefer players not to be too good or too clever at other things. It means they concentrate on football. **❞**

BILL NICHOLSON, 1970

66 The Spurs fans, marching and shouting their way back to the station, banged on the windows of the [team] coach as it threaded its way through the crowds. 'Go on, smash the town up,' said Cyril [Knowles], encouraging them. **99**

HUNTER DAVIES, author of *The Glory Game*, 1972

66 The club call us hooligans, but who'd cheer them if we didn't come? You have to stand there and take it when Spurs are losing and others are jeering at you. It's not easy. We support them everywhere and get no thanks. 99

TOTTENHAM FAN, quoted in *The Glory Game*, 1972

" I read in the papers that Terry Neill says he's going to put the joy back in Spurs' football. What's he going to do – give them bloody banjos? "

EDDIE BAILEY, Bill Nicholson's former assistant manager, 1974

> " We have no desire just to be a football club. That is not the basis for success. "

PAUL BOBROFF, chairman of Tottenham Hotspur plc, 1983

"There used to be a football club over there.**"**

KEITH BURKINSHAW departs as manager in 1984 with a swipe at the club's new owners

66 Spurs as a company
I believe are underpriced
and undervalued. **99**

DAVID SULLIVAN, Birmingham City owner, 2003

66 Even the tea lady was told that she couldn't get the milk for the canteen delivered any more and that she had to get it from the supermarket herself on the way in. That was a complete joke. **99**

STEVE PERRYMAN on the club's financial situation when he left Spurs in 1986

> Interviewer: Which do you prefer, Rangers or Celtic?
>
> Alfie Conn: Spurs.

IT'S ONLY A GAME, TV documentary, 1986.
Conn played for all three clubs

> **"** Spurs were like West Ham used to be, all fancy flicks and sweet sherry. **"**

PHIL SPROSON, Port Vale defender, after scoring against Spurs in their FA defeat to Vale, 1988

> **"** When you finish playing football, young man, which is going to be very soon, I feel, you'll make a very good security guard. **"**

DAVID PLEAT to 17-year-old Neil Ruddock, 1986

66 I like a challenge. If I'd been a woman I would have been pregnant all the time because I can't say no. **99**

ROBERT MAXWELL, on his interest in saving cash-strapped Spurs, 1990

“ Robert Maxwell's record is exemplary... He has always been prepared to invest heavily in football at a time when others are turning their backs on the game. Some people seem to doubt him, but they don't know the man. ”

IRVING SCHOLAR, Tottenham chairman, 1990

" Bastard! **"**

GARY LINEKER to Chris Waddle in a friendly between Spurs and Marseille, 1990. Waddle left Spurs just as Lineker signed

> The expectations of Spurs fans are always high, and if the 'Glory, Glory Days' are long gone, Tottenham fans still presume the team will play Glory, Glory football.

TERRY VENABLES, 1994

> It was definitely the hardest job I had ever had to do, and in the early months, I often shook my head at the scale of the task facing me, and thought to myself: How the hell do I do this?

TERRY VENABLES, 1994

66 When Gazza came to the Spurs training ground for the first time, he got the ball, went round eight players as if they were not there and then smashed the ball into the net. Just to see him play like that made the hair stand up on the back of your neck. Everybody stood there and applauded him. **99**

TERRY VENABLES, 1994

> At White Hart Lane, the two teams were going down the tunnel and I felt this tugging from behind. As I was about to step onto the pitch with 30,000 people watching, Gazza was trying to pull my shorts down. Luckily, they were tied firmly, or I would have made my entrance with my kecks around my ankles.

DAVID SEAMAN, 2000

" Tottenham without Terry is like Westminster without Big Ben. **"**

PAUL GASCOIGNE's reaction to Terry Venables' sacking by Alan Sugar, 1993

> **"** Ask any Tottenham fan today about the team Terry was building and they will tell you it was the best they'd had for years and would have gone on to challenge for major honours in the next year or two. **"**

NEIL RUDDOCK, 1999, on Terry Venables' departure

> Part of his managerial reputation was built on the strength of his Tottenham side beating my lot from Nottingham in the 1991 FA Cup Final.

BRIAN CLOUGH on Terry Venables, 2002

" David [Beckham] said in his autobiography that I wasn't aware of him. Not true. He came out to Barcelona, I chatted to him and to Bobby Charlton. I remember telling chief scout John Moncur about him. John says, 'You've got no chance – we've been after him for years but he's Man United-mad.' **"**

TERRY VENABLES on the one that got away, 2004.
As a kid, Beckham trained with Spurs and won a skills competition which took him to Venables' Barcelona

" To be marooned on a desert island with an endless supply of lager, women and Sky TV. **"**

Spurs goalkeeper, **IAN WALKER**,
describes his chief ambition, 1993

66 Wimbledon with fans. 99

JIMMY GREAVES on the mediocrity of Gerry Francis's side, 1996

66 If he put a mask on, called himself Geraldo Francisco and came back here tomorrow, things would turn around immediately. **99**

ALAN SUGAR, Tottenham chairman, on Francis's resignation, 1997

66 I suppose that will be my epitaph at Spurs: he was always talking about injuries. **99**

GERRY FRANCIS, 1997

66 The day I got married, Teddy Sheringham asked for a transfer. I spent my honeymoon in a hotel room with a fax machine trying to sign a replacement. **99**

GERRY FRANCIS on the stresses he faced at White Hart Lane in the summer of 1997

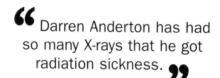

" Darren Anderton has had so many X-rays that he got radiation sickness. **"**

ALAN SUGAR, 1997

❝ I'm 58 and I think even I've played more football than Anderton over the past two years. If the Black Death ever swept through London again, I would not even want to be in the next street to him because you can be sure he would get it. **❞**

JIMMY GREAVES, 1998

" Whenever I break down with injury, it's always 'Sicknote'. People read it and think it's funny. I've been out on the street, just walking along, and they shout, 'Sicknote!' It's not nice. "

DARREN ANDERTON, 1998

" There are days when you think about it more than others and I even find myself talking to my leg, saying, 'Please don't let me down again.' **"**

JAMIE REDKNAPP, 2002

66 I'm amazed he wasn't put on his bike at the end of last season. After another four months of mid-summer muddle, does anyone at Spurs still believe he's the business? 99

DAVID MELLOR on Christian Gross, August 1998

❝ I tried to sign Gareth Barry, but we have been blown out of the water by Manchester City. They offered a far bigger transfer fee and are giving the lad much bigger wages. We could not get near. **❞**

HARRY REDKNAPP reveals that Liverpool were not the only club to miss out on the England midfielder

"It's hard not to have some opinion on Harry Redknapp. Whether you think he's a top geezer, lovely jubbly man of the people; a shifty, underhand dealing crafty chancer; or simply a melting waxwork of his son Jamie, most people can muster up feelings one way or another for him. West Ham fans love him, Southampton fans hate him. Bournemouth fans love him, Portsmouth fans hate him. Tottenham fans love him, Tottenham fans hate him."

A **FAN** opines on Footballfancast.com

66 The trouble with Christian Gross is that no one had heard of him. The communication was not brilliant and I decided, as captain, to explain to him how things worked and what players liked and were used to. I do not believe he listened to a word I said. **99**

GARY MABBUTT, 1999

> One of my big tasks here is to keep the mediocrity away. Tottenham in the last few years have signed mediocre players.

DAVID PLEAT, 1998, on being appointed
Director of Football

" If things go according to plan I won't need to move to a bigger club because Tottenham will be big enough... If we add to the squad we can challenge for the championship in a year or two's time. "

LES FERDINAND, 1997

66 There has been speculation about me being wanted by Spurs and talk of me going back to London. But all that talk about the bright lights of the capital is crap. 99

TIM SHERWOOD, Blackburn Rovers captain, shortly before joining Spurs, 1998

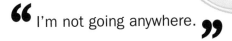

" I'm not going anywhere. **"**

SOL CAMPBELL, November 2000, as speculation mounted
over whether he would sign a new contract

> **66** We will not be pushed around by a bunch of north London yobbos. **99**

RUPERT LOWE, Southampton chairman, shortly before his manager Glenn Hoddle left for Spurs

" If someone wants to give you a bum steer on who we're after, then so be it. If you want to know, ask me, because I have a list of players we want and Robbie Keane isn't on it. **"**

GLENN HODDLE, Tottenham manager, shortly before paying Leeds United £7million for Robbie Keane

66 If Alan Sugar thinks he can just walk in and take West Bromwich Albion's manager, I'll be down that motorway in my car like an Exocet to blow up his bloody computers. 99

Baggies' chairman, **TREVOR SUMMERS**, on Tottenham's interest in Ossie Ardiles, just before he left the Hawthorns for White Hart Lane

> **“** Someone asked me the other day if I would be tempted if a big job came along in London. My answer is that I have taken on this big job at Leeds and will finish it. **”**

GEORGE GRAHAM in the Leeds programme, 1997.
The following year he joined Spurs

> **66** George Graham will not go to Spurs. I spoke with him recently and he assured me he would not walk out on Leeds. **99**

JOHN BARNWELL, chief executive of the League Managers' Association, 1998

66 We like a tackle at Tottenham.
We're not pansies, you know. 99

DAVID PLEAT, caretaker-manager, after the win at Derby 48
hours before George Graham took over as
manager, 1998

66 Sugar posed as the enemy of corruption. He was critical of Arsenal for not sacking George Graham. He tore up Jurgen Klinsmann's shirt on TV because he walked out halfway through a contract. He is now attempting to lure Graham from another club a quarter of the way through his contract. 99

RICHARD LITTLEJOHN, columnist, *The Sun*, 1998

> **"** Short of Margaret Thatcher joining New Labour, it's hard to imagine a more stunning move than Graham going to Spurs. **"**

DAVID MELLOR, 1998

   “ All that stuff about the Spurs tradition for attractive football is just a crutch. They haven't been playing like that for ages. **”**

GEORGE GRAHAM, soon after becoming manager, 1998

I've changed. It's all attack now... only kidding.

GEORGE GRAHAM after Spurs' 5–2 defeat
of Watford, 1999

INTERVIEWER:

" What do you feel you've added
to Spurs? "

GEORGE GRAHAM:

" Me. "

Verbal cut and thrust in an **INTERVIEW** after a draw
at Middlesbrough, 1999

> 66 I want a consistent team, not a flash one. When I was at Highbury, the message from White Hart Lane used to be, 'Let Arsenal win things with boring football, we'd rather play entertainingly and lose.' I want my team to be exciting, and to win week in, week out. I'm working on it. 99

GEORGE GRAHAM, 2000

"Man in the raincoat's blue-and-white army."

CHANT by Spurs fans, reluctant to use the former Arsenal manager's name, 1999

" At least all the aggravation will keep me slim. **"**

GEORGE GRAHAM on encountering fan hostility at Tottenham because of his Arsenal background, 1999

" When you are a person of a certain age, with a certain intelligence, like he is, then why, if you are the manager, would you be jealous of someone who is playing well and is loved by the fans? **"**

DAVID GINOLA on George Graham, 2000

" Graham would always give me hassle. I knew he wasn't a big fan of mine, but he should have respected what I could do. He would try to put me down in front of other players. Even if I had been the best on the pitch, he would point to me and say, 'I expect more from you.' He never did that to anyone else. **"**

DAVID GINOLA on George Graham, 2000

" How can anyone say he's lazy? He is a sex symbol and has all that hair to blow-dry every day. That's an hour's job in itself. **"**

SIMON MAYO, Tottenham fan and broadcaster, on David Ginola, 1998

66 I rugby-tackled him once because it was the only way to stop him. He then gave me three dummies on the trot. I was out of the game for so long I had time to eat two hot dogs. And, to make matters worse, he was polite to me after the game. **99**

Defender **DARREN BAZELEY** on David Ginola after Watford lost 5–2 to Spurs, 1999

66 I know more about schmaltz herring than I do about football. **99**

ALAN SUGAR to outgoing chairman Irving Scholar, before taking over at Spurs, 1991

66 He's a coward who will not stand up and admit mistakes. I got mugged into believing that this Adonis of the football world was the be-all and end-all in management skill and tactics. In my time at Tottenham I made lots of mistakes. The biggest was possibly employing him. **99**

ALAN SUGAR on George Graham, 2001

" He'd said that he bought Spurs on 'a whim' after he and his family had watched them win the 1991 FA Cup final. If he'd known what he was in for in the following ten years, he said, he would never have done it. "

RODNEY MARSH on Alan Sugar, 2001

> **"**Without football I could have made some mistakes. A lot of mistakes. Too many mistakes.**"**

New signing **SEBASTIEN BASSONG** rues his errors. Lots of errors. Too many errors.

" I was so upset – I felt like my life had been hit by a train. **"**

LUKA MODRIC mistakes a fractured fibula for a horrific rail accident

" I thought I had seen it all when it comes to the fickleness of football folk. Then I heard the Spurs fans singing, 'There's only one Alan Sugar.' "

MICK McCARTHY, Millwall manager, 1994

> **"** If I fail, I'll stand up and be counted – let some other brain surgeon take over. **"**

ALAN SUGAR, Tottenham chairman, 1996

66 When I took over, football was not fashionable. Going into the bank and asking for money was like asking a rabbi to eat a bacon sandwich. Now the banks are queuing up to lend. **99**

ALAN SUGAR, Tottenham chairman, 1997

> **❝** I have found Alan Sugar to be one of the least charming people I have ever come across. **❞**

PETER HILL-WOOD, Arsenal chairman, 1997

66 There's a limit to the thickness of the skin of the rhino. I want a goal at the end of the rainbow, or at least to be appreciated. What I won't accept is more abuse. I've been branded a cold, cynical individual with no knowledge of football and no interest in the club's heritage or traditions. 99

ALAN SUGAR after protests against him by Spurs fans, 1998

66 I personally believe Spurs are very lucky to have someone like him. 99

SAM HAMMAM on Alan Sugar, 2000

❝ [Alan] Sugar was hell bent on imposing his will on other people's lives and careers without giving a second thought to their true views or feelings. There were only two sides to an argument with Sugar – his and the wrong one. **❞**

TEDDY SHERINGHAM, 1998

REPORTER:

❝ Is Klinsmann Spurs' biggest-ever signing? **❞**

OSSIE ARDILES:

❝ No, I was. **❞**

Exchange at **PRESS CONFERENCE** to unveil
Jurgen Klinsmann, 1994

66 He was a World Cup winner and no one could believe he was coming to Tottenham. **99**

TEDDY SHERINGHAM on Jurgen Klinsmann, 2002

" We played so well that the Liverpool fans applauded us off the pitch, having seen their team go out of the competition. That was special. **"**

TEDDY SHERINGHAM, 2002, on Spurs' victory at Anfield in the 1995 FA Cup quarter-final

“ At the end of my 1994–95 season with Tottenham Hotspur, I got many letters and calls from teachers. They told me that the German language was becoming increasingly popular at schools. That, I think, is even better than successes on the pitch. ”

JURGEN KLINSMANN, 2002

66 During the season the shares doubled in value but their prices started to fall when the first rumours began to spread concerning my move to Bayern Munich. 99

JURGEN KLINSMANN, 1997, on his first spell at Tottenham

66 I miss playing in England, and I'm not just being polite. The attitude of our coach, Giovanni Trapattoni, is that if we score we must defend immediately. You could say he is the opposite of Ossie Ardiles. **99**

JURGEN KLINSMANN at Bayern Munich before returning to Spurs, 1997

66 I fell in love with the club and it is still my favourite. I was made very welcome there by everyone and the fans were always marvellous. There is always a place in my heart for Tottingham Hotspurs. **99**

OSSIE ARDILES, 2000

" We would be perfect for the club. We'd love to. Osvaldo already had a coaching experience there and I'd be eager to do it. It would be a great challenge. **"**

RICKY VILLA, assistant manager to Ossie Ardiles at Argentina's Racing Club, on managing Spurs, 2003

> **Because we've got Ledley at the back (SOMETIMES!)**
> **We've got Ledley at the back (SOMETIMES!)**
> **We've got Ledley**
> **We've got Ledley**
> **We've got Ledley (SOMETIMES!)**

SPURS FANS update an old classic for their dodgy-kneed skipper

" We do not really practise penalties. **"**

GARETH BALE commits the cardinal sin – telling the truth – after Tom Huddlestone misses a penalty in the FA Cup against Leeds

> "My brother was a West Ham fan. He took me to Upton Park but when I came to my senses at the age of about 12 I became a Tottenham fan!"

TEDDY SHERINGHAM, 2002

" I do hate Arsenal. With a passion. No money in the world would ever tempt me to play for them. **"**

TEDDY SHERINGHAM, Spurs striker and supporter, 1996

> **"** I made Gavin a Spurs fan. It fits: a lot of people who sit in the stadium will be from Essex. I told various people, and the next thing you know, the art department have spent £2,000 in the Tottenham shop, and costume have got me a shirt to wear. **"**

Gavin and Stacey star **MATTHEW HORNE** reveals how art ended up imitating life

66 When I first joined Tottenham I couldn't believe the standard. We've got international players in each position and a really strong squad. **99**

PETER CROUCH reveals Spurs are better than he thought they would be, March 2010

" I used to dread losing to Spurs, especially when a big England game followed soon afterwards. The reason was simple: I shared a room with Glenn Hoddle, and he wouldn't miss a chance to wind me up about it. **"**

KENNY SANSOM, Arsenal and England full-back, 1996

It doesn't matter what else you do, just make sure you beat Arsenal.

SPURS FAN to Terry Venables, on his appointment as manager, 1987

66 A season in which Spurs finished second in the League would be counted as a triumph, unless Arsenal finished first, in which case it would instantly become a disaster. 99

TERRY VENABLES, 1994

66 How am I betraying Spurs? I go to see Spurs win and Arsenal get stuffed. **99**

HUNTER DAVIES, who has a season ticket for both north London sides, 1998

66 What a nightmare. I'm a Tottenham fan and I get cuffed to you. 99

FELLOW PRISONER to Tony Adams on the night the latter was arrested for drink-driving, 1998

66 He hasn't stopped giving me stick since. He's always at it, but I say that's the only one he's scored against me. **99**

DAVID SEAMAN on Gazza's free-kick in the 1991 FA Cup semi-final

" Na-yim, from the halfway line,
Na-yim, from the halfway line. **"**

SPURS FANS mock David Seaman after the ex-Spurs midfielder scored a freak winner for Real Zaragoza against Arsenal in the 1995 European Cup-Winners' Cup final

66 The Spurs fans loved it of course. They still remind me of it when we play them and the goal was the inspiration for their fanzine – *One Flew Over Seaman's Head*. 99

DAVID SEAMAN, 2000

> **"** We're a big club and sometimes you've got to take a chance in life. It's no good being Steady Eddie and standing still, you've got to move on and take a gamble, if necessary. Most of the other big clubs take a chance now and then and it doesn't normally go against them. **"**

SOL CAMPBELL, November 2000, exhorting Spurs to spend more money on players

" Obviously for the good of the team and the good of the club, he's got to come out and say what he's doing. But only Sol knows what's going on. We used to ask him about it all the time and dig him in the dressing room, but he never says anything about it, so we've given up asking. "

STEPHEN CARR, February 2001

" To be fair to Tottenham, they tried everything to get Sol round the table to discuss his contract, but he didn't want to talk. People say, why didn't you sell him? But he wouldn't go. "

GEORGE GRAHAM, 2002

" Judas. **"**

BANNER at White Hart Lane on Sol Campbell's return with Arsenal, November 2001

> **" We hate you so much, cos we loved you so much. "**

Another **BANNER** at White Hart Lane on Sol Campbell's return with Arsenal, November 2001

66 The World Cup one was difficult because we'd never tried to target a specific area of London before and I was nervous about Tottenham being so close. But we got very little feedback from them; I think they just accepted it. **99**

Daily Mirror editor, **PIERS MORGAN**, on running the headline 'Arsenal Win The World Cup', after France's 1998 triumph

" The day I arrived in England I first went to White Hart Lane. I think I had a meeting with Mr Sugar or his assistant. I saw two people and they made me an offer, and two hours later they ordered me a black cab, it was pre-paid ... and I went to see Arsène Wenger at his place. When I arrived he was with David Dein, and two hours later I had given my word to Arsenal. "

EMMANUEL PETIT, the one that got away

❝ I've learned never to say never. Then again, I think I can safely say I wouldn't join Tottenham! **❞**

PATRICK VIEIRA, 2004

> **Oh, Teddy, Teddy. Went to Man United and he won f**k all.**

ARSENAL FANS rib the former Spurs striker after the Gunners win the Double in 1998

> **Oh, Teddy, Teddy. Might have won the Treble but he's still a c**t!**

ARSENAL FANS, after Sheringham won the Treble

66 He is a legend as a player for Spurs, and he will do everything he can to become a legend as manager too. **99**

DAVID GINOLA on Glenn Hoddle's appointment, 2001

66 There were a lot of stories about me going to Tottenham but in my opinion it's not a club with the ambitions I need and PSV is a bigger stage for me at the moment. I want to stop this speculation. Money is not the issue, I want to win plenty of trophies and I don't think I can do that at Spurs. 99

PSV Eindhoven striker **MATEJA KEZMAN**, 2003

> I know Tottenham are not among the biggest clubs in England but they are considered a very good club to play for, a nice place to play.

RIVALDO, 2003

66 I don't think I'm the big bad wolf. I can't produce the money to buy players. **99**

DAVID PLEAT defends Spurs' record in the transfer market, 2003

> **66** No one at Tottenham would shed a single tear if Glenn Hoddle was sacked tomorrow. The only way they will bring success back to Tottenham is through a change of manager. **99**

TIM SHERWOOD, May 2003

> **"** There was certainly discontent
> in the dressing room.
> Everyone knows about his
> man-management skills
> – or lack of them. **"**

NEIL SULLIVAN, September 2003

66 We've had everyone. Managers, agents, mothers, fathers, dustmen, cleaners applying. 99

DAVID PLEAT on the search for Hoddle's successor, 2003

66 The position [Pleat] holds at the club is making it enormously difficult for a manager to succeed. The job will be made just as difficult for any new manager coming in; he should have the job on his own. Let him take on the responsibility and, without his disruptive intervention, the fans might just get their success. **99**

GLENN HODDLE, 2003

" Most people said, 'Thanks and good luck for the future,' but David (who was manager at the time) waited until I left and then criticised me and said Spurs would be a far better team without me. Ironically that season Spurs went on to have mixed fortunes – I won a French Championship medal. "

GLENN HODDLE, 2003, on how his second departure from Spurs was a case of déjà vu

66 Because of his pride, Hoddle wanted to be the best player in training every day – at 46 years of age. I don't think you can see the whole picture when you're training out there among the guys. Can you imagine Arsene Wenger playing with Thierry Henry and the rest? 99

DAVID PLEAT, 2003

> **"** Glenn Hoddle if he was singing. **"**

LES FERDINAND nominates his ex-Spurs boss as the person he'd least like to be stuck in a lift with

> **I didn't know you were a Spurs fan.**

Blackburn boss **GRAEME SOUNESS** to referee Graham Poll during the game at Ewood Park with Tottenham, 2003

> **"** We tried to redden Alex's face a bit more, but were unable to. **"**

DAVID PLEAT after his side's 2–1 loss at home to Manchester United, 2003

66 We're having dialogue – we're not going to shoot him. **99**

DAVID PLEAT on Freddie Kanouté's decision to play for Mali in the 2004 African Cup of Nations

> 66 Our central defenders, Doherty and Anthony Gardner, were fantastic and I told them that when they go to bed tonight they should think of each other. 99

DAVID PLEAT, 2004

" I was sitting just a few feet away from David Pleat at the World Cup. He's a nice fellow, but the man is mad: certifiably, eye-spinningly mad. **"**

DANNY KELLY, co-host with Danny Baker, discussing Tottenham's director of football on a Talk Radio football phone-in, 1998

" You don't have to bare your teeth to prove you're a he-man in football. Some people are morally brave – Hoddle is one of them. I've heard him criticised for non-involvement, but if you can compensate with more skill in one foot than most players have in their whole body, then that is compensation enough. **"**

BRIAN CLOUGH on Glenn Hoddle the player

" Always had a bit of time, make a little bit of space, look up, bang. And you know he could put it on a postage stamp from 40 yards. Mmm... **"**

RON MANAGER, aka Paul Whitehouse, Spurs fan, on Glenn Hoddle, 2000

> **"** He's the reason I support Spurs. My family took me to see Leicester v Spurs and I marked Hoddle as a great player. Not exactly rocket science, but my brother told me it was the first sensible thing I'd ever said about football. **"**

CLARE TOMLINSON, Sky Sports' pitchside reporter, 2002

66 My team used to be Tottenham Hotspur, because I liked the way they played the game. They always used to play entertaining football and would attack all the time. They had some great players like Glenn Hoddle and Ossie Ardiles. **99**

BRIAN LARA, legendary West Indian batsman, 2001

66 He'd think they were cheating, diving, nasty foreign scum. But he'd rather like the English boys. Like that nice Steven Iverson. 99

PAUL WHITEHOUSE on what Ron Manager would make of the Spurs side, 2000

66 Steffen is only 20 and earns too much money for a boy of his age. 99

BENTE IVERSON, the Spurs striker's mother, on her son's £10,000-a-week wages, 1997

66 He gets the little sniff type of goals. **99**

GLENN HODDLE on Steffen Iversen, 2002

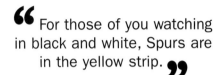

" For those of you watching in black and white, Spurs are in the yellow strip. **"**

JOHN MOTSON

> **66** And in the Cup-Winners' Cup,
> Spurs will play either Eintracht
> or Frankfurt. **99**

ALISTAIR BURNETT, football expert, *News At Ten*, 1982

" I expect the Croats to come out… oh dear, I had better not say fighting, had I? **"**

PETER SHREEVES, Spurs manager, before a match versus Hajduk Split from war-torn Croatia, 1991

" Tottenham are trying tonight to become the first London team to win this Cup. The last team to do so was the 1973 Spurs side. "

MIKE INGHAM, Radio Five Live

" ... and Tottenham ice
their sublime cake with
the ridiculous. "

PETER DRURY, ITV

> There are signs at all vomitory entrances advising that alcohol cannot be taken into the seated area.

The **SPURS PROGRAMME** leaves everybody confused, 2003

> **"** Spurs have been the greatest under-achievers of the original 'Big Five'. **"**

GERRY COX, journalist

> **You know when Spurs last won the championship? The Beatles hadn't even been formed! Bill Haley was Number One in the charts.**

HARRY LANSDOWN, 1996

> **"** White Hart Lane is a great place. The only thing wrong is the seats face the pitch. **"**

LES DAWSON, comedian, 1991

> **"** Hello, my name is Jacques. I am fifty three years old and I live in London. **"**

JACQUES SANTINI introduces himself to the Spurs squad, July 2004

" My time at Tottenham has been memorable and it is with deep regret that I take my leave. I wish the club and the supporters all the best. "

JACQUES SANTINI says 'au revoir' after 13 games at White Hart Lane, November 2004

66 I don't drink or smoke and I've never touched drugs. All I wanted to do was be a footballer. A lot I used to play with have ended up in prison. It's very sad. **99**

JERMAIN DEFOE explains the straight and narrow route he took to the top

> **Boom, boom, boom – everybody say Bale – BALE.**

After a sizzling run of games, the **SPURS FANS** finally welcome Gareth Bale as one of their own with an adaptation of The Outhere Brothers' seminal early-1990s anthem

“ There's no problem with Jermain. I wouldn't swap him for Miss World – he would probably swap me for Miss World though. ”

MARTIN JOL, on rumours of a row with Jermain Defoe in 2006

“ I did really well to hold myself back. I really don't think he realises how strong I am, otherwise he wouldn't approach me with headbutts and everything. **”**

MARTIN JOL, after a touchline confrontation with Arsène Wenger following the April 2006 Spurs–Arsenal match

" Sick As A Marriott "

DAILY MIRROR, headline after Spurs players fell ill at a hotel and lost to West Ham, a result that cost them a Champions League spot for the 2006–07 season

" Tottenham have joined the
quartet of five teams. "

JOE COLE, Chelsea midfielder on Spurs' improvement
in 2006

> **" If you want to play with the big boys, you have to play like the big boys. Spurs don't. "**

Ex-midfielder **EDGAR DAVIDS** on why Spurs are still nearly men, December 2009

66 I wouldn't know what a long-ball team was. We pass the ball to death. **99**

HARRY REDKNAPP responds to criticism from Aston Villa keeper, Brad Friedel

66 If it had missed or gone wide I'd have got it from my strikers for hitting it too hard. 99

PAUL ROBINSON talking about his 80-yard-free-kick goal against Watford in March 2007

66 He is regarded as one of the best left-backs coming through in Spain and Yuri will be a very good signing for us. We have been following him for two seasons now and his signing will continue our strategy of strengthening at all levels of the playing side. **99**

DAMIEN COMOLLI, director of football, on the signing of 17-year-old Spanish left-back Yuri Berniche in June 2007

66 He wasn't born, he was chiselled out of an oak tree. **99**

ALAN GREEN, BBC Radio Five Live commentator, praising Tom Huddlestone during Spurs' game against Manchester United in September 2007

66 Last season the UEFA Cup became our salvation. We started off badly in the Premier League but Europe gave us a good platform and we brought that form into the league. Hopefully that will happen again this time around. **99**

ROBBIE KEANE, showing optimism despite a poor start to the 2007–08 season

66 The first I knew was when I saw my nephew in the tunnel immediately after the game and he pulled me to one side and told me what everyone else seemed to know already. **99**

MARTIN JOL reveals Spurs' unorthodox methods of getting rid of managers (October 2007)

66 The English league has always been my dream and coaching in England is the realisation of that dream. 99

JUANDE RAMOS, on becoming Tottenham's manager in October 2007

66 Juande's arrival is great news for Tottenham Hotspur. He brings with him a wealth of experience, a proven track record and a winning pedigree. 99

Going. Spurs director of football, **DAMIEN COMOLLI** welcomes the arrival of Ramos, July 2007

66 He has recommended Juande Ramos, clearly he will have [to take] responsibility if it doesn't work. **99**

Going. Spurs chairman **DANIEL LEVY** reveals the contents of his crystal ball, August 2007

"We have spent around £175m on new players over the last three years ... Following a meeting of the directors and a full review of our football management structure, I can inform you that Damien Comolli has left the club with immediate effect.**"**

Gone. **DANIEL LEVY** confirms that Comolli follows Ramos out of the White Hart Lane door, October 2008

❝ On the training pitch I speak English and the players understand me perfectly. **❞**

JUANDE RAMOS insists there is no language barrier between him and the Spurs players

" He said about four words to me in two years. With Juande and the Spanish it was a bit hard [to have a proper conversation]. When the manager isn't talking to you it's hard and you start to question their motives. At one stage the training ground was a horrible place to be. Everyone was down, there was no team morale. "

DARREN BENT insists there was a language barrier between the former manager and his troops

> **"** I know I am sometimes criticised for appearing too business-focused, too uncommunicative, or simply for not being emotional enough when it concerns our team... that is simply not my way. **"**

Spurs chairman **DANIEL LEVY** responds to criticism following the sacking of Ramos with an open letter to the fans

❝ I grew up in a Tottenham supporting area and most of my mates follow Spurs. They used to give me all sorts of stick when I played for Arsenal. **❞**

New signing **DAVID BENTLEY** looks forward to finally getting his friends off his back, July 2008

66 I'm an emotional wreck.
I went mad. **99**

DAVID BENTLEY after scoring his first league goal for
Spurs – a 45-yard volley against Arsenal at The Emirates,
October 2008

66 Harry has come in, everyone has had a new lease of life and that has shown in the performances. **99**

DARREN BENT welcomes the arrival of Harry Redknapp as Spurs manager

" How the f**king hell did he miss that? My missus could have scored that ... You keep pussyfooting around with people – what am I supposed to say? Really good try? Really unlucky? He's really done his best with that? "

HARRY REDKNAPP after Bent heads wide of an open goal from five yards out against Portsmouth, January 2009. Still a Harry fan, Darren?

" I must admit myself I think I made a mistake ... I did cane them a bit and it's not really the way I manage. I get more out of the players by telling them what they can do rather than what they can't do. That has always been my way. **"**

Four months later, **HARRY REDKNAPP** apologises to Darren Bent. Sort of ...

❝ I just told him to tell [Roman Pavlyuchenko] to f**king run around a bit. The boy himself just kept nodding his head. He might be thinking inside: 'What's this t*sser saying to me?' **❞**

Either way, **HARRY**'s conversation with the Russian striker's interpreter seemed to do the trick after he scored the winner against Liverpool, November 2008

" You've always got his interpreter running around the training ground. Sometimes you pass the ball through the middle in training and Pava chases it. The interpreter's running alongside him, gets in there, and heads it into the net! **"**

HARRY REDKNAPP discovers he's signed two players for the price of one

66 The lad likes a tackle,
I don't know how he's going
to fit in with this lot. **99**

HARRY REDKNAPP has a warning for new signing
Wilson Palacios, January 2009

" I'll implement a strong rule next season that drinking is a no-no here. Footballers should dedicate their lives to playing. Footballers should not drink. You shouldn't put diesel in a Ferrari. I know it's hard but they are earning big money, they are role models to kids. "

HARRY REDKNAPP puts his foot down after a Ledley King bender makes the front pages, May 2009

" You're just a s**t
Chas & Dave! **"**

SPURS FANS assess the musical merits of Manchester City
fans Liam and Noel, May 2009

" He's been a problem and if Aaron [Lennon] doesn't get injured he probably doesn't play. I played Niko [Kranjcar] at first, because I didn't really feel at that time David deserved to play in all honesty. I suppose other managers probably wouldn't have had the patience that I've shown with him. Everyone's different and I don't bear grudges. "

'ARRY shows those famous motivational skills in his assessment of errant midfielder David Bentley